CLAIMING HIS KISS

Serpent's Kiss Book 4

SHERRI HAYES

Claiming His Kiss (Serpent's Kiss, Book 4)

By Sherri Hayes

ISBN (ebook): 978-1-948471-08-4

ISBN (paperback): 978-1-948471-09-1

Cover Design by QDesign.

Editing by Lawrence Editing.

This is a work of fiction. Names, places, characters and incidents are the product of the author's imagination and are fictitious. Any resemblance to actual persons, living or dead, events or establishments is solely coincidental.

FREE DOWNLOAD

CLICK HERE to join my NEWSLETTER and get WELCOME TO SERPENT'S KISS (SERPENT'S KISS #0) for free.

ABOUT THIS BOOK

What do you do when the woman you love is having problems with her neighbors? You ask her to move in with you.

Daniel Ross has been lusting after Ali for two years, but she's young enough to be his daughter. When her new neighbors begin to cause issues for her, his protective instincts kick in. His house is big enough for both of them. She can have her space and he'll know she's safe. What could possibly go wrong?

Ever since that first night at the private club where they're both members, Allison Foster has wanted to explore the pull she feels toward Daniel, but he's made sure to keep them in the friend zone. She wants more, but every time she's hinted at the possibility, he turns the tables on her and throws her into the arms of another man. That is until he insists she move into one of the spare rooms.

Living in the same house and sharing meals together means there's no running away for either of them. But will their age difference be too big of a gap to overcome...especially when his kids find out about the woman who's moved into their dad's house?

CHAPTER 1

Daniel Ross held the metal frame steady as Drew attempted to line it up with the footboard. It should've been easy, but for some reason the damn thing wouldn't go into the slot.

"Want me to get it?" Justin asked, trying and failing to contain his amusement.

Drew paused long enough to shoot Justin a dirty look, then went back to what he was doing. "Can you hold it a little more to the right? I think I see the issue."

Daniel did as Drew requested and watched as the metal hovered over the wooden slot for the first time.

"Need some help?" Kim's voice caused all three of them to glance toward the doorway.

Another grin tugged at Justin's lips, as he looked her over from head to toe. "I think we've almost got it."

With one last push, Drew forced the metal into the slot. He straightened and rolled his shoulders. "That was more challenging than I thought it would be."

"It was sticking when we took it apart the other day," Justin said.

Stretching out his own back, Daniel tried to ignore the way his muscles protested. As much as he hated to admit it, he wasn't as young as he used to be. At fifty-five, he was twenty years older than everyone else in the room. "Hopefully, you won't be needing to take it apart again for a very long time."

Kim sent a coy look in Justin's direction as she skimmed her fingers over the bed. "I don't plan on going anywhere anytime soon."

Grabbing her hips, Justin pulled her against him. "Damn straight."

Daniel was only half paying attention to the couple. Ali was grinning, happy for her best friend, but there was something off about her today. He didn't know what it was, but he was going to find out.

Kim let out a sigh that said more than words ever could, and he knew it was time for them to make their exit. Daniel cleared his throat. "And with that, I think it's time we said goodbye."

"You don't have to run off—"

"Yes, they do," Justin said.

Everyone chuckled, even Ali, although, again, it felt half-hearted.

Daniel helped Ali with her coat, relishing being able to touch her, even if it was in the most innocent of ways. He waited as she said her goodbyes to Kim and Justin, then escorted her to her car.

They were almost to their vehicles when he noticed her stifling a yawn. "Everything all right?"

She glanced up at him. Her normally bright blue eyes appeared duller than usual, her exhaustion showing. "I'm fine. Just a little tired."

"Why?" he demanded, stopping his progress.

Ali wasn't a party girl. He knew she hadn't been out late the night before. She'd left the private BDSM club where they were both members at eleven o'clock, and she'd gone straight home. He knew this because that's what she'd told him she was going to do and Ali wouldn't have lied to him.

She lowered her eyes to the ground before meeting his gaze once more. He could almost see her mind working behind her eyes. "I've got new neighbors."

"They're keeping you up?"

Ali nodded and tried to hide yet another yawn.

He felt his irritation rising. "Did you report them to your complex management?"

Her shoulders sagged. "I can't."

He crossed his arms in front of his chest. "If they're making noise at all hours of the night, you should report them."

She scraped her teeth over her bottom lip, and he knew from experience what that meant. "It's not…"

"What?" He wasn't letting her leave until he knew what was going on.

After glancing around, she sighed and met his gaze. "They have very loud sex."

Daniel raised an eyebrow.

"She's very vocal and he's…well, he's not quiet either." Her face turned pink as she averted her eyes to look over his shoulder. "I can't exactly call management and report my neighbors for having sex."

His first instinct was to insist that she could do exactly that. He would have. But this wasn't him. It was Ali, and in truth, he couldn't see her marching into her management office and demand they tell her neighbors to quiet down when having sex. "When's your lease up?"

Ali met his gaze again, the blush slowly leaving her cheeks. "Not for another six months." She rubbed her forehead. "It'll get better."

He had his doubts about that. Her neighbors either didn't know or didn't care about the noise they were making. Daniel had thought she looked tired last night, but he'd let it go. Tonight, he wasn't letting it go. He wrapped his fingers around her elbow and guided her the rest of the way to her car. "I'll follow you home."

She stared up at him. "Why?"

"Because you're going to pack a bag and come home with me."

The weary look she'd had before morphed into what could only be wide-eyed disbelief. Her mouth dropped open, and he knew she was moments away from coming up with some excuse.

He didn't give her the opportunity. "Just for a night. I'm sure I can find you something tomorrow."

"But what about my lease? I can't afford to pay rent on two places."

Her paying rent was the last thing he was worried about. If need be, he'd pay whatever was needed. It wasn't as if money was an issue. "Don't worry about it." Opening the car door, he motioned for her to get in. "I'll figure something out."

She slid behind the wheel but continued to gaze up at him. "Daniel, you don't need to. I'll be fine."

Leaning over, he braced one arm on the hood of her car above the door-frame and met her gaze. "You are not fine. Your eyes are bloodshot and you're slouching. You never slouch."

Ali pulled her shoulders back and sat up straight in her seat.

He went on. "That's not to even mention how many times you've yawned since we've been here." He paused, then stood to his full height. "Do you feel awake enough to drive?"

She nodded. "Yes."

Giving her a curt nod, he took a step back. "If that changes, pull over. Understand?"

"Yes," she whispered.

He closed her car door before making his way to his SUV and climbing inside. Backing out of Justin's driveway, he waited for her to do the same.

The drive to her apartment complex was a measure in patience. Twice she'd crossed the white line onto the shoulder before correcting herself. He was tempted to put her over his knee, but he was afraid if he did, he wouldn't be able to stop himself from doing more. Just thinking about her spread out across his lap, her ass in the air, had his cock twitching.

Luckily, they pulled into her complex a few minutes later and he released the tight grip he had on the steering wheel. He was striding toward her before she'd gotten out of her vehicle. "Do you want some help?"

"No. I'll only be a few minutes."

He waited patiently for her to return and took the time to reflect on the situation. Ali would be in his home. Even if it was only one night, she'd be in his space, her scent mingling with his.

Closing his eyes, he took several deep breaths to calm himself. Ali was a beautiful woman. Any fool could see that. But she was thirty-two years old. She was young enough to be his daughter. Hell, his oldest was only five years younger than Ali.

The door to Ali's apartment opened, and he made his way over to her as she locked her door. "I'll take your bags for you."

She turned and met his gaze before allowing him to take her duffle bag and suitcase.

He walked to his vehicle, opened the back, and placed her things inside. "Um?"

Knowing what she was going to say before she said it, he cut off her protest. "I'll bring you back to your car later. Right now, you're not alert enough to be driving."

She pressed her lips together, giving him a hint of that spunk he knew she had but held such a tight rein on. "I made it home, didn't I?"

"Do you really want to stand here and argue about your driving?"

She released an audible sigh and let him open the passenger's door for her. Once she was tucked safely inside, he made his way around the car to the driver's side.

Daniel started the vehicle and glanced over at her. "Are you comfortable?" The evening had become chilly, so he'd turned the seat warmer on for her.

"Hmm."

He grinned at her response and turned on some music. The soothing sounds of one of his favorite cellists filled the small space as he maneuvered onto the road. Before they made it to the highway, she was asleep.

Relaxing into his seat, he concentrated on the road. It was Sunday evening, so traffic wasn't bad. They should be at his house soon and he could get her settled into one of his spare bedrooms for the night.

Daniel was trying not to think about anything other than her getting the rest she needed, but it was difficult to ignore the way his body reacted to her —had always reacted to her. He could have seen her home and left. Ali wasn't his responsibility. She wasn't his submissive. They were friends. He looked out for her at the club, made sure her needs were met, but that was it. That's where their relationship ended.

Ali sighed, drawing his attention, and he looked over to see a smile pull at her lips. Warmth spread through his chest, the urge to brush his fingers along the side of her cheek almost impossible to resist.

He flexed his fingers on the steering wheel and reprimanded himself before returning his attention to the road. "Control yourself, old man."

Once again, his mind drifted to his daughter, and he felt a chill run through him. What would he think if a man his age thought about his little girl the way he did about Ali?

Shaking his head, Daniel pushed those thoughts out of his mind. He turned into his driveway. As the gate opened, he glanced at his passenger, who was still sound asleep, then followed the winding driveway to his house. The sun was going down, creating an orange glow through the trees.

Pulling into his garage, Daniel turned off the engine and he climbed out. He tucked his keys into his pocket and walked around to the passenger's side. Ali's head was resting against the glass, and he didn't want to startle her.

Easing the door open, he crouched down to her level. Her head fell forward, but she didn't wake. The urge to touch her surged to the surface once more, but again he resisted. It was something he had a lot of practice with as he'd been doing it for the last two years.

"Ali? Wake up. We're here."

She didn't move, so he chanced giving her arm a little shake.

"Ali?"

Her eyelids fluttered open, and her brow furrowed with confusion for a moment as she focused on him. "Daniel?"

He smiled, hoping to put her at ease. She'd been sleeping for the last twenty minutes. "We're here. I'll show you to your room, then you can crawl into bed."

She looked around and he saw her eyes widen a little. Ali had never been to his house before. No one at the club had. And no one besides Katrina and her P.I. who ran background checks for her knew how much money he had. Her gaze scanned his four-car garage. "Where are we?

"This is my home." He paused. "Well, my garage."

He stood and extended his hand to help her out.

Ali hesitated for a moment, then unbuckled her seat belt and took his offered hand. Tingles shot up his arm when she placed her hand in his, and once she was on her feet, he released her. While she was in his home, he was going to have to be mindful of not touching her. As much as he tried, Daniel couldn't control his reaction to her.

He went to get her bags from the back of his SUV and she followed him. Ali reached for the duffle bag, but he was quicker. "I've got it."

"I can carry it."

"I know you can, but you don't need to." He shut the door and headed for the house.

Ali followed. She didn't argue with him, but she rarely did. Daniel knew he overstepped a lot, but he couldn't help it. She may not be his, but there was something that made him want to care for her.

Daniel led her into the house, through the living room and kitchen, and down a long hallway to one of his guest rooms—he had four in this wing of the house. The room he'd chosen was the farthest from his. He figured it was safer that way.

Placing her bag and suitcase beside the dresser along the far wall, he turned to face her. She was a foot inside the room with her arms crossed as if she were protecting herself. He frowned. "What's wrong?"

She shook her head. "Nothing. I'm just...taking it all in."

It was a lot, he supposed. "There's a bathroom through that door with a shower, or you can use the one across the hall. It has a bathtub." She didn't say anything, and it occurred to him that she might be hungry. It had been a few hours since they'd last eaten. "Are you hungry, or would you rather go back to sleep?"

"I probably shouldn't go to sleep this early. I'll end up waking up in the middle of the night."

Daniel nodded. "Then come with me and I'll see what I can throw together." He didn't wait for her to agree before heading toward the kitchen, but he heard her footsteps behind him on the hardwood floors.

The kitchen was why he'd bought the house. He loved to cook. On the rare occasions when his children did visit, they would spend hours in the kitchen cooking and catching up. Some of his best memories with his kids happened in that room.

Going directly to the refrigerator, he pulled out sausages and some leftover pasta sauce. It may not be fancy, but it would be filling.

Ali hovered on the other side of the large island, so he nodded toward the stools.

"Have a seat. Dinner will be ready soon."

She lowered herself onto the stool. He could feel her gaze on him as he cooked the sausages, boiled the pasta, and warmed the sauce. She didn't say anything, only watched, following his movements as he tended to the food.

After draining the pasta, he removed two plates from the cabinet and piled a healthy portion of noodles on top, along with the sausages and sauce. Belatedly, he thought he should have made some garlic bread to go with it, but it was too late.

He walked around the island to where she sat and set one of the plates and a fork in front of her.

"Thank you." She smiled and picked up the fork. "It smells good."

Daniel took a seat at the island as well but made sure to keep a stool between them.

Ali pursed her lips and blew on the steaming pasta before bringing the fork to her mouth. He couldn't pull his gaze away from her lips as they wrapped around the fork. Then, she moaned, and all the work he'd done earlier to calm his attraction to her was moot.

He cleared his throat and forced himself to look away. "Eat up, and then you can turn in early. I want you to get plenty of rest tonight."

"The nap in the car helped." She twirled some more of the pasta onto her fork. "This is good."

"I'm glad you like it." He chanced a glance at her again, making sure to keep his gaze away from her mouth this time. "I assume you have to work tomorrow?"

"Yes, I do."

Daniel nodded. "What time?"

"What?" she asked.

Her forehead wrinkled and her nose scrunched up a little in the cutest way. Damn, he had to stop thinking about her like that. He looked away, gathering more food onto his fork.

"What time do you need to be at work?"

"Seven thirty." She paused. "But I need to get my car first."

Again, he nodded. "We'll leave around six thirty. That should give you plenty of time."

They ate the rest of the meal in silence. When she was finished, he gathered their plates and took them to the sink. By the time he faced her again, her eyes were already half closed.

She looked up when he approached.

"Did you need anything before you turn in?"

Ali blinked. "I don't think so."

"I'll be here or in my room." He indicated a hallway off the kitchen. "Should you need anything." He prayed she didn't come looking for him in the middle of the night.

Daniel waited, but she didn't move. He raised an eyebrow, indicating he expected some sort of response from her.

She slid off the stool and began walking toward her room. Then she stopped, turned, and met his gaze. "Daniel?"

"Yes?"

"Thank you for letting me stay here. You didn't have to."

Her blue eyes drew him in, almost begging him to invite her into his bed, but he took a cleansing breath instead. "Good night, Ali."

CHAPTER 2

*A*llison Foster woke with a start, a loud, annoying sound filling her ears. A second later, her heart still pounding hard in her chest, she realized where the noise was coming from. Her phone.

Reaching for the object that woke her from the first sound sleep she'd had in over a week, she turned the alarm off and flopped onto the bed to stare at the ceiling. As her thoughts began to clear, realization dawned. She wasn't in her bed. She was in Daniel's.

Okay, not Daniel's actual bed, but a bed in his house. She'd been so tired after more than a week of listening to her neighbors screwing each other's brains out. Given she was a member of Serpent's Kiss, she was used to loud sex, but her new neighbors would give anyone at the club a run for their money. The banging. The screams. The dirty talk...

She'd heard it all. Every. Last. Word.

The first night wasn't so bad. She'd even giggled a little at some of what filtered through their adjoining wall. But all her laughter had fled when she realized it wasn't just going to be a one and done. Her neighbors had gotten down and dirty three times that first night. And the second night. And the third. She'd been granted a slight reprieve the fourth night when they'd only woken her up twice, but by that time she was so sleep-deprived it had hardly mattered.

Of course, Daniel had noticed her yawning. He noticed everything. The man was as frustrating as he was sexy. In a lot of ways, he treated her as if she were his submissive, but she wasn't and despite her hints to the contrary, he'd never indicated he saw her as anything more than a friend.

Which led her to where she was now, lying in a bed in his house. She'd been too tired to put up any type of a fight last night, not that she was an overly aggressive person. She wasn't. In fact, her best friend, Kim, said she wasn't assertive enough. Kim was constantly trying to get Ali to stand up for herself at work, but Ali didn't have it in her. She didn't like confrontation and never had.

Speaking of work...

She sighed and flipped the covers off. Like it or not, she had to get to work and before that, she needed to pick up her car.

Ali padded into the attached bathroom. She rubbed the sleep from her eyes and stretched before looking into the mirror. Her hair wasn't as wild as it usually was, which meant she hadn't moved much during the night. It was no wonder. The bed had felt wonderful, and she'd been exhausted.

Even still, she ran a brush through her hair before walking to the shower to turn on the spray. As the water warmed, she stripped out of her T-shirt and panties.

Stepping into the shower was an experience in and of itself. There were two shower heads. One overhead and the other on the wall. The way the water cascaded over her body felt heavenly and the shower itself was big enough for three people, but she didn't have time to linger. Not if she wanted to make it to work on time.

After rinsing the conditioner from her hair, Ali turned off the water and stepped out. She reached for the fluffy white towel that was hanging nearby. Moving it over her skin, she couldn't believe how soft it was. And when she circled it around her torso and tucked the ends between her breasts, it was like being wrapped in a cloud.

Ali wanted to relax and enjoy the moment, but she couldn't be late for work. This wasn't a vacation.

It was almost six by the time she'd dried her hair, put her makeup on, and gotten dressed. And best of all, for the first time in over a week, her head didn't feel foggy.

A knock on the door made her heart skip a beat, then beat double time. Not because she was scared, but because she knew it had to be Daniel.

Ali opened the door and her breath caught in her throat. Daniel stood in the hallway wearing a long-sleeved button-up dress shirt, the kind men usually wore underneath suit jackets, and a pair of pressed slacks. His hair was still damp from his shower, and he was freshly shaved. She was struck with the urge to run her tongue along his jaw to his lips to see if they were as soft and smooth as they looked.

He must have caught her staring because he cleared his throat. "I came to make sure you were awake." He glanced behind her and she followed his gaze to the bed. The blankets were in disarray from where she'd pushed them off her earlier. She hadn't bothered to fix them, not knowing if she'd be there tonight or not. If she wasn't staying for another night, he'd no doubt want to change the sheets.

Then, she wondered who changed his sheets. Did he have a housekeeper?

Brushing those thoughts aside, Ali walked to the bed and grabbed her jacket and purse. "I'm ready."

Daniel hesitated for a moment, then met her gaze. His gray eyes almost silver this morning. "I'm making us breakfast."

"You don't—" A pointed look had her stifling her words. "Thank you," she said instead.

She followed him down the hallway to the area of the house that housed his kitchen. Last night his house had felt huge. This morning, it felt even bigger. His kitchen was half the size of her entire apartment. It had a large cooktop with six burners, a double oven, and two separate islands in the center. She'd only seen kitchens like this in magazines.

"Have a seat," he said, pointing to the island where they'd eaten dinner the night before.

Still trying to gather her thoughts on this new information about him, Ali lowered herself onto one of the chairs. He moved about the kitchen with ease and once again she was drawn to the way his muscles moved. For a man his age, he was very well built. She'd spent many nights fantasizing about how they'd feel under her hands, or what he'd look like hovered over her, his muscles straining as he took her.

He glanced over at her and she lowered her gaze. He didn't see her like that and she needed to get over it. Move on. There were other good Doms at the club. She'd played with a few of them. But none of them affected her like Daniel. Maybe she was cursed or something.

"Do you like mushrooms?"

Ali felt heat rise to her cheeks. He couldn't have known the direction of her thoughts, but for some reason it felt as if he'd caught her. "Um. Yes."

She'd been expecting something like a bagel or toast—that was usually what she had for breakfast, but after last night, she should have known better. He tossed a handful of ingredients into a skillet with some olive oil. "Did you sleep well?"

"I did. Very well."

Daniel smiled. "Do you prefer coffee? Orange juice? Milk?"

"Coffee, with some milk and sugar, please." She knew better than to try and get it herself. Daniel didn't even allow her to do that at the club if he was around. Anytime he saw her drink empty, he'd offer to get her another one.

The way he moved around his kitchen told her how comfortable he was in there. She'd never known that about him. If fact, she realized she didn't know much about him outside of the basics. He was a real estate agent—he'd helped Alexander, another Dom at the club, find a building for his medical practice. She also knew he was divorced and that he'd been in the Army when he was younger.

Daniel removed two mugs from a cabinet and filled them both with coffee. After adding cream and sugar to hers, he placed it in front of her.

"Thank you."

"Anytime." His smile caused her stomach to do a little flip.

He finished cooking their omelets, plated them, and carried them to where Ali was sitting. He placed one plate in front of her before taking the same seat he had the night before.

"Your house is beautiful."

He paused, fork in hand. "Thank you. It's rather large given that it's only me, but I love the kitchen, so I keep it."

Ali nodded and dug into her omelet. She contemplated whether she should probe more or if that would be rude. She was his guest after all.

In the end, her curiosity got the better of her. "You like to cook."

Daniel took a bite, chewed, and swallowed before he answered. "I love to cook. It relaxes me." He paused and glanced over at her before returning his attention to his breakfast. "Almost as much as flogging a submissive."

She'd seen him playing with subs many times. The look on his face was so peaceful when he was in the zone. It was always a catch-22 for her. She loved watching him, but she hated seeing him with another woman. "You're very good at it." She paused. "Cooking and flogging."

He let out a half laugh. "Thank you." Then he shoveled the rest of his breakfast into his mouth before standing. "Finish up and we'll go. I'm going to warm up the vehicle."

It took her a few more minutes to finish. She was a rather slow eater. At least, that's what her mother had always told her.

Ali took her empty plate to the sink, rinsed it, and loaded it into the dishwasher. Even though he probably wouldn't mind, she didn't want to make him regret inviting her into his home.

When Daniel strolled into the room again, he was rubbing his hands together. "Did you bring a coat with you? The temperature has dropped quite a bit overnight."

"I have a jacket, but I left my winter coat at the apartment." It hadn't been all that cold yesterday. Spring was around the corner and the days were getting warmer. She hadn't had to wear her winter coat for a couple weeks.

Without saying anything more to her, he disappeared down another hall. How many of them were there, she wondered.

Less than a minute later, he returned with what looked to be a woman's coat. "I think this will fit you."

Ali tried to tamp down the jealousy she felt. They weren't a couple. He'd made her no promises other than providing her a temporary place to stay.

Holding up the coat, he waited for her to slide her arms into the holes before settling it onto her shoulders. Then he turned her around, his hands bringing the two sides together, and he pulled the zipped up.

His fingers brushed against her collarbone, sending little sparks across her chest. Their gazes met a half second before he dropped his arm and stepped away.

"Are you ready to go?" Daniel asked, striking across the living room, heading toward what she knew was the garage. When he reached the other side of the living room and realized she hadn't moved from her spot, he looked concerned. "Ali?"

She searched in his eyes for anything that would indicate he'd felt something when he'd touched her, but his face held nothing but question and maybe a little worry. Letting out a breath, she forced her feet to move.

* * *

Daniel drove Ali to her apartment complex so she could pick up her vehicle. It was a cold morning and all the cars that had been sitting outside had frost covering their windshields. There was a spot open next to her car, so he pulled up beside it. He put his SUV in park and held out his hand. "Give me your keys."

She blinked at him. "I can..." The words died in her throat.

A long moment passed, then she placed her keys in his palm.

He disengaged his seat belt and reach for his door handle. "Do you have a scraper in the car?"

"Yes. It's on the floor behind my seat."

Daniel slid behind the wheel of her car long enough to get it started and to turn the heat on full blast. The cold air hit him square in the face, sending a shiver rippling through his body. He had no idea how people lived in colder climates.

Once the car was running, he retrieved the scraper from the back floorboard and began working on her windows. It came off without too much trouble, and he returned the scraper to where she had it stored.

He could feel Ali's gaze on him as he made his way back to his car. The warm air surrounded him as he lowered himself into the driver's seat. "We'll give it a few more minutes for the heater to do its thing, and then you can be on your way to work."

"Thank you."

"You're welcome."

"In case you get home before I do." He paused. "The gate code is 3030. The code also works on the garage as well."

She didn't know what to say, so she remained quiet.

Ten minutes later, Ali got out of his car and into her own. She gave him a little wave as she drove off to work and he backed out of the space to do the same.

He drove to his office in downtown. It was early and the office was empty, but that didn't mean there wasn't work he could be doing. There were properties to review, research to do, and most importantly, he needed to find Ali somewhere to stay.

At eight o'clock, he placed a call to Rebecca, his property manager. She knew every one of his properties inside and out. If there was an opening at one of his rentals, she would know about it. "Good morning, Rebecca."

"Daniel. I wasn't expecting to hear from you this morning." Her tone was pleasant, but he could hear her curiosity coming through. They met once a month to discuss his properties, but outside of that he only called her if there was an issue, or if he was turning another property over to her.

"I have a situation I'm hoping you can assist me with."

"You know I will if I can."

He tapped his pen on the notepad in front of him. "A friend of mine needs a place to stay for a while. Are any of the rentals available?"

"Let me double-check, but I don't think so." He could hear her typing in the background. "No. Sorry. All your rentals are full."

Not exactly the news he wanted to hear. "Anything available in the next month?"

Again, he heard typing. "There's a four-bedroom house outside of the city that might be available at the end of next month. We haven't reached the thirty-day mark yet, so I haven't spoken to the tenants to see if they were wanting to renew or not."

Daniel's shoulders slumped. "That's all right. I don't want to kick anyone out of their house. I'll...figure something else out. Thank you for checking."

"Of course. That's what I'm here for." She paused. "Did you want me to check on other rentals in the area?"

"No, but thank you." He asked Rebecca a few more questions about the state of his rental properties before disconnecting the call, then turned his attention to other possible options. One of his flip houses was almost complete, but it wasn't ideal. Her commute would be close to an hour.

"Good morning." Kevin, his assistant, knocked on his open door before coming inside. He gave his boss a once-over and frowned. "Did something happen at one of the properties?"

"Just a personal matter. I'll figure it out." He hoped.

Kevin took the information in stride and handed Daniel a stack of papers. "I put the most promising one on top. We can get in this morning if you want to take a look."

The papers were sale listings in the surrounding area. Daniel glanced at each one and returned to the property Kevin had mentioned. He was right. It did look the most promising.

Daniel checked the clock. It was almost nine. The morning was flying by, and he hadn't gotten anything accomplished yet.

Pushing back from his chair, he stood. "Let's go take a look."

Three hours later, he was picking at a sandwich and running the numbers. The house was a mess with trash everywhere and it looked as if it hadn't been remodeled since the seventies, but the layout was good. He'd have to get his contractor out there to confirm, but unless he found something dire, the comps in the area looked good.

Right on cue, Kevin strolled in. "Freddy's going to stop by the house today. He said he can have an estimate together by tomorrow."

"Sounds good," Daniel said. "Cosmetically, the house is in bad shape, but I didn't see any major structural damage."

"I'll start drawing up the offer so it's ready."

One of the downsides this part to his business was that things moved fast. If he saw something that interested him, he had to jump on it. Waiting, even a week, could mean missing out on a great deal.

As four o'clock rolled around, his thoughts returned to Ali. Not that she hadn't been on his mind all day, but he was no longer able to avoid the issue before him. With none of his rental properties available for the foreseeable future, the only option was for her to stay where she was. With him. At his house.

Thinking about it had him feeling panicky and he didn't like it. He'd had trouble falling asleep the night before. He kept imagining her lying in her bed down the hall, the sheets brushing against her skin as she moved.

The ache in his groin began to grow and he knew he needed to change the direction of his thoughts. He needed to get out of there. Do something. Anything to take his mind off her.

Slipping into his coat, he said goodbye to Kevin and headed toward the gym. Granted, he had a workout room at home, but he was in the mood for a good hard swim.

He waved to Carly seated behind the reception desk and made his way to the locker room to change. It was still early, so he had the pool to himself outside of a mom teaching her daughter how to float on her back in the shallower end.

Daniel fixed his goggles over his eyes and dove into the deep end. Water rushed over his ears as he let his momentum carry him. When he popped up for air, he'd traversed almost half the length of the pool. It felt good to release some of the tension he'd been bottling up.

With each lap, he felt better. He concentrated on his breathing, on the way his body felt moving through the water.

He popped out of the water along the pool's edge and lifted his goggles. The mother and daughter had left, but they'd been replaced by a group that looked to be doing water aerobics.

Glancing at the clock, he realized it was getting late. He wanted to be home when Ali arrived.

He groaned and dunked his head under the water to wash away his thoughts. Why was he so attracted to her? Why couldn't he find someone closer to his own age he wanted as much as he wanted her?

Both good questions, but he didn't have an answer to either one of them.

Ducking under the lane markers, he swam to the ladder and hoisted himself out of the pool. While doing laps had helped in the moment, they weren't the solution. He had no idea what the solution was, but swimming hadn't been it. At least, he'd gotten a good workout in.

The drive home only took twenty minutes, but it felt much longer. He kept checking the clock to see how much time had passed. When he finally pulled into his driveway and maneuvered his SUV into the garage, he didn't miss the fact that Ali wasn't there yet. He'd hoped to beat her home, but given it was already almost six, he'd worried she'd be there waiting for him.

The thought occurred to him that maybe she'd stayed in the city. Had she gone to visit Kim? Or...someone else?

The possibilities were endless. She was young, single, and independent. There was nothing and no one tying her down.

That thought conjured up an image of her tied to his bed and he groaned. He had to find a way to stop thinking about her in that way.

Gathering his coat and briefcase from the back seat, he made a beeline for his liquor cabinet and poured himself a shot of whiskey. It burned going down, but he welcomed it.

His phone rang and he removed it from his pocket. The part of him that hoped it was Ali warred with the part that prayed it wasn't.

Flipping the phone over, he realized it was a video call. He clicked on the link to accept and was met with his daughter's smiling face. Her eyes bright with excitement.

"Hi, Dad."

"Hi, honey." He moved into the kitchen and took a seat at the island.

"I wasn't sure if you'd be home yet."

"You have good timing. I just walked in the door." Daniel grinned. "How's Kansas City?"

She glanced over her shoulder at something and then back at him. "It's good, Dad. In fact, I have some news."

Trepidation filled him, but he tried not to let it show. "Oh?"

"Do you remember the guy, Jesse, I was telling you about?"

"The guy you're seeing." He remembered him. The guy seemed nice enough. He was a few years older than Cassandra and worked in accounting at his father's company.

Cassandra nodded. "Well..." She looked over her shoulder again and Daniel realized Jesse must be there with her. "He asked me to marry him, and I said yes!" The last word came out in almost a squeal.

Daniel was trying to figure out how to respond when he heard the front door open. His gaze drifted from the phone and his daughter to the foyer. Even though he couldn't see Ali, he could feel her presence in his home.

"Dad?"

He forced his attention back to the phone.

Cassandra was looking at him with concern. "Are you okay?"

"I'm fine." He could hear Ali's footsteps retreating down the hall.

"What's wrong?" Cassandra asked.

Instead of answering his daughter's question, he asked one of his own. "When do I get to meet him?"

"Um. He's here now if you want—"

"I meant in person." Technology was all well and good, but there were things you could ascertain from meeting someone in person you couldn't over the phone. Not even via video chat. "If you're planning to marry the man, I'd like to meet him."

"Um." She looked off camera again. "Maybe we could come down for a weekend or something. This is our busy season, so it's hard for Jesse to get off work."

Daniel nodded. "Just let me know when works best and I'll rearrange my schedule. I want to make sure this guy's good enough for you."

"Dad." It was said in that tone children use when they're exasperated but resigned with their parents.

He chuckled. "Humor your old man, all right?"

She laughed. "We'll talk about it, and I'll let you know when we'll be down."

CHAPTER 3

li took hold of the doorknob and twisted. The knob turned and she pushed the door open.

It felt strange letting herself into Daniel's house. When she drove up the winding driveway, she realized she would have no idea if he was home if he parked his vehicle in the garage as he had the night before.

She thought about knocking but changed her mind. Daniel had given her the code and if the front door was locked, she'd go through the garage. It wasn't as if she was sneaking in or something.

As soon as she stepped over the threshold, she heard him. He was talking to someone. The other voice sounded feminine.

A momentary pang of jealousy curled in her belly, but she tamped it down. He wasn't hers. She had no claim on him. Not like that anyway.

As quietly as she could, she closed the door and turned toward her room. It was exactly how she left it, messy bedsheets and all.

Tossing her purse onto the mattress, Ali kicked off her shoes and dug in her suitcase to find something comfortable to wear. It had been a long day and all she wanted to do was relax.

Ali dug out a pair of leggings and a long sweater, along with some comfy socks. It didn't take long to change, but now she didn't know what to do with herself. It was after six and she was getting hungry, but she didn't want to disturb Daniel if he was still on the phone.

Biting her lip, she contemplated her options. She could stay holed up in her room all night and starve, or she could venture out and see if he was finished with his call.

The grumbling in her stomach made her decision for her. She hadn't eaten anything since breakfast and her body was protesting. It needed food. Stat.

She entered the large open space that included the kitchen, dining room, and living area to find Daniel working on dinner. He must have heard her approach because he turned and met her gaze. "Hey."

"Hey." She crossed to him, leaving a few feet between them. "Can I help with something?"

He motioned toward the vegetables lying on the counter. "You can make the salad if you'd like."

Ali nodded and went to stand on the other side of the sink. She picked up the knife. "Do you have a size preference?"

"What?" He coughed. "Oh. Not really. Not too small, though. I like to taste what I'm eating."

She snorted. "So size does matter."

Daniel shook his head, his shoulders vibrating, and went back to the chicken he was grilling.

They worked together in companionable silence as they put the finishing touches on dinner. It was simple but delicious. Daniel had made grilled chicken and roasted potatoes to go with the salad she'd put together. He'd also cut up some crusty Italian bread for them. She'd cleaned her plate and polished off three slices of bread.

When she'd popped the last bite of bread in her mouth, she noticed him frowning. "What's wrong?"

"What did you eat today?" he asked.

The last bit of bread felt heavy going down. She knew that look. She'd been a submissive for long enough to recognize it. "Um."

"The truth, Allison."

He'd only called her by her full name once and that was when he'd found out she'd left the club by herself one night without asking Brandon or

Cooper to escort her. Since then, he'd stayed until she was ready to leave and walked her out himself.

"I haven't eaten anything since breakfast this morning."

The lines on his face deepened. "Why didn't you eat lunch?"

She lowered her gaze. "I got busy. It was three o'clock before I knew it and I figured I could wait until dinner."

"Do I need to start bringing you lunch every day?" he asked.

Her eyes widened and she met his gaze. He was serious. "No, I..." She swallowed. "I don't normally miss lunch. Things were hectic today and I lost track of time. That's all."

A grumble sounded from deep in Daniel's chest and for some reason she felt her sex pulse.

He stood and took their plates to the sink. She had the distinct feeling he wanted to turn her over his knee and not in the fun, let's get kinky kind of way.

Ali made herself stay seated. She didn't think he'd welcome her closeness in that moment. "Were you able to find me a place to stay?" she asked instead, figuring the change in subject would be welcome.

His shoulders stiffened. "No. None of my properties are currently available, so you'll stay here. There's plenty of room."

She didn't miss that he'd said *one* of his properties. "How many properties do you have?" Looking at this house, she knew he had to have money, but she had no idea how much. She'd thought he was a real-estate agent. Did he really make that much money helping people buy and sell houses?

"Fifty-four." He paused. "At the moment."

She gasped. "You own fifty-hour houses?"

He rinsed the plates and placed them in the dishwasher. "No. Some are townhouses or commercial buildings. I like to diversify my assets."

"I see."

A heavy silence hung in the air. Daniel wiped his hands on a dish towel, then dropped it onto the counter. "Does the fact I have resources bother you?"

Did it bother her? A little. The last man she'd dated managed a grocery store. He made decent money. Good money, she thought. But nothing like...this.

Not that she and Daniel were dating. They weren't. No matter how much she wished otherwise.

"I'm just surprised. You don't act like you're rich," she said.

"And what is one supposed to act like if they're rich?" He looked amused, which she preferred to him being pissed at her.

She shrugged. "I don't know. Someone who flashes their money around?" She tried to find the right words. "You don't even drive a nice car."

He raised an eyebrow at that, but it was paired with a half-smile.

"What I mean is, it's not a Porsche or anything fancy like that."

Daniel pushed his weight off the counter. "I've never been a car guy. I'll leave that to Justin."

Her friend's boyfriend and Dom was the best mechanic she knew. He also loved classic muscle cars.

Before she could formulate how to respond, Daniel strolled into the living room and turned on the television. He began scrolling through the channels. One of her favorite shows popped up on the screen and she must have made a noise. He paused and looked at her. "Did you want to watch this?"

"That's okay. I don't—"

"Come." He placed the remote onto the coffee table. "There's nothing else on anyway."

She hopped off the stool to join him in the living room. He sat down in the high-backed chair farthest away from the television, so she lowered herself onto the couch.

Ten minutes later, she was curled up on the cushions, her knees tucked under her chin, engrossed in the show. She'd seen the episode before, but it didn't matter.

When the credits appeared on the large screen, she glanced over at Daniel for the first time since sitting down. He had a book open in his lap, reading. A pair of glasses were perched low on his nose and his forehead had the cutest wrinkle in it as he concentrated.

As if he could feel her gaze on him, he glanced up and removed the glasses. "Finished with your show?"

"The episode's over."

Daniel looked at the television, then back at her. "It looks like there's another episode starting. Did you want to watch it as well?"

Sure enough, one of the main characters appeared on the screen as another episode began. Ali bit the inside of her lip, not sure if she should or not. She could sit there all night and binge the show, but she was a guest in his house...

He interrupted her thoughts. "Watch your show. I have my book."

"Are you sure? If there's something else you'd rather watch."

He grinned and put his glasses back on before returning his attention to his book.

She let her gaze drift back to the television and was soon lost, once again, in the story. This time, when the episode ended and the next began, she didn't do more than check to see that he was still engrossed in his reading.

Somewhere along the line, she stretched out on the couch and tucked her hands under her chin. She yawned, having trouble keeping her eyes open. There were more episodes after this one, but she wasn't going to be able to stay up and watch them. She'd finish this one, and then she'd go to bed.

* * *

Every now and then, Daniel would glance up from his reading to peer at Ali over his glasses. She'd been so engrossed in her show she hadn't noticed. Or at least, he didn't think she had.

Halfway through the fourth episode, her eyes began to drift closed. He considered saying something but decided to let it go. If she was sleepy, he wanted her to rest.

Her chest rose and fell, and her mouth relaxed, signaling she was asleep. He continued to read, letting the episode drone on in the background, until he felt his own eyelids growing heavy. Closing his book, he set it on the table beside his chair before getting up.

He passed through the kitchen and made his way down the hall to her room. A faint whiff of cherries and lavender tickled his nose the moment he entered the room.

Daniel flipped on the light, illuminating the space. Her bed was in complete disarray, the sheets bunched in the center of the mattress. He straightened them, making the bed, and then turned down the sheets.

When he returned to the living room, Ali was still sound asleep. He didn't think she'd moved an inch while he'd been gone. Her chest rose and fell with each breath, drawing his attention. She had nice tits. They weren't overly large, but they were slightly more than a handful.

He shook his head, aggravated with himself for even allowing his thoughts to go in that direction. *Too young for you, old man*, he reminded himself.

Bending, he eased his arms under her knees and shoulders before lifting her into his arms. If he'd thought her scent affected him in her room, it was doubly potent with her pressed against his chest. The desire to run his nose along her skin, seeking the source of the sweet fragrance, had his groin tightening. He closed his eyes and forced those thoughts to the back of his mind.

Ali shifted in his arms and her eyes flew open. A soft sigh left her lips, and her arms came up, circling around his neck. Her nose skimmed his collarbone, sending a shot directly to the part of him he was trying to talk down. Daniel tried to steady himself and his body's reaction. He'd never had this much physical contact with her before and he desperately wanted to carry her into his bedroom instead of her own.

His feelings for her were wrong. He knew that. But it didn't change anything, and it never would.

A soft smile graced Ali's lips as she snuggled closer, and his heart clenched. If only he were twenty years younger...

Wishing wouldn't change anything, however, and he needed to get her settled into her bed before she woke up. Or before he did something stupid.

As quickly as he reasonably could without waking her, Daniel carried her to her room. He lowered her onto the bed and gently removed her arms from around his neck. Her lips curved up in a tiny smile and he wondered what she was dreaming about. Then, he realized it was probably better if he didn't know.

He pulled the covers over her sleeping form. Ali released a contented sigh and rolled away from him.

His brain was telling him to leave, but his feet wouldn't move. He wanted to stay and watch her sleep, to listen to the sounds she made, but he knew how creepy that would be.

Turning on his heel, he walked to the door. Hand poised on the light switch, Ali said his name.

He looked toward the bed, but she was still facing away from him. "Sleep," he whispered. "We'll talk in the morning."

"Okay," she mumbled.

Turning off the light, he waited until her breathing slowed once more, then backed out of the room. He closed the door behind him and rested his forehead against the doorframe. He had to find her somewhere else to stay. Having her this close…

He took several steadying breaths. Last night he'd only imagined what she looked like lying in her bed. Tonight, he wouldn't have to imagine.

Granted, she'd been clothed, but it wouldn't matter. Daniel had a very vivid imagination where she was concerned. He could still feel the weight of her body against him and the sweet scent of her lingering on his shirt.

He blew out a deep breath and headed back to the living room. Another episode of the show she'd been watching played on the television. Picking up the remote, he turned it off, then made his rounds.

Daniel turned on his bedside lamp before ambling into his en suite bathroom. He removed his clothes, throwing them in the hamper, and took care of business. As he was washing his hands, he looked at his reflection in the mirror. He was getting grayer with every passing day. His dark hair was speckled with gray hairs and the stubble on his chin had more gray than brown these days.

His body was in decent shape. He tried to swim at least three days a week and could out swim most of the men half his age at the gym.

As he stood there, looking in the mirror, his mind went to Ali as it often did these days. What would she think if she knew the thoughts, he had about her? He'd volunteered to help Kim move because he'd known Ali would be there. And because he knew she'd be there, he'd spent most of the night before dreaming about her.

The way she looked at him sometimes made him forget all the reasons a relationship between them couldn't work. But that didn't change the real fact that it wouldn't. Even if she was willing to try, what would his kids think? They were all adults now, but that didn't mean they wanted to see their father with a woman not much older than they were.

He groaned, flipped off the light, and marched out of his bathroom. Moonlight illuminated the bedroom through the large French doors that led to a private patio. He was tempted to take a dip in the hot tub, but he knew it wouldn't help.

Climbing into bed, he let the sheets cool his heated body. He closed his eyes and tried to relax. But, of course, the only thing on his mind was Ali.

Knowing it was useless to resist, he let his mind go where it wanted to. Normally, when he thought about her, they were at the club, but tonight they were in his living room. He was sitting in his chair as he had been less than an hour before, reading, and she was on the couch. She turned to look at him, her eyes bright and mischievous. He quirked a finger at her, indicating he wanted her to come to him.

Ali arose from the couch, her lithe body calling to him with every step she took toward him. She came to a stop in front of him and he wasted no time tugging her onto his lap. Her legs straddled him, and he could feel the heat of her sex as it pressed against his straining erection.

His cock ached and he slid his hand beneath the covers, taking himself in hand.

In his mind, she'd been wearing a skirt instead of leggings, and he pushed the fabric away so he could touch her. She was already wet, her pussy ready for him. "Please," she begged. "Please, take me, Sir. Please, make me yours."

His hand moved faster up and down his length as he imagined what it would feel like to drive her down onto his cock, to feel her pussy pulsing around him. Her hot, wet...

A strangled moan tore from his chest as he came, cum covering his hand. He rubbed his other hand over his face. This had to stop. He knew it did. Especially with her living in his house. But he had no idea how.

Daniel went to clean up, and then got back into bed. His cock, at least, was satisfied. The rest of him was a different story. He still had no idea what to do about, or with, Ali.

It was well after midnight before he fell asleep. He was out cold when a noise woke him. It sounded like something hitting the floor. Not quite a crash, but a...thump?

He shot out of bed, not bothering to grab his robe or put on any clothes. His alarm hadn't sounded, which meant the noise had most likely come from inside the house. Ali. Thoughts of her falling and getting hurt had his heart pounding. She wasn't used to his house. Had she gotten up in the middle of the night, half asleep, and fallen?

He rushed down the short hall to the main living area. What he saw stopped him in his tracks. Ali was on her knees in his kitchen, paper towels in one hand and his kitchen towel in the other.

She looked up and her eyes grew wider than he'd ever seen them. Daniel took a step forward, then stopped when he realized where exactly she was looking. He slept naked, which meant he was standing in the kitchen wearing his birthday suit.

Ali's lips parted and he thought he heard her whimper. The sound had his cock sitting up and paying attention, but there wasn't anything he could do about it.

"What are you doing?" The question didn't come out as confident as he would have liked, but he chalked it up to being roused from sleep. When she didn't answer, he tried again. "Ali? What's going on? What happened?"

That seemed to snap her out of it. She tore her gaze away and lowered it back to the floor. "I dropped the milk."

Only then did he notice the jug of milk sitting on the counter.

CHAPTER 4

li's heart was pounding, and it had nothing to do with the half gallon of milk she'd just spilled all over the floor. Daniel was standing buck naked not ten feet away from her.

He strolled over to the milk container, picked it up, examined it, then set it down again. She kept her gaze on the floor even though she desperately wanted to look. Even though he played with subs at the club, she'd never seen him without his clothes. Unlike most of the other Doms, she'd never seen him have sex with a submissive.

"Are you all right?" he asked.

She nodded, trying not to look at his impressive erection but failing. "I'm fine. I'm sorry I woke you up. It slipped out of my hand." The milk had migrated down the length of the cabinets, and she crawled to wipe it up.

"I'm not worried about the milk."

The dishtowel was soaked through with milk and so were the paper towels in her hand, and yet there was still more on the floor. She reached for another dishtowel, not wanting to use all his paper towels, too, but he placed a hand over hers.

"Ali, stop."

He was standing so close to her she could feel heat radiating from his body. She closed her eyes and swallowed. It wasn't fair. All she had to do was turn her head and his cock would be right there, begging her to take it into her mouth and...

But he didn't want her. He'd made that very clear over the last two years. She'd done everything she could think of outside of coming out and asking him to be her Dom.

Daniel lifted her chin, forcing her to look up at him. Her gaze lingered on his length before rising to look into his eyes. It was dark in the kitchen, the only light coming from the hallway and the windows along the back wall. She wished she could see his face better. Maybe then she could tell what he was thinking. "What happened?"

"I was getting a bowl of cereal."

He rubbed his thumb along the side of her cheek, and she closed her eyes, relishing his touch.

Then it was gone. She opened her eyes as he took a step back. He picked up the milk, poured it into the bowl she had sitting next to the counter full of cereal, and then placed the gallon jug back into the refrigerator.

"Eat your cereal. I'll clean up the milk."

"I can—"

Even in the dim light, she didn't miss that look. She stood, walked over to a stool, and sat down. Picking up her spoon, she took a bite of her cereal.

Daniel opened the drawer containing the dishtowels and removed several of them. He tossed them on the floor, then kneeled to clean up the mess.

She tried not to look. Really, she did. But her gaze was drawn to his butt as it flexed and moved. She'd seen a lot of naked men at the club, men who were a lot younger, who didn't look as good naked as Daniel did.

When he stood, wet towels clutched between both his hands, he noticed her staring. Without saying a word, he threw the towels into the sink, stepped over the still damp floor, and disappeared through a doorway off the kitchen.

Ali sucked in a breath and blew it out. What a way to start the day.

She smiled and lifted the spoon to her mouth as she took another bite of her cereal. It was already beginning to get soggy, but she didn't care. She'd trade mushy cereal for seeing Daniel in all his glory any day.

When he reemerged several minutes later, he was wearing a pair of loose-fitting pants and a T-shirt. He grabbed a mop and bucket out of a tall closet, then finished cleaning up her mess.

"Thank you for cleaning up the rest of the milk," she said after swallowing the last of her cereal.

He rinsed the mop head, then returned it and the bucket to the closet. "You're welcome." His gaze lowered to the bowel in front of her. "Finished?"

She nodded and got up to take her bowl to the sink. "Again, I'm sorry I woke you."

He shrugged. "My alarm would have woken me up in another half hour anyway."

An awkward silence filled the room and she shifted on her feet. "Um. I'm gonna take a shower and get ready."

"If I'm not in the kitchen when you've finished getting ready, I'll be in my study." He tipped his head toward the other side of the living room to the hall she'd been down twice before—once the night he'd brought her home with him, and the next morning when he'd driven her back to her apartment to get her car. She had to admit she hadn't paid much attention either time. "Come find me when you're done."

Ali took her time in the shower, trying not to remember what Daniel had looked like standing so close to her, his hard cock tempting her. She was tempted to get herself off but hesitated for some reason. It wasn't as if she hadn't masturbated before. She had. Lots of times. But it felt wrong somehow. Like he'd know and be upset with her.

It was stupid. He wasn't her Dom. They had no agreement. Her body was her own and she could do with it whatever she wished.

Unfortunately, that rationalization didn't change anything. She hadn't had sex in almost two years. She'd played with some of the Doms at the club and some of them had even brought her to orgasm, but it had always been with toys or their fingers.

Turning the shower off, she yanked the towel off its holder so hard the end of it snapped against her leg. "Ouch."

She bent to rub the spot on her leg where the towel hit. "That's what I get for letting my stupid emotions get the better of me."

As she wiped the water from her body and began drying her hair, she relived the way he'd touched her cheek. It was a simple touch. Nothing special. But she'd felt cherished. Something she didn't experience often. In fact, the only other person who'd made her feel that way was her grandmother and she'd been gone for almost ten years.

Ali reached for her makeup bag and began applying a thin layer of concealer. She missed her grandmother. Gretchen Foster was everything her daughter was not. It wasn't that Ali's mother, Zelda, didn't love her. She did. In her own way. But Ali would never describe her mom as nurturing.

She finished putting on everything but her lipstick and tucked the rest of her makeup in her bag. As she selected her clothes from those she'd brought with her, she tried to pick something comfortable. She had a feeling today would be a repeat of the day before, which meant heels were out. Even thinking about yesterday caused her feet to ache.

It also made her remember Daniel's reaction to finding out she hadn't eaten lunch. Ali knew she had to do better. Even if he wasn't her Dom, he was still her friend and he cared about her. Even her best friend, Kim, got on her case when she skipped lunch.

It was so much easier for Kim, though. Her best friend had no problem saying no or sticking up for herself. It wasn't that Ali couldn't. It was more she hated confrontation. Most of the time, it was easier to agree than to argue. A copout, maybe, but she'd learned it was easier not to rock the proverbial boat.

Satisfied with her clothing selection, Ali headed into the kitchen looking for coffee. What she found was Daniel, fully showered and dressed in a suit and tie. He was holding two plates of food.

"There you are." He smiled and her belly did a little flip.

"What's this?" she asked, eyeing the plates.

"Breakfast."

She hiked her purse higher onto her shoulder. "I already ate breakfast."

He carried the plates to the table. Pulling a chair out, he sat down and picked up his fork. His gaze met hers. "A bowl of cereal is not breakfast."

"Millions of kids across the country would disagree with you." It was a lame response. She knew that, but it was the best she could come up with.

Daniel took a bite, chewed, then swallowed. "What other people do is not my concern." *But you are,* was implied by the look he gave her as he scooped more food into his mouth.

Ali glanced at the clock, then back at the plate of food he'd prepared for her. It would be rude if she left it, right?

Setting her purse down on the counter, she walked over to the coffee pot and poured herself some caffeine. After doctoring it up with the cream and sugar he already had on the counter for her, she took a sip, then carried it over to the table.

The food wasn't much to look at, but it tasted like heaven. She rarely ate more than a bagel or cereal for breakfast, especially on a workday.

Before she knew it, she'd eaten the entire plate. She must have been hungrier than she'd thought.

She was about to take her plate to the sink when a scraping sound beside her drew her attention. Looking down, she saw a key. Ali looked up to meet Daniel's gaze.

"If you're going to be staying here for a while, then you'll need a key. If there's a power outage or something, the code won't work."

Ali swallowed as she tried to take in everything he'd said. "You're giving me a key to your house?"

One side of his mouth quirked up. "Yes. I'm trusting you not to throw any wild parties while I'm away."

She laughed and so did he. "I'll try to control myself."

"Good." He stood, took a step toward her, and lowered his lips to her forehead.

Closing her eyes, she felt her heart flutter and her belly clench. Then, it was gone. He was gone. Leaving her sitting at the table alone.

WHAT THE HELL was wrong with him?

The sound of the door closing, signaling Ali leaving the house, had him both breathing a sigh of relief and wanting to hit something. If he didn't have a meeting to get to in less than an hour, he would have had a nice, long run on the treadmill. Or maybe he'd spend some time pounding out his frustrations on the punching bag his youngest had insisted he install.

What had possessed him to touch her? That was the million-dollar question. The one that would be eating at him for the rest of the day.

He'd done it on impulse. She'd been upset about spilling half the milk and he'd wanted to vanquish the worry from her eyes. The urge to touch her again had been overwhelming. And then the way she'd smiled at him...he couldn't resist.

Groaning, he stalked to his study, logged onto his computer, and tried to lose himself in facts and figures. It wasn't as if he didn't know the specs on the building he was seeing today. He did. Like the back of his hand. Going over them was merely a way to kill time.

Fifteen minutes later, he realized it wasn't working. Logging off, he set the alarm and headed to his meeting. If all went well today, he'd be the proud owner of a three-story commercial building. It already had long-term tenants, which was appealing, and the price was fair given its location.

His property manager and the current owner were already waiting for him in the lobby. Rebecca saw him first. "Good morning, Mr. Ross." Normally, he and his property manager weren't so formal, but Mr. Birch was an older gentleman in his seventies, who liked such things.

"Good morning, Ms. Clawson. Mr. Birch, it's nice to see you again." He extended a hand to the man.

Mr. Birch took Daniel's hand, giving it a firm shake. "Are we ready to get started with the tour?"

"Lead the way," Daniel said, motioning for Mr. Birch and Rebecca to go first.

The walk through took a little over an hour. Whenever he purchased a new property, he wanted to see everything. It was often the less viewed areas of buildings where issues were hiding, unaddressed, but overall, the property was sound.

They ended their walk around in the basement. The furnace looked to have been replaced within the last few years. That was a major expense he shouldn't have to worry about for a while. "How long since the roof was replaced?"

Mr. Birch didn't have to think about it. "Eleven years ago."

Daniel nodded, impressed by the man's quick recall. As they'd walked around, he'd asked about windows, carpets, elevators, and even electrical and plumbing. There was a small leak in one of the bathrooms, but he thought that would be an easy fix. The only major expense he foresaw were the elevators. They were at least fifty years old. While they functioned fine for now, they were a potential expense he had to prepare for.

Offering his hand again, Daniel thanked Mr. Birch and told him they would be in touch.

"Always a pleasure," Mr. Birch said. "Call me with any questions."

Rebecca followed Daniel out to the parking lot. They didn't speak as they got into their cars and drove to his office downtown. This was a routine they'd practiced many times before.

His assistant looked up from what he was working on when Daniel and Rebecca walked through the door. "How'd the walk-through go?" Kevin asked.

"Good." Daniel took the stack of papers Kevin handed him, not bothering to flip through them. There would be time for that later. Plus, it would give him something to do to keep his mind off what happened this morning with Ali. "Anything promising?"

Kevin shrugged. "There are a couple that have potential, but only if they come down on the price."

Tucking the papers under his arm, he strode toward his office. Rebecca followed behind him.

Daniel took a seat behind his desk, setting the stack of property listings off to the side. Rebecca closed the door and took a seat opposite him.

His property manager was tall, about five-ten, and blond. She looked good in her business suit. It hugged her waist, accentuating her curves. She was pretty. They'd been working together for five years and got along well. And at forty-seven, she was more suited for him than Ali ever would be.

But he wasn't attracted to Rebecca. Setting aside the fact that she worked for him, she didn't spike his heart rate or have his cock straining against his pants. For the last two years, there was only one woman who did that for him.

"I think it's a good investment for you," Rebecca said, pulling him out of his thoughts.

He cleared his throat. "Yes, it seems to be. We need to run some numbers on the elevators, though. They're older than I like to have in my buildings, and I want to be prepared."

"Of course." She typed something into her phone. "I'll get the numbers together and have them for you by tomorrow."

They spoke for another thirty minutes about the property before Rebecca stood, promising to give him a call as soon as she had everything together. As she walked out of his office, he let his gaze linger on her ass. It was nice. But other than general appreciation, his body didn't react. And for the second time that day, he wondered what the hell was wrong with him.

Kevin brought him a sandwich at noon, and he ate it at his desk while going through the new property listings. He tried to concentrate on square footage and the number of bedrooms, but it was a battle. It was almost a relief when his phone rang. "Hello?"

He spent the next hour addressing some tax questions with his CPA. And while he could have passed the task off to Kevin, Daniel had needed the distraction. For the first time that day, he'd been able to push Ali to the back of his mind.

At three o'clock, he said goodbye to his assistant and drove to one of his rehab properties. He wasn't planning to keep this one. It was in an up-and-coming neighborhood and prices in the area were soaring. If he could keep the remolding costs down, he was set to make a hefty profit.

He strolled through the property, making note of the progress. The bathrooms were almost finished, and the kitchen cabinets were installed. If all went well, he should be able to have the house staged and on the market in thirty days.

"I didn't know you were stopping by today," Jeff, his project manager, lowered the drywall screw gun he was holding.

"Looking good."

Jeff glanced at the bathroom they'd gutted and reconfigured. "The tile guys are coming Friday, and then we can get the floor in."

"How are we doing with the schedule?" While Rebecca handled almost everything for his rental properties, Daniel was more hands-on with his flips.

"Two weeks."

To someone who'd never flipped houses, they might think Jeff was saying the house would be done in two weeks. What he was really saying was that they were two weeks behind the initial schedule. Construction was always about delays. Whether it was waiting on materials, uncovering unknown issues that had to be addressed, or problems with subcontractors, things never went as planned. There was always something and two weeks was better than he'd expected.

"I'll let you get back to work," Daniel said. "Call me once the painting's finished. I want to look at it before we put the flooring in." The color his designer chose for the master bath was concerning him, but he was trusting her judgment and moving forward with it.

Jeff nodded, and Daniel took his leave. It was almost four thirty, and he debated whether to head home or stop by the gym. Ali had a key and the code, so it wasn't as if he had to be there when she got home. But he wanted to be.

Daniel pulled into his driveway and maneuvered his SUV into its place in the garage. After tuning off the engine and grabbing his briefcase, he made his way inside.

The house was quiet. Ali wasn't home yet.

Not that he expected her to be. It was only five thirty. Given rush hour traffic, he didn't expect her till around six.

He tugged at his tie as he made his way through the main living area. Once in his bedroom, he shed his suit jacket and removed his cufflinks. They landed with a clinking sound as he placed them in the engraved dish his daughter gave him one Christmas nearly fifteen years before. Then he rolled up his sleeves and headed back to the kitchen to start prepping dinner.

Halfway through chopping the peppers, he heard the front door open and a whoosh of air left his lungs. Ali was home.

No. Not home. She was here. This wasn't her home. It was his home. She was only staying here until he found her somewhere else to live.

Her shoes clicked on the hardwood floors as her steps drew closer. Then, she stopped.

Daniel took what he hoped was a calming breath and glanced over his shoulder.

She met his gaze. "Hi."

He grinned, taking her in and feeling his groin tighten at the sight. "Hi."

Ali shifted on her feet and looked down. "Let me change and I'll help you with dinner."

"That's all right. I'm almost finished prepping everything. Take your time and I'll call you when it's ready."

She scanned the plethora of vegetables on the counter, then nodded and turned toward the hall that led to her room.

Daniel went back to his chopping. As he drizzled oil into the sauté pan and turned on the heat, he tried not to think about how much better he felt now that she was there. His feelings didn't matter. All that matter was what was best for Ali.

CHAPTER 5

*A*fter changing into a pair of leggings and a T-shirt, her favorite after-work attire, Ali dialed her best friend. They talked, at least by text, every day, but she hadn't spoken to Kim since Sunday afternoon. She wondered how her friend was enjoying her new living arrangements.

Granted, Kim and Justin had been living together for almost two months, but now it was official. The lease on Kim's old apartment was up and all her things were either at Justin's house or in storage.

Kim answered on the second ring. "Did you tell your boss where to shove it yet?" The last text Ali sent to her friend had been a rant about her boss, so of course that was where Kim would start their conversation.

"No, I haven't." Her boss was a royal pain in the ass. Today he'd told her to go to the hospital pharmacy and visually verify a medication had been received. The pharmacy had been busy, so it had taken her almost an hour to find what she'd needed. When she'd returned, her boss had been fuming, demanding to know where she'd disappeared to. When she'd tried to explain, he'd cut her off and ordered her out of his office.

"You need to find another job. Or, at least, another position. Doesn't the hospital have anything else you could do?"

Ali sighed and plopped onto the bed. "I've been keeping an eye out, but I have to be careful. If my asshole boss gets wind of it, I might not have a job at all. He'd love an excuse to fire me." She needed to change the subject. The last thing she wanted to do was talk about her jerk of a boss. "How's your new living arrangement?"

She could almost see Kim's smile through the phone. "Really good."

"Oh? Do tell."

"I wish we hadn't waited, Ali. I mean, we wasted so much time when we could have been together," Kim said.

"But you're together now. That's what matters." Even as she said it, Ali's thoughts drifted to Daniel. How long did she have with him?

Not that she really had him. Not like that. But she couldn't stay in his house forever. Even if he was okay with her being there, it wouldn't be good for her mental well-being.

"True." Her friend hummed. "And we're enjoying making up for lost time."

Her friend giggled and Ali joined her. "I bet you are."

"Yes, well, enough about me. How are your neighbors? Still banging the night away?"

Ali rolled her eyes. "I wouldn't know."

The other end of the phone was silent for a long moment. "What do you mean you don't know? Did you get ear plugs to wear to bed or something?"

Biting the inside of her cheek, Ali debated whether to tell her friend about her current living arrangements. Kim would read something into it that wasn't true. As much as Ali had tried to downplay it, her best friend could read her like a book. She knew Ali had feelings for Daniel. "No. I didn't get ear plugs. I sort of...found somewhere else to stay for a while."

Again, she was met with silence from the other end of the line. "Ali, what's going on?"

Closing her eyes as if that would somehow shield her from whatever Kim's reaction would be, she spat it out, "Daniel saw me yawning when we were helping you move on Sunday and..."

"And?"

Ali turned her head toward the door. Daniel was in the kitchen, cooking for her. For them. She closed her eyes and answered her best friend. "I'm staying at his house for a while. Just until I can find something else."

Silence.

Not exactly the reaction Ali was expecting. "You still there?"

"Yeah. I'm still here. I'm just trying to decide if I heard what I thought I did." She hesitated. "Did you say you're at Daniel's house? As in sleeping under the same roof as he is?"

She choked out her response. "Yes."

"Girl, you need to spill and be quick about it."

Ali shrugged, even though her friend couldn't see her. "There's not much to tell. I told him about my neighbors, and he offered to let me stay in one of his spare rooms."

"One of his spare rooms?"

Sitting up, Ali leaned against the headboard. "Yes."

"And where is he sleeping?" Kim's voice dripped with suggestion.

"It's not like that." What Ali had dubbed the milk incident came to mind. She'd replayed that scene in her head hundreds of times. What if she'd opened her mouth, inviting him to slide his cock inside when she'd been on her knees in front of him? Would he have guided her mouth to him and let her suck him off?

Her sex clenched at the thought, and then disappointment filled her once again. He didn't want her that way.

"What's it like then?" Kim's question pulled her back to the present.

"I'm in one of his spare bedrooms." When her friend didn't respond, Ali continued, "His bedroom is at the back of the house."

"And how do you know where his bedroom is?"

Her friend wasn't going to let this go. Not that Ali could blame her. "I told you it isn't like that. He told me his bedroom was down the back hall if I needed him for something."

"The back hall? Just how big is this house?"

"Pretty big. I've seen most of the downstairs. Except for his bedroom, of course. But I haven't been upstairs yet."

"Wow," Kim said. "I never would have guessed. He seems so—"

A knock sounded on her door. "I've got to go."

Kim chuckled. "Tell Daniel I said hi."

Ali didn't bother to respond before disconnecting the call. She scrambled off the bed and went to answer the door.

Daniel looked her over for a long moment before speaking. "Dinner's ready."

"Oh. Thanks." She tossed her phone onto the bed, then stepped out into the hallway.

Daniel turned on his heel and strode toward the kitchen.

The chicken and shrimp stir-fry he'd made smelled delicious. Her mouth was watering before she took the first bite. "This is really good," she said after swallowing.

"Thank you." He lifted the glass to his lips, drawing her gaze.

Ali forced herself to look away and took a couple more bites. She was amazed by how good he was in the kitchen. The only other man she'd met who could cook this good was Drew. He'd brought spaghetti Bolognese to the submissive group once and she'd almost had an orgasm right there. The man could cook. So could Daniel.

"How did you learn to cook like this?"

He scooped up some rice, then stabbed a piece of broccoli. "I took a few cooking classes, but there was also a lot of trial and error."

"Wow. That's impressive. Most single guys would rather live on takeout or ramen noodles."

"If it was just me, I would have been fine with that, but I wanted healthier meals for my kids when they were here."

She almost choked on her food. Kids? Ali reached for her glass of water and drank, downing half the glass. "You have kids?"

"I do. Three of them."

Before she could stop herself, she scanned the room for any signs of children. There were no toys or children's books lying around. Granted, there were parts of the house she hadn't seen, but surely there would be evidence in the living room and kitchen.

And where were they? She had to assume they were with their mother.

Their mother. Or mothers. She had no idea.

So many thoughts were swirling through her head. "Do they live around here?"

He stood and she thought she saw sadness cloud his features. "Not anymore."

"Oh. I'm sorry."

"It's all right. Kids grow up and move away. That's life."

Even though he attempted a smile, it didn't reach his eyes. She wanted to comfort him. "How old are they?"

"Twenty-seven, twenty-five, and twenty-one."

"Oh." Her fork hovered in mid-air as she processed the new information.

He chuckled and turned his back on her. "I'm an old man, Ali."

"You're not old."

He wiped his hands on a kitchen towel before addressing her again. "Did you want more?" He tilted his head toward the stir-fry.

She blinked and looked down at her plate. "No. Thank you. I think I'm good."

Daniel worked to put the remainder of the food away as she finished eating. Ali couldn't stop thinking about what she'd learned. He had kids. Adult kids. Kids she never knew existed.

How many other things didn't she know about him?

His shirt bunched and flexed as he moved around the kitchen, and she felt that same stirring low in her belly. Finding out this new information only made her want to know more. To know everything about him. "Daniel?"

He glanced at her for a moment before placing the leftovers into the refrigerator.

"Have you ever played twenty questions?"

* * *

DANIEL SHUT the door on the refrigerator and paused, thinking about her question. "I don't think so."

"Never?"

He leaned back on the counter, crossing his arms. "Is that one of the twenty questions?"

She laughed. "No."

He smiled, loving the sound of her laughter.

"But seriously, you've never played twenty questions to get to know someone before?"

Grabbing the dishtowel, he wiped the counter, then hung it back in its place. "Not that I can recall, no."

Ali pushed back from the table and stood. She carried her plate to the sink, rinsed it, then placed it in the dishwasher. "Let's play, then."

Before he could respond, she took her glass, still half filled with water, and headed into the living room. She sat down on the couch, tucking her legs beneath her, watching him.

Should he play along? He was probably playing with fire.

"What the hell," he muttered too low for her to hear.

Her smile grew as he walked into the living room and lowered himself into his favorite high-backed chair. "Do you want to go first or should I?" she asked.

"This game was your idea." He had to admit he was curious as to what she'd want to know about him. It wasn't as if they were strangers. Then again, there was only so much of his life he shared at the club.

She sat up a little straighter. "How old are you?"

"Fifty-five." While she may not have known his exact age, she had to have an idea.

Ali nodded. "Okay. Your turn."

What should he ask? He knew how old she was. "What's your full name?"

She grimaced a little. "Allison Margret Foster."

"I take it you don't like your name?"

The sides of her mouth pulled down into the cutest pouty frown. "Not really."

"Was Margret a family name?" He couldn't remember the last time he'd met someone named Margret who wasn't older than he was.

"Yes. And that's three questions in a row. You're only supposed to ask one, and then it's my turn to ask another question."

Daniel chuckled. "Sorry. Go ahead. What's your next question?"

"What's your favorite color?"

"Blue." His gaze was drawn to her blue eyes, and he had to force himself to look away. He took a sip of his water. "Yours?"

"Purple."

That made sense. He'd seen her wear purple a lot at the club. She had this bodysuit she wore sometimes. Then the pretty corset with purple ribbons that framed her breasts.

Luckily, her next question dragged his thoughts away from their dangerous direction. "Your kids. What are their names?"

He knew they'd touch on his kids again and he was okay with that. Talking about his kids reminded him how wrong his attraction to Ali was. "Cassandra, Bradley, and James." And before she could ask the follow-up question he knew she'd ask, he continued, "Cassandra's the oldest. James the youngest."

She looked more interested to find out about his children than he thought she'd be. "Do you see them often?"

"I thought we were trading questions."

Ali narrowed her eyes at him. "You asked three questions in a row earlier."

Daniel laughed. "So I did." He took another drink of his water, wondering if he should have poured something stronger for this game of theirs. "No, not often. Not anymore."

"When—"

"I think it's my turn now," he said.

She nodded and gestured for him to go ahead.

What should he ask? "Have you lived in St. Louis all your life?"

"No. My grandmother and I moved here when I was ten."

His eyebrows rose at that. What had happened to her mother?

But he didn't get a chance to think about that question too much before she asked her next one. "What do you do for a living?" She paused. "I mean, I thought you were in real estate, but..."

He grinned. "But I live in a really nice house?"

"Yeah." She shifted uncomfortably. "I mean, I know you can make a good living as a real estate agent, but...I mean..."

Daniel smiled and released a soft chuckle. "It's all right. I know what you mean. And I am a real estate agent. Although, I don't often look for properties on behalf of other individuals." He hesitated, wondering what her reaction would be. "I'm more of an investor."

She opened her mouth, then closed it again. He knew she wanted to ask another question, but she was trying to play by the rules of the game.

He took another sip of his water. "Tell me about your grandmother."

"That's not really a question." There was a little twinkle in her eyes, and he knew she was messing with him.

"Okay. What was your grandmother like?"

A smile lit her face as she thought of her grandmother. "She was spunky. She'd tell you her opinion even if you didn't want to hear it." Ali's smile faded and a sadness draped over her features.

Daniel was out of his seat before he knew what he was doing. He closed the distance between them, sat down next to her, and cupped the side of her face.

"What is it?"

She waved one of her hands in dismissal. "I just miss her. She always knew what to do, you know?"

He held her gaze, not missing the extra moisture glinting in her eyes. For some reason, he felt as if this was about more than her simply missing her grandmother. "Is there something you wish you could discuss with your grandmother?" He brushed a strand of her hair behind her ear. "I might not be as wise as your grandmother, but I'll help if I can."

Ali shook her head. "You can't help."

"Try me."

She held his gaze for a long moment, then she removed his hand from her face and stood. "I think I'm going to go to my room and read. Thank you for humoring me with the game."

Daniel stood as well. He wanted to reach out to her, but he stopped himself. "Ali?"

"I'm fine. Really. Thank you again. For everything."

He wanted to make her stay and talk to him, but he knew he had no right. "All right."

She nodded, then quickly fled down the hall to her room, leaving him standing alone in the living room, trying to figure out what had happened. One minute, they were playing twenty questions. The next, she was rushing off to her room as fast as her feet would carry her.

Had he said something inappropriate? He didn't think so. They'd been talking about her grandmother. While he understood the sadness in her eyes—he still felt the loss of his own grandmother and it had been more than twenty years since she'd passed—but he didn't think that was it.

Confused and frustrated, he made his way to his liquor cabinet and poured himself a stiff drink. The alcohol burned as it went down his throat, but he welcomed it. He poured himself another, downed it, and then closed the doors to the cabinet. As appealing as getting drunk might sound, he knew better. He wasn't twenty anymore and had no desire to deal with a hangover tomorrow.

It was still early, but the thought of staying in the living room without Ali held no appeal. He checked the doors, the security cameras, and then turned off all the lights except for the one at the end of the hall. There was no sound coming from the direction of her room, so he turned and made his way across the house to the master suite.

He sat on the edge of his bed and gazed out the patio doors, watching the moonlight as it reflected off the pool. As much as he replayed the last few minutes of their conversation in his head, he couldn't for the life of him figure out what had happened.

The muscles in his back were beginning to tense. He rolled his neck and shoulders, but it wasn't helping. He needed to find a way to relax, and he didn't have a sub handy to flog.

Well, technically he did have a sub nearby, but she wasn't an option. So, the hot tub was the next best thing.

He strolled onto his patio, turned on the hot tub, and headed back inside to give it a few minutes to warm up. While the calendar said it was spring, there was still a bite in the air. He hadn't tested the water in the pool, but if he had to guess, it was probably close to forty or fifty degrees. Still too cold for an evening swim.

Ten minutes later, Daniel stripped out of his clothes and padded naked outside to slip into his hot tub. He lowered himself into the warm water, lining one of the jets up with his lower back. Sighing, he tried to let the warmth work its magic.

Ali knew she couldn't avoid Daniel. It was his house after all. But she made sure to wait until the last minute before venturing out of her room and heading to the kitchen for breakfast the next morning.

Last night, all the feelings churning inside her had come to the surface. It wasn't only about her grandmother. It was about Daniel, too. Her feelings for him. The longing to have him hold her, comfort her.

It was difficult enough being around him, knowing he didn't feel the same way about her that she did him. When he'd touched her...the look in his eyes...it was too much. She'd wanted him to take her in his arms, brush his lips against her skin, and then carry her off to his bedroom.

She hadn't been able to control the emotions that felt like a weight on her chest and so she'd escaped, running off to her room.

As Ali rounded the corner, Daniel came into view. He was at the cook-top, his back to her. She stood there frozen as she watched him flip several pancakes.

She gritted her teeth and stepped into the kitchen, plastering a smile on her face. "Morning."

Daniel laid the spatula on the counter, turned, and looked her over from head to toe. His brow creased in concentration. Had he been worried about her?

Of course he had been. He took care of her. That's what he did. That was who he was.

She sat down at the island, trying to look casual. "Pancakes, huh?"

He stared at her for a long moment, then grabbed the spatula again and removed the pancakes from the griddle. "I thought maybe you could use some comfort food this morning. I also made eggs and sausages." He nodded toward a covered plate already on the table.

Ali felt as if she needed to apologize. She wasn't sure why, but she'd obviously upset him when she'd run off. "I'm sorry about last night. I shouldn't have left like that."

"It's all right. I was close to my grandmother, too."

He thought she'd left because they were talking about her grandmother. She wished that were true, but she also wasn't going to correct him.

He carried a plate full of pancakes to the table, and she followed.

Taking her seat, she didn't say any more and tucked into her pancakes.

Three hours later, Ali was sitting at her desk, going through an email her boss had sent her the night before. Twenty items. All numbered.

She'd managed to get through the first six before he called her into his office. "You wanted to see me?"

"Did you get the list I sent you last night?" Grant Jacobson asked.

"Yes. I've been working on it." Why he asked, she had no idea. Every morning when she came into the office, she had an email from him waiting for her.

He nodded but didn't look up from whatever he was working on. "What are you doing Thursday night?"

His question was unexpected. "Um..."

Her boss didn't give her time to formulate any more of a response. He handed her an envelope, then went back to what he was doing. "One of the hospital's largest donors is holding a fundraiser. Normally, I take my wife."

She stared at the envelope in her hand. Was he asking her to go with him? "Um..." She sounded like a broken record. Why couldn't she say something?

"Since I'm unable to go this year, you'll need to go in my place."

Ali breathed a sigh of relief. He wasn't asking her to be his date. Thank heavens. She wasn't sure if she could stand next to him for hours and pretend she liked him.

He went on. "It's black tie. Do you have a dress you can wear?"

"Yes. I—"

"Good." He paused. "And you'll need a date." Finally glancing up from his papers, he looked her in the eye for the first time. "Surely that won't be a problem. You have a boyfriend or...something?"

The way his gaze raked over her made her skin crawl. "Um. I'm sure I can find someone to go with me."

Lowering his gaze, he began scribbling something on the paper in front of him. She had no idea how long she stood there, but apparently it was too long. "Don't you have work to do?" he asked.

"Yes." Ali turned on her heels and scrambled out of his office.

Her heart was pounding by the time she returned to her desk. She turned the envelope over and lifted the flap. Removing the invitation, she read over the details.

The fundraiser was being held at one of the posh hotels downtown. She'd never been there herself, but she'd heard they had a huge crystal chandelier in the lobby. The dinner started at seven o'clock, which meant she would have to get home, change, and make it back downtown in two hours. While not impossible, it was going to be tight.

And then there was the issue of a date. Ali chewed on her bottom lip. Maybe Justin could go with her.

As soon as the idea came to her, she knew it wouldn't work. Mr. Jacobson said it was black tie. Justin wasn't a formal type of guy. She doubted he had a tux hanging in his closet and there wasn't time for him to rent one and have it fitted.

Peeking in her boss's office, he had his back to the door, his phone to his ear. That meant he would be on the call for a while. She grabbed a stack of papers that needed to be shredded and stuffed the invitation in her purse before slinging it over her shoulder.

As soon as she stepped into the elevator, she pulled out her phone. Kim answered on the second ring. "What's wrong?"

Kim and Ali texted back and forth throughout the day, but it was rare either of them called the other. Between Kim's meetings and Ali's boss, texting was easier...and safer. "Can you meet me for lunch today?"

"Are you okay?" The concern in Kim's voice was impossible to miss.

"Yeah. I just need to run something by you, and it can't wait."

"Okay. Let me check." She paused. "When did you want to meet?"

Ali checked the clock on her phone. It was only ten thirty. She normally didn't take lunch, if she took a break at all, until one. But she didn't want to wait that long. "Noon?"

"At the usually place?" Kim asked.

The elevator dinged, letting her know she'd reached her floor. She exited, still holding the phone to her ear. "Definitely." Ali was in desperate need of some chocolate, and no one had better chocolate mousse than Giorgio's.

"Are you sure you're okay?"

"Yeah, but I've gotta go. See you at noon." Ali disconnected the call before her best friend could grill her any more. It wasn't that she didn't want to spill everything to Kim, but there were too many people around and she didn't want someone to overhear.

Like clockwork, one of the biggest gossips in the hospital strolled out of the mailroom. "Ali!" Joyce's smile was friendly, but Ali knew better. The woman would throw anyone under the bus if it suited her.

"Hi, Joyce."

"Picking up mail?" she asked.

"Nope. Just dropping off some papers to be shredded." Ali lifted the stack of papers in her left hand.

"That little bit?" She waved her hand in dismissal. "Isn't your boss keeping you busy enough?"

Ali forced herself to keep smiling. "Speaking of busy, I need to get moving. Have a good day, Joyce."

Brushing past the woman, she entered the mailroom, found the shred bin, and dumped her stack into it. Luckily, Joyce was nowhere to be seen as she headed back to the elevator.

The next hour and a half dragged. But her boss, thank heavens, left her alone.

At eleven fifty-five, Ali logged off her computer, grabbed her things, and made a beeline for the elevator. Unfortunately, Grant Jacobson decided to leave at the same time. His mouth turned down in a disappointed frown as he got on the elevator and pushed the button for the parking garage. He glanced at his watch. "You're taking lunch early."

"I'm meeting a friend."

He didn't comment.

The elevator jerked as it reached the first floor. The doors opened and she couldn't exit the elevator fast enough.

It took her another five minutes to reach the restaurant. Kim was already there waiting, and Ali slid into the seat across from her. "I already put in our order."

They always got the same thing when they came here. "Thanks," Ali said.

"You're welcome. Now, tell me what's going on." Kim paused. "And don't tell me nothing because I know better."

Ali removed the fundraiser invitation from her purse and pushed it across the table toward her friend.

Kim examined it, then handed it back. "I take it you have to attend?"

"Yes." Ali bit the inside of her cheek. "And I'm supposed to bring a date." She leaned closer as if she were sharing some secret. "Justin doesn't happen to have a tux tucked away in his closet, does he?"

Her friend laughed. "Not that I've seen." Then Kim sighed. "Although, he would look really good in a tux."

Ali flopped back in her chair. "Drat!"

Kim stared at her friend. "I bet I know someone who might have a tux hanging around. And who will go with you if you'd ask."

"You do?"

Her friend nodded, pressing her lips together, trying to suppress a smile.

It took Ali a few moments to realize why. When it hit her, she shook her head. "No. I can't."

"Why not?" Kim was no longer hiding her amusement. "You said the man has money, so he most likely owns a tux or can get his hands on one quickly."

"Yes, but—"

"But what?" Kim paused long enough for their server to bring their food and leave them alone again. "Look, you don't have many options here. This fundraiser's in two days, right?"

Ali's shoulders slumped. "What if he says no?"

Kim snorted. "You need him. He's not going to say no."

Her friend was right. Daniel would probably say yes if she asked him to go with her. The thought of asking him had her stomach doing summersaults, but it wasn't as if she had a lot of options. "Okay, I'll ask him."

"Great!" Kim twirled her pasta around her fork. "Now tell me how you got roped into this in the first place."

* * *

It was after seven by the time Daniel drove his SUV into his garage. Mr. Birch had countered his offer and Daniel had spent a large portion of the day going over figures and deciding how to proceed. He opened the door to his home and was immediately hit by the smell of food.

He took a deep breath, enjoying the scent of roasted chicken and something sugary. But it wasn't the promise of good food that had his heart rate accelerating.

Tossing his keys onto the side table, he removed his jacket and headed toward the kitchen. As he emerged from the hall, he heard a noise, then a mumbled curse. Ali came into view, her dark hair pulled back into a ponytail, exposing the curve of her neck.

She reached for a paper towel to clean up whatever she'd spilled on the counter. A smile spread across his face as he watched her move. She was wearing the apron his daughter had given him for Christmas several years ago. It was too big for her, the fabric wrapping all the way around her and hanging past her knees.

He must have moved or something because her gaze drifted in his direction a moment before she jumped, letting out a little gasp. Then she composed herself.

"I didn't hear you come home."

Her cheeks were flushed, but he wasn't sure if that was from the shock of seeing him or the heat of the stove. "I didn't mean to startle you."

"It's all right. I guess I was too focused on what I was doing."

Daniel walked toward her, taking in the mess on the counter. It was littered with flour, both white and brown sugar, and chocolate chips. "Are you making cookies?"

"Chocolate chip." She wiped her hands on the apron, then crossed to his pantry cabinet. "You like cookies, right?"

"Of course. Doesn't everyone?" When his kids were younger, they'd made cookies every weekend. It was part of their special time together. One of the rare bonding moments he'd had with them once they'd become teenagers and it wasn't cool to hang out with their dad.

Ali took a deep breath and released it before removing a bag of pecans. "Nuts or no nuts?"

He was beginning to feel as if he were missing something. She was smiling, but it wasn't reaching her eyes.

Daniel removed the bag from her hand and placed it on the counter. "Tell me what's wrong?"

She averted her eyes. "Nothing's wrong."

"Ali, look at me."

Obediently, she met his gaze. There were worried lines around her eyes.

He stood and waited.

She shifted her weight and started to look away, then caught herself.

Daniel waited.

"I need to ask you a favor." Ali closed her eyes. "I have to attend a fundraiser on Thursday night and…" She paused. "I have to take a date."

Several thoughts swirled in his head at once. Thoughts of her in a beautiful dress, smiling and mingling. Then his mind went to places it shouldn't.

But before he could go too far down the rabbit hole, she continued, "It's black tie and I don't know anyone else who might have a tux." She sucked in a breath and looked at him again. "I mean, I don't know if you have a tux either, but I figured that maybe you would. If you don't, though, I would understand. I don't—"

He placed a finger over her mouth, stopping her mid-sentence. Her warm breath fluttered against his skin, making him think very impure thoughts.

She opened her eyes, gazing up at him. The look in her eyes told him he hadn't misunderstood what she'd said. Or what she was asking, but he wanted to clarify anyway. "You want me to be your date for the fundraiser?"

Daniel still had his finger over her lips, so she just nodded.

All those impure thoughts he'd been having moments before sprang to the surface again and he felt himself growing hard. He gazed into her eyes, getting sucked in, wanting nothing more than to kiss her.

But instead, he dropped his hand and took a step back. He needed to get his head on straight, now more than ever. "I'd love to escort you, Miss Foster."

She let out the cutest giggle. "Thank you. I appreciate it. I'll make it up to you. I promise."

He chuckled, pushing away thoughts of just how she could make it up to him. "Taking a beautiful woman to an event isn't exactly a hardship."

A light shade of pink stained her cheeks, and she returned her attention to the counter. "Do you like nuts in your chocolate chip cookies, or should I leave them out?"

"Nuts. Definitely nuts." He opened the bag of chocolate chips, took a handful, and popped them into his mouth.

She smiled, the tension in her posture easing. "Nuts it is."

He excused himself for a few minutes, disappearing into his room to change out of his suit and tie. Luckily, he didn't have to wear it most days, but when there was a lot of money on the line, he made sure to dress the part.

By the time he returned, Ali had removed the chicken from the oven. "Would you like some help?" he asked.

She rolled the last of the cookie dough between her palms and placed it on the baking sheet. "Can you carve the chicken?"

As he sliced the chicken, Ali placed the cookies into the oven and put the finishing touches on the rest of the meal. She'd roasted a variety of vegetables and used his air fryer to make baked potatoes.

He removed two plates from the cabinet and placed a healthy portion of chicken on each. Ali added a potato and a scoop of vegetables.

They carried their food to the table. Daniel waited until they were a few bites in before he asked more about this fundraiser. "What is the fundraiser for?"

Instead of answering, she hopped out of her chair and walked over to her purse. She removed an envelope and brought it him. "I'm not sure. That's all my boss gave me."

He removed the invitation and read over it. However, other than the where and when, it didn't say much else. "Are you coming back here to change, or would you like me to pick you up at your apartment?"

"I was thinking about that." She took a drink of her water. "I don't get off work until five and we have to be there before seven."

"I'll pick you up at your apartment then."

"Are you sure?" she asked. "I mean, I can come back here if that's easier."

"Nonsense. We have to drive into the city anyway, and I don't want you rushing," he said.

The alarm on Ali's phone went off and she got up to take the cookies out of the oven. The room was filled with the delicious aroma of sugar and chocolate.

Ali returned to her stool, picked up her fork, and smiled at him. "They should be cool enough by the time we're finished eating."

He tried to ignore the way his insides reacted to her beautiful smile. "I hope you made enough."

"Are you trying to tell me you have a sweet tooth?" she asked.

Daniel chuckled. "I admit nothing."

She snorted. "I'll have to make you cookies more often then."

"Guess that means I'll be spending more time at the gym."

"I need to get back to exercising. I haven't worked out since I've been here," Ali said as she ate her last bite of chicken.

He stood with his empty plate and offered to take hers as well. "I'll show you where the gym is upstairs."

"Upstairs?"

His house wasn't what you'd call traditional, but that's one of the reasons he loved it. The main part of the house was all on one level, but there was a staircase that led to what was essentially a separate living area. Daniel should have had her stay there, but the thought hadn't even occurred to him. He didn't want to examine too closely why that was. "Come. I'll show you."

Each with a cookie in hand, they made their way down the hallway past her room, the laundry area, and a second sitting room to the back staircase. She stopped at the top of the stairs to look out the large windows into the backyard. "I had no idea this was here." She met his gaze. "I mean, I saw the house was two stories from the outside and I knew there were stairs, but..."

"It's all right. I don't come up here much. I've thought about moving the gym downstairs, but my son likes to work out at all hours of the night when he comes to visit."

"Bradley or James?"

She'd remembered. For some reason, that made him happy. "James." He crossed the open area to the largest room along the back of the house. The room was originally supposed to be a bedroom, so the windows didn't go to the floor, but the view was still great. Daniel flipped on the lights, illuminating the room. "He's training for a fitness competition, so everything's about watching his food intake and how many squats he can do."

"I hate squats. The only thing worse than squats are burpees."

Daniel laughed. "He does those, too."

She shuddered, and his gaze went directly to her tits. She had the most perfect breasts. In his weaker moments, he'd imagined what they would feel like in his hands—what they would taste like.

He tore his gaze away from her and turned toward the treadmill. "The treadmill and bike are easy to use and there are weights going from five to fifty pounds along the wall. I also have some resistance bands and a yoga mat in the corner. If there's something else you need, just ask."

Ali didn't respond right away, and he turned to see if something was wrong. She took a step toward him, then stopped herself. "I should probably get back in the kitchen and clean up."

"No. You cooked. I'll take care of cleaning up. You can use the time looking around." Before she could say anything to make him stay, he bound down the stairs and got to work in the kitchen.

CHAPTER 7

*A*li remained in the gym area for a few more minutes, looking over the machines. They didn't look all that different than what she was used to. Her apartment complex had a small gym attached to the office and she tried to utilize it at least twice a week. She probably needed to go more often, but she hated working out.

Venturing back downstairs, she went to her room. She debated staying there for the evening, but after asking Daniel for a favor, she didn't think it would be good manners to hide out in her room.

She grabbed the book she was currently reading, then walked to the main part of the house. Daniel was still in the kitchen. He glanced over at her as she walked past, then went back to what he was doing.

The best part about her spot on the couch was that she had a perfect view of the kitchen. Daniel put everything away, including the cookies—but not before eating another one—and then wiped down the counters.

Ali had her book open, pretending to read, but she was really watching his every move. He started the dishwasher, then turned to find her staring.

"Enjoying your book?"

Blushing, she looked down at the page in front of her. "It's a good story."

"Are you sure about that? You've been on the same page since you sat down."

He'd noticed that? "I got distracted watching you cleaning up."

Daniel sat down in his chair and reached for his own book. "I can't imagine watching me put food away was all that fascinating."

She didn't know about that. Watching him move about the kitchen, bending and reaching, his slacks pulling tight against his ass making her muscles pulse and clench. "I like watching you."

His face fell and she regretted her confession. But instead of commenting, he nodded toward her book. "What are you reading?"

"Oh." She felt her cheeks heat again. "Um. It's a romance."

He raised an eyebrow. "Let me see."

Ali hesitated. Then she stood and handed it to him. She worried her bottom lip, waiting for his reaction. The romances she tended to read weren't exactly pure and wholesome.

Daniel took it and skimmed over the page she was supposed to have been reading. Things were beginning to heat up between the hero and the heroine, but they hadn't done more than kiss yet.

He flipped the page, read some more, and then flipped again. She knew the moment he got to the good part. His mouth tightened and his fingers flexed. He read for several minutes, not saying anything, and kept reading.

Butterflies began to flutter in her stomach as she awaited his reaction. She knew he wouldn't be mad or anything, but would he be disappointed? That would almost be worse. Even though he wasn't her Dom, she respected him, and she wanted his respect in return.

Daniel glanced up, his eyes searching hers for a moment before holding out the book for her to take.

The tips of her fingers brushed against his as she reached for the book, and she felt warmth spread up her arm. She closed her eyes and tried to will the feeling away as it worked its way down her arm to the pit of her stomach.

"Allison?"

She opened her eyes and met his gaze. "Yes?"

His eyes darkened and her breath caught in her throat. She felt something pass between them for a moment, but then he looked down, and it was gone. "Go sit down and read your book like a good girl."

Blowing out a breath, she turned her back to him, clutching her book to her chest. "I think I'll go read in my room." She had to bite off the 'Sir' she wanted to add and left before she could embarrass herself any further. Running away from him for the second night in a row.

The next morning, he greeted her with a smile, serving her an omelet and some fruit. She thought about bringing up what had happened the night before, but what if it was all in her head? Maybe it was the part of the story he'd read that had caused that look in his eyes. She'd finished reading the chapter last night in her room, so she knew exactly what he'd seen on the page. The hero had lit candles and drizzled wax all over the heroine before going down on her and fucking her with a toy. It was so hot she'd had to dig her vibrator out of her luggage.

But it didn't matter if the look she thought she saw in Daniel's eyes had been because of the book or if she'd imagined it altogether. It didn't change anything. "I won't be here for dinner tonight. I need to run to my apartment, so I'll just go through a drive-thru or something."

He finished chewing before he responded. "How late do you think you'll be?"

She shrugged. "I don't know. I need to make sure I have everything for tomorrow night."

Again, he didn't answer right away. "I'll most likely be working late again as well. I'll pick something up for both of us and meet you at your apartment."

The impulse to ask him if he was sure was on the tip of her tongue, but she stopped the words from escaping. She knew he hated it when she did that. So instead, she thanked him and moved on. "Do you work late a lot?"

"Only when I'm closing a deal."

"A new investment?" she asked.

He finished his omelet. "I'm attempting to purchase a building down-town and we're in the middle of negotiations."

"Does that happen a lot?"

Daniel grinned at her as he walked to the sink with his plate. "Sometimes."

"I don't think I'd be good at something like that." In fact, she knew she'd be horrible at it. Ali didn't like confrontation. In fact, she avoided it whenever she could. Even when it came to scenes at the club, she had difficulty with negotiating. That's one of the reasons why, when he'd offered, she'd let Daniel negotiate the scenes for her with the other Doms. She'd told him what she wanted, what her limits were, and he set it up.

"Are you finished?" He nodded to her now empty plate.

"Yes. Thank you."

He took her plate, then continued their previous conversation. "It takes practice like anything else. A lot of it can be learned, but some of it is instinct."

Ali stood and strolled toward him, wanting to get more water. She filled her glass, then turned to face him. "I bet you're really good at it."

Her words trailed off as he gazed down at her. They were standing close—so close she could feel the heat radiating off his chest. "I'm really good at a lot of things," he said.

The feeling from last night was back. Maybe she hadn't been imagining it.

"Ali?" His voice sounded a bit hoarse.

She swayed a little closer to him. "Yes?"

"You're going to be late for work."

It took a second or two for his words to register, but when they did, she blinked out of whatever trance she'd been in. Glancing at the clock, she realized he was right. If she didn't leave right now, she was going to be late.

Confused about what had happened between them, she set her still full glass on the counter and backed away. "I'll see you later."

Ali didn't wait for him to reply before grabbing her things and rushing out the door.

* * *

THE FIRST THING Daniel did when he arrived at the office Wednesday morning was check all his properties to see if something, anything, had changed. It hadn't. All his tenants were in the middle of their leases. His newest rehab would be ready before any of his rentals became available and that was still at least a month away.

Things were getting tricky with Ali. Reading part of her book last night hadn't done anything to help his attraction to her. The scene had begun innocent enough but had devolved into a hot scene involving candles being dripped over the heroine's body.

Daniel loved wax play, but he hadn't done it in a long time. His last submissive was scared to death of fire. They'd tried it once and she'd screamed her safeword before he'd gotten the wax anywhere near her.

Of course, those thoughts had led to Ali lying there, waiting for him to drip wax on her naked body. His cock twitched thinking of what her breasts would look like and her reaction to the hot substance gliding over her skin.

He groaned and rubbed his palms over his eyes, trying to will the image from his brain. Thinking about her like that would get him nowhere.

A knock on his door diverted his attention and he was grateful. "Come in."

Kevin strolled into the room. "Gail called and said there's a problem with the cabinets she needs to talk to you about."

His interior designer didn't normally call him for minor issues, which meant they'd most likely be picking out new cabinets. That would shoot his timeline to hell. "Tell her I'll meet her at the job site around two."

"Will do."

The rest of his morning was uneventful. He went through his emails, scanned the newest property listings, and made a list of those that looked interesting. Timing was key when it came to flipping houses. The ones in decent neighborhoods with potential tended to get snatched up fast. That, or the buyers wanted too much considering the work that needed to be done.

At twelve thirty, he signed off his computer and drove to the dry cleaners. His tux had been hanging in his closet for a few years and could use freshening up.

After several assurances they could have it ready for him by noon tomorrow, Daniel grabbed lunch, then headed to the job site. He walked the backyard, wanting to stay out of the areas being worked on, and came up with a game plan for the lawn. It was a decent size, but at the moment it was covered in weeds.

Gail showed up right on time and they spent the next hour figuring out what to do with the cabinet situation. The door style they'd originally picked was no longer available, so he had to pick another. That sounded easy enough, but of course what he liked didn't come in the color he wanted. By the time they were finished, he could feel a headache coming on.

He said goodbye to Jeff and walked Gail to her car, then drove to the gym. Ali was still working, which meant he had time for a swim.

He plunged into the pool, letting the water engulf his body as he glided through the water. Coming to the surface, he engaged his muscles and pushed himself through the water.

A half hour later, his muscles were burning, and he was breathing hard. He pulled himself out of the pool and noticed a woman staring. She gave him a shy smile but didn't look overly embarrassed she was caught ogling him.

She was pretty. Maybe ten years younger than he was. She was wearing a one-piece bathing suit, but it showed off her curves as it hugged her waist. But other than acknowledging how attractive she was, he didn't feel any great pull toward her. Not like he did Ali. Stifling a groan, Daniel walked to where he'd left his towel and began to dry off.

It was almost five o'clock by the time he made it back to his vehicle. Ali would be leaving work and making her way to her apartment. The thought of seeing her again had his heart rate increasing. He wanted to see her, even though he knew he shouldn't.

Daniel drove to his favorite Greek restaurant, ordering a variety of his favorites. He had no idea what Ali would like.

The closer he got to Ali's apartment, the more that feeling in the pit of his stomach began to grow. He needed a distraction.

Out of all his children, his oldest son, Bradley, called him the least. He'd graduated from law school last year and was working at a firm in Chicago. Being the lowest on the totem pole, he worked long hours. Daniel worried about him overdoing it, but as Bradley always reminded him, it would get better once he made partner. But in the ten or so years that would take, Daniel would worry. It was a father's prerogative.

It took five rings for his son to answer. "Hey, Dad."

"Are you busy?" Daniel asked.

Bradley snorted. "I'm always busy, but what's up?"

"I just haven't heard from you in a while. Have you talked to your mom?" While Daniel had been divorced for fifteen years, he was still on good terms with his ex-wife. And even if he wasn't, he wouldn't say anything bad about her to his children.

His son didn't answer right away. "Um. I think I talked to her a couple of weeks ago." He paused. "I should call her."

"Yes, you should."

Bradley chuckled. "Did you call to yell at me for not calling Mom?"

Daniel chuckled. "No. I called because I haven't heard from you either. I wanted to make sure you were still alive."

"Sorry. I'm always knee deep in work and—"

"I know," Daniel said. "But you can't let life or relationships pass you buy. Before you know it, you'll be my age."

"I think I've got a little time."

His son was twenty-five and still thought he had all the time in the world. Daniel remembered being that way at his age. Little did he know that three years later he'd have a newborn daughter. "Just don't work too hard. That's all I'm saying. You need to live your life, too."

"Says the man who does nothing but work."

The words were mumbled, but Daniel heard them. "I do have a life, you know." Daniel sighed. "Besides, we're not talking about me. I don't want you to wake up one day and realize you're forty and have nothing to show for it." He paused. "Your mother and I worry. That's all."

"I know. And I do go out with some of the guys here sometimes."

"Good." A car pulling in the parking lot drew his attention. Ali was here. His heart skipped a beat as she got out of her car and walked to her apartment, her hips swaying in her heels. "And give me a call every now and then, so I know you're okay." His words came out soft and distant.

"You okay, Dad?" Bradley asked.

Ali unlocked her door and a moment later she was gone from his sight. "Yeah, I'm good. I should probably let you get back to work so you can get home at a decent hour."

Bradley chuckled. "I'll try to call you more often."

"And call your mom."

"I will," his son promised.

"I love you."

"Love you, too, Dad."

They disconnected the call and Daniel's gaze went toward the door Ali had disappeared behind. Warmth spread through his chest and anxiety filled his belly. But before he could overthink it, he grabbed the bag of food from the passenger seat and climbed out of the vehicle.

CHAPTER 8

A knock had Ali stopping in her tracks. She'd barely removed her coat. Turning on her heel, she went to answer the door, hoping it was Daniel.

She looked through the peephole, then unfastened the chain. Pulling the door open, she stepped back to let him inside. "I wasn't expecting you yet. I just got home."

He moved past her, walking into her humble apartment. It was nothing like his house. The complete opposite, in fact. Daniel's home was all big open spaces, while her two-bedroom apartment felt tiny in comparison. It wasn't that she disliked her apartment. It was fine. She'd lived there for two years now. But it was still a small space with very basic furniture, and she couldn't help but wonder what he thought of it.

Daniel placed two bags on her kitchen counter, then removed his coat.

"Here, let me take that," she said.

He let her take his coat and she hung it beside hers on a wood coat rack near the door.

By the time she returned to her kitchen area, he'd removed all the food from the bags and had it lying on the counter. "I hope you like Greek food."

She eased around him to get to the plates. Her hip grazed his in the tight space and she sucked in a breath. Blowing it out, she tried to sound casual. "Did you get any baklava?"

He chuckled, not seeming affected in any way by their bodies brushing against each other. "You can't eat Greek food without baklava."

Ali smiled and handed him a plate. "No, you can't."

They loaded up their plates with food and carried them over to her table. It was then she realized they had a problem. She'd forgotten about the project she'd been working on at her dining room table. Her canvas and paints were covering every inch of the wood surface. "Um."

She was still contemplating what to do when he walked over and began looking at what she'd painted.

"You did this?" he asked.

"Yes. Sorry. I forgot I'd left my paints out." She set her plate on one of the chairs and began loading her paints into a shoebox.

Daniel held his plate in one hand and picked up the canvas to examine it. "I didn't know you liked to paint."

"It helps me relax."

He nodded. "We all need something that helps us deal with stress. For me, it's swimming."

She hadn't known he liked to swim, but looking at him now, she could see it. He was trim and fit, but not in a way that said he spent hours every day in a gym. Ali could imagine him in a pair of Speedos, his naked chest heaving as water droplets danced along his chest after doing laps in the pool.

Her sex pulsed and she pressed her thighs together. She turned her back to him as she felt her cheeks heat. "I'm gonna put these in the other room. Be right back."

Rushing down the hall to the spare bedroom, she placed the box of paints on the shelf in her closet and took a moment to try and catch her breath. She used to think being around him at the club was difficult. Not that it was easy. Especially when she saw him go upstairs with another submissive. But the more she was around him, the more she wanted him.

"Ali? Are you all right, sweetheart?"

She closed her eyes at his endearment. He'd called her that twice before and every time it nearly broke her heart. She knew he didn't mean it the way it sounded—like she was his. "Yeah. Just putting the paints away."

Ali felt him as he approached, then he was turning her to face him. She opened her eyes and got sucked into the depths of his gaze.

Daniel cupped the side of her face and she leaned into his touch. It was sad how much she cherished these moments. They didn't mean the same to him as they did to her, but it didn't matter. She'd take what she could get even if that made her pathetic.

He took a step closer, her chest touching his. She could feel his breath against her face as he exhaled.

Time seemed to stop as they stood there. He didn't remove his hand and she feared with every breath she took he'd stop touching her.

He rubbed the pad of his thumb along her cheek several times, then slid his hand to the back of her neck, tilting her head up. She saw something flash in his eyes a moment before his lips caressed hers.

Ali's heart stopped for a moment before restarting in double time. A desperate whimper left her throat as the feel of his lips spread white hot lightning through her veins. She wanted more and she wasn't beneath begging for it. Not when it felt like this.

A groan tore from his chest a split second before his other hand wrapped around her waist, pulling her flush against him and his mouth crashed over hers. Ali's hands gripped his waist, holding on tight. His lips glided against hers with the right mix of heat and tenderness, his tongue teasing the seam on her lips, enticing her tongue to come out and play.

She could feel his hard length pressing against her stomach. The urge to press against it, to get closer to him, was too much to bear, but before she could do anything about it, he ripped his mouth away. "No. I can't."

Then he was across the room, and she was left standing there with swollen lips and an ache between her legs she wasn't sure would ever go away. Her heart was beating a mile a minute and she was struggling to catch her breath, but she knew she had to say something. Anything.

"Why?" It was the best she could do under the circumstances. She'd never been kissed like that before and he hadn't even put his tongue inside her mouth.

Daniel looked at her. Pain, and what appeared to be regret, crossed his face. "I can't," he said again, then he darted out of the room.

Ali leaned back against the wall, attempting to settle her breathing and bring her heart rate back to normal. He'd kissed her. Kissed her, kissed her. Not a sweet peck on the lips like you'd give a friend, but a toe-curling kiss that had her wanting to sink to her knees in front of him.

Had Kim been right? Did he want her the way she wanted him?

The memory of his erection pressed against her suggested he did. But the look on his face and his declaration that he couldn't, had her confused.

She sifted through everything she knew about him, but nothing stuck out. He wasn't married anymore, but did he have a girlfriend she didn't know about? If he did, Ali hadn't seen any sign of her. Not at the club and not at his house.

Of course, she hadn't been in his bedroom, but certainly there'd be a picture or some other evidence a woman had been in his home. Right?

Her head was beginning to hurt, and her stomach let out a growl, reminding her she hadn't eaten dinner. She pushed off the wall and made her way down the hall.

Looking around, she didn't see him at first. Then, she saw him sitting on her couch, his head in his hands. His shoulders were slumped, and he was mumbling to himself.

Ali sat down beside him, keeping a few inches between them. He stopped talking to himself and glanced in her direction. Her chest clenched at the look of pain in his eyes.

She wanted to reach out to him, comfort him, but she wasn't sure her touch would be welcomed. "What's wrong?" Her voice was barely audible, but she knew he heard her.

He released a tortured sound before looking at the wall opposite where they were sitting. His chest rose, then fell again in an exaggerated breath. "I'm sorry. I...I don't know what came over me." He stood, taking her off guard. Straightening his shoulders, he looked down at her, all the previous emotion gone from his face. "It won't happen again."

She blinked several times. "I don't understand."

Daniel shook his head, then walked into the dining room.

Ali followed, confused and still incredibly turned on. "Did I do something wrong?"

"No." He rubbed a hand over his chest. "No. You did nothing wrong, Allison. It's me. I…"

Nothing was making sense. He'd kissed her. She'd kissed him back. "Do you have a girlfriend?"

"What?" He looked stunned by her question. "No."

"Then why did you stop kissing me?" she asked.

The muscle in his throat contracted as he swallowed and the vein in the side of his neck pulsed. "It was wrong. I'm sorry. I don't know what came over me."

The confusion was back. "Why was it wrong?"

He shook his head. "Our dinner's getting cold. We should eat."

She was hungry, but not for food. At least, not only for food.

Taking a chance, Ali went to stand in front of him. He didn't back away, although she got the impression he wanted to. There was a question she'd been wanting to ask him for a while now, but she hadn't had the courage. She tilted her head up, meeting his gaze. "Why won't you play with me at the club?"

"Allison, I think—"

"I think I deserve an answer." This wasn't like her, but she was taking a page out of Kim's book. Her friend always told her that if you wanted something, you had to go after it. She wanted Daniel and the only thing that had kept her from going after him was because she'd thought he wasn't interested in her that way.

He closed his eyes, took a breath, and released it. "It's easier that way."

Instead of clearing up her confusion, his responses were making it worse. "You're attracted to me."

Again, he swallowed. "Yes."

It would be difficult for him to deny it. He was still hard. His erection called to her as it tented his slacks.

Going on instinct, she lowered herself to the floor, kneeling in front of him. He must have sensed the movement because he gazed down at her, his eyes wide with what looked like fear.

Ali brought her mouth level with the bulge in his pants and looked up at him, letting her desire show in her eyes. "May I please suck your cock, Sir?"

He didn't answer.

She pressed her face against his crotch, rubbing her cheek against him. It was a dangerous game, but she had to take the chance.

Nothing happened for several very long moments. Ali was beginning to doubt herself, then he threaded his fingers through her hair. The feel of his hand cupping the back of her head had every submissive instinct in her body purring.

Her lips brushed against his length, and he moaned out a strangled, "Yes."

Ali didn't know what he was saying yes to, but she took it as an answer to her question. She reached for his belt, releasing the buckle and then going for the button on his slacks. His cock peeked its head above his boxer briefs as she lowered the zipper. She closed her mouth around the tip, sucking gently, and she felt his fingers grip the back of her head.

Heat surged in her belly as she pushed his underwear down his legs, letting his cock spring free. She closed her eyes and focused on the feel of him on her tongue as she took more of him into her mouth. With excruciating slowness, she explored every inch of him.

He held himself rigid, not moving except for his fingers as they flexed against her scalp. But after a while, she began to see patterns in his reactions. Figuring out what he liked sent a rush of excitement and arousal through her. She wanted to please him, to make him tremble the way she did when she fantasized about him being inside her.

Circling her hand around the base of his cock, she moved it up and down with the motion of her mouth as she licked and sucked and hummed along his length.

Daniel fisted her hair, sending delicious shots of pain down her scalp as his breathing grew more labored. She knew he was close—could almost feel the vibrations of his impending orgasm under her tongue.

Sucking him down as far as she could, letting the head of his cock hit the back of her throat, caused him to increase his hold. She was so wet. She wanted so desperately to touch herself, but she wouldn't. This was about showing him what she wanted. What she needed.

As if a dam broke inside him, Daniel took hold of her head with both hands and began pumping his hips. She released her throat and let him take control, using her mouth however he wanted.

It didn't take long. He'd already been on the edge. Cum shot out of his cock, the tang of it hitting the back of her tongue and throat as she swallowed it down.

Ali was basking in the glow of serving him when he stumbled backward, his back hitting the wall. Daniel looked down on her with what looked like horror for several moments before he closed his eyes and let out a mumbled curse.

Tucking himself back into his pants, he refastened his belt, then pushed off the wall.

He held out a hand and helped her stand. All the emotion was gone from his face.

"What's wrong?" she asked, getting to her feet.

He made sure she was steady, then took a step back, putting distance between them once more. "What happened tonight. What I let happen." Daniel paused and blew out a breath. "It was my fault, and I'm sorry."

CHAPTER 9

*A*li looked at him for a long time, her eyes full of questions, and Daniel couldn't blame her. He'd fucked up. "Why are you sorry?"

A part of him wanted to turn the clock back an hour before their relationship got turned on its head, but then he wouldn't know what it felt like to kiss her or have her lips wrapped around his cock. He was going to hell, but there was no helping it. "Because I'm old enough to be your father."

Her brow creased as she considered what he'd said. "You're not my father."

"That doesn't matter."

The wrinkles in her brow got more pronounced. He could see the confusion written all over her face. "I've seen you play with women younger than I am at the club, but you won't play with me. I don't understand."

He didn't miss the slight hiccup in her voice at the end and he had to force himself not to pull her into his arms. "It's not the same. That's just…"

"Just what?"

As difficult as this was, she deserved the answer. "I don't have feelings for them."

An energy filled the room as he awaited her response to his admission, but when it finally came, it wasn't what he'd expected. "I want you to be my Dom."

His heart skipped a beat as fear and excitement took hold of him at the same time. "That's not a good idea."

Ali closed the short distance between them. She stood close enough to touch and his fingers tingled with the desire to get his hands on her again. Her blue eyes sparkling in the light as she gazed up at him. "Why not?"

He didn't answer.

"Did I not serve you well?" she asked. Her lips and her question bringing back the vision of her lips around his erection. "It's been a while since I've given a blowjob, but—"

Hearing her question herself was the last straw. He covered her lips with his and kissed her again. It felt so right, and yet so wrong at the same time. He shouldn't want this. He shouldn't be enjoying this. And yet he didn't want to stop kissing her.

Resting his forehead on hers, he held her gaze as she fisted the front of his shirt. "Nothing about this has to do with you. You were perfect. You served me well." Too well. His body was still humming from his climax. It had been years since he'd come so hard in a sub's mouth.

"I don't care about our age difference," she whispered. "I want you." Then she lowered her lids, breaking eye contact. "And you seem to want me."

He had no idea what to do. Holding her like this—touching her—was a dream come true, but it was destined to break his heart and probably hers as well. He could deal with himself, but he didn't want to hurt her. Still, he couldn't let her think she'd done anything wrong. This wasn't about her. "I do want you, Ali, but I wouldn't be a good Dom for you."

"I don't want to play with anyone else. I want to play with you."

Could he give her that? Play and nothing else? Keep the emotions out of it?

He doubted it. His emotions were already involved when it came to this woman. She owned him whether she knew it or not. "You want to be my submissive?"

Her gaze met his again and he saw something there he didn't want to hope for. He shouldn't want her to say yes. He shouldn't want any of this. "Yes." She placed her palm flat on his chest and toyed with one of the buttons on his shirt. "I..." She looked down, then back up again. "I want to be the only sub you play with, though."

Daniel swallowed. He played with a lot of subs at the club. He was the best flogger and subs often approached him, wanting him to flog them. She'd never asked him, though. Not directly, anyway. Ali would say she wanted to play, and so he would find another Dom to play with her. Every time it nearly killed him, but he did it knowing it was the right thing for Ali. But now, she was standing in front of him asking if he would take care of her needs.

"You don't want to play with other Doms at the club?" Saying the words left a sour taste in his mouth, but this wasn't about him. Ali's happiness was all that mattered.

"No. Just you."

His heart felt as if it would burst from his chest. He wanted this more than anything, even though he shouldn't. But as usual, he couldn't say no to her.

He cupped her face and pressed a soft kiss to her lips. "Send me your list."

She smiled. "Hold on."

Then she was out of his arms, leaving him feeling emptier than he had in a long time. The more he touched her, the more he wanted to touch her. But he had to set some boundaries. For her sake as well as his own.

Ali returned a few minutes later holding a printout of her limits list. She handed it to him, then went to where their uneaten plates of food sat on her table. He'd completely forgotten about dinner.

"I'll go warm these up in the microwave for us." She ducked into her kitchen, leaving him to look over her limits list.

Daniel tried to concentrate on the long list of items she'd marked, but it was difficult when he could hear her in the other room. He needed to look at her list, but his body didn't care much about anything except getting his hands on her again. Of course, that was fighting with the part of his brain that was still yelling at him about how wrong it all was.

The microwave dinged, and he heard her moving things around. He shook his head and read over the first page for the tenth time. Because he'd arranged for her to play with other Doms at the club in the past, he knew a lot of her limits. Or at least, the tamer ones. But Ali had some kinks on here he wasn't aware of.

She strolled out of the kitchen a few minutes later with a plate in each hand. "I'll get us some water."

Taking a seat in front of one of the plates, he put her list aside for the time being. It would be easier to look over when he was alone.

Ali handed him a glass of water and sat down beside him. She glanced over at him before picking up her fork. "Can I ask you something?"

"Of course." His response was automatic, but once it was out there, he wondered what she'd want to know.

"Is that why you wouldn't play with me at the club? Because of the age thing, I mean."

"Yes." That and because if he played with her, he knew it would only increase his feelings for her.

She thought about that while chewing some of her food. "That explains a lot."

It was his turn to be confused. "It does?"

Ali nodded. "I always thought you weren't interested in me sexually. That you thought of me as more of a sister type. But both Kim and Justin said you wanted to play with me but were holding back for some reason."

Apparently, he must not have been hiding his interest as much as he thought. "I don't think of you as a sister."

She smiled. "Good."

He wasn't so sure about that. It would be much easier if he did think of her as a sister.

Before he could think of what to say next, there was a noise from the apartment next door. It sounded like something, or someone was being slammed against the adjoining wall. It happed twice more, and then he heard a woman's voice yell, "Yes! Harder!"

He looked at Ali, raising his eyebrows in question. "Your neighbors?"

"My neighbors."

It was impossible to continue their conversation over the racket coming from next door. It was no wonder Ali couldn't sleep if that was what she heard every night. He couldn't remember the last time he'd heard a scene at the club that loud and that was saying something.

They finished the rest of their dinner in silence. He waited until she'd finished eating, then stood. "I'll clean up while you do what you need to with your outfit for tomorrow." He began gathering their dishes. "Then we'll head home."

She shot a glance at her neighbor's apartment. They'd quieted down, but who knew how long it would last. According to Ali, it wasn't usually a one and done. "I won't be long."

* * *

ALI PLUGGED IN HER STEAMER, then pulled her dress out of the closet, along with the shoes she'd need for tomorrow night. While the steamer was warming, she went to her underwear drawer and debated which pair she should choose. Normally, she'd go for comfort, but she was hoping Daniel would be seeing said underwear. She didn't want him to peel her out of her dress only to find her in a pair of cotton briefs.

Her fingers grazed over a red bra and matching panty set. She'd bought it to wear at the club, but she'd never gotten up the courage. It was sheer and didn't cover much.

A huge grin stretched her face as she removed it from the drawer and placed it on the bed. They were going to knock his socks off. She was going to make him forget all about their age difference.

The light on the steamer lit up and she quickly gave her dress a once-over, relaxing the wrinkles. She was hoping her dress would get a reaction out of him as well.

After finishing with her dress and making sure everything was prepped and ready to go for tomorrow night, she went to find Daniel. He was sitting at her table, waiting patiently for her, her limits list in his hand.

Noticing her, he stood. "All set?"

"Yep. I think I have everything I'll need laid out."

Walking to the coat rack, he removed her coat and held it out for her. She slipped her arms into the sleeves, closing her eyes as his breath brushed against her ear when he settled the coat on her shoulders. "Is there any way you can leave work early tomorrow, so you'd have more time?"

Ali shook her head, unable to form words. No man had ever made her feel like this besides Daniel.

After donning his own coat, he followed her outside. He waited patiently as she locked up and escorted her to her car. "Surely your boss would understand. He is the one who wants you to go to this fundraiser, isn't he?"

She climbed behind the wheel of her car. "He is, but it's just easier this way."

Daniel frowned. "We're going to need to talk more about this boss of yours, but I want us to get home before dark." He leaned in, brushing his lips against her forehead, which sent tingles rippling through her, warming her from the inside out. "I'll be right behind you."

He closed her door, and she watched him walk to his SUV. She wanted to call Kim, but her friend would ask Ali questions she didn't have the answers to. Not yet anyway.

Traffic was light as they made their way out of the city to Daniel's home. She had no idea what the night would hold, but if it involved more of Daniel's kisses, she was all for it. As long as he didn't push her away.

The sun was setting by the time they drove up his driveway. It had been a long day in more ways than one, but she wasn't ready for it to end. The fear that he was going to shut her out again was still there. She didn't want to wake up tomorrow morning and go through the motions as if nothing had happened between them.

Daniel looked stoic when he came in from the garage and her worries returned. He met her gaze, holding it for a long moment before lifting the bags of food in his hand and nodding toward the kitchen. "Let me put this away, and then we'll talk."

She removed her coat and made her way into the living room. Other than the light in the foyer and the one in the kitchen Daniel had turned on, the rest of the house was shrouded in shadows.

It didn't take him long to store the leftovers from their dinner in the refrigerator, but instead of joining her on the couch, he walked past her, turning on the light as he went, and disappeared into his study. She was about to go after him when he reappeared holding several papers in his hand. It didn't take a genius to realize what they were.

He handed her his limits list, and then sat down in his chair several feet away. She understood the need to have some distance between them for this conversation, but she didn't want distance. She'd had enough of that over the last two years.

But instead of saying anything, she began reading. Their lists were extremely compatible, more so than any other Dom she'd played with. She glanced up to find him watching her. "I don't think there's much to negotiate."

"No. I don't think so either. We seem to have similar kinks." That didn't seem to make him happy.

She decided to ignore that for now, figuring he was still hung up on the age thing. "Should we talk about our differences?"

There was a long pause before he answered. "We should."

Ali thought he'd go on, but he didn't. "I don't like to be gagged." He'd listed it as love. She listed it as a soft limit, although she'd been tempted to change it to a hard limit.

"Tell me why."

She blew out a breath. "My second Dom gagged me once. He had me tied up and gagged, then started torturing my breasts." She met Daniel's gaze, not wanting to tell him the next part because she knew what his reaction would be.

"Go on." To someone who didn't know him, she doubted they'd notice the edge to his voice, but she did.

"He started using needles, something we'd never discussed. I panicked and started crying. I tried to say my safeword, but I just started coughing. He'd pierced me with five needles before he stopped to check on me."

Daniel's face was pulled tight, and his fists were curled against the arms of his chair.

"I'd never been a fan of gags before then, but after that, I steered clear. Any time a Dom suggested using one in a scene, I would just back out of the scene and say I'd changed my mind and didn't want to play anymore."

"Was this a Dom at the club?"

Ali shook her head. "No." She lowered her head, then looked up at him through lidded eyes. "He was the last man I played with before I joined Serpent's Kiss. I wanted a place to play where I felt safe."

He nodded and relaxed a little. She could tell he still wasn't happy, but he seemed to be letting it go. At least for now. "I will want to select the clothing you wear at the club."

She swallowed and lowered her gaze.

"This doesn't work if you don't talk to me." He paused. "Or have you changed your mind about wanting me to be your Dom?"

"No," she said. "I haven't changed my mind."

"Then explain your reaction."

She met his gaze for a moment before lowering it again. "I dress pretty conservatively at the club."

"I know."

Ali figured she needed to come right out and say it. "I'm not comfortable being on the main floor of the club naked. Or nearly naked."

"But you're okay being naked upstairs." It wasn't a question.

"Upstairs is different."

His eyebrows lifted a little, but other than that, he gave no reaction, but she knew he was waiting on more of an explanation.

"I just feel more...exposed. In a playroom I can focus on me and the Dom I'm playing with. On the main floor, it's different."

Daniel waited until she looked up again. "I will take that into consideration."

Not exactly the assurance she was hoping for, but at least he hadn't outright said he was going to make her prance around naked. Some Doms required that of their subs. Or, even if they allowed them to wear clothing, it was so see-through or skimpy, they might as well be naked.

Several moments passed before either of them spoke again. "Was there anything else you wanted to discuss regarding my list or yours?" he asked.

She glanced down again at his list. They really did have similar kinks. It was uncanny. "I don't think so."

He nodded. "We need to talk about the arrangement. Boundaries."

"Boundaries?" Ali didn't like the sound of that.

Daniel nodded. "I think it's best if we keep it to playing at the club."

Was he serious? One look at him told her he was. The thought of only being able to have that type of connection with him two nights a week—one really, given she worked one of the two nights the club was open, left her feeling hollow inside. Now that she'd gotten a taste of him, of how good it could be between them, she wasn't willing to limit that to the club. "No."

"No?"

"No." She placed his list on the couch cushion and came to stand in front of him. He looked up at her with wary eyes. "I want more than just playing at the club." He held her gaze and she realized if she wanted a relationship with him—one that went beyond play and friendship—that she was going to have to fight for it. For him. "I want you. All of you."

CHAPTER 10

li crawled onto his lap, took his face between her hands, and kissed him.

She was expecting to encounter some reluctance, but it was the opposite. He gripped her hips, pulling her closer. His lips danced with hers as his fingers dug into her ass.

He ran his tongue along the seam of her lips before cupping the back of her head and taking over the kiss. Ali moaned as he lined up her sex with his hard length and ground against her core. She was so wet after their kisses and having him come in her mouth earlier, she was ready to explode.

Daniel ripped his mouth away from hers and she whimpered. He held tight to the back of her head, sending shots of delicious pain down her scalp. "Are you sure?" he asked her. "This is really what you want?"

There was no hesitation. No doubt in her mind. "Yes, I'm sure."

A second passed, and then he stood, taking her with him. She held on tight as he carried her to his bedroom.

He paused for a moment at the door and flipped on the light. Ali had never been in his room, and she was tempted to look, but there would be time for that later.

Setting her on her feet next to the bed, he ran his hands up her sides and over the curve of her breasts. "What's your safeword?"

"Red."

He nodded and began unbuttoning her shirt. As he released each button, revealing more skin, he brushed his fingers over the newly exposed area. When he finally parted the flaps of her blouse, her breasts were feeling heavy, wanting to be touched.

Her shirt fell to the floor, and he made quick work of removing her bra. Cool air grazed her nipples, causing them to harden even more, and he leaned down to suck one into his mouth. Ali almost cried when he didn't linger. It had been so long since a man had really played with her breasts.

But then he was unbuttoning her pants, sliding the zipper down. He wasted no time pushing the fabric from her hips and letting it fall to the floor. In a matter of minutes, she was standing before him in nothing but her panties while he was still fully clothed.

Daniel's gaze raked over her for a long moment and he didn't disguise the heat in his eyes. He wanted her as much as she wanted him.

He snaked his hand down the front of her panties, cupping her sex, and he hummed his approval. "So wet."

Ali swayed a little as he rubbed her swollen flesh, making sure to circle her clit with each pass. He circled an arm around her waist to steady her as she grabbed onto his forearms for support. "Do you like that, Allison?"

"Yes, Sir. So good."

His lips brushed against her ear and he removed his hand. "Lie down on the bed."

It took her a moment to register what he'd said, but when she did, she did as he asked. He walked into what she assumed was his closet and returned a moment later with a dildo. Placing the items on the mattress, he climbed onto the bed, spread her legs, and buried his nose against her soaked panties. He took a deep breath before pressing his lips against her clit. She sucked in a breath, wanting him to do it again.

He hooked his thumbs in the sides of her panties and eased them down her legs, revealing her pussy to him. Daniel tossed her panties to the side, then made himself comfortable between her spread thighs. He took a long lick, circled her clit with his tongue, and then did it again.

Ali closed her eyes and let herself feel everything that was happening. Daniel was playing with her. He was licking her pussy.

His thumb rubbed her clit as he continued to lick and suck and kiss, the pressure building inside her with each lap of his tongue. Then she felt the head of the dildo entering her, stretching her. He nipped and sucked at her clit as he moved the toy in and out of her, bringing her closer and closer. She tangled her fingers in his hair, silently begging him not to stop.

"Are you going to come for me?" he asked.

She looked down to find him watching her, his eyes dark, his face covered in her juices. It was one of the hottest things she'd ever seen. "I'm so close, Sir."

"Tell me what you want." He bit down on her clit, sending a mixture of pain and pleasure right where she needed it most.

"More. Please, Sir. Just more."

Then she felt vibrations insider her. She fisted the sheet and arched her back.

He draped a hand over her stomach, holding her in place as he fucked her with the vibrating dildo and continued to put pressure on her clit with his tongue. That was all it took. She went flying.

* * *

ALI LAY naked on his bed, her dark hair spread out on his pillow. He felt as if he were dreaming, but the taste of her on his lips was too real.

He crawled up her body until his face was even with hers. Her chest rose and fell with exaggerated breaths from her orgasm. So many times he wondered what it would be like to watch her come undone—to see her body flush as her climax took hold of her. It was a moment he'd never forget.

She gazed up at him and smiled, sending a mixture of warmth, arousal, and guilt mixing in his gut. This was so wrong, but he wanted it. Had wanted it for a long time. "You're beautiful, sweetheart."

Her smile grew wider. "May I touch you, Sir?"

He shouldn't allow her to touch him. It would be easier if she didn't. But heaven help him, he wanted her to touch him. "You may."

Ali rested one hand on his back. She glided the other up his chest in a move that felt way too sensual than it should have. He captured her mouth with his, letting her taste herself on his tongue.

Her soft moans had his cock begging to get free. He wanted to be inside her, to feel her inner muscles gripping him.

Cupping her ass with one hand, he hiked her leg over his hip and pressed his erection against her core. He ground his cock against her, needing some relief.

Her fingers grazed the waistband of his pants. She lingered near the clasp, silently asking for permission since he currently had her mouth occupied. Then she brushed her fingers against the head of his cock, and he lost his conviction to not let this go any farther. He released the button on his slacks and guided her hand beneath the fabric.

Ali covered his erection with her palm and then gave it a little squeeze. He jerked his hips and released a tortured moan. If she kept doing that, he wasn't going to make it inside her.

Breaking the kiss, he rolled off her, putting a little distance between them. She met his gaze, question in her eyes.

Daniel tucked a lock of hair behind her ear. "Undress me."

She sat up, her tits bouncing as she moved, drawing his attention. The urge to suck on them again had him leaning forward and capturing one of her nipples in his mouth as he moved her to sit astride him. Her fingers faltered as she tried to unbutton his shirt, but he didn't relent. How had he gone so long without touching her like this?

He caressed her left breast as he continued to suck on her right. It was making it slow going as far as undressing him went, but he wasn't complaining. Her reactions were worth the snail's pace. Every time he'd nip at her nipple, she closed her eyes and let out a moan that went straight to his cock. He never wanted to stop hearing those sounds from her.

Releasing the last button, his shirt fell open, his chest bare. Her fingers danced up his torso, tangling in the hair on his chest. "Sir?"

"Yes," he said around her breast.

"I don't think I can get to your pants with you sucking on my breasts."

She was sitting astride him, leaning forward to give him access to her tits. To reach his slacks, she'd have to lean back and that would cause her to pull away from him.

Daniel did a quick assessment of his options. He kissed the tip of her nipple and lay back on the bed. "Finish undressing me and be quick about it."

Ali lifted herself off him and went to work on removing his pants, underwear, and socks. Once that was done, she returned to his top half. She unbuttoned the cuffs of his shirt and then waited for him to sit up so she could finish the job.

As she looked at his naked body, he wondered what she saw. Daniel was in great shape for his age, but that didn't mean he looked the same as he did at thirty or even forty. He wasn't vain, but he wanted her to like what she saw. He shouldn't, but he did nonetheless.

She grazed her finger along his pecks, down to his abs, and then lower. When she reached his hard length, she bent her head and kissed the tip, much as he'd done her nipple.

His cock jerked at the feel of her lips. He wanted to give her time to explore. Hell, he wanted hours to explore her body, but it was going to have to wait for another time.

He stretched to reach the drawer beside his bed and prayed there was a condom in there. It had been a while since he'd had sex in his own house, but he tried to be prepared. His finger wrapped around the square packet he was looking for and he sighed in relief.

It took him a matter of seconds to tear open the packet, remove the condom, and roll it down his erection. Ali stared, unmoving as he put the condom on, then once he was sheathed, she looked up to meet his gaze.

Daniel lifted her from under her arms and sat her astride him again. He brought her mouth to his and reached between them to line himself up with her opening.

Ali moaned as the tip of his erection pushed into her, stretching her. Being inside her for the first time had him biting back a groan of his own.

She sank down on him until his balls grazed her ass. The feel of her surrounding him was better than he'd imagined it would be.

His hands went to her hips as he began guiding their movements. With each of his upward thrusts, she tilted her hips, riding him.

The feel of her tits brushing against his chest, her hard nipples teasing his own. He slid one hand up her side to cup her breast. Taking her nipple, he rolled it between his thumb and forefinger.

Her inner muscles pulsed in response. She liked breast play. It was one of the first scenes he'd arranged for her at the club. He'd stood in the hallway, watching over her as another man had covered her tits with little metal clothespins before smacking them off with a crop one at a time.

Thinking about it had him thrusting into her harder, twisting her nipple between his fingers. He had no right to be jealous of her playing with the other Doms at the club. She wasn't his. Not then. But for now, for as long as it lasted, she was his and only his. She didn't want him playing with other subs and he sure as hell wasn't letting her play with other Doms. It had been hard enough to watch before. Now? Now that he knew what it was like to be inside her?

Without warning, he flipped them over and began driving her into the mattress. He was being rough, but she didn't seem to mind. Ali held on to him, meeting him thrust for thrust. Her nails scraped against his back and she gasped for air when he abandoned her mouth to bury his face against her neck.

Daniel felt his climax building, knowing he wouldn't last much longer if he kept up this pace. He couldn't stop, though. He needed to claim her.

His thumb found her clit and her nails bit into his skin. "Come. For. Me." Each word was punctuated with a thrust of his hips. He wanted to feel her, needed to know it was good for her, too.

Ali sucked in three hard breaths and then let out a cry that had his entire body quaking with need. Her head fell back, and he watched her ride out her orgasm. But this time he felt it, too. Her pussy spasmed around his cock as she came.

He waited until the last quiver left her body before letting go. Energy surged up his cock. He pumped his hips once more as his climax hit him.

Daniel fell forward, barely catching himself before crushing her. His breaths were coming quick and fast. It was a good thing he worked out regularly.

Once he was able to speak again, he propped himself up and gazed down at her. She was beautifully disheveled. "Are you okay?"

She snorted, then grinned at him. "I'm more than okay. How about you?"

He smiled, feeling happier than he had in a long time. "I have you in my bed."

"You do."

She ran her hand along the side of his face, and he leaned into it, kissing her palm. "I need to go clean up."

Daniel eased out of her before getting to his feet. Bending down, he gave her a soft kiss, then headed for the bathroom.

A loud gasp from her stopped him in his tracks and he turned to see what was wrong. Her eyes were wide as she stared at him. She sat up and threw her legs over the side of the bed, making her way to him.

"Ali?"

Lifting her hand, she touched his shoulder and turned him around.

He was about to ask her again when she finally whispered, "Your back."

CHAPTER 11

li inspected the long claw marks—and that's the only way to describe them—her nails had left on his back. A few of them were bleeding, but most of them were nothing more than surface scratches. "I can't believe I did that," she said.

Daniel turned his head to look, but she doubted he could see much. The worst of it was down the center. "I'll have a look at it in the mirror." He cupped the side of her face and kissed her again. "I'm sure it's fine."

"I broke the skin."

"Hm. It does sting a little." He took her hand. "Come. You can help patch me up."

He winked and she giggled, some of the worry leaving her. She'd never gotten that carried away before.

In the bright light of his bathroom, the scratches looked worse. Very gently, she washed his back and applied ointment to the ones that were bleeding.

Ali handed the supplies to him to put away. "I think I got them all." She still couldn't believe her nails had done so much damage. His entire back was covered in red marks.

Daniel returned the ointment to the medicine cabinet and threw the washcloth into the hamper before returning to her. He rested his hands on her hips and pulled her to him. "Next time I'm going to have to restrain those hands of yours."

There was amusement dancing in his eyes, and she smiled up at him. "Probably a good idea. Especially if sex is going to be like that."

He chuckled. "Good to know." He kissed the tip of her nose, took hold of her hand, and led her back into the bedroom. "Get into bed. I'll be back in a minute."

She hadn't been sure he'd want her in his bed. After his comment about boundaries, she'd been sure he wouldn't.

Ali slid under the blankets, pulled them around her chest, and waited for him to return.

She didn't have to wait long. Only a few minutes passed before he was easing in beside her.

The king-sized bed meant there was plenty of room for both of them, but she found herself being gathered against him, her back to his chest. He didn't say anything, just pressed his lips to the back of her head and settled in with one hand cupping her breast.

THE BED DIPPED BESIDE HER, dragging her sleep-muddled brain into the present. She had no idea what time it was or even what day it was, but she knew something was different.

Soft, warm pressure along her back, and then a hand snaking around her waist brought last night back to her. Daniel.

"Good morning," he whispered in her ear.

She hummed. "Morning. What time is it?"

"A little after five." He slid his hand up to her breast and began kneading it with his fingers. "You didn't move at all last night. I must have worn you out."

Ali arched her breast into his hand. "Yes, Sir."

He scraped her earlobe with his teeth, and she felt it low in her stomach. "How much time do you need to get ready for work?"

His hand had abandoned her breast and was now making its way down her body to the junction between her legs. She opened her thighs, giving him full access to her. "About forty minutes, Sir."

"That means I have thirty minutes to make you scream."

Then his hand was gone, and she felt something circle her wrists. She opened her eyes to see him attaching cuffs. The bed dipped again as he lifted her hands above her and attached the cuffs to something on the bed she couldn't see.

She met his gaze as he hovered over her. Daniel hadn't turned on the lights, so his body was mostly in shadow. He lowered his head to her neck while his hands went to work on her breasts. But unlike the night before, everything was featherlight—his touch—his kisses.

It was torture. Ali wanted to touch him, but he seemed content to keep her tethered to his headboard.

He worked his way down her torso, lingering at her stomach. His tongue traced a line from her belly button to the crease of her hip before licking his way back up. Then he repeated it on the other side.

She was trying very hard not to move, but it was proving impossible. She clenched her fists and gritted her teeth to get her body to obey. He hadn't told her not to move, but she thought it was implied given he'd secured her hands. Then again, maybe he was only attempting to prevent her nails from causing more damage to his flesh.

Her hips lifted off the bed of their own accord as he drew near her clit, and he chuckled. "Patience. I'll take care of you. I promise."

Ali closed her eyes and blew out what she hoped was a steadying breath. Her sex pulsed when he rested her legs on his shoulders and spread her lips.

"Are you sore this morning?" he asked.

He'd fucked her hard the night before and she wouldn't lie and say she was fine. She was feeling it this morning, but it was a good soreness. "A little, Sir."

She felt his tongue move along her folds, almost massaging her sensitive flesh. It felt good and somewhat relaxing, even though it had her pussy desperately wanting more.

As he continued to lick her, he positioned his thumb on her clit and began applying pressure. It was light at first and she raised her hips, seeking more.

Daniel gave her more, but not in the way she wanted. He dipped his tongue into her pussy, running it along her opening before easing up and placing a kiss on her clit.

After he repeated this action several times, she thought she was going to go insane. Her blood was pumping in her ears and her sex was swollen and hot. She had no idea how long he'd been between her legs, and he seemed in no rush.

Ali was about to begin begging, wondering if that was what he was waiting for, when he sucked her clit into his mouth and began sucking hard. She let out a scream and arched her back, digging her heels into his already abused back.

But he didn't let up. If anything, he increased the suction, which she didn't think was possible. It was a mixture of pain and pleasure, and after everything else he'd done, she couldn't hold on anymore. A loud wail erupted from her lips as her orgasm took control of her body.

He didn't stop until the last shudder rippled through her. Then he pushed himself up the length of her and released her wrists. Her arms fell limply on the bed. She didn't feel like she had any bones in her body anymore. He'd sucked them all out.

His mouth found hers and gave her a long, lingering kiss. Ali could smell herself on him, blocking out her concern about morning breath. He coaxed her mouth open with his tongue and filled her mouth with the taste of her sex. She wrapped her arms around him and kissed him back, letting her tongue tangle with his.

Then, he removed his lips and pushed himself off her. "As much as I'd love to spend the rest of the morning lying in bed with you, we both have work."

Ali groaned. Work. The last thing she wanted to think about was dealing with her boss when she was still floating on her orgasm cloud.

Daniel noticed her reaction and bent to give her another quick kiss. It was only then she realized he was fully dressed. The only thing he was missing was his tie and jacket. "Grab a shower and get dressed while I prepare breakfast."

He didn't give her a chance to respond before striding out of the bedroom. She propped herself on one arm, watching him leave before forcing herself to get out of the comfy bed. Daniel's comfy bed.

Gathering up her clothes from the night before, she made her way into the main area of the house, passing Daniel in the kitchen on her way to her room. She didn't miss how he stopped working and watched her until she disappeared down the hall.

As she stepped into the shower, Ali couldn't believe how much had changed in the last twelve hours. To think she'd been ready to sit down and have dinner with Daniel as nothing more than friends last night, and now she'd spent a night in his bed, and he'd agreed to be her Dom.

Ali rinsed the conditioner from her hair, unable to wipe the smile from her face. She couldn't wait to see what would happen tonight when they attended the fundraiser. And then, her mind went to Friday when they'd be at the club where she'd make her first appearance as Daniel's submissive. It was certainly going to be an interesting couple of days.

* * *

DANIEL FOUND himself grinning at random times throughout the day for no apparent reason. He and Ali had eaten breakfast together that morning, and then he'd walked her to her car and kissed her goodbye. The way she'd looked at him as she slid behind the wheel of her car had heat spreading through his chest. He'd wanted to drag her back to his bed and keep her there.

At three o'clock, he said goodbye to Kevin and drove to the cleaners to pick up his tux before heading home. Daniel spent some extra time shaving, making sure there were no stray hairs poking out behind his ears or anything. He'd been to plenty of these types of functions over the years, but tonight he wanted to make an extra effort for Ali.

Tugging his jacket into place, he checked his reflection in the mirror and adjusted his bowtie. It liked to tilt to the left for some reason.

Once it was as straight as it was going to get, he tucked his wallet into his pocket and grabbed his keys. Ali would be getting off work right about now and heading to her apartment. He still couldn't believe the noise her neighbors had made when they were there the evening before. It was no wonder she hadn't been able to sleep.

The drive into the city wasn't bad until he reached the outer belt. It was five thirty and everyone was trying to make their way home. He kept glancing at the clock as the traffic inched forward.

Twenty minutes later, he reached the exit he needed to take and breathed a sigh of relief when traffic was moving at a normal pace. He turned into Ali's apartment complex at six thirty on the dot. As long as they didn't run into any more traffic, they should have no trouble arriving at the hotel before seven.

He strolled up to her door and knocked. A minute later, it swung open to reveal a semi put together Ali. He'd expected her to be ready, but she seemed flustered. "What's wrong?" he asked, stepping inside.

"Nothing. I'm just running a little behind. I didn't get out of work until five fifteen." She rushed down the hall toward her room, leaving him standing in her small foyer. "I need another five minutes."

Seven minutes later, she reappeared, her hair pinned up with little curls framing her face and sparkly earrings dangling from her ears. She stopped in front of him and released a loud breath. "I think I'm ready."

Daniel looked down at her flushed cheeks and the way her chest was rising and falling against the fabric of her dress. "Breathe."

She did—her shoulders rising and falling with the exaggerated movements.

"Good girl. Now, where's your coat?" Her long red dress left her arms bare, meaning she would need a covering. The weather was warming, but the nights were still chilly.

"The back of the couch."

He crossed to the couch and picked up the black dress coat draped over the back. When he returned to her, she turned her back to him and allowed him to help her put it on. He pulled her against him and kissed the top of her hair. "You look beautiful."

She gathered the coat in front of her, tying it at the waist. "Thank you."

Daniel weaved his way through traffic to the hotel. The place was hopping, but that was to be expected when there was a big event like this. He pulled up to the front and stepped out as the valet handed him a ticket. "Good evening, Sir. Are you here for the event?"

"Yes."

The valet nodded and took his keys.

Making his way to the other side of the SUV, Daniel opened Ali's door and helped her out. She placed her hand in his and he wrapped his fingers around her palm. He wanted to pull her into his arms and kiss her, but he controlled himself. "Ready?" he asked, tucking her arm in his.

"As ready as I'll ever be."

They made their way into the hotel and toward the elevator that would take them to the ballroom. There was a line, so they had to wait their turn. "Thank you for coming with me tonight."

"I would do anything for you. I hope you know that."

Ali met his gaze, but before she could respond, the doors opened, and it was their turn to step inside.

They rode the elevator up with four other couples, all dressed in ball gowns and tuxes. The doors opened and everyone exited into the large open area full of people.

Daniel scanned the room to see if there was anyone he recognized and was shocked to see a familiar face he wasn't expecting. Or a somewhat familiar face. One he hadn't expected to see in St. Louis.

The other man didn't notice him, so he refocused on the woman at his side. She was looking at him. "Everything all right?"

He gave her arm a squeeze. "Of course."

Ali didn't look overly convinced, but she let it go. "We should probably find a place to put our coats."

The coat check was easy enough to find. He slipped the ticket the man handed him into his jacket pocket, then guided Ali toward the ballroom.

Ali removed the invitation from her purse and handed it to the man standing near the double doors. He scanned the paper and looked at the woman at his right. "Table fifteen." Then he turned back to them and smiled. "Madeline will show you to your table."

Daniel rested his hand on Ali's lower back as they were led to their table. It was smack dab in the middle of the room near the front.

"Here you are." The woman's smile was polite and professional. "Enjoy your evening."

"Thank you," Ali said, but the woman was already walking away.

Each of the place settings included napkins folded in the shape of a dove. He'd done a little research on the fundraiser when he'd got to the office that morning. The organization behind it was out of Minneapolis. They raised money to help cover medical costs for those who couldn't afford the expense. It was a worthy cause and he understood why the hospital would want to have a presence.

Daniel pulled out one of the chairs, inviting Ali to sit. She lowered herself into the chair and he sat down next to her.

She looked around, a slight frown on her face. "I'm not really sure what I'm supposed to do."

"These functions are usually more about networking and drumming up donations." More people were filtering into the room and taking seats at the various tables. "After dinner, we'll mingle a little."

A man and a woman at least twenty years older than Daniel joined them at their table. The man helped his wife into her seat before easing into the chair beside her. Another couple approached the table and sat down, leaving only one set of seats empty.

Everyone at the table introduced themselves and the older woman, Gladys, complimented Ali on her dress. As the conversation began to flow naturally, he felt Ali begin to relax.

The servers came by to take drink orders when the final couple showed up. Daniel swiftly hid his reaction as the man held out the seat for the woman and the two sat down. The other man, however, wasn't as good at covering shock at seeing Daniel.

Another round robin of introductions began with everyone else at the table introducing themselves to the newcomers. When it came around to them, Daniel acted as if he didn't know the other couple. "I'm Daniel Ross, and this is Ali Foster."

"It's nice to meet all of you," the woman said with an air of excitement. She hadn't reacted the way the man had to seeing him, which made him wonder if she didn't recognize him or if she was just better at concealing it than her partner. "It's so much warmer here than it is back home. I was able to get away with a simple wrap tonight. Back home, I'd still be stuffed into a winter coat." She paused. "I'm Lily, by the way. And this is my husband, Logan."

It had been five years since Daniel had seen Logan and Lily. He'd been visiting a friend in St. Paul and had been invited to a party. The two hadn't been married then. In fact, if he recalled, Logan was very new to the lifestyle.

"Where are you from, my dear?" Gladys asked.

"Minneapolis," Lily answered. "I work for The Coleman Foundation as their events coordinator." That turned the conversation to the fundraiser itself and all the work the foundation was doing. The Coleman Foundation was growing, expanding to help more people, and Lily was more than happy to share.

Dinner was served and he was impressed. The food was excellent.

"You did well, baby," he heard Logan whisper to his wife.

She beamed. "Thank you."

Daniel cleared his throat. "How long are you two in town for?"

Logan was the one to answer. "We leave Sunday." He gazed lovingly at his wife. "Lily's never been to St. Louis, so we thought we'd take in some of the sites."

"Let me know if you need some recommendations. I know of a few private venues you may be interested in checking out."

The other Dom didn't miss the implication. "We'd defiantly be interested."

It was a quick exchange and everyone else was occupied with their meals. No one else at the table had any idea what they were talking about.

Ali, however, wasn't as oblivious. She leaned in, whispering low in his ear, "You know them."

"Yes." He left it at that and allowed her to fill in the blanks. She was smart and it didn't take long for her to put two and two together.

By the end of the meal, everyone was ready to get up and move. Unfortunately, they had to sit through several speeches and a slide show. He didn't miss how Lily's lips moved with the timing of each slide. Based on that and Logan's comment earlier, Daniel was guessing she'd had a hand in tonight's event.

Once the presentation part of the evening was over, a small band started playing in the corner of the room and people began to get up from their seats and mingle. He stayed put, waiting for the other couples to leave first. Then, he took out a business card and handed it to Logan. "Give me a call tomorrow and I'll give you more information."

Logan tucked the business card in the pocket of his tux. "Sounds great." Then he looked at Lily. "Did you want to chat with anyone?"

She stood, not waiting for him to assist her. "I need to talk to Cheryl. Oh, and I should probably find Greg, too."

Logan chuckled. "Hopefully, we'll see you both around."

Daniel watched as they disappeared in the crowd, shaking his head. He definitely remembered Logan and Lily.

CHAPTER 12

ali didn't know what to make of the couple who'd just left. He was quiet and reserved, while she was friendly and talkative. If Daniel was right, and she had no doubt he was, then they were in the lifestyle. While not all submissives were demure and quiet, Lily seemed the opposite of submissive. Then again, Ali would guess they weren't playing tonight.

"Is there anyone you wanted to talk to?" Daniel asked, pulling her out of her thoughts.

"Um. I should probably see if I can find some of the other executives from the hospital. At least so there's proof I was here."

Daniel frowned. "Why would you need to prove you were here?"

She hadn't told Daniel much about her boss. He knew she was an executive assistant for one of the senior vice presidents at the hospital, but that was about it. The last thing she wanted to do when she wasn't at work was talk about it. "In case my boss decides to check."

His frown deepened.

She knew he was going to ask questions she didn't want to answer, so she stood, hoping he would follow. It took a moment, but he did. Daniel took a step toward her. He ran his hand over her shoulder and down her arm in a light caress that had thoughts of her boss evaporating. "I'll let it go for now." The implication was that they would be talking about it later.

He took hold of her hand and let her lead them through the throng of people until she saw someone she knew. Luckily, it was the hospital CEO. Mason Barrett was a handsome man in his early fifties. He noticed her approaching and smiled. "Ali. I didn't realize you'd be here tonight."

"Mr. Jacobson and his wife couldn't come, so he asked if I'd step in." That was the nice way of putting it.

She introduced Daniel to Mason and his wife.

"You look vaguely familiar," Mason said to Daniel. "Do you work for the hospital?"

"No. I'm in real estate."

"Commercial? Residential?" Mason asked. "The hospital's always growing and expanding."

"I dabble in a little of both."

The hospital's CEO didn't seem fazed by Daniel's less than specific answer. "Do you have a card?"

Daniel produced a business card out of what seemed like thin air. He handed it to Mason. "I'll help if I can. And if I can't, I have some other contacts who might be a better fit."

A man tapped on Mason's shoulder and whispered something in his ear. Mason nodded, then turned back to them with a smile. "If you'll both excuse us. Thanks again for the card."

Mason and his wife followed the other man through the crowd.

"Is that enough proof, or do we need to seek out more people?"

Even though his tone was pleasant, Ali knew him well enough to know he wasn't happy. "I think I'm good."

She looked over his shoulder, not wanting to meet his gaze, and saw Logan and Lily gliding over the makeshift dance floor. Daniel turned his head to see what had drawn her attention. "Would you like to dance?" he asked.

Ali loved to dance, but none of her previous boyfriends had been interested. Especially not to the type of music currently being played. "Yes, please."

Daniel led her over to the edge of the dance floor and twirled her into his arms, causing her to giggle.

He grinned and she felt some of the tension leave his body as he began moving them in time with the music. The bottom of her dress flared out as he turned them in a circle, weaving them around the other couples effortlessly. He was confident on the dance floor, which surprised her. Ali had never seen him dance at the club. "You're good." She paused. "Dancing like this, I mean."

"I took ballroom dancing lessons years ago."

"Really?" she asked.

He chuckled, amused by the shock on her face. "Yes. I didn't want to embarrass myself at my own wedding."

Oh. His wedding. That made sense.

They hadn't really talked about his marriage or his ex-wife beyond the basics. Ali stared at his bowtie as questions swirled in her mind. They were together now. It would be okay to ask questions about his previous relationships, right?

Daniel brought their joined hands under her chin and tilted her head up so he could look into her eyes. "Ask me."

"How long were you with your wife?"

He released her chin but kept their hands tucked between them. The back of his hand rested against her chest, and it made Ali wish they were alone instead of surrounded by all these people. "We were together for twenty-two years. Married for almost twenty."

She tried not to be jealous of this woman she didn't know, but it was difficult. He'd obviously loved her. Why else would he have stayed with her for twenty years?

Ali was trying to figure out what to ask him next without it sounding weird, but he seemed to know what was on her mind. "We were very much in love. Then, our lives were taken over by the kids. Over time, we lost each other, and we couldn't get it back."

"Do you still love her?" Ali asked, even though she wasn't sure she wanted to know the answer.

"No. I haven't felt that way about her in a long time." He guided them toward the edge of the dance floor. "We're friendly for the sake of our kids, but given they're all adults now, we rarely have contact with each other. The last time I saw her in person was at James's high school graduation."

So, Ali probably wouldn't come face-to-face with the ex anytime soon. That was good news.

Again, seeming to be able to read her mind, Daniel pressed a kiss to her temple and whispered in her ear, "There's no need to be jealous, sweetheart. She and I haven't been together for fifteen years."

She knew he was right, but it didn't change the urge she had to tear off all his clothes and stake her claim on him. For two years she'd wanted him, and now that he was hers, she had every intention of keeping him.

But one question plagued her—one he hadn't answered yet. "How did it end?"

Daniel dropped the pretense of dancing and took her by the hand. "Are you ready to go?"

A little taken aback by his sudden desire to leave, it took her a little longer than it should to respond. She nodded and let him guide her out to the lobby.

They retrieved their coats, then made their way downstairs. She stood beside him as they waited for the valet to bring their car around, curiosity eating at her.

A young man drove Daniel's SUV to a stop in front of them, climbed out of the vehicle, and jogged over to them. He handed the keys to Daniel, and in return Daniel handed him a tip.

"Thanks," the young man said.

After helping her into the passenger seat, Daniel walked around the vehicle, opened his door, and slid into the driver's seat. He eased them into traffic, then picked up the conversation where they'd left off as if time hadn't passed. "Jessica, my ex." He glanced over at Ali before refocusing on the road. "She found someone else."

Ali's eyes widened. "She cheated on you?"

"No." He paused. "At least, she says she didn't. But we'd drifted apart, and she'd fallen in love with someone else."

Given how Ali felt about Daniel, it was hard for her to imagine a woman not loving him. He was extremely lovable. Polite. Charming. Protective. "So the divorce was her decision?"

"It was." He paused. "Looking back now, I can understand. We were just occupying the same space. We barely talked unless it was about one of the kids. That isn't the way to have a lasting marriage."

There was one more thing Ali wanted to know about his past relationship. "Was she your submissive?"

Daniel guided the vehicle onto the highway out of town. "We dabbled, but it wasn't anything formal."

"So you embraced the lifestyle after your divorce." It wasn't really a question. He'd implied as much.

"Yes. When I started dating again, I realized I needed to find women who liked the same things I did in the bedroom."

Ali was trying to process all the information she'd obtained in the last hour. For some reason, she'd pictured his ex as a horrible person who'd been a nightmare to live with. It was easier that way.

She was still mulling things over when they arrived home. Ali waited for him to open her door, then took his offered hand as he helped her out of the vehicle.

Her heels clicked on the concrete floor of the garage as they made their way inside. Daniel eased her coat from her shoulders and down her arms, hung it up for her, then removed his own. He loosened his tie as he strolled down the hall toward the kitchen. Removing two glasses from the cabinet, he filled one of them with water. "Water or something stronger?"

"Water's fine."

He nodded, handed her the already full glass, then filled the other one. After downing half of his water, he leaned against the counter, facing her. The look in his eyes told her she wasn't going to like what was coming and she was right. "Tell me about your boss."

* * *

DANIEL WATCHED Ali's face pale. Her gaze darted around them room, looking everywhere but at him. "Um. He's my boss."

"Yes. But why would you need to have proof you attended tonight's event?" Her nervous assertion after dinner had all his protective instincts on alert.

She lowered her gaze, focusing on the clear liquid in her glass. Was she searching for words because she didn't want to tell him? That didn't sit well with him at all.

The silence was almost deafening while he waited for her response. He'd stay there all night if he had to. Luckily, she didn't make him wait that long. "He'll want to confirm I was there."

"Why?"

Ali scraped her teeth over her bottom lip, a nervous habit of hers. "Because he wanted me there."

Daniel sighed, set his glass on the counter, then strode toward her and lifted her chin to meet his gaze. There was a note of fear in her eyes and those protective instincts went from concerned to wanting to throttle someone—namely her boss. "Allison, we are going around in circles."

"Please." Her desperate whisper did nothing to calm him. "I can't lose my job."

Alarm bells were going off all over the place. He clenched his jaw, keeping a tight rein on his temper. "Has he touched you?"

Genuine shock crossed her face, which helped to soothe him a little. "No. It's not." She paused, trying to find the right words, and he wished she'd just spit it out already. He didn't care if it was pretty. He only wanted to know what was going on. "He's never touched me or said anything...inappropriate."

"Then what?"

She averted her eyes again. He didn't like it when she didn't look at him, but he gave her time to gather her thoughts. When she answered, it provided him no more information than what he'd had before. "He's picky."

Daniel was losing patience. "Look at me."

Her gaze found his and he saw the mix of emotions raging behind her eyes.

"We are not leaving this kitchen until you tell me what is going on with your boss, do you understand?"

"Yes, Sir."

"Good." He dropped his hand, letting his arm fall to his side. "Now, out with it."

"I'm not sure I can explain it." When he didn't respond, she went on, realizing he wasn't going to accept that vague dismissal. "He likes to micro-manage everything." She paused. "Including me."

Daniel crossed his arms. "Explain."

Ali sighed, resigning herself to his interrogation. "Every morning when I get to work, I have an email waiting for me with a list of tasks I need to do. Most of them are the typical stuff I do every day, but there are always some other things mixed in there as well. He says he likes to keep me busy."

He nodded for her to go on.

"It's not what he says, exactly. It's more how he says it. He's very...condescending. When he told me about the fundraiser, he didn't ask me if I would go. He told me I needed to go in his place."

Daniel's eyebrows nearly rose to his hairline.

"But that's not unusual. He does that stuff all the time. He assumes I have no life outside of work and that if he needs something, I should be able to accommodate him. I'm his assistant after all."

The way she said that last sentence, as if she were repeating her boss's words, made him see red. And it had nothing to do with the dress she was wearing. "Being his assistant doesn't give him the right to mistreat you."

"I know." She bit her lower lip again. "I keep thinking it will get better. That he just needs to settle in and realize I'm good at my job."

"How long have you worked for him?" Daniel asked.

He saw her shoulders relax a little. "About six months." Then, she went on, filling in more blanks for him. "My old boss retired. Baily was great to work for. I loved my job. Now..."

"Now?"

"Now, I dread going to work every morning." Worry creased her face when she realized how that sounded. "But I can't lose my job."

"Yes, you mentioned that."

Neither of them said anything right away. He was contemplating his options. Although he'd agreed to be her Dom, that didn't mean he could run her life. But it also didn't mean he could sit by and do nothing.

"What are you going to do?" she asked.

Daniel reached for her hand and led her toward his bedroom. "I haven't decided yet."

He needed to think about what would be best for her. The only thing he did know was she wouldn't be working for...

Walking into the bedroom, he flipped on the lights. "What's your boss's name?"

"Grant Jacobson."

Grant Jacobson. Why had he heard that name before? It wasn't as if he had a lot of contact with the hospital or its administration.

He dropped her arm, leaving her standing in the middle of the room, and walked over to the closet to hang up his jacket and finish removing his bowtie. Ali stood, watching him as he removed his cuff links and dropped them into a dish on his dresser. Her gaze followed his every movement as he unbuttoned his shirt and shrugged it off his shoulders and down his arms.

The heat in her eyes grew as he continued to undress. He wasn't making a show out of it, simply removing his evening attire, but seeing him stripping out of his garments seemed to be turning her on. That wasn't something he was going to complain about.

Naked from the waist up, he crossed to her, her gaze tracking his every move. She'd been teasing him in her dress all night. He couldn't wait to get her out of it.

"This is a very pretty dress," he said, tracing the outline of fabric from her shoulders down to the dip between her breasts. There was only a hint of cleavage, but he knew what lay beneath. He'd played with dozens of women over the years in various stages of undress, but it was Ali who had his heart pumping as she stood before him completely clothed. The anticipation was killing him, but so sweet at the same time. "Turn around."

She presented him with her back and lifted her hair. He kissed her neck, causing her flesh to break out in goose bumps.

The back of the dress wasn't quite as daring as the front. It wrapped around the lower half of her torso, cradling her and showing off her waist. He ran his finger down the center of her back while he placed more kisses at her nape.

Finding the zipper, he began lowering it, revealing what she was wearing underneath. He wasn't sure what he'd been expecting, but the lace and sheer fabric he encountered wasn't it. Maybe it was wishful thinking on his part.

Ali tended to dress somewhat conservatively at the club, at least compared to the other subs. But most of the time she was working, so that made sense.

He remembered her saying she wasn't comfortable walking around naked at the club when they were discussing their lists. The few times he'd negotiated play for her with other Doms, her club attire had covered all the important bits. It was only once she entered one of the playrooms that she'd removed the necessary clothing. And since the Dom she played with wasn't her own, his control over her clothing was limited to the scene.

Daniel tried not to think about her playing with anyone else. It had been difficult enough at the time, but he'd endured it because she'd wanted to play. The last time it had happened, nearly six months ago, it had taken him three days to get rid of the sick feeling in the pit of his stomach.

But she was here now. His. As long as she wanted him, he would take care of her needs. He would be the only one she played with. And when that changed—when she realized he couldn't give her everything she wanted—he'd let her go.

The dress dropped to the floor in a whoosh of fabric, leaving her standing in a red bra, garter belt, and panties. His cock strained against his pants, begging to be free, but he took the time to appreciate the sight before him. Red might be his new favorite color.

The garter belt hugged her hips, framing them perfectly. He rested his hands over the lacy material, toying with the strings on the sides of her panties. From over her shoulder, he could see her breasts, barely contained in the matching bra. This woman was going to kill him.

His original plan had been to strip her, but now he was reconsidering. He really liked the way she looked in her lingerie. He slid his right hand lower, lingering on her ass before finding the heat between her legs.

CHAPTER 13

li spread her legs wider as Daniel rubbed her already sensitive folds through the sheer material of her panties. His fingers glided over the wet fabric as he caressed her. She'd hoped he would like her underwear selection, but she hadn't been at all sure. Both times they'd been together, he'd stripped her naked, not paying much attention to what she had beneath her clothes.

Tonight, she'd chosen one of her sexier bra and panty sets. Red was her second favorite color. She looked good in it. And by his reaction, Daniel thought so as well.

His finger found her clit and circled, adding the right amount of pressure. She sucked in a breath and moaned as she embraced her body's response to his touch. As the muscles began to tighten in her belly, he removed his hand, and it took everything in her not to plead for him to keep going.

"Turn around and place your hands on the bed." His voice was crisp and clear. If not for his erection that had been pressing into her backside moments before, she would think he was completely unaffected.

She did as he asked, bending to put her hands on the mattress. The sounds of him moving around the room had her straining to hear what he was doing. She wanted to look but kept herself in position.

Then she felt his hand on her ass. He cupped her cheek, massaging it, and then raised his hand before bringing it back down in a stinging blow.

The action startled her, and she let out a little yelp. "You will not keep things about your life from me in the future. Do you understand?" He gave her other cheek a solid smack.

Both sides of her ass were now tingling. "Yes, Sir."

"Good. Because next time I won't be so easy on you."

While she knew he hadn't hit her that hard, she still felt the weight of his disappointment. She hadn't meant to keep things from him. Only her best friend knew how bad her boss was, and even then, she didn't tell Kim everything. But things with Daniel were different now and while he was acknowledging that in the past she was under no obligation to tell him anything, now she was.

He lifted the string along the edge of her panties, pulling them taut, and then she felt them give. "I'll buy you a new pair." Then, he cut the other side as well. Her panties fell to the floor at her feet.

There was more movement behind her, and then she felt the tails of a flogger along her back. Daniel was a master flogger. Subs at the club were always asking him to flog them, but Ali never had. She'd wanted to, spent countless hours wondering what it would be like, but she'd been too afraid he'd refuse.

Daniel took his time, dragging the falls along her back, her butt, and the backs of her thighs. He tapped the inside of her thighs, letting her know he wanted her to spread wider. She opened her legs, pushing her ass higher into the air.

A sound of appreciation rumbled from his throat. He placed a hand on the small of her back, then flicked the flogger along the inside of her thighs.

Ali took a deep breath in and almost sighed. It had been so long since she'd been flogged, and she'd forgotten how much she loved the thud against her skin.

He began slowly, building as he moved along her legs and her hips. Some of the falls tangled with her garter belt, creating almost a tickling sensation, but that only added to the play. She leaned into the bed, bracing herself, waiting for the next kiss of the flogger as he worked his way over her body.

Before long, she was on fire. Sweat glistened on her skin and her pussy ached to be touched. She was breathing hard and riding on a sea of endorphins.

The sound of a zipper resounded in her ears and the flogger landed with a thud on the floor. She wanted to look, but her entire body felt heavy. It would take too much effort to move, even to tilt her head.

Then, she felt his cock pressing into her. He gripped her hips with both hands, his fingers digging into her flesh as he seated himself deep inside her. One of his hands reached up to gather a handful of her hair, lifting her head off the bed.

Ali released a strangled cry as shots of pain raced down her scalp. Her nails raked over the bedcover, trying to find purchase, but he was pounding into her so hard. Every time she thought she had a grip of the blanket, she'd lose it.

Eventually, she collapsed onto the bed, unable to hold herself up. But still, he didn't stop. Her pussy contracted around his length and her clit pulsed almost painfully, wanting so desperately to be touched.

But he hadn't touched her there. Not since before he'd removed her panties. And she was plastered to the bed, face down. She wasn't even sure she could snake an arm between them if she'd wanted to.

Then, he rolled a little to his side long enough to pull her leg up, bending it beneath them. "Touch yourself." His gruff voice growled in her ear, making every muscle in her body clench with need.

She forced her fingers to release the blanket she'd been clinging onto and lowered her arm into the narrow space he'd created. Her clit was slick and incredibly sensitive. At the first brush of her fingers, her pussy spasmed, leaving them both groaning.

Her fingers worked her clit as his harsh breathing tickled her ear. "Come." The word was said through gritted teeth, adding another layer to her arousal.

The climax she'd been waiting for hit her hard. It was almost painful as the ripples of pleasure vibrated through her body. A scream tore from deep in her throat and tears streamed down her cheeks.

Daniel's grip on her hair tightened, sending another spasm rocketing through her. A moment later his own orgasm overtook him. He held himself deep inside her for a long time, his weight pressing her into the mattress.

Streaks of moisture covered her face as she lay, trying to catch her breath. Her body felt used, and she loved it.

"Are you all right, sweetheart?" His lips brushed against her hair.

"Yes, Sir."

He pressed a kiss against her neck. "I need to clean up and get rid of the condom. Stay where you are."

"Okay." At least she thought she said okay. She was still riding the high, so she couldn't be sure.

A shiver ran through her when he pulled out of her body and removed his heat. Then, he draped a blanket over her, and she sighed. It wasn't the same as having him pressed against her, but it helped with the chill that was beginning to creep in.

What felt like several minutes later, she was being scooped up into a set of arms. She rested her head on his shoulder as he carried her to the other side of the bed and laid her down. He climbed in beside her and gathered her to him, holding her close. "How are you feeling?"

"Tired, Sir." She snuggled into his warmth. Being with him like this felt so good. Her body ached in the best way.

"I want you to drink some water. Then you can sleep."

Ali nodded and forced her eyes open as he brought a glass of water to her lips. She took a drink, letting the liquid rehydrate her dry throat. All she wanted to do was sleep, but she knew she had to drink.

It took a while, but eventually she finished her water. Daniel set the empty glass on the nightstand and lowered them both so they were lying flat in the bed.

She let her eyes drift closed, sleep calling her. "I'm sorry I didn't tell you."

He kissed the top of her head. "Go to sleep, now."

"Okay." Her words were mumbled, and she had no idea if he'd heard her, but it didn't matter. He'd heard her apology. That's what counted.

* * *

A LIGHT DRIZZLE tapped against the windows as Daniel eased himself out of the bed the next morning. Ali had clung to him for most of the night, snoring softly against his chest.

He tucked the covers around her shoulders, letting her sleep a little longer as he padded to the bathroom to take care of business.

It was a little after four. Too early to be awake, but his mind had other ideas.

Changing into his workout clothes, he headed upstairs to the gym and stepped onto the treadmill. The sound of his feet hitting the rubber as he slowly increased the speed and incline brought with it a sense of steadiness.

A half hour later, he was drenched in sweat and breathing hard. He wiped the moisture from his brow and grabbed a bottle of water from the mini refrigerator, downing it in one go. Then, he headed over to the weights.

As he moved through his strength training, Daniel let his thoughts drift to what Ali had told him about her boss. He was still positive he'd heard the name Grant Jacobson before, but he had no idea where.

The logical answer would be somewhere through his work, but that was a broad scope. He worked with contractors, other real estate agents, HOAs, inspectors…

The list went on and on.

At five o'clock, he called it quits and went downstairs to grab a shower. That was where Ali found him.

He hadn't heard her at first. It wasn't until she opened the door, drawing his attention, that he realized she was in the bathroom.

She stepped into the shower, and he reached for her, pulling her against him. He cupped the back of her head, lowering his mouth to hers. She tasted of mint, which let him know she'd been awake long enough to sneak off to her room and brush her teeth. "Good morning."

Ali smiled up at him. "Good morning."

He kissed her again, unable to resist, before tilting her head back into the spray. Once her hair was wet, he reached for the shampoo and began massaging it into her scalp. "How are you feeling this morning?"

She hummed.

He wasn't sure if that was in response to him washing her hair or in answer to his question. "I'm going to need more than that, sweetheart."

"I feel like I've been thoroughly fucked."

The blissful look on her face had him tightening his hold on her hair.

Her mouth opened, forming an O, and his cock pulsed. He needed to change the direction of their conversation, or he'd have her pressed against the wall of the shower in a matter of seconds. "You get off at five today?"

"Four thirty." She let him tilt her head back again, rinsing the shampoo from her locks. "I have to be at the club by five thirty tonight."

"You're working tonight?" He'd memorized her schedule a long time ago. She and Bridget traded off so neither had to work both nights the club was open.

As he retrieved the conditioner from the shelf, she answered, "Bridget asked if I'd cover her prep work tonight. She had an appointment or something and can't get there until six thirty."

That was good. He had plans for her tonight. "I'll drop you at work this morning and pick you up."

"You don't have to do that. I can—" The look on his face must have been enough to stop her because she lowered her gaze. "Yes, Sir."

Daniel finished washing her and himself, then turned off the water. He grabbed his towel and began drying her off, starting at her hair and working his way down…lingering on the important bits. He lifted one of her feet to dry it, and she held on to his shoulders. His muscles rippled in response to her touch. He wanted her again. It would be so easy to turn her around, bend her over the counter, and take what he wanted, but instead, he finished drying her before padding to the closet to get another towel for himself.

Ali headed to her room to dress, while he did the same. He knew it was a good idea to keep things as separate as possible. She needed her space. They shouldn't get too comfortable with each other. It would be easier when this thing between them was over. But he wanted her things mingled with his. He wanted to see her lacy undergarments in his dresser.

Shaking those thoughts away, he finished tucking his shirt into his pants, then headed into the kitchen to start breakfast.

He dropped Ali off in front of her office at seven twenty, then drove to one of his renovation projects. The contractors were getting set up for the day, the sound of boots thudding on the subfloor at the back of the house greeting him the moment he walked through the front door.

Daniel followed the sounds, knowing he'd find his project manager. Luke had been with him for the last five years and the man had a memory like no one else he'd ever met. If there'd been some sort of interaction with Grant Jacobson regarding one of Daniel's remodeling projects, Luke would know.

When he didn't see the man, he called out, "Luke?"

"Over here." The voice came from one of the back bedrooms.

Heading in the direction of Luke's voice, Daniel entered the master bedroom, but there was no one there. "Where the hell are you?"

The sound of Luke's laughter led him to the master bathroom.

When he stepped into the connecting room, he found his foreman standing in the floor. Not on the floor. In the floor. "What happened in here?"

Luke pushed himself out of the hole. "I noticed the tub was leaning a little last night and was going to investigate it this morning. But when I got here, I found this."

The bathtub had busted a hole in the subfloor and was now sitting on dirt. Thank goodness they had the water turned off, or they would have even more issues.

It wasn't the first time they'd found something like this, and it wouldn't be the last. Many of the houses Daniel took on were in less than stellar condition. It was why he could get them at a good price. Of course, that also meant an unknown number of surprises along the way. "Send me an estimate on how much fixing this is going to add to the budget."

"Will do." Luke stood and brushed off his jeans. "So what brings you out to the job site this early in the day? I wasn't expecting you to stop by till next week."

They left the disaster of a bathroom behind, making their way into the main part of the house. "Do you recall ever having dealt with a man named Grant Jacobson?"

Luke thought for a long moment. "Not that I can recall. No." He paused. "Why?"

Daniel shook his head. "The name sounded familiar, but I can't place it."

"Well, you've met a lot of people over the years. It's possible you've had dealings with him, and I haven't."

That was true. And it also narrowed down the possibilities of where he may have encountered the person or the name. Either that, or he'd met him before he'd brought Luke on board. "I'm sure it will come to me."

Luke nodded. "Do you want to see the rest of the house while you're here?"

Daniel spent the next thirty minutes going through the house with Luke. They talked about adding a patio onto the back and discussed what he wanted to do with the yard.

It was after nine before he made it to the office, but that wasn't out of the ordinary. Daniel didn't keep normal business hours. Kevin looked up as he walked in. "I put today's listings on your desk. And James called about fifteen minutes ago."

His youngest son had a habit of calling his office rather than his cell. He had no idea why. "Thanks."

James answered on the first ring. And instead of saying hello, he dove right into the conversation. "You made it into the office."

Daniel chuckled. "I did. But you know you can always call my cell phone."

"That's okay. It wasn't an emergency or anything. I wanted to ask if you were doing anything next weekend."

"I don't believe so," Daniel said. But even as the words came out of his mouth, he thought of Ali. "What's next weekend?"

"I have an event in St. Louis and I wanted to know if you'd like to come."

"Of course. I'll get your room ready at the house." Again, his thoughts went to Ali. He'd never introduced his kids to women he'd dated. It was different now, he knew. They were all adults, but still. What would they think of him being with a woman almost half his age?

"No need. I have to change between events, so I'm sharing a room at the hotel with a friend."

Why did it feel as if fifty pounds had been lifted off his shoulders? "All right. Well, let me know where I need to be and when."

"I'll email you the info. Thanks, Dad." James paused. "I should go. I need to get some extra training in before next week."

After saying goodbye, Daniel considered what to say to Ali. He'd told her about his kids, but telling her about them and meeting them were two different things. Would she even want to?

Running a hand over his head, he pushed those thoughts aside. There would be time enough to figure out what he was going to do once James sent him the information.

He scooped up the listings Kevin had placed on his desk but didn't see anything of interest. Setting them aside, he moved on to other pressing matters. Grant Jacobson.

A quick computer search didn't garner him much information. He now had the man's employment history, but that was about it. Grant Jacobson had worked in nearly every aspect of healthcare administration, floating from position to position, not spending longer than two years at any given job. But with every move, he'd worked his way up the ladder and was now the senior vice president of marketing at the largest hospital in St. Louis.

Daniel didn't know what he'd been hoping to find—maybe a huge lawsuit from a former employee—but there was nothing. To make matters worse, the man looked like a choir boy. His blue eyes smiled at the camera, presenting a likable and approachable image.

Then, there was something in the man's smile. A note of recognition tickled the edge of Daniel's brain again. He had seen the man before. The place was still evading him, but they'd met. If he could figure out where, that would go a long way to figuring out his next move.

CHAPTER 14

Ali was counting down the minutes until she could leave. Her boss was being a special kind of irritating today. He'd started off by grilling her about the fundraiser. What time had she got there? Who had she sat with? How long did she stay?

Then, as the day progressed, he had her running from department to department, trying to get surveys filled out regarding the current marketing materials each department had. Her suggestion to send the survey via email to each department head was met with a scowl and a quick dismissal. She'd spent the better part of four hours walking through the entire hospital. Her feet were killing her.

At four o'clock, her boss called her into his office. "Yes, Mr. Jacobson?"

"I need you to stay late tonight and go through this stack of surveys. All the data needs imputed into a spreadsheet. I need it ready for my meeting Monday morning." He handed her the surveys she'd put on his desk two hours earlier.

Ali took the papers but didn't move.

When her boss realized she hadn't left, he looked up, frowning. "Is there a problem, Ms. Foster?"

"I can't work late tonight. I already have plans."

118

"Your date can wait." He turned his attention back to whatever he was working on.

She didn't know what to do. Staying wasn't an option. Not only was Daniel coming to pick her up in half an hour, but she'd also promised Bridget she'd cover for her.

"You're still here."

Ali cleared her throat. "I'm sorry, Mr. Jacobson, but I really can't stay tonight. When is your meeting Monday morning?"

He scowled at her. "Ten o'clock."

She breathed a sigh of relief. She could come in early on Monday and get it done. Three hours should be plenty of time. "I'll come in early Monday morning and get everything entered. Would you prefer a printout, or would you like me to email it to you?" She sounded confident, but inside she was shaking.

Grant Jacobson stared her down and she almost gave in. If it weren't for her other commitments, she would have. "Both."

Blowing out the breath she'd been holding, she nodded, turned on her heel, and hightailed it out of there before he could demand something else from her.

Her boss was still sitting behind his desk when she logged off her computer at four thirty. Ali gathered her things and headed to the elevator. She chatted to a few people she knew on the way down to the lobby, but all she wanted to do was get out of there.

As soon as the elevator doors opened, she made a beeline for the front doors. Daniel was parked out front, waiting for her. A feeling of calm came over her at seeing him sitting behind the wheel.

He watched her as she approached the vehicle, his gaze raking over her from head to toe. She opened the door to the SUV and slid into the passenger seat. Once she was buckled in, he pulled away from the curb and headed toward the club. It wasn't until they were on their way that he spoke. "What happened?"

"How did you know something happened?" she asked.

Daniel gave her a look that said he expected an answer.

Ali sighed and leaned back in her seat. "My boss had me running all over the hospital today, so my feet are killing me. And I have to come in early Monday so I can get a spreadsheet ready for a meeting he has at ten."

"Why did he have you running all over the hospital?" His tone was even and to someone who didn't know him, they would think he was only making conversation. She knew better. He wasn't happy.

She told Daniel about the surveys. His response had been the same as hers. "Why not just email them to each department?"

"He said he couldn't wait for the department heads to get around to it when they felt like it. That he needed it done today."

Daniel frowned as he pulled into the parking lot of Serpent's Kiss. From the outside, the club blended into its surroundings. The brick building had been there for over one hundred years, as had several other buildings in the neighborhood.

She waited in the passenger seat until Daniel came around to help her out of the vehicle. He retrieved her bag from the back seat with her change of clothes and placed a hand on her low back as they walked toward the club. "We're going to discuss your job situation this weekend in more detail, but I want you to forget about it for the rest of the night."

He opened the door, letting them inside the small foyer. She didn't say anything as he swiped his membership card to let them into the lobby area where she typically worked the coat check. No one was there, of course. It was still early. Club members wouldn't begin arriving until six thirty or seven.

Helping her out of her jacket, he hung both items behind the coat check, then handed Ali's bag to her. "I need to speak to Katrina about something, but I'll be around if you need me."

"Yes, Sir." They may not be playing right now, but they were in the club and he was her Dom.

Daniel brushed his thumb along her cheek, then bent to give her a soft kiss. Opening the door that led to the club, he motioned for her to enter.

Ali waited until he disappeared down the hallway that led to Katrina's office before making her way to the locker room. She needed to change into her club attire.

Her heels echoed in the empty locker room. She set her bag on the bench in front of her locker and began removing her clothes. When she opened her bag, she found a note.

Meet me upstairs at six forty-five. Room four.

She knew they would most likely be playing tonight, but the note had blood pumping through her veins in anticipation. The urge to get her work done so she could be ready for him had her moving with renewed energy.

Knowing she wasn't working the entire night and that she now had a Dom, Ali had chosen an outfit she thought Daniel would like. After his reaction to her red lingerie the night before, she'd chosen something similar. The bra was all lace. It came up high, giving the illusion of modesty, but it was anything but. The lacy flowers on the panties were strategically placed to hint at the important bits but keep them hidden.

Over her bra and panties, she wore a purple dress. It was tight, hugging her curves and hiding what she had on beneath.

After taking a long look at herself in the mirror, Ali folded her dress clothes into her bag and shoved all of it into her locker. She had a lot of work to do before she could play, and she needed to get started.

* * *

KATRINA SAT AT HER DESK, her wavy blond hair cascading over her shoulders as she read the paper in front of her. He tapped lightly on the doorframe, and she looked up.

"Got a minute?" Daniel asked.

"Sure. Come in." She tucked the papers into a folder and pushed them aside. A new application, no doubt. "You're here early tonight."

"Ali agreed to cover the prep for Bridget tonight." Daniel closed the door behind him before taking a seat across from her.

One side of the club mistress's mouth lifted in a smirk. "I see."

"I've agreed to be Ali's Dom." He figured he'd put it out there. It wasn't as if she wouldn't have figured it out in an hour or so anyway. News traveled fast in the club. He had no doubt that within minutes of him entering a playroom with Ali, Katrina and over half the club would know about it.

Katrina sat back in her leather chair. She was already dressed for the night in her signature corset and even over the desk he could appreciate the way the silk and lace hugged her body. It was why she had the uncollared male subs in the club drooling after her. "I'm assuming you don't need me to provide either of you with a limits list, so what is it I can do for you this evening?"

"I need a background check ran on someone and I need it to be discreet."

She nodded, not asking him who or why, and turned her attention to her computer, her fingers flying across the keyboard. When she was finished, she returned to her relaxed position. "He should be giving you a call within the next twenty-four hours. It'll be from an unknown number."

"Thank you. I appreciate it." Daniel had met the private investigator Katrina used to screen applicants once before by chance. She didn't advertise who she used, and Daniel knew he was one of the few members who'd had any direct contact with him.

He walked to the door, closing his hand over the knob. As he was walking out the door, he heard Katrina's parting words. "Don't break her heart."

Daniel strolled into the hall, leaving the door open behind him. He headed to the main room, following the sound of ice being poured into the large wells behind the bar.

As he approached, Brandon grinned. "I'm not quite ready yet, but I'm sure I can whip you up something."

Taking a seat at the bar, Daniel waved his hand in dismissal. "I'm good. Just killing some time. Is Ali still upstairs?"

Brandon nodded. "She should be down in ten minutes or so."

Daniel spent the next fifteen minutes chatting with Brandon as he prepared garnishes and stocked the bar. The click of heels on stairs drew his attention. He watched as Ali eased her way down the staircase, her steps more tentative than usual. *Why the hell is she still wearing those damn heels?*

She glanced toward the bar and met his gaze. Daniel quirked his finger, beckoning her to him.

Ali made her way over, and he could have sworn he saw her wince a couple of times. She came to a stop in front of him and he wasted no time with pleasantries. "Take off your shoes."

Bracing herself on one of the bar stools, she stepped out of her shoes.

Daniel was keenly aware of their audience, but he didn't care. "Put them in your locker with the rest of your things. You won't need them for the rest of the night."

"Yes, Sir."

She bent, picked up her shoes, and headed toward the locker room.

"Well, now. That's a new development," Brandon said once Ali was out of earshot.

Daniel figured this was going to be a reoccurring theme throughout the night. He didn't have time to discuss it with him, though. "Is Cooper here yet?"

Brandon chuckled, not missing the dismissal and not bothered by it. "Yeah. Upstairs."

Nodding, Daniel stood and made his way to the second floor. One of Ali's jobs was to set up any rooms that had been reserved for the first half of the night. He'd reserved room number four, but he'd given no instructions as to how he wanted it set up.

Cooper, the dungeon monitor, was making some adjustments to a pair of chains hanging from the ceiling in room three when Daniel found him. The other Dom noticed him as soon as Daniel appeared in the doorway. Cooper finished what he was doing and removed his keys from his pocket. "I'm guessing you need supplies. I saw you had room four reserved."

Daniel followed him to the storage room at the end of the hall. It had enough toys to supply a club twice the size of Serpent's Kiss, which meant there was never a shortage of implements to choose from. All of them had been cleaned and sanitized, ready for the evening's play.

"What were you needing?" Cooper asked.

"Wax."

Cooper went to the far end of the room. "Body or pussy?"

"Both. In a variety of colors."

A few minutes later, they exited the room, their hands full of supplies. Ali had marked wax play as something she'd done before. However, he was guessing it had been a while. He knew all the men she'd played with for the last two years and none of the scenes had involved wax.

Of course, it was possible she'd played with someone outside of the club, but he didn't think so. One of the reasons Ali had joined the club was for safety and because she knew Katrina vetted every member.

Cooper placed the supplies on the table along the far wall and left Daniel alone. One of the downsides to playing at the club was they couldn't have open flames. Having a bunch of mini crockpots lined up wasn't exactly as sexy as holding a burning candle over his submissive's body while the wax dripped down, but it still got the job done.

Once Daniel was satisfied everything was the way he wanted it, he headed downstairs. He scanned the large room for Ali, but she was nowhere to be seen. There were a few members beginning to filter in and Brandon had turned on the music. One couple was already on the dance floor, and he had no doubt they'd be making their way upstairs soon.

"Looking for your girl?" Brandon asked with a smirk when he approached the bar again. "I think she's out front."

"Has Bridget arrived yet?" It wasn't quite six thirty, but it was getting close.

"I haven't seen her."

Daniel nodded. "Four bottles of water, please."

Brandon opened the refrigerator and removed four bottles of chilled water. He placed them on the bar in front of Daniel. "You playing tonight?"

"Yes."

"With Ali?" the bartender asked.

"Yes." Daniel took the bottles of water and turned on his heel, not giving the other Dom the chance to make any additional comments.

He'd known there would be some reactions to him and Ali playing together. Especially since he'd made it his mission over the last two years to negotiate play for her with other Doms. Brandon, of course, had been one of those Doms.

Daniel had watched that scene. Watched as the other Dom had bound her and played with her tits.

The memory hit him hard. At the time, he'd convinced himself it was for the best despite the way it had made him feel seeing her playing with someone else. Now that he'd been with her—now that she was his—replaying it in his head had him wanting to punch something.

As he reached the second floor once more, he could already hear a whip cracking inside one of the rooms. Cooper stood, arms crossed, as he watched the scene taking place inside. He glanced over at Daniel and gave a curt nod before turning back to what was going on inside the room.

Cooper was the club's dungeon monitor. He was in his forties and had been a Dom for a decade before coming to work at the club. Unlike Brandon, Ali, and Bridget, he didn't rotate his shifts with anyone so he could play. A lot of the members speculated on why that was, but as far as Daniel knew, no one knew for sure except Katrina.

Leaving Cooper and the rest of the club behind, Daniel entered room four and did a final inspection to ensure everything was exactly the way he wanted it. In the short time he'd been downstairs, the wax had melted in the warming pots and he'd made sure to have plenty of towels on hand. Playing with wax could get messy.

He checked the clock again. Six thirty-five. Ali would be along soon.

Taking a seat, he settled in to wait for his sub.

CHAPTER 15

*B*ridget burst through the door at six thirty on the dot. "Sorry I'm late. I got stuck behind an accident on the other side of town." She stripped out of her coat and hung it up on one of the hangers. "I need to change. Can you cover for me for a few more minutes?"

Ali looked at the time. "I have to be upstairs in fifteen minutes." Then the clock changed. "Make that fourteen."

Grabbing her bag, Bridget ducked into the nook that housed the coat check. "I'll change here, then."

Before Ali could react, Bridget was halfway undressed. She shook her head. "I would have waited, you know."

"Yes, but then you would have been late." She heard some rustling, then Bridget asked, "Who are you playing with?"

Heat rushed to Ali's cheeks, anticipating her friend's response. "Daniel."

Bridget peeked out from behind the partition, her eyes wide. "Girl, you have got to tell me how you managed that, but for now you'd better get your butt in gear or you're going to be late."

Sure enough, Ali only had six minutes to get upstairs. "I'll catch you later." She eased out from behind the coat check and headed into the club.

Her bare feet slapped against the floor as she hurried toward the staircase. Daniel hadn't looked pleased earlier when he'd seen her wearing her heels. Normally, she didn't have an issue. She was used to heels. But after being on her feet so much earlier, her feet had been begging her for mercy. Even now, her feet hurt, but being out of the constricting heels helped.

The door to room four was closed when she approached. Cooper saw her and smiled. "He's waiting for you inside."

"Thanks," she said and let herself into the playroom.

The lights were dim, but she spotted him right away. He sat in the corner, his eyes trained on her.

Ali walked over to him, kneeled, and lowered her head. He lifted his hand, resting it on top of her head. She closed her eyes, leaning into his touch. The back of his other hand brushed the side of her face before tilting her chin up. "Why are you breathing hard? Were you rushing?"

"Yes, Sir. Bridget was running behind and I didn't want to be late."

He nodded. "How are your feet?"

"Sore, Sir."

"You shouldn't have been wearing your heels earlier. You need to take better care of what's mine."

"Yes, Sir," Ali whispered. It had been a long time since she'd had a Dom. She was used to taking care of herself. Pushing herself to meet others' expectations.

"We need to talk before we get started with tonight's scene." He rubbed his thumb along her bottom lip. "I know you've done wax play before. Are there any body parts that are hard limits?"

She'd noticed the warming pots on the table as she'd entered the room and wondered if that's what was on the menu for tonight. Thinking about the warm wax dripping onto her skin filled her with anticipation. "No, Sir."

Daniel stood and offered his hand to help her up.

She took it and let him lead her to the long table he'd set up on one side of the room. Without a word, he lifted the dress she was wearing over her head and discarded it on the floor. His gaze roamed her body, taking in the bra and panty set she'd chosen for the evening. Her nipples were straining against the sheer fabric of her bra, aching to be touched.

He used his index finger to trace the edge of her breast before moving in to circle her left nipple. Then, his finger was gone. She snapped her eyes open, not even realizing they'd drifted closed.

"Turn."

Ali did as he asked, presenting her back to him so he could unhook her bra. But instead of pushing it off her shoulders once he had it unfastened, he cupped her breasts from behind and massaged the fabric against her tits. The lace scraped against her nipples, adding to the sensations coursing through her. He held her against him, tugging at her nipples before dragging the bra down her arms to pool on the floor.

Cool air hit her back as he stepped away and she held her breath, waiting to see what he'd do next.

She didn't have to wait long. The feel of him behind her returned, and then his hands appeared in front of her face. He held the end of a scarf in each hand and placed it over her eyes. In a matter of seconds, her vision was gone.

The fabric of the scarf pulled against her hair as he secured it behind her head. His fingers brushed her hair from her shoulders, and then soft lips grazed her newly exposed skin.

She sucked in a breath as his hands came around her from behind to palm her breasts. A tiny sigh left her lips as he massaged her already sensitive flesh.

"Don't hold back tonight. You are free to move and make as many noises as you want." He rolled her nipples between his fingers, sending a shot of electricity to her pussy.

"Thank you, Sir." The words barely made it out. All she wanted to do was relax against him and let him play with her body however he saw fit.

But then he removed his hands again, and the next thing she knew, she was being lifted off the ground. Ali squeaked at the unexpected movement, but she didn't have time to do much more than that before she was spread out on the table.

The hard wood had been draped with towels to help with the cleanup after. They also provided a little padding.

Fingers hooked into the sides of her panties and slowly dragged down her legs. Then, he was removing her stockings. She hadn't worn a garter belt tonight, thinking the thigh-high stockings would be easier to remove.

Once she was completely naked, she waited. A few seconds passed, then he began to move his hands on her body, rubbing oil over her skin. He took his time, massaging her shoulders, kneading her breasts, and dipping his hand down to caress the sensitive area between her legs.

Ali sighed when he removed his hands and as she listened to him moving about the room, her mind wandered. How many people were watching them from the hall? She wasn't an exhibitionist like Grace or John, but she didn't mind playing in front of others for the most part. Not at the club, anyway. The people here wouldn't judge her for her desires.

She had been so wrapped up in her own thoughts that the first drizzle of hot wax startled her.

"Too hot?" he asked.

"No, Sir."

She'd barely gotten the words out before the next drizzle hit her chest. This time it was a bit hotter. The wax followed the curve of her left breast, tightening as it cooled. She loved the feeling of wax on her skin. The warmth followed by the constriction had her body coming alive.

Drip by drip, he used the wax to draw on her body. Dried wax cascaded over her nipples, encasing her breasts. Her stomach muscles flexed as the wax rained down, warming her and making her want to move away at the same time.

There wasn't much of her torso that wasn't covered in wax and she could only imagine what she looked like. A lot of Doms liked to use different colors of wax to create pictures or faux clothing on their subs. She had no idea what all the wax on her looked like, but she was willing to be his canvas anytime he wanted her to be.

Then, she felt wax drip between her thighs and by instinct she began to close her legs. A hand stopped her, spreading her open and moving the wax so it hit her pussy.

Ali arched her back and held on to the sides of the table.

"That's it. Embrace it."

Another drop hit directly on her clit and she cried out. Hot wax dripped between the folds of her most sensitive flesh. It felt...

She didn't have time to think before he opened her leg and drizzled wax along the inside of her leg. She was completely open to him, exposed. Not that he hadn't seen her before, but between the wax and the position and knowing people were watching her had her on the edge of something. What, she didn't know.

Her chest was rising and falling rapidly, pulling at the wax on her breast. It only added to the sensation, and she felt every inch of her body.

The feel of his hands running over the wax created an entirely new feeling. He was barely touching her, but it felt so intimate she wanted to cry.

"You look so beautiful, sweetheart." His hands caressed her sides, tracing the lines made by the wax.

Ali arched against his hands, needing his touch.

His fingers skimmed over her wax-covered clit, moving the hardened wax about, sending shots of pain mixed with pleasure directly to her core. She knew herself well enough to know it wouldn't take much for her to come. Her body was primed.

Then, his hands were gone. She wanted to cry out, but she didn't. Instead, she bit her bottom lip and waited to see what he would do to her next.

* * *

WATCHING her reactions to the wax had Daniel grinning. It also had his cock straining against his jeans. He picked up the massage oil and flipped the lid open. Wax could be removed in a variety of ways, including with a flogger. He'd considered that option, but flogging wax off created a hell of a mess.

Depositing a good amount of oil into his palm, Daniel rubbed his hands together before running them up Ali's thighs. The wax gently pulled away from her skin, leaving the shiny oil in its place as he worked his way up one thigh and then the other.

Ali sighed, her legs falling open, giving him full access to her body. As he moved over her, massaging as he went, he removed the dried wax and placed it on one of the extra towels.

He took his time, making sure to remove as much as he could from the dips and valleys between her legs. When he began caressing her pussy, the sounds coming from her lips changed. Her soft sighs became moans. He could feel heat radiating from her sex that had nothing to do with the wax.

Spreading her wide, he used both hands to rub up and down her labia before moving his attention to her clit. It was out from beneath its hood, swollen, and begging for some attention. He brushed his thumb against it several times, thrilling each time she sucked in a breath, then moved his attention higher, leaving her hanging.

A soft whine left her throat, and he chuckled. "Patience, sweetheart."

She bit her bottom lip again as his hands roamed over her stomach. Wax had pooled in her belly button, and he took his time getting as much of it out as he could.

Ali squirmed as he skimmed up her sides, his touch tickling her, but he could tell she was trying her best to keep still. She was a good submissive and having his hands on her was doing nothing to make him want her less. No, the more time he spent with her, the more he had of her, the more he wanted.

He shook his head, trying to push those thoughts from his mind. Thinking about the future wouldn't do him any good. He had to focus on the present. Right now, she was here with him. His. He would enjoy it while it lasted.

His hands covered the swell of her breasts, pulling and pushing them together, working the wax loose from its hold on her skin. She tilted her head back, releasing a low moan as his hands glided over her tits.

Daniel wiped his hands on a towel and used a clean one to wipe as much of the remaining wax from her body as possible. She'd need a shower after the scene, but he wasn't quite ready to be done with her. His cock was straining painfully in his pants, and he wasn't about to end the scene until he'd finished what they'd started.

Going to the wall of toys, he selected a flogger. With most of the wax removed, he didn't have to worry about it flying everywhere.

He stood over her, taking in her beautiful form. She was absolutely perfect. Her nipples stood erect, and her sex gleamed, wet and wanting. He cupped the side of her face. "Are you doing all right?"

She leaned into his touch. "Yes, Sir."

He bent to kiss her, letting his mouth linger and pulling a sound out of her he felt all the way down to his toes. She was slowly breaking all his resolve. All he wanted to do was bury himself inside her, to feel her heat wrapped around him.

Dropping his hand, he stood to his full height and moved to the opposite end of the table. She had the smallest feet. He thought of her wearing her heels, running all over the hospital on her boss's errand. She'd been out of her heels for almost two hours, but he could still see evidence of her pain.

With his free hand, he took his thumb and gently pressed it into the sole of one foot. She flinched before she could stop herself.

He didn't reprimand her, though. She was hurting and there was only one person to blame for that. "From now on, you will take a pair of flats with you to work. If you need to run around the hospital, you will change into those. Do you understand?"

"Yes, Sir."

Daniel removed his hand and trailed the ends of the flogger over the tops of her feet. The leather brushed her skin, and he saw her muscles relax.

He moved the falls of the flogger up her body, letting them touch every inch of her exposed skin. The ends dipped between her legs, teasing her pussy before he shifted them up to caress her stomach. Her breathing slowed as all the tension left her body. The only thing on her mind was the feel of his flogger. Exactly the way he wanted it.

The leather kissed her breasts before he ran it up her neck and face. Her mouth fell open and she turned her head to the side, silently begging for more.

One of the things he loved most about floggers was how versatile they were. The sensations he could create with a flogger ranged from a barely there brush of the leather to a thud that bordered on the edge of pain. It was all in the technique, the location, and the type of flogger.

The one he'd chosen to use on her tonight was on the lighter side. When he was flogging her ass and the backs of her thighs the night before, he'd used a heavier flogger. Those areas of a woman's body were ripe for a good, hard flogging.

He lifted his wrist and took aim at one of Ali's breasts. The impact startled her, but it only lasted a moment. At the second hit, she tilted her head back as her nipples, already sensitive from the wax, embraced everything he was giving her.

Her chest a healthy rose color, he changed his focus to her pussy. It was in desperate need of attention. He spread her legs, placing one foot on either side of the table, and went to work.

As he continued to flog her pussy, he could see her arousal coating the falls. Little sounds began from deep in her throat and he knew what he wanted. It had been years since he'd had sex in front of an audience, but in the moment he didn't care. He needed to be buried deep inside her and he didn't want to wait until they were in the privacy of his home.

Dropping the flogger to the floor, he swiped a condom from the room's ample supply and returned to stand at the end of the table. When Katrina designed the playrooms, she tried to think of everything. While the table Ali was lying on had a wood top, the base was metal and could be adjusted to whatever height the Dom preferred.

Daniel grabbed hold of Ali's legs and pulled her toward him, her ass sliding against the towels with ease. She let out a little yelp at the sudden movement, but otherwise didn't react. He used the foot pedal to bring her to the height he wanted and placed her ankles on his shoulders.

Popping the button on his jeans, he quickly pushed them out of the way and rolled on a condom. He gripped the base of his cock and guided it to her sex. Her pussy welcomed him as he slid inside, primed and ready for the beating it was about to take.

He didn't waste time. Playing with her like this, having had his hands on her for the last hour, he was ready to explode.

The sound of their bodies slapping together as he drove into her filled the room. With every thrust of his hips, her body moved on the table. Ali held on to the sides, trying to push back against him, but unable to get the leverage she needed. That was okay. He had no problem doing all the work.

Feeling the beginnings of his orgasm, he peeled one of her hands from the table and placed it between her legs. "Make yourself come."

Her fingers circled her clit, drawing gasps from her as he continued his relentless assault. She was close. He could tell. Even though they'd only been together like this a few times, he knew her body. He knew her.

"Come for me," he growled.

As soon as the words left his mouth, he felt his own orgasm surge forward. Luckily, Ali was right there with him. The beautiful sounds of her climax filled the room, mingling with his.

CHAPTER 16

Ali's body was buzzing in the best possible way.

"Are you all right?" He reached up to run his thumb over her bottom lip.

"Yes, Sir. I'm better than all right."

Daniel was still inside her, so she felt the vibrations as he chuckled at her reply. He bent to press a kiss to her lips and remove the scarf from over her eyes before easing out of her and going to dispose of the condom.

Thanks to the dim light in the room, it didn't take long for her eyes to adjust. She followed his movements as he refastened his jeans. He'd taken her fully clothed while she'd been spread out naked on the table.

As realization hit, her gaze went to the large window. No one was standing there now, watching, but she knew they had been. Wax play was rare at the club given how messy it was. Most Doms understood the cleanup involved and didn't want to mess with it, even if they left it to their submissives.

Daniel, however, had removed the wax in a way that required the least amount of cleanup. Besides the towels, the rest of the room was clean.

A hand cupped her face and she shifted her attention to the man in front of her. "Are you okay to stand?" he asked.

"I think so, Sir."

She sat up slowly, just in case her equilibrium was off after their scene. Other than feeling as if every inch of her skin was alive, Ali didn't notice any lingering effects.

Daniel stood close as she slid her feet onto the floor, reaching a hand to steady her. That was good considering her legs buckled.

His arm went around her waist, keeping her upright. She fisted his shirt and nuzzled her nose in the fabric. He smelled of sweat and sex.

Lips pressed against the top of her head. "Do you need to sit down?"

Ali shook her head. "I don't think so, Sir. I think I'm okay."

He didn't let her go right away and she was okay with that.

Once he was confident she wasn't going to fall, he helped her into a thin robe. It didn't hide much, but at least he wasn't going to make her walk downstairs naked.

He handed her a bottle of water. "Drink that, and then you can head downstairs to shower."

She took the bottle from him and began to drink. He opened his own bottle and downed it in under ten seconds.

While she drank her water, he turned off the warming pots so the wax could cool. Someone would be in tomorrow morning to clean the club from top to bottom. They would take care of the leftover wax in the pots.

Daniel picked up her undergarments and handed them to her. She polished off the rest of her water and took them from him. He tilted her chin up so she could meet his gaze. "Shower and put the bra, panties, and stockings back on. Then, come find me on the first floor."

She swallowed but didn't say anything.

When she stood there, unmoving, he raised an eyebrow. "Problem?"

Ali sucked in a breath. She could do this. "No, Sir."

"Good. Now go shower. I'll be waiting for you downstairs."

Clutching the flimsy lingerie to her chest, Ali scrambled out of the room.

No one said anything to her as she passed, but she did get a few looks. Some of them seemed happy, others confused, but all of them knowing. They knew she'd played with Daniel. And if they hadn't witnessed the scene themselves, they'd heard about it.

She breathed a sigh of relief when she entered the locker room, but it was short-lived. As she rounded the corner to the showers, Kim stood there, waiting for her.

Ali dropped her bra, panties, and stockings on the shelf outside one of the shower stalls and pulled the curtain back. She turned the water on to warm, then faced her friend. "I guess you heard about my scene with Daniel."

She nodded but didn't say anything. When Kim had revealed she'd slept with her boyfriend and Dom, Justin, Ali had been hurt given her friend had been crushing on her older brother's best friend for well over a decade. And while Ali's feelings for Daniel hadn't been brewing for as long, that didn't change things.

"Are you mad?" Ali asked.

"No." Kim motioned toward the shower. "You'd better get in there."

She was right. Daniel wouldn't be happy with her if she lingered.

Stepping into the shower, she pulled the curtain closed and began to wash off the wax. "I'm sorry I didn't tell you. These last couple of days have been crazy."

"I do hope you know I want all the details. And you'd better not leave anything out."

Ali laughed. "I promise."

"Lunch tomorrow at Georgio's?"

"Twelve o'clock."

The sound of heels clicking on the tile floor let her know Kim had left the room. She finished washing, removing the remnants of the wax from all the crevices of her body. It took longer than she thought it would but digging all the wax from her belly button had taken a while.

She dried off and dressed in her bra, panties, and stockings. A quick look in the mirror told her what she'd already known. Her outfit didn't cover much. A flower over each nipple and a grouping of similar flowers at her crotch were the only things keeping her goods from being on full display.

Blowing out a breath, she threw her wet towel in the hamper and went in search of her Dom.

* * *

MOST OF THE scenes Daniel had been involved in over the last two years had been rather tame. At least, on his side. Even before he'd met Ali, when he had indulged in a sub's mouth or pussy, it had never been like it was with her. When he was inside Ali, it was as if he couldn't get deep enough. He wanted to consume her. For her to consume him. It scared the hell out of him, but not because he didn't want it. Because he wanted it too much.

It would be different if Ali didn't seem to enjoy their rough play, but she did. The force of her climaxes was impossible to ignore. Daniel knew he was in deep—deeper than he'd ever meant to be with her.

As he turned to go, Katrina was standing in the doorway. The look on her face said more than words ever could, but she said them anyway. "I hope you know what you're doing." Then, before he could respond, she'd walked away.

Daniel didn't miss the looks he received as he made his way down to the main floor of the club and could only imagine Ali had experienced the same. He glanced toward the women's locker room, but he knew she wouldn't be finished yet. It was too soon.

Resuming his progress toward the seating area, he came face-to-face with Justin. "Sorry. I wasn't watching where I was going."

"Looking for Ali?" Justin asked.

"No. She's showering. She'll join me when she's done."

The other Dom nodded. "I thought you two were just friends."

"Things change."

Again, Justin nodded. "Kim went to check on her."

Of course, Justin was worried about his own sub. Kim was Ali's best friend. It was because of Ali Kim had joined Serpent's Kiss. "I'm assuming Kim heard about our scene."

"Everyone heard about your scene. You two are the talk of the club tonight."

Brilliant.

Justin laughed. "Come on. I'll buy you a drink while we wait for our girls."

He followed Justin to the bar. Brandon had a shit-eating grin on his face. "What can I get you, gentlemen?"

"I'll take a beer," Justin said.

Brandon looked at Daniel.

"Make it two."

The bartender nodded and turned to get their beers. He popped off the tops and set them in front of them within a matter of seconds.

Justin took a pull from his beer and Daniel did the same. They sat at the bar, drinking their beers and waiting on their subs to emerge from the locker room.

Kim appeared first. She scanned the crowd until she located Justin. She was wearing a light pink dress that barely covered her ass. As she approached, Daniel could see the outline of her hard nipples pressing against the fabric of her top. She walked straight to her Dom.

Justin set his beer on the bar, spread his legs, and pulled her against him. One of his hands snaked under her skirt to cup her ass while the other cupped the back of her head. "Did you talk to Ali?"

"Yes, Sir. She's taking a shower." Her last word came out in little gasp and Daniel realized the other Dom's hand had moved lower.

"I think you owe me something," Justin said.

"Yes, Sir."

He moved his hands away and Kim dropped to her knees. She reached for the button on his jeans but looked at him before continuing. A sub going down on their Dom in the club wasn't unusual, but he'd never seen Kim and Justin have sex of any kind with an audience.

Kim's mouth closed over Justin's cock when Daniel saw Ali walked out. He resisted the urge to stand and go to her. She looked uncomfortable standing in her underwear, but she would get used to it. He'd make sure of that.

Her eyes locked on his and she made her way through the crowd. He didn't miss her reaction to seeing Kim on her knees sucking Justin off, but she recovered quickly.

Daniel held his hand out to her, bringing her close to his side. "Would you like a drink?"

"Yes, please."

He signaled to Brandon and tilted his head toward Ali. The bartender nodded and soon appeared with a Sprite.

Daniel moved Ali to stand between his legs, her back to his front, and handed her the drink. He brushed her hair away from her neck as she took a sip. "Would you like to stay and watch?"

He wasn't sure how she'd feel watching Kim and Justin, but he had no issues watching if she didn't. It was obvious to him from the exchange that the blowjob was payment for allowing Kim to go check on Ali. While it may not be a punishment, Justin was making her work for it. Every time she tried to speed up, he'd slow her down.

"No, Sir."

Sliding off his stool, Daniel picked up his beer. "Thanks for the drink," he said to Justin.

The other Dom lifted his chin but didn't break his concentration as he guided his submissive's mouth over his erection.

Instead of heading toward the seating area where their friends were no doubt eagerly waiting, Daniel found a quiet area in the corner. It was behind the bar on the far side of the dance area. Only one other couple was there, no doubt decompressing from a scene.

The other couple didn't spare them a glance as Daniel sat down on one of the couches and lowered Ali onto his lap. He placed his beer on the small table, then took her drink and set it down as well.

Stretching out, he pulled her against him, resting her head on his shoulder. "Did you have any trouble removing the rest of the wax?"

"I had to dig a little in my belly button, but that was the hardest part."

The feel of her against him in this outfit had him growing hard again, which was insane. He wasn't twenty anymore, but sometimes she made him feel like he was. "How are your nipples and pussy? Are you sore anywhere?"

"My nipples and pussy are tender, Sir, but in a good way."

The front of her body had a slight redness to it from where the hot wax had been. He ran his hands over her midsection, remembering how the multicolored wax had dripped over her skin. How could he want her again this soon?

To try and distract himself, he changed the direction of the conversation. "You didn't tell Kim you'd asked me to be your Dom."

"We haven't texted much over the last couple of days with everything going on at work and the fundraiser." Ali sighed. "I should have told her. Then she wouldn't have had to suck Justin in the middle of the club."

"She made her choice."

Ali didn't say anything for a long time and he let her have her quiet. They watched as people danced, grinding against one another to the music. The beat moved through his blood as his hands caressed the woman molding against him.

"We need to talk about our scene. Was there anything I did you didn't like?" he asked.

She took her time answering, but he was grateful she was taking his question seriously. "I've never had wax on my pussy like that before, but I liked it."

"You marked on your list you've had experience with it before."

"I have, but it wasn't the same." She paused and turned to look up at him. "You used a lot more wax."

Ali held his gaze and he felt the pull between them. What was it about this woman that had him all tight up in knots, wanting her even though he knew he shouldn't?

He lowered his mouth to hers, coaxing her lips to open for him as he slid his tongue inside. She tasted sweet from the pop she'd been drinking. "We should talk more about our scene."

"There was nothing you did I didn't like, Sir." She twisted in his arms, tangling her fingers in his hair, and their lips came together again.

Eventually, he broke the kiss, cupping her face in his hands. Her lips were swollen, and she was breathing as hard as he was. As tempting as it was to stay hidden in the corner with her for the rest of the evening, they needed to get the next part of the evening over with. "Are you ready to face our friends?"

The light in her eyes dimmed a little. She knew what was coming. Not that they wouldn't approve, but there would be questions.

Ali nodded and reluctantly eased herself from his lap. He stood and laced his hand with hers as they headed toward their group seated on the other side of the room. They were all there. Beth and Drew. Justin and Kim, Nicole and Jeff. And even Alexander and Grace.

Kim saw them first, but it didn't take long for the rest of the group to notice their approach. Daniel ignored them for the most part and sat on the couch next to Kim and Justin, adjusting Ali on his lap.

No one said anything for several minutes. He was about to break the silence when Alexander spoke up. "It's about fuckin' time."

All their friends laughed.

"Next round of drinks is on me," Nicole said. "What's everyone having?"

Her submissive, Jeff, took their drink orders and headed toward the bar.

"So how long have you two been hiding this from all of us?" Beth asked.

"Oh, I think this is new," Drew said.

Beth played with the hair at the nape of his neck as she smirked at Daniel and Ali. "You might be right."

Ali looked at him and he nodded, letting her know it was okay to share. He'd much rather have her give her version of their arrangement since he was still trying to figure it out himself. "It happened this week."

A pleased look crossed Drew's face.

Grace leaned forward. "I'm happy for you both. Sir's right. It's been a long time coming."

Daniel sat and listened to his friends talk, asking questions here and there, but mostly sharing how pleased they were he and Ali had finally 'taken the plunge.' Justin's words. All the time Daniel had thought he'd hidden his feelings for Ali behind the veil of friendship, he'd apparently been hiding nothing.

At eleven o'clock, Daniel instructed Ali to go change. Beth and Drew had left an hour ago, as had Alexander and Grace. Nicole and Jeff had ventured upstairs, leaving him, Ali, Justin, and Kim alone in the seating area.

Justin patted a hand on Kim's hip. "Go with Ali and change. I want to get you home."

Both women headed toward the locker room, leaving Daniel and Justin alone.

"I know you care about her," Justin said out of the blue. "I'm not sure why you dragged your feet for two years, but I'm sure you had your reasons. I just hope whatever they were, you've resolved them. If you hurt her, it will upset my girl and I don't like to see my girl upset."

The man didn't mince words and Daniel could appreciate that. He didn't have a response, however. The last thing he wanted to do was hurt Ali. His feelings for her were getting more complicated by the day. Every moment he spent with her had him wanting to entwine her more in his life and never let her go.

Ali and Kim strolled out of the locker room together several minutes later, both dressed in street clothes. Kim walked to Justin and Ali to him.

Daniel took her bag from her and circled an arm around her waist. They said a quick goodbye and headed out.

Later that night, Ali tucked into his side as she slept, Daniel knew he was screwed no matter what he did. If he let her go now, he'd hate himself for not enjoying her while he could. If he let things go on, when she did move on, the pain would probably kill him.

"Everything okay?" she murmured against his chest.

"Everything's fine, sweetheart." He pressed his lips to her forehead and tightened his hold on her. "Go back to sleep."

She hummed and moments later her breathing evened out.

Closing his eyes, he memorized the feel of her in his arms and finally admitted what he'd been avoiding for far too long. He loved her. Had for a long time. And even though it might be easier, better for them both if he ended things now, he couldn't. He was selfish enough to take what she offered. He'd figure out the rest later.

CHAPTER 17

Ali strolled into Georgio's at eleven fifty-seven. She'd planned to get there earlier, but Daniel hadn't let her out of bed until she'd been unable to feel her limbs. And after she'd dragged herself from his bed to shower and dress, he'd pressed her against the wall and given her a toe-curling kiss that had her wanting him to drag her back to bed.

Remembering that kiss had all her woman parts tingling. She had no idea how she could still be horny given how many orgasms he'd given her in the last twenty-four hours, but she couldn't seem to get enough. Maybe it was her lack of explosive orgasms over the past two years that had her body going haywire.

The hostess escorted Ali to a table in the middle of the restaurant where Kim was already seated. Ali sat down across from her friend and got down to business. "I went to my apartment Wednesday night to get my dress and everything ready for the fundraiser and he brought dinner."

Kim raised her eyebrows. "Were you the one on the menu?"

Ali snorted. "No." Then she blushed.

"Un-huh. Spill."

Luckily, their server appeared, and she was given a momentary reprieve. "What can I get you ladies today?"

"Two orders of fettuccine Alfredo," Kim said.

Their server nodded and took the menus they hadn't even glanced at. "I'll get this put in and be back to check on you shortly."

As he walked away, Ali shook her head at Kim. "Sometimes I wonder if you're not a switch."

"No idea, but I have no interest in finding out." Then, Kim leaned in. "All the details."

She didn't need to clarify which details she was wanting. Ali knew. "I'd left my art supplies on the table, so I gathered them up and went to put them away."

Kim hadn't moved. She had one elbow on the table and her chin resting in her palm.

"I was embarrassed about him seeing my paintings. He noticed I was upset, so he followed me."

"And?"

"And..." Ali met her friend's gaze. "He kissed me."

"He kissed you."

"Yes." The word came out on a sigh as she remembered the kiss. As wonderful as all their other kisses had been, she wasn't sure she'd ever forget that first one. The way his mouth had felt moving against hers, the surprise she'd felt, and how her body had softened as he'd teased her lips with his tongue.

"Hello?" Kim waved her hand in front of Ali's face.

"Sorry."

Kim chuckled. "Must have been some kiss."

That was an understatement.

"What happened next? Did he carry you into your bedroom and have his wicked way with you?"

That got a laugh out of Ali. "I wish." She picked up her water and took a sip before continuing. "He stopped and said, 'I can't.' Then, he ran out of the room."

Her friend's eyes widened in shock. "What?"

"I followed him back out to the living room and..."

When she didn't go on, Kim groaned. "Woman, you're killing me."

Not wanting the entire restaurant to hear what she was about to say, she leaned forward and lowered her voice. "Long story short, I had a pre-dinner snack."

"Holy—" Kim cut herself off. "I would've loved to see that."

Given she'd witnessed Kim doing the same thing to Justin the night before, Ali wasn't so sure. Then again, Kim's hang-ups about sex were different than Ali's.

"Back up. What happened between him running out of the room and you having your pre-dinner snack?"

This was the part Ali didn't really want to talk about. "He kept apologizing, saying it wouldn't happen again."

Kim's brow furrowed. "Why was he sorry? 'Cause after seeing you two together last night and hearing about your scene, it's not because there's a lack of chemistry between you two."

"No. That's not it." And Ali was beginning to realize that was never it. All the time she'd spent thinking he didn't want her the way she wanted him and that hadn't been it at all. "He thinks he's too old for me."

Her friend was quiet for several, very long, moments. "How much older is he?"

"He's fifty-five."

She could see Kim doing the math in her head. "That is a bit of an age gap, but I've also seen the way you two look at each other."

Ali smiled, glad her friend understood. But she was done talking about herself. She wanted to know about Kim. "Speaking of servicing your Dom…"

Kim gave her a look that said she knew exactly what Ali was doing. "The club was buzzing saying you and Daniel were upstairs in one of the rooms. I wanted to make sure you were okay."

Ali knew her friend didn't mean physically okay. "You didn't have to—"

"Yes, I did. And I understood the choice I was making." She blew out a breath. "It was awkward knowing people were watching, but I got through it."

"You get used to it. You may even learn to like it."

"Maybe." Then Kim turned the focus back on Ali. "But how are you really? How are things between you and Daniel? Besides the sex part. 'Cause from what I gathered, there are no issues there."

Her friend winked at her and Ali blushed. "Things are good, I think. I mean, it's only been a few days."

"True."

Their conversation was interrupted yet again by their server. This time, he came bearing food.

The creamy fettuccini noodles covered in alfredo sauce made her mouth water. She hummed as the first bite hit her tongue. It was heavenly.

"I never remember how good this is until I taste it," Kim said, with a contented smile on face.

"I know. They must have some magic potion back there or something to make it this good." Ali swirled some more pasta on her fork and shared another tidbit of information. "Daniel can cook."

"Like he can whip up a good breakfast or he's a five-star chef?" Kim asked before stuffing a huge bite of pasta in her mouth.

"More than just breakfast, but not quite a five-star chef." Ali paused. "He learned to cook so he could feed his kids when they were staying with him."

She saw Kim hesitate, but her friend recovered quickly. "How old are his kids?"

"Twenty-one, twenty-five, and twenty-seven."

Again, Kim seemed to be considering her next line of questioning. "So is this thing with Daniel serious or is it just, you know, a play arrangement?"

Crap. "We're still trying to figure it out."

Kim put her fork down, which considering Georgio's fettuccini Alfredo was to die for, meant her friend was about to lay it out for her. "So that tells me that while you want it to be serious, he's not completely on board."

"It's not—" But Ali didn't know what it was exactly. They'd talked about it. Kind of. She'd let him know she wanted more than a play only relationship. Not to mention she'd spent every night since their first kiss in his bed. That had to mean something, right? "Can't I just enjoy being with him?"

Her friend sighed and covered Ali's hand with hers. "Of course you can, but I don't want to see you get hurt."

"This sounds like a very familiar conversation."

Kim laughed. "Yeah. Well, you were right to be concerned when I was in the thick of it. Justin's relationship with Mark still isn't the same as it was before."

When Mark, Kim's older brother, found out about her relationship with Justin, he hadn't exactly been thrilled. In fact, he'd punched Justin.

Before Ali could say anything, Kim went on. "If he's not as invested as you are, I'm worried you're going to get hurt. He has adult children. I'm assuming he's been married before."

"They divorced a long time ago."

"Has he had any serious relationships since then?" Kim asked.

Ali frowned. "I don't know. I haven't asked."

"Are you planning to meet his kids?"

Again, she didn't know. They hadn't talked about it. "We haven't gotten that far."

Neither said anything for a long time. They finished their pasta and Kim motioned for the bill. "My treat."

"Thanks."

They made their way out of the restaurant and stopped on the sidewalk. Kim pulled Ali in for a hug. "Call me if you need anything, okay?"

"I will. Promise."

Ali made her way to her car, her mind full of everything she and Kim had talked about. As she drove to Daniel's, she couldn't stop thinking about one thing Kim had brought up. Daniel's kids. Would he want her to meet them? And, if so, what would they think of their dad having a much younger woman in his life?

* * *

AFTER ALI LEFT for her lunch with Kim, Daniel went into his study to get some work done. When he logged onto his email, he noticed one from James.

Hey, Dad.

I've attached a flyer about the event and two tickets. I sent Mom two tickets, too. My competition starts around noon and goes till two.

James

Daniel printed the flyer and the tickets. He hadn't mentioned the event to Ali yet. It was something he'd been struggling with, but he needed to decide.

Leaning back in his chair, he ran through his options—a mental list of the pros and cons. But at the end of the day, the only thing that mattered was that he wanted Ali by his side.

He spent the rest of his alone time skimming over some online listings that had cropped up in the last twenty-four hours. One looked promising, and he emailed the homeowner to schedule a viewing. Some of his best finds had been through nontraditional sites most realtors avoided. These were often for sale by the owner and needed major work or, at the very least, extensive updating. He wasn't afraid of either.

The front door closing brought his head up. He glanced at the clock to find it was almost two. Pushing away from his desk, Daniel went to find Ali.

He found her kicking off her shoes in her room. Her back was to him, which gave him a stunning view of her round ass in a pair of fitted jeans. Then, she leaned forward to grab something from the bed and he was a goner.

Crossing the room in two strides, he grabbed hold of her hips and jerked her against him. She giggled. "Hello to you, too." Her eyes twinkled as she looked over her shoulder at him.

"Your ass looks amazing in these jeans." He ground his erection into her backside.

"They're my favorite jeans. I figured I needed all the confidence I could get."

He stepped back, pulling her with him. She stood and twisted in his arms. Daniel wasted no time kissing her. "How'd it go?"

Her fingers played with the hair at the base of his neck, sending tingles down his spine. "Okay. I told her what happened at my apartment."

"So you told her how you seduced me." He was teasing her.

"I didn't seduce you."

He raised an eyebrow.

"I didn't." She pulled herself onto her tiptoes and brushed her lips against his. "You kissed me first, remember?"

Daniel chuckled. "I guess I did."

He covered her mouth with his, letting their tongues dance and explore as he held her against him. The feel of her in his arms, her touch had him forgetting everything else.

But the world wasn't ready to be ignored. He'd tucked his phone in his pocket earlier so he'd have it in case Ali called him. Now, it was the interruption he didn't want.

Groaning, he dug in his pocket and pulled out his phone. Ali buried her face in his neck, her tongue darting against his skin as he checked the caller ID. It was his ex-wife. She was likely calling about next weekend. He had to take it.

"Sweetheart, I need to take this."

Ali's hands slid down his chest as he tapped the screen to accept the call. "Jessica."

"Daniel." She paused. "Did you get an email from James? He said he sent you the information about his event next weekend."

"I did." He felt Ali begin to pull away, but he held her tighter. She glanced up at him and he pressed a kiss to her forehead.

"David and I are flying in Saturday morning. We wanted to know if you'd like to meet for lunch."

He'd met David, Jessica's new husband, but it wasn't as if they were overly friendly. "Something going on I should know about?"

Jessica blew out a breath. "I'm assuming Cassie called and told you about her engagement."

"She did."

"Have you met him?" she asked.

"No. Not yet." Ali was stiff in his arms. He didn't like it, but there was no way he was letting her go. "She's supposed to bring him for a visit soon." He paused. "Is there something I should know?"

Instead of answering his question, she said, "I think it's better we talk about this in person."

As much as he wanted to know what was going on, Daniel let it go. He could get through a meal with his ex-wife and her new husband. "James said his event starts at noon. That's not going to leave a lot of time for lunch."

"Brunch, then. Why don't we meet you in the hotel restaurant at ten? That should give us plenty of time to talk and still make it to the event on time."

Daniel nodded even though Jessica couldn't see him. "I'll see you then."

He disconnected, then slipped the phone back into his pocket. Wrapping his arms around Ali, he rested his chin on the top of her head. "That was Jessica, my ex-wife."

"I know." There was something in the tone of her voice he didn't like.

"My youngest son, James, has a fitness competition next weekend here in town and his mother and her new husband are flying into St. Louis to attend."

Ali didn't comment.

He was done doing this when he couldn't see her face. Taking a step back, he guided her to the edge of the bed and sat down. "James sent me two tickets. I'd like for you to come with me."

She stared at him for a moment before answering. "You want me to meet your ex-wife?"

"You meeting Jessica is irrelevant." He blew out a breath and admitted something he'd only recently admitted to himself. "I'd like for you to meet my son. Or rather, I'd like for him to meet you."

"Really?"

Daniel smiled. "Really." He brushed a strand of hair behind her ear. "You said you wanted more than just us playing at the club."

"I do." She looked down at her hands, then back at him. "I just wasn't sure if you'd be ready for me to meet your kids."

He wasn't sure he was ready either, but he wasn't going to hide her. She wasn't his mistress. "I'm ready if you are."

Ali smiled and it lit up her face. "Tell me about James?"

The tension he'd been holding in his shoulders relaxed. "Out of all my children, he looks the most like me."

"So he's handsome."

Daniel chuckled. "I told you how he's obsessed with fitness. He measures out his food and drinks protein shakes on a regimented schedule. Especially when he's getting ready for a competition."

"Does he make a living by doing these competitions?" Ali asked.

"No. The competitions are for fun, he says, and bragging rights. He went to school for physical therapy and nutrition."

She asked question after question, wanting to know everything from where he went to school to what he'd been like growing up.

As they'd continued to talk, they'd moved farther onto the bed. They lay on their sides, arms tucked beneath their heads, talking for hours.

When she'd run out of questions about James, she'd moved on to his other kids. She wanted to know everything and as a proud dad, he loved talking about them.

The light in the room began to fade and she grew quiet. "Have you finally run out of questions?"

"For now."

He leaned in and pressed a soft kiss to her lips. "Thank you for listening to me drone on about my kids."

"I liked learning about them." She scooted closer. "Plus, it gave me some more insight into you."

"And what, pray tell, did you learn?"

"That you're a big softy underneath that Dom exterior." Her lips hovered over his, tempting him.

Daniel took the bait. He rolled her over, pinning her to the mattress. "A big softy, huh?"

"Uh-huh."

Gathering her arms above her head, he secured them with one hand as he brought the other to cup her jaw. He kissed her hard.

Ali bucked against him, urging him on. Not that he needed it. His body had been ready the moment he'd stepped into the room and seen her in those jeans hours ago.

Daniel turned her head to the side, exposing her neck to him. He grazed his teeth along her skin where her pulse was beating wildly. If he snaked his hands into her jeans, he knew she'd be wet. Ready. For him.

He ground his erection against her center. "Do I feel soft to you?"

She gasped. "No, Sir."

"That's right, sweetheart. Not soft at all."

He didn't draw it out. Within a matter of minutes, he had her out of her clothes and his cock buried inside her. He fucked her hard and fast as he held her down on the bed.

Ali took what he gave her, exploding in a climax that had her toes curling against the backs of his thighs. He swallowed her cries and emptied himself inside her, as his own orgasm hit him with equal force.

As he came down from his high, realization struck him. He'd not used a condom. And while he knew Ali was on birth control, it didn't change the fact that he'd not even thought about suiting up.

She noticed him stiffen. "What's wrong, Sir?"

Hearing her use his title made him feel even worse. It was his job to take care of her. She'd put her trust in him and he'd let her down. At the very least, they should have discussed it first.

His gaze met hers and he knew the moment she realized. "I didn't use a condom."

CHAPTER 18

$\mathcal{A}$li looked up at him, still trying to clear the fog from her brain after coming. As her breathing slowed, what he said finally registered. "I'm on birth control."

"I know, but that's no excuse. We should have discussed it."

While this was true, Ali wasn't concerned. She wasn't playing or having sex with anyone else, and neither was he. "It's oaky." Then, when she saw he was still beating himself up over it, she added, "I like knowing your cum is inside me." She hesitated, not sure if she should say more, but he was still intimately connected to her. "It's like you're marking me as yours."

His cock pulsed inside her, letting her know how much he liked that idea as well.

Daniel pressed his lips to hers. "I'm going to clean up. Stay here."

Before she could say anything, he was pulling out, leaving her feeling the loss. She turned her head to follow his movement into the connecting bathroom. He was gone for less than a minute before returning with a damp cloth.

"Spread your legs for me, sweetheart."

She did as he asked and sighed as he used the warm cloth to clean her. It felt good and more intimate than the sex had been. "Thank you, Sir."

He smiled down at her. "Take your time getting dressed. I'll make us some dinner before we head to the club." After giving her another light kiss and returning the wet cloth to the bathroom, he left her alone in her room.

Ali dragged herself off the bed and into the bathroom. She jumped in the shower to rinse off and redressed in the same clothes she'd had on earlier. It took all of five minutes for her to pack her bag with the outfit she'd wear that night at the club, and then she was ready to go.

Slinging the bag over her shoulder, she turned off the light in her room and made her way into the kitchen. Daniel was standing at one of the islands, spreading sauce onto a pizza crust. She snuck up behind him and wrapped her arms around his waist.

He gave her arm a little squeeze, pressing it against his side. "What do you like on your pizza?"

"Do you have pineapple?"

He shot her a look of horror over his shoulder.

She laughed. "I'm kidding." Kind of. She did like a good Hawaiian pizza every now and then. "I'm fine with just about anything except anchovies."

Daniel nodded and went back to what he was doing.

"Did you need me to do anything?"

"You could set the table."

She gave him a squeeze, and then went to the cabinet to find what she needed.

While the pizza was in the oven, Daniel whipped up a salad faster than she thought possible. He carried it to the table as the timer went off, letting them know the pizza was ready.

They polished off their dinner and headed into the city. Normally when Ali worked at the club, she had to be at the club early. Since she'd covered for Bridget the day before, tonight Bridget was returning the favor.

Halfway to the club, Daniel's received a text. Five minutes later, his phone dinged with another incoming message. He ignored both until they reached the club.

She couldn't see what either text said, but he didn't appear bothered by whatever the messages were. After typing a quick reply, he tucked the phone in his pocket.

He went to get her bag from the back, then came to the passenger side and opened her door. She took his offered hand and let him guide her into the brick building that housed Serpent's Kiss.

Bridget was in place in front of the coat check when they entered the lobby at six thirty on the dot. She greeted them both with a knowing smile but kept her comments to herself. For now. Ali knew that would change once they were alone.

Daniel handed Ali her bag, gave her a lingering kiss that had her head spinning, then disappeared into the main part of the club, leaving her heart racing and her feeling a little dizzy.

When Ali finally turned around, Bridget was fanning herself. "Now I know why everyone was talking about your scene last night."

Ali felt her cheeks heat.

Bridget laughed. "Go get changed. I'll watch the front for you."

Not arguing, and needing a few minutes to collect herself, Ali ducked into the club and made a beeline for the locker room. Daniel was at the bar, getting a drink. He looked up as she passed, and she could feel his gaze follow her as she traversed the main floor of the club.

The dress she'd chosen for tonight was black with sheer long sleeves and reached mid-thigh. She'd worn it many times before. In fact, it was one of her favorite club outfits. No doubt, Daniel would prefer her in something a little more revealing.

Changed, she made her way out of the locker room and was halfway to the door leading to the lobby when she spotted Daniel talking to Shara. Ali didn't know the other submissive that well, but she did know that Daniel had played with her before.

Jealousy spiked inside her and she froze in place, unable to tear her eyes away. Daniel looked up and met her gaze. He said something to Shara and walked over to where Ali stood.

He stopped in front of her, taking in her outfit. "Is something the matter?"

Ali shook her head. "No, Sir. I was just going to relieve Bridget."

Daniel nodded and she made her exit.

Bridget was chatting with Ryan when Ali emerged from the club. "There she is," Bridget said.

"Sorry I took so long."

"No worries." Bridget nodded in Ryan's direction. "I was picking Ryan's brain."

Ali stepped behind the tall desk. "Are you having legal trouble?" Ryan was a lawyer at a large firm in the heart of downtown. She wasn't sure what type of law he practiced.

"Not me. My sister's having some issues with her neighbor."

"Do you have something to write on?" Ryan said. "I'll jot down my number. Have your sister call me and I'll see if I can help."

Bridget handed him a notepad and he scribbled his number on the paper. "Thanks. I appreciate it."

"Anytime."

Ryan slid the paper with his number on it across the desk to Bridget as the door leading to the club opened. It was unusual for people to be exiting the club this early in the evening—most members were arriving, not leaving—so everyone's head turned to see who it was.

Mistress Katrina stepped through the opening. She grinned at Ali and Bridget. "Good evening. Ladies." She paused, her smile not quite as bright as she greeted Ryan. "Ryan."

Rumor had it that something went down between Katrina and Ryan months ago, but no one seemed to know what. They used to play together all the time, but they hadn't since whatever happened, happened.

They all returned the greeting, then Ryan took a step toward the door Katrina had entered from. "I should get inside." He looked directly at Katrina, and he lowered his voice. "Excuse me, Mistress Katrina."

Katrina nodded, keeping her back to him as he left.

"Was there a problem, Mistress Katrina?" Bridget asked.

The club mistress smiled. "Not at all, but I was hoping to have a word with Ali."

"Oh, of course." Bridget shot Ali a look, then scampered off into the club.

Once they were alone, Katrina moved behind the desk and took a seat. Ali felt awkward standing when Katrina was sitting, but there was nowhere for her to go except on the floor and that didn't feel right either. "What can I do for you, Mistress Katrina?"

"I wanted to see how you're doing?"

Ali knew what she was referring to, but she asked anyway. "You're talking about me and Daniel?"

Katrina nodded.

"Things are good." She paused. "I mean, we're still trying to figure things out, but that's normal, right?"

"Yes. Very." Katrina crossed her legs and rested her hands on her knee. The new position pushed her breasts together, amplifying her already generous assets. "I witnessed some of your scene last night."

Ali lowered her gaze as heat once again crept up her cheeks.

Katrina chuckled. "There's no need to be embarrassed. No one here will judge you."

"I know. It's not that."

Katrina waited for her to go on.

"Whenever he and I are together it feels so..." She searched for the right word. "Private."

"I see."

Ali crossed her arms in front of her. "That sounds silly, doesn't it?"

Katrina's response didn't come as quickly as Ali expected. "No."

She waited for Katrina to elaborate, but she didn't. "When I'm in the moment, I don't think about anything but him. It's only after when people talk to me about it that I want to bury my head in the sand."

"This thing between you and Daniel has been brewing for a long time."

Ali shook her head. That wasn't true. Was it?

"It has."

Ali didn't argue.

"Given the arrangement you two had prior to last night with him negotiating scenes for you, it's bound to cause people to talk."

Ali nodded. Her arrangement with Daniel, if one could call it that, was somewhat odd, especially for someone who wasn't new to the lifestyle. Before Daniel, she'd negotiated her own scenes. But the first time she'd approached him, he'd turned it around on her. He'd made it seem as if she was asking him to find her a Dom to play with rather than asking him to play with her. She hadn't corrected him, and it had become a pattern.

"Once the newness of it wears off, people will get used to it. You won't be the topic of club gossip forever."

Ali groaned.

Katrina stood and placed a hand on Ali's arm as Beth entered the foyer. "If you need someone to talk to, I'm always here to listen."

"Thank you."

Making her way to the door leading to the club, Katrina swiped her card. "Good evening, Lady Beth."

"Good evening, Mistress Katrina." Beth was alone tonight, which meant Drew was working. He had a crazy schedule as a captain with the St. Louis Fire Department and Ali could never keep track of when he was working and when he wasn't.

Beth handed Ali her jacket and purse, along with her membership card, as Katrina disappeared into the club.

Ali moved without thinking, hanging Beth's jacket up and placing her purse into one of the secured lockers. She entered Beth's card, then handed it back to her.

"Everything okay?" Beth asked.

"Yeah. I'm good." And she was. Sort of. But she couldn't get her mind off Shara talking to Daniel. He said he wouldn't play with anyone else, and she trusted him. She trusted him more than she'd trusted any other man. But that didn't stop her from wanting to be inside the club, staking her claim. She'd never felt that way before.

* * *

DANIEL SPENT most of the evening hanging out with friends. Two submissives he'd played with previously had approached him, asking to play, and he'd turned them down.

In the past, he avoided playing with submissives when Ali was around. He'd wait until she was working the front desk. The club's submissives soon figured out not to come to him asking to play if Ali was around.

With Ali working the lobby tonight, some of the subsmissives figured he was still available. Apparently, his and Ali's scene the night before hadn't been a big enough signal things had changed.

He glanced at the clock. Eleven thirty. He still had another thirty minutes to go before Ali was finished with her shift and he could take her home.

Katrina ambled toward him.

He tipped his head up in greeting.

"I heard you had quite the night."

Daniel frowned. "I don't know what you're talking about."

"Breaking hearts left and right." She turned to Brandon. "A Jack and Coke, please, Brandon."

"I'm not aware of any broken hearts," Daniel said before taking a swig of his water.

Katrina chuckled. "I'm told you made it clear tonight that you're off the market for the foreseeable future. There are a lot of disappointed subs."

"They'll get over it. There are other available Doms."

She smirked. "True."

Brandon set the Jack and Coke down in front of Katrina and she took a sip.

The club had cleared out, leaving only a handful of members on the main floor. He and Katrina sat in silence, watching the group across the room. There were two couples and a submissive who, to his knowledge, was unattached to a Dom. The vibe coming off the group gave him an indication of what was coming.

Sure enough, less than two minutes later, the unattached submissive had a Dom sitting on either side of her. One had his tongue down her throat while he played with her breast and the other had a hand up her dress. The other two other submissives kneeled in front of their Doms, taking their cocks into their mouths.

It was rare to see a group scene like this on the main floor of the club, but given they were the only ones left besides Daniel and the club staff, it wasn't as public as it could have been.

As Daniel continued to watch the scene, his need for Ali grew. He wanted to sink his cock into her again. Heaven help him, he need to come in her again.

Hearing her say she liked his cum inside her earlier had done something to him. He wanted that. He wanted to mark her as his. His woman.

Needing a distraction, he tore his attention away from the action on the couch. "Do you know a Sarah Evans?"

His question seemed to take Katrina off guard. "I don't think so. Why? Should I know her?"

Daniel shook his head. "She used to be active in the lifestyle several years go."

"May have been before my time."

Brandon moved toward them as he wiped down the bar.

"You may want to ask Brandon. He may remember her."

Brandon perked up at hearing his name.

Daniel figured it wouldn't hurt. While Logan had texted him to explain he and Lily were going to have to pass on the invitation, he'd asked Daniel if he'd be willing to help a friend of his. "Do you know a Sarah Evans? She used to be active in the lifestyle several years ago."

The bartender stopped what he was doing. Daniel could see the wheels turning in his head. "I do recall a Sarah, but I don't remember her last name. Do you know anything about her?"

"No. Just that I've been asked if I could help her get back into the lifestyle again."

Brandon nodded. "Dominant or submissive?"

"Submissive."

"Could be the same one." Brandon began wiping the bar again. "Besides, we can always use more subs around here."

Katrina rolled her eyes. "If you decide to reach out to her and she's interested in joining the club, let me know."

Cooper made his way downstairs, putting a rope across the stairs to let people know the playrooms were now closed. Daniel glanced at the couch to find only the two Doms, both with very pleased smiles on their faces.

The club's dungeon monitor strolled over to where he and Katrina were sitting. "Do you have a moment?"

The tone in Cooper's voice said it all. There'd been an issue tonight. It was hard to say if it was big or small, but either way Katrina would want to know about it.

Katrina stood and handed her drink to Brandon. "Have a good evening, gentlemen."

The three submissives who'd been involved in the couch scene walked out of the locker room in their street clothes. As the group exited the club, Daniel downed the last of his water.

"Waiting on Ali?" Brandon asked.

"Yes."

The bartender smiled but didn't comment.

Ali walked into the club two minutes later. She found Daniel sitting at the bar and came directly to him. "I need to change and get my things, Sir."

He ran a finger down the front of her dress, tracing the outline of the material covering her breasts. Her outfit covered too much, in his opinion, but that didn't mean she didn't look sexy as hell in it. "Go get your things, but don't bother changing."

"Yes, Sir."

Brandon had disappeared into the back, leaving him alone in the club. This wasn't the first time he'd stayed late to wait on Ali. The only difference was this time she was going home with him.

It didn't take long for Ali to get her bag from her locker and make her way back to him. He helped her into her jacket and placed a hand at her back as they walked to his vehicle.

Her eyes began to close as he veered onto the highway leading out of town. She'd had a long day, but it wasn't over yet. He'd let her sleep on the drive home, then he was going to have fun getting her out of that dress.

CHAPTER 19

*A*li stretched, glancing over at the empty space next to her. She was in Daniel's bed as she'd been every night for over a week.

His side of the bed was cold, which meant he'd been up for a while. Shifting to look at the clock, her heart skipped a beat. It was after eight. They were supposed to meet his ex-wife and her new husband in less than two hours.

As if he knew she was awake, Daniel strolled into the room. His hair was still wet from his shower, and he was dressed in jeans and a black button-down shirt.

He took a seat on the edge of the bed. "Good morning, sweetheart. Did you sleep well?"

"Yes." But before she could say any more, his hand cupped her breast, and he began playing with her nipple. She closed her eyes and hummed.

Daniel ran his hand down her side and rested it on her hip. "I'm tempted to blow off brunch and fuck you instead."

Ali sighed. She'd be good with that.

His lips caressed hers, coaxing her mouth open, but before it could go any farther, his phone rang.

Daniel groaned and removed the phone from his pocket. He checked the caller ID. When he met her gaze again, she knew their fun would be put on hold. "I need to take this."

He stood and walked out of the room, leaving her alone.

Ali stared up at the ceiling and blew out a breath. She dragged herself out of Daniel's bed and picked up the T-shirt she'd worn the night before. Slipping it on, she went around the room, picking up her discarded clothing.

As she passed by the kitchen, Daniel looked up from his call. His eyes sparkled as his gaze roamed her body. She felt her sex pulse. Then the person he was talking to said something, and he turned his attention back to the phone.

It took her twenty minutes to shower and another twenty trying to figure out what to wear. While Ali shouldn't care what Daniel's ex thought of her, she kind of did, but more than that, she wanted to make a good first impression on James.

In the end, she took a page from Daniel's playbook and went with her favorite jeans and a button-down shirt. Most of the outfits she'd brought with her from her apartment were either dress clothes for work, club attire, or T-shirts and leggings for lounging around the house.

A knock came at her door as she was putting in her earrings. "Come in."

Daniel walked in, his gaze scanning over her. He held out a hand, and she went to him. "Not sure which I like more. You running around in nothing but a T-shirt, or your ass in these jeans."

Ali laughed.

He pulled her into his arms and kissed her. "Ready to go?"

"Yeah."

The drive to the hotel took less than thirty minutes. Finding a place to park in the parking garage had taken another twenty-five. By the time they made it to the hotel restaurant, they were ten minutes late.

Daniel gave the man at the host stand his ex-wife's name and they were escorted into the restaurant. Ali wasn't sure what she'd been expecting, but the woman sitting at the table they were taken to wasn't it.

The woman had short red hair with streaks of gray around her temples that framed her features. She was dressed casually in jeans and a T-shirt with a huge yellow smiley face on it.

They stopped in front of the table and Daniel held out a chair for Ali. She didn't miss how Jessica's face changed as she registered Daniel wasn't alone. "Who's this?" she asked.

Daniel made the introductions. "Ali, this is Jessica and her husband, David." He picked up the menu from the table. "My apologies for our tardiness. It took longer than expected to find a parking spot."

"It's nice to meet you, Ali," David said.

Ali replied in kind. "You, too."

David smiled, but Ali couldn't read the expression on Jessica's face. It wasn't exactly hostile, but it wasn't overly friendly either. Ali picked up her menu and scanned over the offerings.

After placing their orders, Daniel got down to business. "So what is it about Cassie's fiancé that you wanted to make me aware of?"

Jessica seemed to hesitate, but after giving Ali a side-eye, she said, "I'm not sure he's right for her."

"What makes you think that?" Daniel asked.

"He works all the time, for one thing. And I don't like the way he talks to her."

Daniel took a sip of his coffee. "I need specifics, Jessica."

She huffed. "About a month ago, we were talking on the phone. She forgot to hang up and I overheard some things." She paused and Daniel waited. "It sounded like he was hitting her."

Ali glanced at Daniel, but he didn't take his gaze off Jessica.

"So I called one of her friends under the pretense of getting her mom's number to see if she was interested in helping me with a project." Jessica tapped her fingers on the table. "Olivia said she hadn't talked to Cassie in almost six months and you know how close they used to be."

"Did she give any reason why?"

Jessica shook her head. "Not really and I didn't feel like I could push without giving too much away."

Daniel nodded.

"We're concerned," David said. "He seemed like a nice guy when we met him, but some people can be good at hiding their true selves."

"I'll talk to her."

A few moments later, their food arrived. Ali had gone with yogurt and granola. Daniel had told her James would want to go out after his competition, so she didn't want to stuff herself.

"How long have you two been together?" Jessica asked.

The question was directed at Ali. She swallowed her bite of food and answered, "About two weeks."

Jessica's eyes went wide.

While his wife recovered from her apparent shock, David picked up the conversation. "Have you met James yet?"

"No," Ali said. "Daniel's told me about his kids, but I've never met any of them."

"James is the most laid-back of the three, but don't be surprised if he tries to put you on some sort of nutrition plan."

Ali laughed. "I'll keep that in mind."

They spent the rest of the meal talking about James and his competition. Ali learned a lot, including more about the competition itself. She'd never been to one of these things before, so she'd been clueless about what to expect.

When the server came with their bill, Daniel pulled out his card and handed it to the man, not bothering to look at the amount. Jessica and David made no move to stop him or chip in even though the meeting had been their idea.

Daniel stood, pulled out her chair, and offered his hand. She took it and got to her feet.

"It was nice meeting you, Ali," David said.

Ali laced her fingers into Daniel's. "It was nice meeting you, too."

They made their way out of the hotel's restaurant and followed the signs for the fitness competition. A long hallway led to another long hallway. If not for the signs, she would have gotten lost for sure.

As they turned down yet another hall, this one full of people, Daniel brought their linked fingers to his lips and kissed the back of her hand. "You ready for this?"

No. She wasn't sure she was. But instead, she met his gaze and nodded.

When they entered the room, there were five women standing on the stage. They were all wearing bikinis and heels. But it wasn't their clothing that stood out to her the most. It was how tan they were and the fact they all looked as if they could bench press a truck.

Okay, maybe not a truck, but she'd never seen women with so many muscles before. Their arms and legs were as big as most men's, and they all had six-pack abs.

They found seats about halfway back and watched as the judges picked their winner out of the five women. Once the women left the stage, several people in the audience left, clearing out a good portion of the room.

"Thank you for coming with me today," Daniel said. He hadn't let go of her hand when they sat down.

"You're welcome." She'd do anything for him. All he had to do was ask. Then she noticed his posture. "Are you nervous?"

He turned to look at her, then back to the empty stage. "Maybe a little."

"Why?"

Daniel's chest vibrated in a suppressed chuckle. "I've never introduced a woman to my kids before."

"Never?"

He shook his head. "I don't...date...a lot."

A warm feeling spread through her chest. "I'm honored you want me to meet them."

More people entered the room, filling up the seats around them. She saw Jessica and David sit on the other side of the room, two rows back. Commotion on the stage drew everyone's attention and within minutes things were getting started.

If she'd thought the women's bathing suits were skimpy, the men's were even more so. The strip of fabric didn't hide much of anything. In fact, it hid nothing. As they flexed to show off their muscles, Ali was surprised certain parts of their anatomy didn't fall out.

Then it was James's turn on stage. To say he was the spitting image of his dad was an understatement. Add some gray and a few years and they could be twins. He even had his dad's gray eyes.

In the end, James got third place. The two guys who come in first and second were bigger than he was, but that was the only difference she could see. Then again, she had no idea what she was looking for.

Like before, as soon as the contestants left the stage, people began to leave. Daniel stood and guided Ali into the hall. He moved them away from the entrance and leaned back against the wall, pulling her against him.

Jessica and David came to stand beside them, and she couldn't miss the big smile on Jessica's face. David stood next to her while they waited, his arm around her shoulders.

People milled around, going in and out of the room. Then, a door opened down the hall and Ali recognized some of the men who'd been on stage. They filtered out in groups of two or three. She had no idea how many men passed by them before the door opened and James walked out.

He saw them almost immediately and hiked the duffle back higher on his shoulder. "Hey."

Jessica moved in. She pulled him into her arms for a hug. "I'm so proud of you."

"Thanks, Mom." His gaze moved to his dad, then to Ali. He took a step toward her and held out a hand. "Well, hello there. I don't think we've met. I'm James Ross, and you are?"

* * *

DANIEL PUT a possessive hand on Ali's back. "James, I'd like you to meet Ali."

"Ali." James took Ali's hand and held it in both of his.

Daniel had never been jealous of either of his sons before, but he was now. It was stupid, but love did that to you.

Ali laughed. "Hi, James. Your dad's told me so much about you."

James looked at Daniel, then at Ali. He took in Daniel's hand on her back and his grin grew even bigger. "Well, Ali, I hope you're hungry because I'm starving." He hooked his arm in Ali's and tugged her down the hall with him. "So, tell me everything."

Daniel sighed and followed behind them. He didn't miss the laugher coming from Jessica.

"What do you want to know?" Ali asked.

"How'd you meet my dad?"

Ali glanced over her shoulder, meeting his gaze as they all entered the lobby. James tended to crave certain foods after his competitions. He'd often scope out the restaurants in the area and knew exactly what he wanted. "We met at a club."

James stopped and Daniel almost ran him over. His son turned to look at him, shock on his face. "You went to a club?"

Daniel raised an eyebrow. "I may be old, but I'm not dead."

His son chuckled, then continued on his way.

After a brief stop at James's hotel room so he could drop his bag, they were off again. Outside the hotel, they took a left. The streets were bustling with traffic, but they only had to cross once.

James continued to ask Ali questions as they walked. Where had she grown up? What did she do for a living? It was an interview.

They stopped in front of a burger joint. Daniel had never been there before. He liked cheeseburgers, but he didn't eat them very often anymore. If he was going to eat beef, he preferred steak.

His son kept Ali next to him when they all sat down at a long table. He included her in the conversation, even when it turned to his siblings.

Daniel went to get a refill on his and Ali's drinks. He was putting the lids back on the containers when James came up beside him, cup in hand. "I like her."

He met his son's gaze but didn't comment.

"She makes you happy, right?" he asked.

It was strange having this conversation with his youngest son. "She does."

James smiled, put the lid back on his cup, and took a sip from his straw.

They finished their meal and walked back to the hotel. Once again, James commandeered Ali. This time the two chatted about music. "What was that band you had me listen to the last time I was at your house?"

"Guns and Roses," David said. "Only one of the best hair bands of the eighties."

Ali scoffed. "I don't know about that."

He didn't hear David's response because Jessica placed her hand on his arm, drawing his attention. "She's good for you." Before he could find something to say, she went on. "You deserve to be happy, Daniel. I know things didn't work out between us, but that was both our faults."

That was true. He and Jessica had drifted apart and they'd both had a part in that. At any time, they could have changed course, made time for each other, kept the connection. They hadn't.

"I see the way you look at her." Jessica stopped and he did the same. "You're in love with her."

He didn't deny it, but he didn't confirm it either.

"Don't let this opportunity pass you by, okay?" With that parting comment, she began walking again.

James was flying out early tomorrow morning, as were Jessica and David, so Daniel and Ali said their goodbyes at the hotel. "Call me if you need anything."

"I will," James said, embracing his father. Then, he turned to Ali, pulling her in for a hug as well. "Take care of him."

Ali nodded.

James, Jessica, and David made their way to the elevators, leaving him and Ali alone. Daniel checked his watch. It was after six thirty. "It's getting late. We need to get moving."

Leaving the parking garage was a breeze. The competition had wrapped up two hours before, so most of those who'd come to watch the show had already left. That was good, considering the time.

While there wasn't a set time they needed to be at the club given Ali wasn't working this evening, he wanted to enjoy the time with his sub. He had plans for her tonight and after having to keep his hands to himself all day, he was ready to play.

He'd picked out her attire for tonight and he couldn't wait to see her in it. It was purple, her favorite color.

"I love your outfit," Bridget said as they entered the lobby.

Daniel handed over their jackets for Bridget to hang up. While the days were warm enough, the evenings were a crap shoot.

After Bridget scanned his membership card, Daniel swiped his card and entered the club. Since they were later than usual, the main floor was full of people. He cupped Ali's ass, pulling her against him. "Get changed, then come find me."

"Yes, Sir."

Ali took her bag and he watched her hips sway as she made her way to the locker room. She'd worn his favorite jeans today and he was going to have fun making her pay for teasing him.

"I was wondering if you guys were going to show tonight."

Daniel turned to find Alexander coming toward him. He was using his cane. Most nights he was fine without it, but the injury he'd sustained during his time in the Army acted up when he pushed himself too hard. "My son had a fitness competition today and wanted to go out after."

"Ah."

"Where's your girl?" Daniel asked, not seeing Grace anywhere on the main floor.

"Changing. We just got here ourselves."

Daniel nodded. "I was going to get a drink. Care to join me?"

Alexander motioned for Daniel to lead the way.

While Daniel ordered a water, Alexander ordered a Scotch for himself and a piña colada for Grace. That told him more about how the other Dom was feeling than anything he could have said. He and Grace wouldn't be going upstairs tonight.

"How's business? Any issues growing your practice?" Daniel asked.

"Slow, but steady. We've been asking for referrals, so that's helping." Alexander was a doctor. In the Army, he'd treated wounds caused by gunshots and IEDs. When he decided to open a practice here in St. Louis so he could be with Grace, he'd chosen to switch his focus to pediatrics.

"That's the way to do it." He twisted the top off his water bottle and took a drink. Mid swallow, he saw Ali exit the locker room and almost choked.

Alexander clapped him on the back, then stood. "Have fun, man."

Oh, he planned to have a lot of fun.

CHAPTER 20

Ali wanted to cover herself. The baby doll Daniel had selected for her to wear tonight had a sheer top. Her hard nipples were on full display.

And if that wasn't bad enough, he'd given her no panties to wear. The négligée barely covered her butt. Heaven help her if she had to bend over.

Taking a deep breath, she forced her feet to move. Daniel was waiting for her.

He followed her movement as she weaved through the other patrons, not taking his gaze from her. She focused on him and not all the people around her. Why she could be completely naked upstairs in one of the rooms and not be bothered, yet want to hide in the corner down here, she didn't know. It was just different.

She came to a stop in front of him and waited.

His gray eyes darkened, and his nostrils flared. "You are a walking temptation." He lifted a finger to her lips. "You will not speak unless I ask you a direct question or to use your safeword, do you understand?"

"Yes, Sir."

Daniel slid off the stool and took her hand in his. She thought they would head upstairs, but instead, he led her to the dance floor. He stopped in the middle of the floor, facing her. "Put your arms around my neck."

She did as instructed, which only made her outfit ride up higher on her thighs. Cool air tickled her sex as he brought their bodies together, making her very aware of how exposed she was.

His hands snaked under the short hem of her outfit and cupped her ass, massaging the flesh under his hands as he moved their bodies to the music. The skirt of her dress bunched and lifted, giving anyone who was looking a view of her backside. She tensed.

"Relax," he whispered in her ear.

He held her tight as they swayed to the music. His hands didn't leave her ass, but eventually, her nerves eased a little.

Dipping his head, his mouth found hers and she gladly lost herself in his kiss. He crushed her against him as his lips and tongue explored her mouth. Her nipples scraped against his chest, the thin fabric of her nightie doing nothing to dull the sensations surging through her.

He removed one hand from her backside and rubbed a thumb over her nipple, making it harder. He swallowed her gasp and gave her nipple a hard pinch.

"I want you, Ali. I want you like I've never wanted anything before." He cupped her breast in his hand. "This is mine."

She moaned and he deepened the kiss. All thoughts of the people around them gone.

Removing his hand from her breast, he returned it to her ass, giving both cheeks a firm squeeze. "This is mine." His voice sounded deep and strained as he ground her against him.

They danced like this, kissing and grinding through two songs. Then one of his hands moved lower and lifted her leg. He hooked her leg around his waist, exposing her even more.

Ali pressed her face against his neck as her heart raced and her sex pulsed. Without his lips on hers, she began to feel self-conscious again. People were all around them and she knew at least some of them were watching.

But her body didn't seem to care. She was wet despite how self-conscious she was. Her body and her mind were at war with each other.

Then, Daniel shifted, and she felt his hand brush against her sex. Her fingers gripped the back of his skull, hoping he wasn't going to do what she thought he was going to do, but hoping he was going to do it at the same time. "This is mine."

She sucked in a breath as he caressed her sensitive flesh.

"You are mine."

He slipped a finger inside her and she held on tighter to him. Her mind was racing with what he'd said, and her body was throbbing with need.

He pushed another finger inside. "You make me feel things I haven't felt in a long time."

Her heart clenched. Her pussy contracted. She wanted to say something. Assure him she felt the same way. That she'd never felt this way about anyone before. Only him.

Pressing her lips to his neck, she sucked at the vein pounding out the rhythm of his heart. He groaned and she did it again.

"I need to fuck you."

Again, her pussy clamped down on his fingers. She wanted that too, and she didn't care if he took her right there on the dance floor.

But instead of doing that or taking her somewhere he could have his way with her, he remained where he was. He continued to move his fingers in and out of her while he ground her against his erection. If he kept it up, she was going to come.

The music pumped in the background, driving her closer and closer like a beating drum. Her dress had ridden up to the point it wasn't covering anything, but she was too far gone to care. She felt herself climbing, reaching toward the peak and wanting to fall over the edge.

He grazed his lips over her ear, scraping his teeth over her lobe. "You're close. Your pussy's gripping my fingers, begging me for more."

She ground against him, telling him without words what she wanted. Her orgasm was so close. So close she could already feel her body vibrating in anticipation. All she needed was a little more pressure to her clit and she'd find her release.

But it didn't come. She didn't come.

He removed his fingers from inside her and brought them up to her lips. She knew what he wanted without him asking and sucked them inside, tasting herself.

Her pussy was aching from the denied release. The need to come making her quiver.

Daniel removed his fingers from her mouth and took her hand in his. He twisted and led her from the dance floor to the stairs.

As they ascended the staircase, another couple followed them up a few steps behind. She tried not to think about the fact there they had a perfect view up her dress.

He turned right into room one and closed the door. The lights were on full strength, meaning there would be no hiding in the shadows.

Her gaze went to the window and there were already people gathering outside to see what Daniel had in store for her. "Remove your dress."

She slid the straps of her baby doll from her shoulders. The silky dress fell to the floor, leaving every inch of her exposed.

He moved to the center of the room. "Come here."

Ali closed the distance between them, coming to a stop in front of him.

His eyes were full of heat as he stared down at her. He dipped his head to whisper in her ear, "You will not come until I say."

It wasn't a question, and she felt her entire body respond. A wave of desire rippled through her belly and her breasts felt heavy. She wanted him to touch her.

Instead, he walked behind her. She remained where she was, waiting to see what he would do next.

What felt like minutes, but was probably only a few seconds, went by before he came up beside her. He had a pair of leather cuffs in his hands. "Wrists."

She presented him her wrists, and he placed the cuffs on her. A metal chain connected the two leather restraints, meaning she couldn't separate her hands more than a few inches.

As soon as he'd secured the last cuff, he lifted her arms above her head. Ali knew what was coming. She'd arranged this room many times for the Doms of the club.

Metal touching metal resonated in the room as he placed the chain over the metal hook above her. The hook could be raised or lowered depending on the height of the submissive and how much the Dominant wanted to stretch him or her. Daniel surveyed her position and seemed to be satisfied with where she was.

His gaze went to hers. "Are you doing all right?"

"Yes, Sir."

Before moving to the wall of toys, he disappeared behind her. She couldn't see what he was doing, but she heard a drawer open and shut. Moments later, he walked over to the wall of toys and removed two floggers. He tested their weight in his hands, giving them each a flick with his wrists. Knowing what was coming had her body aching in anticipation.

His movements were deliberate. He circled her several times, brushing the flogger against her skin every so often.

Her breathing quickened as he continued to tease her, letting the falls caress her like fingers. She wanted it so bad she was on the verge of begging.

He brought one of the floggers up to her face, letting it slide along her check before moving it over her shoulder. "Are you ready, sweetheart?"

"Yes, Sir. I'm ready." She sounded breathless.

Daniel placed a kiss on her neck. She let out a sigh, and a moment later she felt the first flogger hit the left side of her ass.

There was a pause, then a hard thud hit her right cheek.

Gradually, the rhythm picked up and she let her head fall forward as she got lost in the sensation. She felt alive as he worked her back, ass, and legs. Tension she hadn't realized she'd been holding onto after meeting his son and ex-wife faded away and all she could think about—feel—was the thud of the flogger.

She had no idea how long it lasted, but she'd been worked over well. Her entire body was covered in a sheen of sweat and her backside was tingling.

His hands came from behind her to cup her breasts, kneading them, pulling at her nipples. He kissed up the back of her neck, then down her spine.

Something pressed between her legs, and then she felt it being inserted into her pussy. It stretched her in the best way, but it wasn't him. She wanted—needed to feel him inside her.

Moments later, the thing began to vibrate. She gasped at the unexpected sensation and closed her eyes, trying to keep her orgasm at bay.

His hands never left her as he came to stand in front of her, caressing her body, adding to the ache between her thighs. Lips covered her right nipple, sucking, licking, biting. He played with her left breast, pulling and twisting, the sweet pain going straight to her clit.

She was breathing hard, biting her lower lip, trying not to come. Knowing he'd be disappointed in her if she let go before he gave her permission. She wanted to please him. Wanted to show him and everyone at the club she was the right submissive for him.

He took her nipple between his teeth and tugged. A whimper left her lips as she felt her control slipping. She felt the telltale sign of her climax moments away. She wasn't going to be able to stop it.

Then his hands and mouth were gone. He reached up, lifting the chain connecting her leather cuffs from the hook. Her body began to collapse, but he caught her, placing her arms over his head.

Before she could register what was happening, she was on her back with her hands secured above her and legs spread, her knees bent. Daniel stood between her legs, pulling the vibrator from her pussy. She heard him unzipping his pants and her body buzzed with anticipation of his cock.

Ali moaned as he pushed inside her, loving the feel of him. He used her legs for leverage as he thrust, the hard wood of the table she was lying on scraping against the sensitive skin on her back.

She dug her fingers into her palms, chanting to herself not to come.

Then, he pressed a vibrator to her clit and said the words she'd been longing to hear. "Come for me."

* * *

ALI BUCKED, her back arching off the table as she let go. The scream that came from her lips was everything he'd hoped it would be. Her pussy spasmed around his cock, putting an end to what little control he had left.

His head fell back as he let the flood of energy surge through his cock. After that first time when he'd forgotten to use a condom, he'd planned to go back to using them. Ali, however, had begged him not to. He'd been torn. Birth control wasn't one hundred percent effective. Him wearing a condom would provide another layer of protection. But he couldn't deny how he felt knowing he was leaving a part of himself inside her even if it was stupid.

So they'd stopped using condoms and he wasn't sure he ever wanted to go back. Not with her.

She lay limp on the table, her eyes closed and the most serene look on her face. He eased out, feeling a sense of male pride as he saw some of his cum dripping from her opening. Again, it was stupid, but he wanted to mark her as his in every way possible.

Daniel fixed his jeans, then moved to the head of the table. He released her wrists from the cuffs and pressed a kiss to the inside of each. Her eyes flittered open, watching him. "How are you feeling, sweetheart?"

"Like Jell-O, Sir."

Daniel chuckled, placing a soft kiss to her lips before retrieving her nightie from the floor. He helped her to sit up and put it back on. Then, wrapped her in a blanket and steadied her as she stood.

She held tight to his waist, not trusting herself to stand on her own. He'd worked her hard and she'd been amazing.

He held her for several minutes, letting her get her legs under her again. She smelled of sex and sweat and that sweet mixture of cherries and lavender.

They needed to get downstairs. She needed water and so did he. "Lean on me."

Ali nodded.

They made their way to the first floor, taking their time on the stairs. She seemed steady enough, but he wasn't going to take a chance.

Brandon saw them coming and had two bottles of water waiting for them along with some chocolate. Daniel handed over his membership card for the bartender to swipe, then took the waters and the chocolate and headed to the same corner they'd decompressed in the week before. He placed the waters and chocolate onto the small table next to one end of the couch, lifted Ali into his arms, and sat down.

She cuddled into his chest, pressing her nose against his neck. He took one of the waters, twisted off the top, and handed it to her. "Drink."

Ali obediently took the bottle and drank. After she got a few sips in her, he handed her the chocolate. She took a bite, and he felt a shiver run through her.

He pressed a kiss to her forehead and reached for his own water. "How are you feeling?"

"Cold, Sir."

Daniel placed his water back on the table and wrapped his arms tighter around her, rubbing a hand along her arm.

She pressed closer and he cherished the feel of her against him. How long would she be his?

He tried not to think about it—to enjoy what they had for as long as they had it. Worrying over the future wouldn't change anything.

They sat for a long time as her body regulated itself. When he felt her body warm, he tilted her head up and brought his lips to hers for a slow kiss.

He could taste the chocolate as his tongue explored her mouth. She was putty in his hands, relaxed, sated, and utterly beautiful. "Feeling better?"

"Yes, Sir."

"You can speak freely now." He combed his fingers through her hair, still damp from their earlier activities. "How did you feel about me drawing out your orgasm?"

"I was afraid I wouldn't be able to hold on." She looked up, meeting his gaze. "I didn't want to disappoint you."

"You did very well tonight. Seeing you come that hard with my cock buried inside you was something I want to repeat again and again."

Ali slid her arm out from under her blanket and placed it on his check. "I'll do my best not to disappoint you, Sir. Not ever."

His lips descended on hers, unable to stop himself. He was never going to get enough of her. "Ready to go mingle with our friends?"

She nodded and stood on her own.

He took her hand and led her across the room to where their friends sat. They all smiled as he and Ali approached but continued with their current topic of conversation.

At ten thirty, they said goodbye and made their way to his car. He got her situated in the passenger seat before going to the driver's side and climbing behind the wheel.

Since Daniel knew their play would be intense and that he'd want to spend the evening with Ali in his arms, he'd left his cell in the vehicle. Opening the center console, he picked up his phone and powered it up.

Almost immediately, it went crazy. Message after message came in.

As he scrolled through, he realized all the messages were from his kids. He didn't read them all, but he read enough to get the gist. James had told them about Ali.

He sighed.

"What is it?"

Daniel placed the phone down, started the engine, and backed out of the parking lot. He glanced over at her, then back at the road. "James told Cassie and Bradley about meeting you."

"Oh." She looked confused. "Did you not want him to?"

He shook his head. "I figured he'd tell them. I just wasn't expecting them to blow up my phone."

Ali bit her bottom lip. "Are they upset?"

"I don't think so. I didn't read all the messages. But they'd like to meet you."

She lowered her gaze to her lap, lacing her fingers together in front of her.

He placed his hand over hers and squeezed. "Do you not want to meet them?"

"No, I do. I just...when?"

Bringing one of her hands into his lap, Daniel rubbed this thumb over the pad of her palm. "Soon." Then he brought their hands up so he could kiss the tips of her fingers. "I'm not going to worry about it tonight, though. I'll call them in the morning, and we can set something up."

She nodded and sank back into her seat to watch the scenery go by.

He focused on the road, trying to push the message from Bradley out of his mind.

CHAPTER 21

li wasn't sure she could move. Her body felt well used. When they'd gotten home the night before, Daniel had led her into the shower and proceeded to wash her. By the time he was finished, she was hot and bothered again and needing him.

She rubbed her thighs together, remembering how she'd asked if she could have his cock inside her again. He'd dried her off, carried her into his bedroom, and spread her out on his bed. She could still remember the look in his eyes as he'd given her what she'd asked for, holding her gaze as he'd sunk deep inside.

Sighing, she forced her eyes open and turned to look at his side of the bed. Empty as always. Daniel was an early riser, even on days he didn't need to go to work.

It was Sunday and they had no plans. Daniel had the pool serviced earlier in the week, so it was ready for the season. Maybe they could do a little skinny dipping. She grinned at the thought.

Unfortunately, her stomach decided it was more concerned about food than her sexual fantasies. She hadn't eaten anything since their late lunch the day before and she was starving.

Throwing off the covers, she headed into the bathroom to take care of business. When she walked back into his bedroom a few minutes later, she'd half expected him to be there.

He wasn't.

Figuring he was either working out or making them breakfast, Ali threw on her robe and headed for the kitchen. Even if he wasn't there, she could start breakfast. He'd come find her when he was finished with whatever he was doing.

But as she neared the kitchen, she heard voices. At first, she thought Daniel was talking to someone on the phone, but the other voice was too clear. The words she heard stopped her in her tracks.

"What? I'm not allowed to come visit my dad anymore?"

Dad?

One of Daniel's kids was at the house, and she was in nothing more than her robe.

Ali didn't know what to do. Should she go back into Daniel's room and wait for him to come get her? She could put dirty clothes on. Her jeans would be fine, but her blouse was probably wrinkled beyond saving. When Daniel wanted her out of her clothes, he tossed them on the floor, not caring where they landed.

She could try to get to her room unseen and change, but she wasn't hopeful. Daniel's room was at the back of the house. Her room was at the front. And the only way to get to her room from his was to go through the kitchen.

There was also the option of ignoring the fact he had company and make her way into the kitchen as she had planned? It wasn't as if they were teenagers sneaking around.

This was a first for her. She'd never been in a position of meeting a boyfriend's children, let alone the potential of meeting them wearing nothing but a thin layer of silk.

Her stomach growled again, not caring about her awkward dilemma. She looked behind her to his room, and then toward the hallway that led to her bedroom.

The voices became more muffled, sounding as if they were moving away from her. She bit the inside of her cheek. If they were in the living room, maybe she could make it. She'd have to be fast and quiet.

She peeked around the corner, careful not to make a sound. Scanning the kitchen, she confirmed it was empty. Then, she made a run for it.

Halfway across the room, a voice drifted across the room, loud and clear. "Is that her?"

Ali looked up to see a man she didn't know striding toward her. He had light brown hair and looked to be in his mid-twenties. His gaze never left hers as he closed the distance between them. Daniel was right behind him. Side by side, there was no doubt these two were related. As the younger man grew closer, she saw more of Daniel in his features. While he wasn't the spitting image of his father, Bradley Ross was still his father's son.

Bradley stopped a few feet away from her. He took in her appearance. It didn't take a rocket scientist to know she'd come from Daniel's bed. Not exactly the greatest first impression.

Daniel pushed past his son and came to stand at her side. "Good morning, sweetheart."

Her look of concern must have shown on her face. He opened his mouth to say something, but Bradley spoke first. "You must be Ali."

Trying to put on a brave face, she met the other man's gaze. "Hi."

The younger man didn't say anything, just continued to watch her.

Daniel frowned. "Ali, this is my oldest son, Bradley. He decided to come for an unannounced visit."

"It's nice to meet you, Bradley." Then she turned to Daniel. "If you'd both excuse me, I need to get dressed."

She backed away and hurried down the hall toward her room.

"Where's she going?" Bradley asked.

"To her room."

There was a long pause. "She lives here?"

Ali didn't wait to hear Daniel's response. She grabbed clean clothes, ran into the bathroom, and locked the door. She needed a few minutes alone.

* * *

DANIEL WENT to the drawer and grabbed a skillet. "She's staying here, yes."

"Do you think that's a good idea?"

In the short time Ali had been living in his house, they'd settled into a comfortable routine. He loved knowing she was there, sharing his space. He'd become accustomed to her being there, seeing her smiling face across from the table, or how she curled up on his couch at night, getting lost in her television shows.

So no, it probably wasn't a good idea for her to still be living there. Not for his long-term mental health. But he wasn't going to share that with his son.

Placing the skillet on the stove, he went to the refrigerator to get the ingredients he'd need for omelets.

"Dad?"

"What?"

Bradley gave his dad a frustrated look before plopping down on one of the barstools. "I asked if you think this is a good idea. Her living with you. James said you've only been together two weeks."

"Son, this is my house."

"That doesn't answer my question."

The sausages hit the pan with a sizzle. After spreading them out in the pan, he reached for the onion and began slicing it. "It's all the answer you're going to get."

This time, Bradley let out an audible groan. "She's like twenty-five."

Daniel stopped cutting the onion and released a steadying breath. He was trying to be patient. "She's thirty-two."

"That's still a huge age difference, Dad. Couldn't you find someone your own age?"

Daniel fixed his son with a look he'd used often on his children when they were younger. "Let's get one thing straight right now. It is none of your business who I date. Ali and I are both consenting adults and what we do is none of your business. Nor is it Cassie's or James's. You're my children, and I love you, but you do not get to dictate my love life. Do you understand me?"

He turned his attention back to breakfast and waited for Bradley's response. It took a while, but when it came, the sound of utter horror shocked him. "You've fallen in love with her."

Bradley was the second person to say that to him and as with the first, Daniel didn't contradict him.

Neither man said a word to each other as Daniel finished cooking. He went to get some plates out of the cabinet. "Are you eating?" he asked Bradley.

"Sure."

Daniel removed three plates from the cabinet and divided the omelet. He carried his and Ali's plates to the table. "Help yourself. You know where the silverware is. I'm going to check on Ali."

She'd been gone for a while. Ali wasn't a big hair and makeup person. It usually didn't take her that long to get ready in the morning unless she was taking a shower.

He found her in her room, fully dressed, sitting on the edge of her bed. "Hey."

Ali glanced up. "Hey."

It was then he noticed her bag and suitcase were sitting beside her. "What's this?"

"I don't want to cause tension between you and your son. If he's here to visit with you, then maybe I should leave you two alone."

The thought of her leaving sent a pain stabbing his chest. He took her hands and pulled her onto her feet. "I made us all omelets."

"I'm sure you and Bradley can finish it all." She smiled up at him, but it didn't reach her eyes. "Your omelets are really good and I know how much you can eat."

He gave her side a little pinch at her sass. "While that may be true, I don't want you to go."

Not giving her time to protest, he covered her mouth with his and put everything he was feeling into the kiss. She skimmed her hands up his chest to tangle in his hair. His need for her, even now when he knew his son was down the hall, had him considering how long it would take him to get her naked.

Her belly growled, and they separated with a laugh. "See, even your stomach wants you to stay."

She nodded and he led her out of her room before she could change her mind.

When they entered the kitchen area, Bradley sat at the table, waiting for them. Each plate had a knife and fork beside it, along with a glass of orange juice and a cup of coffee. A part of him was pleased. The other part questioned his son's motives.

Daniel pulled out the chair across from his son for Ali and waited for her to sit before taking his own seat. He took his first two bites in blissful silence before Bradley picked up the conversation. "James says you're an executive assistant."

Ali swallowed before answering. "Yes, I am."

"Where do you work?"

She glanced at Daniel, then at Bradley. "At the hospital. I work under the senior vice president of marketing."

"That's impressive. How long have you worked there?"

"About three years," Ali said.

Bradley nodded. "Did you grow up around St. Louis?"

Daniel didn't miss that Bradley was interrogating Ali. While he understood it to a certain extent, he also knew his son.

"I moved here with my grandmother when I was ten." Ali glanced over at Daniel, then back at Bradley. "Before that, we lived in Kentucky."

"Did you lose your parents?" Bradley asked.

Ali shook her head. "No. I've only seen a picture of my dad. I've never met him. And my mom? Let's just say she wasn't ready to be a mother."

He could see the wheels turning in Bradley's head and he didn't like it. "What are your plans for the day?" Daniel asked his son.

"I haven't decided." Bradley looked at Ali. "What were your plans for the day?"

Before Ali could answer, Daniel interrupted. "I need to check on a few projects."

He didn't miss how Ali's eyes widened at this announcement. They'd planned to stay in, but that was before his son showed up.

"Mind if I come with?" Bradley asked.

"Not at all."

After they finished their breakfast, Bradley offered to clean up. Daniel took the opportunity to talk to Ali alone in his bedroom.

"Maybe I should go to the meeting today so you can have some time alone with your son." Ali was talking about the submissive meeting that met on Sunday afternoons at Beth's café. She'd been going more often since her best friend had joined the lifestyle, but she didn't go last weekend, nor had she planned to go today.

Daniel pulled the T-shirt over his head before kneeling in front of her as she sat perched on the edge of his bed. "Do you want to go, or are you running away?"

"I don't think Bradley likes me very much."

Tucking a hair behind her ear, he waited until she met his gaze. "What he thinks doesn't matter. He'll get over it."

"But he's your son."

"Exactly. He's my son. He has no say over who I'm with, who I have in my house, or in my bed."

Ali lowered her gaze.

Moving to sit next to her, he reached for her hand and held it in his lap. "Bradley is suspicious by nature. It's what makes him a good lawyer. But it can also make him a nosey pain in the ass."

She laughed.

"If you want to go to your meeting, go, but I'd like to show you around some of my properties." He squeezed her hand. "Show you some of what I do."

Meeting his gaze, she nodded. "I'd like to see these houses you've been telling me about."

Daniel grinned and brought her in for a kiss, then stood and finished getting ready.

Almost an hour later, they were standing in the middle of his newest construction project. He'd decided to stop at this one first because A it was the farthest of all his projects, and B because it was still in the demolition stage. All the walls that needed to come down were either gone or stripped to the bare studs. Bathrooms were being reconfigured and the kitchen layout was being flipped on its head. When it was completed, it would look amazing. Now, it looked like a war zone.

He held Ali's hand as they walked through the construction site. Since it was a Sunday, no one else was there. The quiet gave him time to reflect on his vision for the space. "I have big plans for this kitchen."

"It doesn't look like much to me," Bradley said.

"That's because you have to visualize it in your mind."

"Not really my thing."

Daniel chuckled. "Yes, I know."

"Oh, wow." Ali moved away from Daniel toward the patio door. "Look at that view."

The thing that had sold him on the property was the view. The house sat on almost an acre of land and had a small creek toward the rear of the property. Behind that, were trees. It gave an air of privacy hard to come by this close to the city.

Ali glanced back at him, her hand on the patio door. "Do you mind?"

Daniel motioned for her to go ahead. He watched out the kitchen window as she walked to the back of the property and stood staring into the woods. Her back was to him, but that didn't matter. He still felt drawn to her.

As if sensing him watching, she turned and met his gaze through the window. She smiled and made her way back inside.

They spent the rest of the day visiting the rest of his active construction sites. The last house, a three-bedroom, two-bath ranch, was almost finished. Less than a month and he'd be able to put this one on the market.

"When will this one be ready, Dad?" Bradley asked.

"Within the next month."

Ali had needed to use the bathroom, so the two men stood alone in the living room. Bradley had asked questions as they'd visited each house, so this one wasn't unusual. Which was why what he asked next caught Daniel off guard. "Why is she living with you?"

The way he asked it was as if it were no big deal, but Daniel wasn't born yesterday. Instead of answering, he raised an eyebrow at his son.

"Does she not have a place of her own?"

"You're walking a very thin line, Bradley Allen Ross."

His son ran a hand through his hair. "I'm trying to understand, Dad. Really, I am, but I just don't see her angle."

"There's no angle. She needed a place to stay. I have plenty of room."

"So you asked her to move in with you?" The look on his face was almost comical.

While he didn't want to have this conversation with his son, he figured it was better to get it out of the way. "Ali has an apartment, but she's having issues with her neighbors."

"Were you sleeping with her before or after she conned you into moving her into your house?"

Daniel stepped forward, getting in his son's face. "You will not speak about Ali in that way, do I make myself clear?"

Something flashed behind Bradley's eyes. "Yes."

Ali felt the tension when she entered the room. "Everything all right?"

Daniel didn't back down. He held Bradley's gaze and waited for his son to break it.

"Yeah. Everything's fine," Bradley said.

She looked toward Daniel, wanting confirmation. He met her gaze. "Ready to go?"

"Sure," she said, not sounding sure in the slightest.

Bradley walked to the door and opened it.

Daniel started to follow him, but she stopped him. "Hey, are you sure everything's okay?"

"I'm sure." Daniel grabbed her hand and tugged her toward the door. "Let's get home so we can eat. I'm starving."

The ride home was only about fifteen minutes, but it felt much longer. Bradley sat in the back seat, his brow furrowed, but luckily silent. Ali didn't miss the chill in the atmosphere, but she didn't say anything. He knew he'd have to share what happened with her, but he wanted to do it when they were alone.

Once they arrived home, Bradley was on his best behavior. He even smiled a couple of times at Ali and had a long debate about which police procedural was the best.

Daniel stayed close, not trusting his son wasn't going to pounce, but the rest of the evening passed without incident.

At nine o'clock, Bradley took his bag and headed upstairs, crashing in the room James typically used. Daniel gave his son ten minutes before he stood and gathered Ali into his arms. "Time for bed."

She shifted and averted her gaze. "Maybe I should sleep in my own bed tonight."

"No."

"No?"

"No." He lifted her chin so she was looking at him. "You're sleeping in my bed. That is not up for negotiation."

"But your son—"

"Has absolutely nothing to do with you and me." Before she could argue further, he took her by the hand and led her to his room.

CHAPTER 22

$\mathcal{A}$li stood at the foot of Daniel's bed, her thoughts on the day they'd spent going around to Daniel's properties with Bradley. Everything seemed a bit awkward, but okay until the last house. Something had happened while she was in the bathroom, and she knew it had to do with her.

Daniel strolled out of the en suite, naked from the waist up. He took in her stance and made his way to her side. "Why are you still dressed?"

She knew better than to suggest going to her room again. "Can I borrow one of your T-shirts to sleep in?"

"No, you may not."

There went that option.

She bit her bottom lip and met his gaze. "This feels wrong. Me being naked in your bed with your son upstairs."

"We are not having this discussion again." He went to the hamper and pushed his jeans off his hips, his back to her.

Ali removed her jeans, taking her time folding them and placing them on the end of the mattress. He finished undressing and climbed into bed, his gaze fixed on her as she finished removing her clothes. She took her time gathering her things and placing them on a chair beside the door.

"Come here," he ordered.

She walked to his side of the bed and let out a squeak when he picked her up and deposited her onto the mattress beside him.

He rolled over, pressing her into the sheets. She could feel his erection against her thigh and her body respond despite the reservations swirling in her head. His lips brushed against her neck, and she turned her head, silently begging him for more.

"That's my girl." He trailed his hand down her side and then back up to cup her breast.

"Sir?"

He worried her earlobe with his teeth. "Yes, sweetheart?"

"Do you think Cassie will have a problem with us being together?"

His chest vibrated against her. "No. She and her fiancé, Jesse, are coming to visit in two weeks. According to her texts, she can't wait to meet you. She wants the two of you to go shopping."

"I'd like that."

He pressed a kiss to her forehead. "Are we done talking about my children now?"

"You don't like talking about your children?"

"Not when I have you naked in my bed." He slid his hand down to cup her ass. "I can think of a lot of other things I'd rather be doing."

"What if your son hears?" She wasn't exactly quiet. He tended to tease her until she lost all semblance of control.

"Then he'll know his old man has a very healthy sex life."

Ali gasped as he rolled onto his back and lifted her to sit astride him. Then, to her surprise, he slid down the bed, bringing his head between her legs.

She reached for the headboard to steady herself as he sucked her labia into his mouth. His tongue lapped at her sensitive folds, darting inside her pussy before making his way to her clit.

He continued to explore, taking his time licking and sucking. His fingers dug into her hips, holding her where he wanted her. She tried to grind against his face for more friction, but he wouldn't let her.

When she thought she couldn't take any more teasing, he picked her up and turned her around. She was still straddling his head, but this time she was staring directly at his cock.

Ali didn't need more of an invitation. She was so turned on, desperate for him, she gripped the base of his erection and lowered her mouth onto his cock.

Daniel moaned as her lips surrounded his length and sucked him into her mouth. He spread her open and buried his face in her pussy. The stubble on his chin scraped against her clit, sending a mix of pain and pleasure directly to her core.

She hummed against the hard length of him in her mouth and he lifted his hips, driving his cock farther down her throat.

His lips locked onto her clit and sucked. Hard.

She lost her rhythm, but it didn't matter. He pumped his hips, fucking her mouth. She gagged, not able to focus on her breathing, but it didn't matter.

Tears ran down her cheeks as her climax hit her and she let go. Her cries were muffled by his cock still in her mouth, thrusting with abandon, seeking his own release.

He sucked on her clit until the last ripple of her orgasm dissipated. Her body was ready to collapse, but he wasn't finished.

Pulling his erection from between her lips, he helped her to sit up and moved her down his body until her pussy was in line with his cock. She was facing away from him, staring at the mirror along the far wall. Her hair was a mess, her face was flushed, and she could see his cock moving inside her, surging and retreating.

"Play with your tits," he ordered.

Ali lifted her hands, cupping her breasts. She pulled and twisted her nipples.

"Harder." His voice was gruff as he drove her down onto his erection.

She took her nipples between her fingers and pinched them as hard as she could. Pain and pleasure mixed into one and she could feel another orgasm approaching.

Daniel wrapped his hand around her hair and tugged. She fell backward, landing on his chest. He grunted at the impact but didn't miss a beat.

He lifted his legs, bending his knees to spread her open and keep them connected. One of his hands cupped her sex, feeling them come together. It was intimate and erotic, and the new angle was putting pressure on her clit from the inside.

His other hand circled her neck, forcing her head to the side. He placed his mouth right above her collarbone and sucked. Pleasure went directly to her clit and she felt heat deep in her belly. Her fingers dug into his sides, trying to anchor herself.

He gave her neck one last nip with his teeth, then turned her head in the opposite direction. Bringing their lips together, his tongue plunged into her mouth. It was a take no prisoners type of kiss. He demanded her compliance. She was lost in his mouth, the way his hand gripped her neck, applying just enough pressure to hold her where he wanted her, and the feel of him trusting inside her.

Then his thumb was grazing her clit and she was flying. His own grunts mingling with her screams as he took his own pleasure.

As he stopped moving his hips, his lips grew softer, his kiss gentler. He slipped out of her, letting his legs fall to the bed, and circled his arm around her waist. Rolling to his side, he positioned her so her back was to his front. He brushed the hair away from her shoulder and kissed right behind her ear. "I'm going to have to eat your pussy more often."

Ali chuckled. "I liked it, too."

He kissed the base of her neck. "I know."

Neither said anything for several moments. She was enjoying the feel of him surrounding her, but she felt they needed to talk about the elephant in the room. Or, at least, the elephant in the house. "At the last house. When I came out of the bathroom, there was a lot of tension between you and your son."

"There was."

"What happened?"

Daniel groaned.

"Please?"

She could tell he was trying to decide how much to tell her.

"Please."

"My son overstepped, and I told him so."

Her chest clenched and not in a good way. "What did he say?"

"This is the one and only time we're discussing this."

Ali nodded.

"He's concerned you're using me."

That surprised her. "Using you?"

"For my money."

"Oh." Ali tried to look at it from Bradley's point of view. He didn't know her. And while she and Daniel had never talked about his finances, she knew he was wealthy. "He's trying to look out for you."

Daniel huffed.

"He doesn't know we've been friends for two years. As far as he's concerned, we've just met."

Rolling onto his back, Daniel took her with him. She rested her head on his chest as he ran a hand down her back. "I'm not sure it would matter. Bradley always thinks people have an ulterior motive."

"He loves you."

"I know that, too," he said.

"Maybe it would be best if I went back to my apartment while he's visiting. I don't want to cause problems between you two."

"What did I say earlier about my son having nothing to do with you and me?"

"I don't want to cause problems for you," she whispered.

* * *

DANIEL DIDN'T WANT to be having this conversation, but he didn't want her worrying about it either. "Bradley is under the misconception that I've been blinded by love and can no longer think for myself."

She didn't respond right away. "Why would he think that?"

Propping himself up, he cupped her face in his hand, turning her head so he could look at her. "Because he sees the way I look at you."

Her blue eyes stared up at him, drawing him into their depths. He knew right then he wanted her in his bed for the rest of his days. His heart didn't care if it was logical or if it was what was best for her. He loved her and he needed her to know.

Daniel opened his mouth to say the words when he heard a noise outside.

Ali turned her head toward the patio door, obviously hearing it, too. "What's that?"

She'd no more asked the question when his outside lights came on. Given where his property was located and that in the years he'd been here there'd only been one other time something like this had happened, it didn't take much to figure out who was in his backyard.

The next thing he knew, music began to play from his outdoor speakers. If it were the middle of the day, it wouldn't be a big deal, but it was after ten o'clock at night and both he and Ali had to work in the morning.

Getting out of bed, he threw on a pair of underwear and made his way to the patio door. He slid the door open and walked out onto his deck. The sound of someone entering the pool caught his attention and drew his gaze in that direction. He crossed to the edge of the pool and waited for his son to surface.

Bradley swam to the edge of the pool and turned, not noticing his father standing there.

Walking over to the outdoor kitchen, he turned off the music. Then he returned to the side of the pool, this time with the skimmer in hand. When Bradley approached, Daniel brought it down on his head.

His son popped out of the water as if something was trying to attack him. "Wh-what?" He tossed the net off him and soon found his father looming over him. "What was that for?"

"What the hell are you doing out here swimming at this time of night?"

"I couldn't sleep, so I figured I'd go for a swim."

"A swim doesn't require music. Nor does it require you to turn on every outside light," Daniel said. "And you know my bedroom is right there." He tilted his head behind him. The back of the house wrapped around the pool, which Daniel had loved when his kids were younger.

Bradley didn't back down. "I like to listen to music when I work out."

"You can't hear it when you're underwater."

It was then his son noticed what Daniel was wearing. His face twisted into a grimace. "Dad, are you in your underwear?"

Daniel didn't bother acknowledging his son's comment. "Get out of the pool and turn everything off. Ali and I have work in the morning, which means we need to sleep. We can't do that if you have the backyard lit up like its midday and music blaring." He began to walk away. "And put the skimmer back where it belongs." Not waiting for a response, Daniel headed back to his room.

When he entered his bedroom, Ali was sitting with her back against the headboard. "Is everything all right?"

"Everything's fine." He removed his underwear and climbed back into bed. "My son decided it was a good idea to take a swim before bed."

He pulled her against him, and she nuzzled against his chest. Brushing his lips against the top of her head, he lowered them onto the mattress and pulled the blanket to cover them. She ran her hand along his chest, playing with his hair, and he knew she was thinking. "My mom and I don't have a great relationship."

Daniel had wanted to ask about her mom for a long time, but it had never seemed like the right time. He'd picked up some bits and pieces over the time they'd known each other, like he knew her mom visited her on occasion, and it stressed her out. "Tell me about her."

"She's the exact opposite of me. Where I like schedules, she hates them. Grandma used to call her a free spirit." Ali glanced up at Daniel. "That was her being nice."

"Did you see her very often growing up?" he asked.

"Sometimes she'd stay for a week or two. A few times she even promised to stick around." Ali paused. "That never lasted long."

"I'm sorry." His parents had always been there for him growing up. If he'd needed something, they'd done their best to make it happen.

"It's okay. I had my grandma."

He felt her smile.

"She was the best."

"I'm glad you had her in your life."

"Me, too." Ali's hand stilled on his chest. "I don't want to ruin the relationship you have with your son."

"You won't." He could feel the argument coming, so he continued, "He'll come around."

She pulled herself up, so her face was level with his. "And if he doesn't?"

"He will."

Her teeth dug into her bottom lip, drawing his gaze to her mouth. He brought her lips down to his.

Daniel threaded his hand in her hair, holding her to him. "I don't want you to worry about this. We'll figure it out, okay? I want you in my life and my bed."

"I want that, too."

Emotion rose in his chest. He loved this woman so much.

He kissed her again. "We need to sleep."

She glanced over at the clock beside his bed, and he followed her gaze. It was almost eleven.

When she looked at him again, her eyes were full of warmth. Her lips brushed his. "Good night."

"Good night, sweetheart." I love you was on the tip of his tongue, but he bit it back.

Holding her against him, he combed his finger through her hair until her breathing evened out, letting him know she'd fallen asleep. He placed one last kiss on the top of her head and stared at the ceiling.

He had no idea what he was going to do with his son. While Daniel figured Bradley would be the hardest sell when it came to Ali, he hadn't expected him to dig in his heels quite so much. He got where he was coming from. That was part of the problem. If Daniel were on the outside looking in, he might have the same reservations.

If someone had told him they'd been dating a woman for two weeks and she was now living in his house, he would seriously question the man's sanity. But it wasn't as if he and Ali had just met. They'd known each other for two years. They were friends.

And maybe that was the issue right there. Bradley didn't know about their past, their history. They hadn't lied about where they'd met, only the when.

His kids didn't know about his lifestyle, and he planned to keep it that way. His sex life wasn't any of their business. He'd kept that part of his life separate from his family, including the women he'd played with.

Ali was the first woman he'd introduced to his kids since he and Jessica had divorced. Although he'd had a few arrangements over the years before joining the club, none of them had been serious. Not until Ali.

Bradley would come around. When he realized he was wrong, that Ali wasn't after his money, he'd relax. Or was that wishful thinking?

The woman in his arms stirred. "Are you still awake?"

"Go back to sleep. You have work tomorrow."

"Mmm. You, too."

He hugged her closer and closed his eyes, willing his mind to shut off so he could get some sleep.

CHAPTER 23

*B*radley was sitting at the kitchen island sipping a mug of coffee when Ali made her appearance the next morning. She'd left her robe in her room the day before, so she'd had to borrow one of Daniel's shirts. It was better than walking naked through the house, but not by much. If he was going to be around for a while and she continued to sleep in Daniel's room, she was going to have to ask him about moving her clothes into his bedroom.

Daniel stood next to his son when she came into view. Both had intense looks on their faces, so she knew she'd interrupted another discussion and it most likely involved her.

Noticing her first, Daniel's expression softened. "Good morning, sweetheart."

She smiled and tried to forget she wasn't wearing all that much. "Good morning."

Bradley slid off his stool and walked to the coffeemaker. "I'm sorry if my using the pool last night disturbed your sleep."

His apology was unexpected, and she didn't know what to say. "No. I mean…" She paused and looked at Daniel, but he was watching his son.

"Did you want some coffee?" Bradley asked her. Again, this was unexpected.

"Yes, please." She didn't know what to make of it. One minute, he acted as if he wanted her gone. The next, he was offering her coffee?

He removed another mug from the cabinet and filled it with the hot liquid. "Cream or sugar?"

"Both. Thank you."

Bradley placed the coffee on the island, along with the cream and sugar.

"Thanks." She doctored her coffee with the right amount of cream and sugar before taking a sip. Normally, she waited until after her shower to down caffeine, but this wasn't a normal morning.

Daniel moved to the stove. "Did you want to shower and change before breakfast?" he asked.

She glanced at the clock. "That's probably a good idea."

"What time do you have to be at work?" Bradley asked.

It seemed like such an innocent question, but the look Daniel shot at his son, she wondered if there was more to it. "Seven thirty." She took another drink of her coffee, then sat it down on the island. "If you'll excuse me."

Then, before either one of them could comment, she hightailed it down the hall to her room.

Breakfast was uneventful, mainly because it was only her and Daniel. When she'd returned to the kitchen, fully dressed for the day, Daniel informed her Bradley had gone into town. "Did you two have another argument this morning?"

"No. I wouldn't call it an argument. I just told him he needed to apologize."

"He seemed to be on his best behavior this morning."

Daniel frowned.

"That's not a good thing?" she asked.

"Given his other actions, no."

Ali considered that. "Maybe he's changed his mind about us."

He picked up her hand and brought it to his lips for a kiss. "You, sweetheart, are an optimist."

It was true. She always tried to see the good in people. Even her mother who'd disappointed her more times than she could count.

They finished their breakfast and were headed out the door when she brought up their sleeping situation. Or rather, her clothing situation. "If

Bradley's going to be staying for a while, would it be okay if I moved some of my clothes into your room? This way I don't have to pass by the kitchen in my robe or one of your shirts."

Daniel paused as he opened the door to her car for her. "You want to move your things into my room?"

"If you're not okay with that, I can pick out my outfit for the next day and just hang that up in your bathroom or something. I just don't—"

He took her face in both hands and kissed her silent. "We'll move your things into my room tonight when you get home."

"You're really okay with that?"

Daniel chuckled. "Yes, I'm okay with that."

"Okay," she whispered as his lips descended again.

He stepped back, allowing her to slide behind the wheel. "Have a good day at work."

"You, too."

Three hours later, she wanted to cry. She'd arrived at work to find her usual list of twenty things to do, only five of those twenty things were projects that would take her days to complete. Then, at nine, her boss had informed her he would be unavailable for the next four hours and that she was to hold his calls. Normally, this would be fine, but his phone hadn't stopped ringing for more than five minutes since he'd forwarded them to her.

"Ms. Foster." Grant Jacobson stood in his office doorway with a scowl on his face.

"Yes, Mr. Jacobson?"

"I've been trying to reach you for the last ten minutes. Why haven't you been answering your phone?"

"I'm sorry, Mr. Jacobson. I was on a call and—"

He marched to her desk and placed a stack of papers in front of her. "I need you to research each of these companies and have a report on my desk first thing in the morning."

There were five companies on the list. She'd done this type of research before and knew what all it entailed. There was no way she was going to be able to do that, watch the phones, and make a dent in the list he'd given her that morning. "Mr. Jacobson, I'm not sure I can do that with the other stuff you've already asked me to do."

"Are you refusing to do your job, Ms. Foster?"

"No, sir. It's just—"

"If you want to keep your job, Ms. Foster, I suggest you figure out how to get it done." He turned on his heels and disappeared into his office, closing his door behind him.

Ali bent over, clasping her hands to her knees. She couldn't lose her job, but there was no way she could do this.

Panic began to set in as the phone rang again. With frayed nerves and a trembling hand, she pressed the button and answered the call. "Mr. Jacobson's office."

The caller needed to talk to her boss, of course, so she jotted down a message and let the person know she'd inform him of the call as soon as he was free. When she hung up the phone, she was shaking like a leaf.

Digging her phone out of her purse, Ali texted Kim.

Ali – I'm going to get fired.

Another call came in, so she didn't get to check her phone right away. This time it was one of the other executives—one she liked—vice president operations. After telling her what he needed, he asked, "Allison, are you all right? You sound upset."

She wasn't about to cry to another executive about her troubles, so she downplayed it. "It's just been really busy around here today."

"Well, if you need a break, forward your calls to one of my admins and go get yourself a coffee or something. You don't want to burn out."

"Thank you, Carl. I appreciate the offer."

"I mean it. You're a good admin, but we all need a breather occasionally."

It was almost noon by the time she remembered to look at her phone again. Kim had texted her not once. Not twice. But three times.

Kim – What do you mean you're going to get fired? What happened?
Kim – Can you meet me for lunch?
Kim – Or maybe I should send Justin over there to kick your boss's ass.

Normally, that would make Ali chuckle, but it made her eyes well up with tears for the second time that day.

Taking Carl's advice, she called one of his admins and asked if she could forward her phones to her long enough for Ali to get something downstairs at the café. She didn't have time for a proper lunch break, but if she didn't eat something, Daniel wouldn't be happy.

On her way down in the elevator, she typed a message back to Kim.

Ali – I can't do lunch today. Too busy. I have to research five companies and write a report by the end of the day. Plus, I'm watching his phones and working on five other big projects.

She didn't need to say who *he* was. Kim would know she was talking about her boss.

Kim – That's insane. He needs to get someone else to help you. You need your own assistant.

Ali – Not going to happen

Three little dots appeared on the screen, letting her know Kim was typing.

Ali got off the elevator and made her way to the cafeteria in the basement of the hospital. She got herself a coffee, a sandwich, and some chips, then headed back upstairs. Her boss didn't like when she ate at her desk, but if she had any hope of getting everything done, she needed every minute she could get.

Kim – You need to find another job.

Ali snorted.

Ali – It's not that easy.

Kim – Sure it is. I could probably find you something here. You deal with marketing already. It wouldn't be that big of an adjustment.

While Ali did work with marketing, being the administrative assistant for the vice president of marketing was vastly different than being an administrative assistant for an ad executive who lived and breathed marketing for multiple companies all day.

When Ali didn't respond back, Kim sent her another text.

Kim – Have you talked to Daniel?

The elevator dinged and the doors opened to her floor.

Ali – No.
Ali – I've got to go. Later.

To her great relief, her boss's office was empty when she returned to her desk. She had no idea how long he'd be gone, so she hurried to eat her lunch and took a few minutes of quiet to try and get herself organized before she took the phones back.

Two hours later, she glanced at her phone again and saw Kim's last text.

Kim – Talk to Daniel.

* * *

DANIEL BACKED up his things and was on his way out the door when Kevin appeared in the doorway. "There's a currier here. He has a package for you that requires your signature."

He thought it odd he was coming to tell him this. Packages came all the time, some requiring signatures, and Kevin signed for them. "Is there a reason you can't sign for it?"

"The man said it has to be you, or he will try and delivery it another time."

Daniel nodded. He slipped into his jacket and made this way to the front where a young man no more than twenty-five waited. "You have something for me?"

"Are you Daniel Ross?"

"I am."

The man extended a clipboard to Daniel.

He took it and noticed the sender's name. Peter Sanders.

His heart rate accelerated, knowing what had finally arrived. When he'd spoken to Katrina's private investigator, he'd said it could take a few weeks to compile a detailed history of Grant Jacobson. It was three weeks more than he'd wanted, but if it provided him answers, it would be worth it.

Signing his name, he handed the clipboard back to the man. After a brief look, the man reached into a messenger bag and pulled out a large envelope. He handed it to Daniel and turned to leave.

"That was strange," Kevin said once the man was out the door.

Daniel didn't comment. He wanted to rip into the information immediately, but he had something he had to attend to first. "I'll see you in the morning. Have a good night."

Kevin nodded and went back to his desk.

Tucking the folder under his arm, Daniel made his way to his car and headed home. His phone had alerted him his code had been used to enter the property twenty minutes ago. There were a limited number of people who had that code. His gardener wasn't due till later in the week, nor was his poolman, and Ali was at work. That left his kids, namely Bradley.

He took the time in the car to prepare himself for the conversation ahead. They'd been interrupted this morning when Ali had come into the kitchen and hadn't gotten to finish what they'd started. It was time to set some boundaries.

Sure enough, when Daniel drove into his garage, Bradley's car was there. He left the envelope in the vehicle for now and went to find his son.

After searching inside the house, he went to the pool. Bradley was sitting under the awning, his laptop open in front of him.

He looked up when he heard the patio door open. "Dad. You're home early."

"We need to continue our discussion." He was done beating around the bush.

Bradley closed his laptop and leaned back in his chair.

Daniel took the seat across from him. "You're my son and I love you, but I will not have you disrespecting me or Ali. I understand your concerns about my relationship. However, this is my house and Ali is my guest. You will treat her with respect. Do I make myself clear?"

"Crystal." Not exactly the response he'd been hoping for. It was like his teenage years all over again.

He took a moment to assess the situation. "Do you expect me to be alone for the rest of my life?"

That got a reaction out of him. A small one, but it was something. He recovered quickly, though, returning to his stoic expression. "It has nothing to do with that."

"Then explain it to me."

He sat there, watching, but Daniel waited him out. His son came by his stubbornness honestly. They'd gone head-to-head many times during Bradley's teenage years, but he wasn't a kid anymore. "I've told you my concerns."

"Yes, you have. And I've explained to you Ali isn't like that. We've known each other for two years and she's never asked me for a dime."

He saw something flash in his eyes, and then they grew hard again. "James said you'd been dating for two weeks."

"We have. But we met two years ago."

"At a club."

"Yes."

His son looked at him for a long moment. "What club?"

"It's a private club. One that vets its members thoroughly."

"She doesn't seem like the type to frequent a cigar club."

A laugh escaped Daniel. The image of Ali strutting around in a cigar club in one of her club outfits amused him. But he knew what his son was trying to do. "Stop fishing."

They stared at each other for a long time. Most people would have caved, but he knew better. "There's nothing I can say, is there?" Bradley said.

"To change my mind about Ali? No. She's the woman I've chosen to have in my life. You don't have to like it, but you do have to respect it." He looked at his son with a pointed expression. "That means no more evening dips in the pool or anything else that would make her uncomfortable. Got it?"

"Got it."

Daniel stood. While he wasn't sure he'd changed his son's mind about Ali, he was hoping his message had gotten across. He really didn't want to have to kick his son out. "Ali should be home shortly. Are you joining us for dinner?"

"Yeah. I'll be here."

Nodding, Daniel went inside and started to prep the vegetables for dinner.

Three hours later, he was pacing the floor. Ali wasn't home yet. He'd called her cell twice, but she hadn't answered. He'd even tried her work phone. Nothing. Dinner was ready, but he refused to sit down without her.

"Maybe she had another more pressing engagement," Bradley said from the couch.

Daniel picked up his phone again. This time, he dialed Kim.

She answered on the first ring. "Is she okay?"

Unease creeped up his chest. "That's what I was hoping you could tell me. She's not made it home yet."

There was a long pause. "I bet she's still at work."

"It's after seven. Why would she still be at work?"

He heard someone in the background. Justin, he assumed. Then he heard Kim say, "It's Daniel. Ali isn't home yet." There was another pause, then she was talking to Daniel again. "She had a rough day at work. Her boss—who's an ass—gave her so much work there's no way to get it done. And he told her if she didn't get it to him by tomorrow morning, she'd be fired."

Daniel saw red. "He what?"

Out of the corner of his eye, he saw Bradley stand.

Grabbing his keys, he was halfway out the door before he realized Bradley was following him. He slid behind the wheel of his car, not reacting when his son got into the passenger seat. "See if you can get a hold of her, and if you can, call me back. I'm heading to her work now."

"You won't be able to get in without a keycard. Not this time of night."

Daniel wasn't worried about getting inside. He'd find a way.

He hung up the phone and backed out of his garage.

"Where are we going?" Bradley asked.

"To the hospital administration building."

"Where Ali works?"

"Yes," Daniel confirmed.

"Why?"

Daniel's nostrils flared. Instead of answering his son, he reached into the back and retrieved the envelope from earlier. He handed it to Bradley. "I need you to read this and give me an overview."

His son opened the envelope and pulled out a stack of papers an inch thick. "What's this?"

"A report on Ali's boss."

Instead of questioning why he would have such a thing, Bradley began combing through the papers. "What am I looking for?"

"I don't know." What he wanted to find was something he could use to get the man fired. Or better yet, arrested. He was making Ali's life miserable, and it was going to end one way or another.

CHAPTER 24

*D*aniel focused on the road while his son flipped through the first few pages. "His full name is Grant Edward Jacobson. He's forty-eight. Grew up outside of Chicago."

Bradley flipped through a few more pages. "Good grades. Got detention for skipping class his senior year."

"What about after he graduated?" Daniel asked.

"Let's see." Bradley read several more pages before continuing. "Got a job in management straight out of college. Looks like there was some family connection to the company. Three years later, he moved to Columbus Ohio and took a job in hospital administration."

"How long was he there?"

"Four years."

Daniel merged onto the highway. Luckily, the bulk of the traffic had dissipated. The majority of what was left was headed out of the city, not into it. "Does it say why he left?"

"No, but I'm assuming it had something to do with the pay of his new job."

"Where was that?"

"St. Louis."

Bradley read Daniel the rest of Grant Jacobson's work history, but nothing was ringing any bells. "What about where he lived? His hobbies?"

"Dad, what is it about this guy? I haven't seen you this upset since Cassie snuck out of the house her junior year to go to that concert."

Daniel flexed his fingers against the steering wheel. "He took over Ali's department about six months ago. She used to love her job. Now she hates it."

"You're this upset because your girlfriend hates her boss?"

Daniel snorted, wishing it were that simple. From what Ali had shared with him, her boss was a passive aggressive ass. "Two weeks ago, her boss informed her he needed her to go to a charity event in his place."

"And she didn't wanna go?"

"That wasn't the problem." Daniel looked over his shoulder before changing lanes. "He gave her a day and a half notice. Told her she had to bring a date." He took the exit ramp, the hospital building in his sights. "I'd known things weren't great with her boss before that, but then the night of the event she was nervous and told me she had to mingle so she'd have proof she was there."

Silence filled the SUV as his son took in that piece of information. "That's fucked up."

Daniel didn't comment.

As he turned into the parking lot of the hospital administration building, he searched for Ali's car. He tried her cell once more, but it went to voicemail. Again. "Dammit."

"Still no answer?"

"No." He parked in one of the visitor's spots and got out. "Stay here."

Not waiting to see if Bradley agreed or not, he jogged to the sliding glass doors. They were locked, of course, but he was hoping he could find a security guard or something.

No such luck.

Blowing out a breath, he made his way down the walkway to the hospital's main entrance. With every step he took, he became more irritated. Where the hell was she and why wasn't she answering her phone?

The large glass doors at the hospital's main entrance opened and he stepped inside. A security guard sat behind the large reception desk. He looked up as Daniel entered. "Evening."

Daniel worked to keep his voice pleasant. Or at least calm. "Is there any way to find out if an employee in the administration building has left for the day?"

"I think they're all gone. Most of them dart out of here as soon as the clock hits five."

"I understand, but my girlfriend works as an executive assistant, and I'm worried about her. She hasn't come home, and she isn't answering her phone. Her best friend hasn't heard from her since this morning, either." He was hoping adding the part about her friend would provide context for his concern.

The man whose name tag read Charles, twisted his mouth as if he were considering his options. "I can call up to her desk. See if she answers."

Daniel shook his head. He'd tried that already. She wasn't answering her desk phone either. "Is there any way we could check? In person."

"You want to go up there?" he asked.

"Yes." Then he added. "I need to know she's okay. It's not like her not to come home, or at least call."

Again, the man seemed to be thinking out his response. "What's your girlfriend's name?"

"Allison Foster. She works on the fourth floor."

The man's eyes widened. "You're Ali's boyfriend?"

"I am."

After a quick once-over, the man pulled out his radio. "Phil, where are you?"

"Just finished walking sixty-five. I'm about to head to the basement. You want anything from the cafeteria?"

Charles shook his head even though Phil couldn't see him. "No. I'm good. But I've got a guy here looking for Ali, Mr. Jacobson's admin. You see her up there anywhere?"

Several seconds went by before the radio crackled again. "Nope. It's quiet as a mouse up there."

"Thanks," Charles said, then turned his attention back to Daniel.

Before he could say anything, though, Daniel responded, "Thank you for checking. I appreciate it."

"No problem." Daniel had already turned to leave, but he heard the man yell, "Good luck."

Less than a minute later, he was back in his vehicle. "No luck?" Bradley asked.

"She's not here." Daniel backed out and left the parking lot. "Did you find anything useful?"

Instead of answering, Bradley asked a question of his own. "Where to now?"

"Her apartment." If she wasn't at work and she wasn't with Kim, that left her apartment. If she wasn't there, he wasn't sure where to go next. She had no other family in town.

He was trying not to get ahead of himself, but he didn't like not knowing where she was. Picking up his phone, he pulled up her cell number and tried her again. It went straight to voicemail.

Bradley was staring at him. He glanced over. "What? Did you find something?"

"No. It's just..."

"Just what?" Daniel asked.

"Nothing." Turning his attention back to the stack of papers, Bradley continued to read.

Normally, Daniel would press his son to get on with whatever he was going to say, but he wasn't sure he could take more of his son's immaturity at the moment.

The drive to Ali's apartment usually took fifteen minutes. He got them there in less than ten. He may or may not have run a few yellow lights.

His gaze zeroed in on Ali's car parked in her spot outside her apartment. He was swamped with a mixture of relief and wanting to turn her over his knee.

Daniel found a parking spot and climbed out. As he approached her door, he heard raised voices.

He paused for a moment, wanting an idea of what he was walking in on. The voices were muffled, but he picked out at least two. One belonged to Ali. The other to another woman.

Not willing to wait any longer to find out what was going on, Daniel used the key Ali had given him and opened her door. When he stepped through, two heads turned to face him. Ali's was full of relief. The other woman's—older than Ali by at least twenty years—was not nearly as pleased with the intrusion.

"Get out!" the other woman yelled. "I don't know who the hell you are, but we don't want you here. This is a man-free zone."

Ali ignored the woman, coming to him and wrapping her arms around his waist.

He embraced her, ignoring the other woman. "I've been trying to call you. Why aren't you answering your phone?"

"She took it. I've been trying to get it back for the last two hours."

Daniel looked at the other woman. When she swayed to the left, he caught sight of something purple peeking out of her back pocket. He was betting it was Ali's cell phone.

Before he could ask who this was or how the woman had come into possession of Ali's phone in the first place, the woman spoke again. "Did you not hear me? Get out! We don't want you here. Right, Ali? Go on. Get."

That was when he realized she was drunk. Or at the very least, on her way to being that way.

His gaze landed on a bottle of vodka on the coffee table. Someone had made a decent dent in it, and he didn't smell any alcohol on Ali's breath.

"Mom, stop it." Ali paused. "Please."

At this revelation, Daniel took another long look at the woman. Now that Ali had pointed out the relationship, the similarities were obvious. The other woman's hair was the same shade of brown as Ali's. She was a little taller but had the same build. She also had Ali's beautiful blue eyes, although they looked full of sadness.

"Why didn't you tell me your mother was coming to visit?" He asked the question, but he was already positive he knew the answer. She hadn't known.

Zelda Foster threw her hands up and plopped down on the couch, sitting on Ali's phone. She reached for the bottle of vodka and brought it to her lips.

"I didn't—"

"Who the hell are you anyway, barging in here like you own the place or something? That's the problem with men. They think they can take anything they want. Take, take, take. Well, fuck 'em. Fuck 'em all."

It was obvious he wasn't going to be able to have a conversation with Ali while her mom was in the same room. He turned to his son, who'd followed him in. "Could you stay with Ms. Foster while Ali and I talk?"

Bradley glanced at Zelda, who was narrowing her eyes at them. "Yeah."

Not waiting for any further remarks from Zelda, he took Ali's hand and led her into her bedroom. Closing the door behind them, he got down to business. "Now explain what's going on."

* * *

ALI WAS SO glad to see Daniel. She knew he'd be upset she hadn't called, but her mother had her cell and she didn't have a landline. "I needed to get a few things, so I swung by my apartment after work. I was almost ready to leave when there was a knock on my door. It was my mom."

"I'm assuming you had no idea she was coming?"

She shook her head. "I never do. She just shows up and it...it's like this." Ali bit her lower lip. "I'm sorry I didn't call. I tried, but she took my phone."

"Why did she take your phone?" he asked.

Ali averted her eyes, but he didn't let her. He lifted her chin and forced her to look at him.

"Because she wanted my attention." Ali paused. "Her latest boyfriend broke up with her."

Daniel knew Ali's relationship with her mom was screwed up, but he hadn't expected it to be this bad. Ali's mom was a mess. "Is it like this every time?"

"Pretty much."

He looked at her for a long moment. "We'll discuss this more when we get home."

"I-I can't leave her. She—she needs me. I—"

Before he could say anything more, a familiar sound came from the adjoining apartment. What started out as a loud thud of someone being pushed aggressively against the wall was quickly followed by moans and demands of harder and a stream of yeses.

Then, her mother's voice was added to the mix. "Shut the hell up, you perverts! No one wants to hear you going at it like rutting bulls."

The noise from next door stopped. Ali held her breath, not knowing whether to go to her living room or hide under her bed.

A door opened next door seconds before there was pounding on her door. Ali and Daniel looked at each other, then exited the bedroom. By the time they got to Zelda and Bradley, Bradley had an arm wrapped around Zelda's waist, trying to hold her back as she attempted to get to the door.

Daniel placed a hand on Ali's arm to stop her. She met his gaze. "Deal with your mother. I'll handle the neighbors."

She wanted to argue, but given the look on his face, she held her tongue. He wasn't in the best mood given the circumstances, and she couldn't blame him.

Going to her mom, she stood in front of her, looking her in the eye. "Mom, stop it. This isn't helping anything." Her mom didn't stop, so she tried again. "Mom! Stop it. Now."

That got her attention. Finally.

But then her mom collapsed on the ground, nearly taking Bradley with her. She curled up into a ball and burst into tears.

Ali kneeled in front of her. "Mom, are you okay?"

"No, I'm not okay. Nothing is ever okay."

Not knowing what to do, she stayed with her mom on the floor while Daniel talked to her neighbors outside. When he came back in, he stood over her and her mom. He held out a hand for Ali, which she took, and he helped her to stand. Then, he offered a hand to Zelda. "Ms. Foster, you need to get up."

"Why?"

"Well, I suppose you can stay here if you choose, but we're leaving. If you'd like to remain with Ali, then you'll be accompanying us."

"I'm not going anywhere with you." Then she glared at Bradley. "Or you."

"Very well." Daniel grabbed hold of Ali's hand and began walking toward the door.

Ali didn't move. "Wait—"

"We're leaving," he said.

She nodded. "I know, but I need to get the things I came for. They're in my bathroom."

He released his hold on her hand. "You have two minutes."

Rushing down the hall, she ducked into her bathroom and grabbed the bag she'd stuffed all her things into earlier. After a quick double-check, she made her way back to Daniel.

When she reentered the living room, her mother was no longer on the floor. She was staring Daniel down. Her mother's gaze didn't soften when she noticed her daughter. "Who is this and why does he think he can order us around?"

"Mom, this is Daniel and his son, Bradley. Daniel and I..." She glanced at Daniel, then back at her mom. "Daniel and I are seeing each other."

Her mom's eyebrows shot into her hair, and she pointed at Daniel. "He's your boyfriend?"

Ali nodded. "Yes."

Daniel was still wearing his slacks, but he'd rolled up the sleeves on his dress shirt. "How old are you?"

"Fifty-five."

"And you're dating my daughter?"

"Yes."

She could see the wheels turning in her mom's head and she didn't like it. "Mom, if you'd rather stay here, I can..." She wasn't sure how she was going to finish that sentence. If she insisted on staying, she knew there would be hell to pay.

"What the hell," her mom said. "Lead the way, Mr. Boyfriend."

Her mom picked up the bottle of vodka in one hand and a suitcase in the other. She began making her way to the door.

Bradley swiped the bottle out of her hand. "This is staying here."

Zelda shot him daggers with her eyes, but then turned on the charm when looking at Daniel. "I'm sure you have something better than cheap vodka at your house, right?"

"I do," Daniel confirmed.

Her mom was out the door, not waiting to see if they would follow.

Daniel reached for Ali's hand again.

"I'm sorry—"

He cut her off. "We'll talk at home."

While Daniel locked up her apartment, Bradley bumped her elbow. Ali turned to see what he wanted and found him holding her phone.

"I thought you might want this back."

She took it and smiled. "Thanks."

He grinned back at her. "You're welcome."

Daniel opened the passenger's door for her while Bradley and her mom got in the back. He paused for a moment, and she realized there was a stack of papers on the seat. She wouldn't have thought anything of them, but she saw the name on the top of one of the pages. Grant Edward Jacobson.

Ali wanted to ask him about it, but not with her mother within earshot. This evening was already bad enough. She didn't need to add to it.

He gathered the papers and slipped them back into a manila envelope, placed them under her seat, then helped her into the vehicle.

The drive home was intense. Not because of the topic of conversation, but because there wasn't any. None of them said a word as Daniel drove them out of the city toward his house. It wasn't until they pulled up to the gated driveway that she heard a peep out of her mom.

"You live here?"

"I do," Daniel said and typed in the code.

The gate opened and they proceeded down the long, winding driveway. She couldn't see her mom's expression when they pulled up to the house, but she could imagine it. His house was impressive, including the four-car garage he drove his SUV into. It was bigger than some houses.

They walked into the house and she saw her mom's eyes light up, dread pooled in the pit of her stomach. Her mom had a horrible track record when it came to men, and not only the men she dated. For some reason, she thought she knew what men wanted when she didn't have a clue.

"Ali, why don't you show your mom to your old bedroom. She can sleep there."

"Her old room?" Zelda asked.

"Yes." Daniel didn't elaborate. He strolled off, leaving Ali and her mom alone.

Her mom didn't say anything until they entered the room where Ali had stayed in the wing of the house. "Why didn't you tell me you'd landed a rich sugar daddy?"

Ali's heart sank. Now she not only had to deal with Bradley's judgments, but her mother's as well. The only difference was that Bradley saw her dating his father as a negative and her mother most certainly didn't.

CHAPTER 25

As soon as Ali disappeared down the hall with her mom, Daniel returned to his vehicle to get the file. He didn't know Zelda Foster very well, but what he did know about her didn't impress him. The last thing he wanted to do was clue her in regarding the problems Ali was having at her job. Not, at least, until he got a better read on the situation.

Bradley was in the kitchen when he returned. He was heating up their uneaten dinner. His son moved with skill in the kitchen—something he'd taught all his kids.

His son set a plate in front of him.

"Thank you."

Nodding, Bradley went back to the stove. "Should I make plates for Ali and her mom?"

Daniel had no idea if Ali's mom would want to eat. From what she'd said at Ali's apartment, the only thing she was interested in consuming was more alcohol. He noted, however, that she hadn't yet asked about his liquor cabinet since they'd arrived at the house. Nor had she spoken on the drive here, which had him concerned on an entirely different level.

Bradley sat down beside his father at the kitchen island with a plate of food. "So that's Ali's mom."

"Yes." Daniel took a bite of his dinner, not wanting his son's efforts to go to waste. He'd make sure Ali ate after she got her mother settled.

"You never met her before tonight?"

Daniel shook his head. "No. Ali's told me a little about her, but this is the first time we've met."

His son didn't say any more. He ate his dinner, then slid off the stool and took his plate to the sink. "I'll be upstairs if you need me."

Tilting his chin up, he let his son know he'd heard him.

Bradley jogged up the stairs, leaving Daniel alone in the kitchen to finish his meal and contemplate what had become a clusterfuck of an evening.

Twenty-seven minutes later, Ali appeared looking frazzled. She stopped in her tracks when she saw him at the island.

Standing, he went to the stove to make her a plate. It was cold again, so he stuck it in the microwave. She sat down at the island without a word.

"Thank you," she said when he put the plate of food in front of her. Looking up at him, he could see remorse in her eyes. "I'm s—"

"Eat your dinner. Then we'll talk."

Her shoulders slumped, but she picked up her fork and began to eat.

Daniel left her alone, taking the file he'd carried in earlier to his room, along with the bag Ali had brought with her from her apartment. When he strolled back into the kitchen, she was loading her plate into the dishwasher. She turned to face him, waiting.

"Does your mother have everything she needs?"

"Yeah. I showed her where the bathroom is and how to work the TV. She should be okay for the rest of the night." Ali opened her mouth to say more, then closed it again. He knew there was another apology on the tip of her tongue, but he didn't want I'm sorry. He wanted answers.

"Bedroom."

She lowered her gaze and walked past him as she made her way to the master bedroom.

Before he followed her, he sent a text to Kim, letting her know Ali was home. As irritated as he was, he didn't want Kim to worry about her friend.

Ali was kneeling on the floor when he entered. It was a good start.

Daniel locked the door behind him and crossed to the patio door. He locked that door as well and pulled the curtains closed. The last thing he needed was an audience. Or interruptions. He'd told Bradley no more evening dips in the pool, but they now had another house guest, and something told him she was going to be a handful.

Taking a seat on the end of the bed, he took a moment to gather his thoughts. He'd had submissives misbehave before, but it had never caused such a reaction in him. Not being able to reach Ali tonight—not knowing where she was—had him feeling out of control and he didn't like that.

When he felt calmer, he called her to him. "Come here."

She crawled to him, keeping her gaze on the ground. Sitting back on her heels, she waited.

He didn't make her wait long. "Why didn't you call me to tell me you were going to your apartment after work?"

"I started my period today and needed supplies. I was only going to be a few minutes, so I didn't call. Then my mom showed up and when I tried to call you, she took my phone."

While he understood her need to go to her apartment, it didn't excuse her misstep. She wasn't new to the lifestyle. She knew what she'd signed up for when she'd gotten into this relationship. "You should have called me."

"Yes, Sir."

"You call me whenever you deviate from your normal routine, so I know where you are, and I don't have to go to your work looking for you."

"Yes, Sir."

He took a moment to prepare himself for the next conversation they needed to have. "Tell me what happened today with your boss."

She jerked, but then began to speak. "He gave me a project and said he needs the report on his desk first thing tomorrow, but he'd already given me five other large tasks that needed my attention. Then, he forwarded his phones to me for most of the day. I brought everything home with me, thinking I could work on it after dinner." She gasped. "I left everything in my car. I—"

"You'll get it in the morning."

"But." She stopped herself. "Sir, I can't lose my job."

"If you lose your job, we'll find you another one."

Ali bit her bottom lip. He knew she wanted to argue with him, but also knew it would only land her in more trouble.

"I know you saw the files in the car earlier. I had a private investigator look into Jacobson."

She didn't say anything.

"Even if I don't find anything on him, you won't be working for him much longer."

Her head came up, and then she forced it down again. "Sir, I—"

"Allison, I will not have you working for someone who abuses you. No one deserves that."

He could feel the tension radiating off her. "Tell me what's going on in that head of yours."

"If I lose my job, I won't be able to support myself," she said.

"That isn't a problem. You're already staying here. You have no real need for your apartment. That should free up enough of your funds until you find a new position."

"Then Bradley will hate me even more."

He was going to kill his son.

Taking a calming breath, he lifted her chin, so she was looking at him. "This isn't about Bradley. Or your mom. Or anyone else for that matter. I've told you before. I want you in my bed. Not occasionally. Every night."

She held his gaze. "What if you get sick of me or need your space?"

Something pulled at his gut. She thought he'd get sick of her? "Sweetheart, I've yearned for you for two years. If I need some space, or you do, this house is huge. You can keep the other room if you want, so you have a space that's your own."

Something flashed in her eyes. Guilt? Fear? Maybe a mixture of both.

"Tell me."

"My mom. She—she agrees with Bradley."

It took him a moment to process what she was saying. "She thinks you're after my money?"

Ali pressed her lips together and closed her eyes. He gave her chin a gentle squeeze, letting her know it was okay. Whatever it was, it couldn't be as bad as she thought it was.

She didn't open her eyes. "Mom thinks I've landed myself a sugar daddy."

He dropped his hand, and she opened her eyes to look at him, all her emotions clear on her face. Her mother was a piece of work. "What your mother, or Bradley, or anyone else thinks of our relationship doesn't matter. What matters is how we feel about it."

She lowered her head to his lap. "I don't know what to do."

He knew she wasn't only talking about her mom now. She had an apartment she couldn't stay in because of her neighbor, her boss made her job something she dreaded going to every day, she'd embarked on a new relationship dynamic with him only to have to deal with his son's judgment, and now she was adding her mother to the mix. And that didn't take into consideration she was also dealing with her menstrual cycle, something he'd learned way too much about raising a teenage daughter.

Daniel ran a hand over her hair. "I want you to let it go tonight. Tomorrow morning, you are going to go into work and do the best you can. If your boss starts to harass you, I want you to call me immediately."

"Yes, Sir."

They sat there for a while, him stroking her hair, letting go of all the stress the day had caused for both of them. He wasn't exactly looking forward to what had to happen next, but it needed to be done.

Raising her head, he waited for her gaze to meet his. "Remove all your clothing except your panties. You may leave those on."

* * *

Daniel rose from the bed, leaving her kneeling on the floor. He walked into his closet, and she knew what was coming. She'd screwed up today. After everything that had happened at work, she'd thought she could drop by her house, get the things she needed, and be back at his house in no time. Then, her mother showed up.

Ali got to her feet and began removing her clothes. She knew the only reason he was allowing her to keep her panties on was because she'd told him she'd started her period. Otherwise, she had no doubt she would be naked.

Folding her clothes and placing them on the floor a few feet away, she returned to stand beside the bed with her head bowed. He strolled out of the closet with wooden paddle in one hand and a ball gag in the other.

She'd known discipline was coming. He'd spanked subs he'd played with at the club for less and they had no agreement outside of the designated play. She was his. His to pleasure and his to punish. But the ball gag...

He placed both the paddle and the gag on the bed, then returned to where he'd been sitting before on the edge of the mattress. Her heart was going a mile a minute. Had her misstep warranted being gagged?

"I brought the gag in case you wanted to use it to stay quiet," he said, as if reading her mind. "The choice is yours."

She glanced at the gag and thought about what he'd said. This was not going to be a pleasure spanking. It would hurt and not in a good way. If she cried out, Bradley and her mom might hear her. The gag would muffle the sound.

Even knowing this, she couldn't do it.

"Thank you for offering, Sir, but I would rather not be gagged."

He nodded. "Across my lap, then."

Over their short time playing together, he'd flogged her, poured hot wax on her, tied her up and teased her, but this was the first time he'd punished her.

She placed her knees on the bed and lowered herself across his lap. Resting her head against the mattress, she fisted the covers, preparing herself.

Daniel shifted, adjusting her where he wanted her. Then, he rested the paddle on her thighs. "Do you know why you're being punished?"

"Yes, Sir," she mumbled against the blankets. "I didn't call to let you know I was deviating from my schedule."

"The last time you kept things from me, I told you there'd be consequences if it happened again."

The memory of their conversation in the kitchen felt like ages ago. She'd told him about her boss, and he had in fact told her there would be consequences the next time she kept things from him. When she'd decided to run to her apartment after work, she hadn't thought about calling him. She hadn't thought it would be a big deal. In hindsight, she could see her error. "Yes, Sir. You did."

"I won't make you count out loud tonight out of respect for our house guests."

It was something and she'd take it. "Thank you, Sir."

He brought the paddle to her ass. "You will take twenty hits of my paddle."

Tears were already beginning to sting her eyes and he hadn't even done anything yet. She'd seen the relief in his eyes when he'd walked into her apartment. He'd gone to her work looking for her. She'd caused him distress. She would take his punishment, whatever it was. "Yes, Sir."

Her words hung in the air for a long moment, and then he lifted the paddle and brought it down hard on her backside. She pressed her lips together, trying to stay quiet as he landed another blow to her flesh.

By the tenth hit, her ass was burning. She buried her face in the covers, biting the fabric as tears streamed down her face.

Eventually, he stopped, his hand coming to rest on her hot cheeks.

She didn't move.

He ran a hand over her head. "Allison, look at me."

Relaxing her jaw, she let the blanket fall from her mouth and opened her eyes to look at him. He swiped at the tears running down her face. "You did well."

She held his gaze for a long moment. "I'm sorry. I didn't mean..."

Daniel continued to brush at the moisture on her cheeks. "Come here."

Rolling to her side, he helped her to sit up. The new position put pressure on her ass, reminding her of her punishment.

He wrapped his arms around her, tucking her head beneath his chin. His lips grazed the top of her hair as he held her, letting her cry. It wasn't only the physical pain she cried about, but also the weight of disappointing him. She should have called him, or at least sent a text.

Her tears began to ebb and her breathing returned to normal, matching its rhythm to his. "Feeling better?" he asked.

"Yes, Sir."

He tilted her chin up and gave her a soft kiss. "Get yourself ready for bed. I'm going to make sure everything's locked up for the night."

Ali nodded and got off his lap. Her backside was still burning, but she knew it would be. He hadn't held back when he spanked her, and she would still feel it in the morning.

She took her time in the bathroom washing her face, brushing her hair, and taking care of business. Remaining in only her panties, she headed back into the bedroom and crawled into bed.

The sound of people talking drew her attention, but they were far enough away she couldn't make out what they were saying or even who they were. She figured one had to be Daniel but was the other one Bradley? Or worse, her mother?

The urge to throw on a robe and investigate was there, but she pushed that notion back where it came from. Daniel had told her to get ready for bed. And while he hadn't specifically told her to wait for him in bed, it had been implied and she wasn't about to disobey him again. Not only couldn't her bottom take it, but neither could her heart.

It felt like an hour before the bedroom door opened and Daniel walked through, although it was probably more like ten minutes. His gaze landed on her in his bed and from the look on his face, she knew she'd made the right decision.

He strolled to the hamper and began removing his clothes. His back was to her, and she watched as his muscles flexed with each movement.

When he turned around, he caught her staring. A small smile pulled at his lips. "Roll onto your stomach. I want to put some cream on your ass before bed."

Ali did as he requested, carefully getting into position.

He moved one side of her panties out of the way and rubbed the cream into her backside, then did the same to the other side. She bit the inside of her cheek. Even though he wasn't pressing hard, it was still tender.

Returning the cream to the nightstand, he went into the bathroom. She stayed where she was while he was gone. Part of her didn't want to move because every time she did, her sensitive bottom scraped against the sheets. The other part wanted to stay there to give the cream time to soak in. It wouldn't do any good if she rubbed all of it off on the sheets.

She was still in the same position when Daniel emerged from the en suite. He walked to his side of the bed, pulled the covers back, and lay down. "Come here."

Without hesitation, Ali moved closer to him, turning on her side so she could rest her head on his shoulder. He circled his arms around her, holding her tight. She could hear his heartbeat beneath her ear, and she let the steady beat relax her. "Good night, Sir."

He pressed a kiss to the top of her head. "Good night, sweetheart."

CHAPTER 26

The sun wasn't up yet when Daniel crawled out of bed the next morning. Ali was sleeping soundly, the covers tucked under her chin as high as they could go.

After a few minutes in the bathroom, he slipped into his swim trunks and made his way out to the pool. The morning air was brisk, and he wasted no time tossing his towel onto one of the lounge chairs and diving into the water.

One of the things Daniel loved most about swimming was how he could either push himself until his muscles ached and his lungs burned, or he could glide through the water and let his mind drift. This morning, he needed to blow off some steam, so he pushed himself hard. He didn't stop until his lungs felt like they were going to burst out of his chest.

Resting on the edge of the pool with his forearms pressing against the cool tile, he watched the sun rise over the back of his property. It was a new day, and he knew it was going to come with a new set of challenges. Ali's boss needed to be dealt with. He'd cleared his calendar for the morning and was going to spend the time going through the folder Peter had sent him.

Normally, he'd stay at the house to do that, but he feared that would be a bad idea. Ali's mom was an unknown factor. He didn't know enough about her to get a read on her next move, which meant he needed to be cautious.

Zelda Foster thought her daughter had landed herself a sugar daddy. Something he didn't think had the same negative connotation in Zelda's mind as it did in Bradley's. From what Ali had shared with him, her mother tended to bounce from man to man, returning to Ali only when each relationship came to an end.

The French doors at the back of the house opened and he turned to see Bradley. His son had thrown on a pair of jeans and a T-shirt and was carrying two cups of coffee.

"You're up early," Daniel said.

His son placed one mug down on the table and took a sip of the other. "I could say the same for you."

Daniel swam to the other side of the pool and hoisted himself up. He climbed out of the pool, water dripping from his limbs. "I'm always up this early."

Bradley waited until Daniel dried himself with the towel and picked up his coffee before he said anything more. "I overheard you talking to Ali's mother last night."

Taking a drink of his coffee, Daniel waited to see what his son had to say. His conversation with Zelda Foster had been interesting to say the least.

"I can't believe she asked you how much you're worth."

The sad part was he could believe it. She looked at him, at his house, and she saw dollar signs. And if he read her right, she wasn't only seeing them for her daughter, but for herself as well.

When he didn't respond, Bradley ran a hand through his hair, making it stand up on end. He'd done that a lot growing up. Bradley was the most serious of his children and he often became frustrated when things weren't going the way he thought they should. "I did some digging—"

Daniel stopped with the mug halfway to his mouth. "The next words out of your mouth better not be, I did some digging on Ali."

A guilty look crossed his face.

"Bradley."

"Look, I know you're probably mad."

Daniel narrowed his eyes at his son. "Probably?"

"Okay, I knew you'd be mad, but I was concerned. You're my dad and—"

"And I can think and act for myself. I'm not feeble and senile, yet."

"Dad, would you listen? Please?"

"If you're going to try and convince me again that Ali's after my money, then you're wasting your breath."

"No." Bradley blew out a breath. "I mean, I still haven't made up my mind about her yet, but I'm more concerned with her mom."

So was Daniel, but he didn't say it.

"Ali's mom...she's...well, she's almost a ghost."

"A ghost?"

Bradley rolled his eyes like he had when he was a kid. "A ghost. She has next to no work history. I can't find any record of her buying a house or renting an apartment for the last twenty years, and her credit rating is zero."

Daniel processed that. No work history could mean two things. She was either working and getting paid under the table, or she was getting money by other means. He tried not to think what those other means might be.

The woman he saw last night hadn't looked strung out on drugs. In fact, aside from the drinking, she seemed well put together. Older than Ali, sure, but she took care of herself. Zelda Foster wasn't living in back alleys and eating from a dumpster.

"Who, at her age, has a zero credit rating and no work history."

Bradley said it as a statement, not a question, but Daniel answered it anyway. "I don't know."

"I bet Ali does."

Daniel narrowed his eyes at his son. "Watch yourself."

Bradley blew out another breath. "She has to be getting money from somewhere."

He couldn't disagree with that. Zelda Foster showed up on Ali's doorstep every time one of her relationships du jour ended. It was possible she hitch-hiked her way from wherever she was, but what about food?

Glancing over his shoulder, he looked toward his bedroom where Ali was still sleeping. Did she know where her mother was getting her money, or had she learned long ago not to ask? Knowing Ali, he was betting on the latter.

Daniel turned back to his son. "I'll talk to Ali about it. For now, though, I want you to stay out of it. We have enough problems right now without adding to them."

"Did you look over the file?" his son asked, switching subjects without blinking.

"No. Not yet."

Bradley nodded. "If you need any help..."

"Thanks."

Slinging his wet towel over his shoulder, Daniel checked his watch. He needed to grab a shower and wake Ali. They had to pick up her car at her apartment this morning. "Are you going to be hanging around the house today?" he asked his son.

"Yeah, I'll be around."

"If you want something to do, keep an eye on Zelda and make sure she doesn't get into anything. I need to head into the office and Ali has work."

His son relaxed his shoulders. "I can do that."

Nodding, Daniel turned to go, leaving his son to enjoy the rest of the sunrise on his own.

* * *

SOMETHING soft brushed against the inside of Ali's thighs. It worked its way higher, and then it was between her legs, brushing over her clit. She tried to press her legs together to ease the ache growing low in her belly, but there was an obstacle in her way.

She groaned, irritated she couldn't put pressure where she needed it most when the pressure on her clit increased. Her eyes flew open.

Daniel stared down at his hand between her legs. She tried to reach for him but realized her arms were secured above her head.

Arching her back, she gasped as he drove her higher toward her peak. She could feel her climax knocking on the door. How long had he been touching her before she'd woken up?

He increased his speed, making her pussy pulse with pleasure. His eyes never left hers as he drove her higher with nothing but his fingers. The need to release so close she could taste it.

"Do you want to come?"

"Yes, Sir." The words came out breathy. She sounded desperate and she was.

He didn't give her permission right away, making her wait. "Come."

With permission given, she let go, letting her body have what it desired. He gave her the pressure she needed to send her flying. A high-pitched whine pealed from deep in her throat as she rode the wave of her climax.

Daniel didn't remove his fingers until the last ripple of her orgasm dissipated, then he leaned down and captured her lips with his.

As he continued to kiss her, she realized he was already dressed. She gazed up at him as he hovered over her, her arms still tied to the headboard.

He smiled. "Good morning."

"Good morning, Sir."

Daniel chuckled. "How's your ass feeling this morning?"

"A little sore."

He nodded. "You need to shower and get ready, so we have time to swing by your apartment and get your car."

Her car. And her project. She'd almost forgotten.

She tried to pull her arms down, but they were still in the ropes. He untied her, kissing the inside of each wrist as he freed them.

With one last kiss, he rolled off her and stood. "Your things are in the closet." He nodded toward his big walk-in closet that was almost as big as the bedrooms in her apartment. "I'm going to get breakfast started."

After he left the room, she scrambled into the bathroom to shower. She usually spent several minutes standing under the spray trying to wake up, but she didn't need to do that this morning. Daniel had taken care of waking her up in the best possible way.

The warm feeling in her chest grew as she washed and dried her body. He made her feel loved. Wanted. Needed, even. When it was only them, she felt as if she were the most important person in the world to him. She'd never had that before.

Going to his closet, she walked in to find all her clothes on one side. Her suits for work were hung up, along with her T-shirts. Her jeans and leggings were stacked neatly on three shelves. For some reason, seeing her stuff there, mingled with his, had her close to tears. She loved him so much, had for a long time, but she never thought anything would happen between them. Not like this. This felt like a dream. One she was afraid she'd wake up from.

Taking a moment to get hold of herself, Ali removed her favorite suit from the hanger and got dressed. When she opened the bedroom door, she could smell cinnamon. Her mouth watered as she made her way into the kitchen.

Daniel was putting cinnamon rolls onto a large plate when she strolled into the kitchen. He heard her and turned. His gaze raked over her, male appreciation in his eyes as a slow grin pulled at his lips. She knew exactly what he was thinking.

She walked toward him, and he opened his arms, welcoming her into his embrace. He pressed his lips to the top of her head before tilting her chin up to give her a proper kiss. "Take a seat. I'll bring everything over."

Bradley came in while they were eating. He grabbed a plate, plucked a cinnamon roll from the serving dish, and sat down. "Morning."

"Morning." She gave him what she hoped to be a friendly smile before going back to her breakfast. They were on a time crunch this morning and the last thing she needed was to be late to work. Her boss was already going to be ticked off because she didn't have his report finished. Her only hope was that he would come in late. Another hour or two and she'd have it done.

As they were cleaning up, her mother made an appearance. She was dressed, and her hair and makeup were done, something Ali had never seen from Zelda this early in the day. Typically, the first twenty-four hours after her mother's return were all about wallowing. It was rare she even brushed her hair, let alone styled it.

"How's everyone on this beautiful morning?" Zelda asked the room at large as she helped herself to coffee.

"We're good, Mom." Ali paused. "What are you doing up this early?"

Her mom giggled. Giggled.

Ali frowned, but her mom didn't notice.

"It's a beautiful day. Why would I spend it in bed?" Zelda went to the refrigerator, opened it, and removed the milk. "Are those cinnamon rolls? They smell divine."

Before Ali could think of anything to say in response, Daniel stepped in. "Help yourself to the cinnamon rolls. Ali and I need to get to work, but Bradley will be around if you need anything."

Her mom waved a dismissive hand. "Oh, don't worry about me. I'm sure I'll find something to keep myself busy."

Daniel placed a hand on the small of Ali's back. "Come on. We need to get going or you're going to be late."

That got her moving. She grabbed her purse, and they hurried out the door, leaving Bradley and her mother alone in the house.

Once they were in the car and heading into the city, Daniel spoke, "Did your mother get any type of inheritance from your grandmother?"

Ali shook her head. "No. Grandma didn't have much, but what she did have she left to me."

He nodded.

When he didn't say anything more, she asked, "Why? Did she say something to you?"

Daniel glanced at her before returning his attention to the road. "She did, but that doesn't have anything to do with my question. Not directly, anyway." He paused as he took the exit ramp. "I'm more concerned with her transient lifestyle. Where does she get her money when she's not with you?"

"Her boyfriends," Ali said right away. She'd seen how her mom used the men she was with. Zelda Foster had no shame. She'd seen her mom talk a man she'd known less than a week into taking her to Paris.

"What about after the relationship ends?"

It took her a moment to put the pieces together as to what he was asking. "You mean how does she get to me from wherever she was?"

He nodded.

That was a good question and one she'd never asked. She'd always assumed her mom had some access to money, but Ali realized she had no idea what it was. "I don't know. When my mom shows up on my doorstep, it's like a whirlwind. And by the time I get my head wrapped around it, she's usually found another guy and is off again."

"How does she meet these men?" Daniel asked.

She shrugged. "Lots of places. She met the last one at a bar. The one before that at a park. Then there was one she met doing yoga outside my apartment. He was visiting one of my neighbors." Ali sighed. "That was a little awkward."

"I imagine so."

They pulled into her apartment complex. He parked and came around to open the passenger's door for her. "Thank you."

He stood at her side while she unlocked her car and threw her purse onto the passenger's seat. The day was warming up nicely, but she felt a chill move through her. Daniel noticed and pulled her into his arms. He rubbed his hands along her back, warming her from the inside out. She wanted to stay right there forever.

But she couldn't. She had to go to work. "I need to go," she mumbled against his dress shirt.

He lifted her chin and pressed his lips to hers. "I'll see you later, sweetheart."

She went up on her tiptoes, giving him another peck on the lips before sliding into the driver's seat. He stood patiently as she started the car and backed out.

Before she turned out of the parking lot, she glanced into her rearview mirror. He was still in the same spot, watching her. Something pulled at her heart, and she sat there an extra moment, taking in the sight of him. "I love you," she said to herself. He couldn't hear her, but saying it helped.

She turned onto the road toward the hospital. The sun climbing in the sky let her know she didn't have much time to prepare herself.

It was a little after seven when she got to her desk. That gave her an hour to get the report finished before her boss made his appearance. Hopefully, she could get it done by then.

Wasting no time, she logged onto her computer and got to work. She'd done all the research yesterday, so this morning was about compiling the data.

The clock on her computer seemed to mock her. It ticked closer and closer to eight while her fingers flew over the keyboard.

At eight o'clock, she was still working on the report. The end was in sight, but she needed at least another fifteen minutes.

Ignoring everything around her, she concentrated on what she was doing. She didn't unforward her phone, even though she was supposed to, because she couldn't have any distractions.

As she was typing the last paragraph, summing up the information, Ali heard the elevator ding. Without looking, she knew it would be her boss.

Clicking save, she waited a moment for the computer to do its thing before hitting print. Her heart was racing as his footsteps got closer. He stopped at her desk, glaring down at her. "Do you have my report?" he snapped.

She tried to hide the fact she was shaking. "On the printer, Mr. Jacobson."

A flash of surprise crossed his face before he schooled his features. He marched to the printer and removed the papers. After a quick scan, he went into his office, shutting the door behind him.

It was then she realized he'd wanted her to fail.

CHAPTER 27

*D*aniel made himself comfortable and began going through the file Peter had sent the day before. It was thorough. When he'd told the man he'd wanted to know everything about Grant Jacobson, including what he ate for breakfast, he hadn't expected quite this much detail.

Peter hadn't only run a background check on Jacobson. He'd also followed him. Or at least, had him followed. There were huge eight by ten photos of him sitting in restaurants, going into what Daniel assumed was his condo building, even one of him working out at the gym.

After doing a quick scan of the documents, Daniel began going over the information, line by line. He didn't want to miss anything, so he took his time. Kevin was holding his calls and he had no pressing matters to attend to unless Ali called. By the end of it, he was going to know more about Grant Jacobson than he did any other human being.

It was almost eleven o'clock when he stumbled onto what he was looking for. Seven years ago, Grant Jacobson had lived in a neighborhood where Daniel had purchased a house to flip. He remembered it well. It was the only house he'd ever sold without completing the renovations.

He'd lost his entire crew, too. Not because of anything he did, but because they'd been harassed by the neighbors. Or more to the point, one neighbor. The man who'd lived next door, one Grant Jacobson.

Daniel had only spoken to the man face-to-face once because he never seemed to be home, but Jacobson had made working conditions unpleasant for his crew. He'd leave them notes nit-picking that they'd left something in his yard, things there was no way they'd left, and then he'd 'return' them to the house they were working on.

While annoying, it wasn't the only issue. Somehow, the man had organized with the other neighbors and would often take up all the parking on the surrounding streets. Trucks delivering supplies couldn't get through, and when they stopped on the street long enough to unload their goods, the police would show up and force them to move. It had been frustrating and eventually, one by one, his guys quit.

Daniel set the papers down on his desk and leaned back in his chair. The man was a colossal pain in the ass then and now.

What he didn't understand, however, was why Grant Jacobson was targeting Ali. She was his assistant. She was there to help him. The house renovation, he could almost understand. Some people didn't like the noise or mess that came with construction. But that didn't explain his attitude toward Ali.

He took a quick break, then continued reading. It wasn't until he got to the details of the man's work history that something stood out. Peter had not only provided where he'd worked, his position, and his length of time there, he'd also, somehow, gotten his hands on performance reviews. The ones about him and the ones he'd written about his employees.

Daniel couldn't believe what he was seeing. One name kept cropping up over and over again. Brenda Renyolds.

Not wanting to wait for Peter to do more digging, Daniel did a quick internet search. Her picture came up, much as it had for Jacobson.

He followed the links to her work history, and sure enough, her list of employers mirrored Jacobson's for the last eleven years. And when he looked at the dates, Jacobson always started first, then three to six months later, she would start at the company as well.

Although he didn't know the connection between the two, he now understood what was going on. Grant Jacobson was trying to get Ali to quit. And while he wasn't averse to that plan given the situation, he wasn't all for Jacobson continuing whatever this was he was doing. Ali was able to leave. He'd take care of her. But what about the next person he did this to?

With that in mind, he found the names of the people who'd been in the positions Brenda Renyolds had filled prior to her arrival at the companies. The first, a Kylie Brant, had been twenty-three and fresh out of college. She was currently working for an insurance company in Chicago.

The second, Mary Ortega, was a paralegal working at a small law firm across town.

But it was when the search came back on the third woman that his heart sank into his stomach. He clicked on Michelle Olson's obituary.

As he read over the post, short as it was, he wanted to see Grant Jacobson pay. The date of her death was less than three months from the date Brenda Renyolds started working in Michelle Olson's previous position.

He dug a little more and found some old social media posts that were still up. As he scrolled through, the need to do something grew. She'd been a single mom and as he read the comments on her last post, one about her kid's dad taking her daughter away from her because she didn't have a job, he realized her death hadn't been an accident. Michelle Olson had committed suicide.

Daniel wanted to punch something. Preferably Ali's boss, but he wasn't sixteen anymore. It wasn't hard to put two and two together. Her job loss had led to her losing custody of her child and that all led back to Grant Jacobson.

Out of curiosity, he read over Michelle Olson's performance review and felt as if he were having déjà vu. Unable to complete tasks on time. Refusal to follow through on instructions. Unavailable to meet the requirements of her position.

Given what Ali had told him and what he now knew of Michelle Olson's situation, he could see the pattern. Ali was killing herself trying to meet Jacobson's demands. He made her nervous. And as a single mom, Michelle Olson wouldn't have been able to drop everything at a moment's notice and attend functions outside of office hours.

Daniel switched gears, wanting to look more at the first company where Jacobson and Brenda Renyolds worked together. Upon closer inspection, he realized Brenda had started as a clerk according to her online résumé. Her previous job had been along the same lines. Then, two months after starting, she'd been promoted to an administrative assistant for Jacobson. And surprise, surprise, her performance reviews while she worked under Jacobson were glowing.

But what he found even more interesting were the huge gaps in her work history. She'd quit when Jacobson left each company, then she didn't work again until he hired her.

Sitting back in his chair, Daniel tried to put the pieces together. Brenda Renyolds was beautiful. She had long blond hair in the picture, looked to be in her thirties, and had, what looked to be, deep brown eyes.

Was she a long-lost sister or something? They didn't look alike in any way, so he didn't think that was the connection. He needed more information.

Shooting Peter a text, he waited for the man to respond.

Daniel – Do you have any additional information on Brenda Renyolds? A connection between her and Jacobson?

It took less than a minute for Peter's response to come through.

Peter – Pictures 10 and 17.

Snatching up the eight by ten photos Peter had included in the file, Daniel found number ten and number seventeen. The first was of Jacobson sitting in a restaurant with a woman. The second was of the two of them going into a building together. He hadn't thought much of either of them before, but he now realized the woman was Brenda Renyolds.

As he studied the pictures, he began to pick up on the little things. They were sitting a little too close at the restaurant. The flirty smile on her face as she looked at him. And the way the tips of his fingers touched her back as they were going into the building. These two were lovers.

The pieces began to fall into place. Grant Jacobson was inserting his lover into a position where he always had full access to her...and on the company's dime.

He had no idea if Brenda Renyolds was a good administrative assistant, but he was now realizing that wasn't the biggest qualification required to work for Jacobson. Ali had assured him Jacobson hadn't made any sexual advances toward her, so in some twisted way her boss must have some sense of loyalty to the woman he was sleeping with. That didn't, however, solve Daniel's problem.

A quick look at his clock told him it was almost noon. Grabbing his suit jacket, he slid it on and headed out the door. He hadn't seen Jacobson in seven years, and he was thinking a second meeting was long overdue.

* * *

ALI WAS SITTING at her desk, trying to work on the list her boss had sent her when she heard the elevator ding. The footsteps grew louder at the person's approach, and she looked up, expecting to see one of the other executives or their admins. Her heart rate kicked up a notch when she saw Daniel. "What are you doing here?"

"I came to take you to lunch."

She glanced at her boss's door, then back at Daniel. "I don't usually take lunch until one."

"Is that a rule?" he asked, quirking an eyebrow.

"No. It's just..." She looked toward her boss again and her eyes grew wide as he got up and headed toward her. He was looking down at a piece of paper—most likely something else he was going to have her do. Like what he'd already given her wasn't enough.

"Ms. Foster, I need you to—" He took in Daniel standing in front of her desk. She knew he was trying to figure out if Daniel was someone he needed to impress or not. Despite Daniel not wearing a tie, he had an air about him that screamed he was important. "Do we have an appointment?"

"No." Daniel never took his gaze off her boss. "I'm here to take Ali to lunch."

Her boss's mouth twisted in displeasure. "I don't think Ms. Foster will be taking a lunch today." He turned his attention to her. "She's rather busy."

Ali didn't know how to respond. On one hand, her boss was...well, her boss. But her backside was still feeling the effects of her punishment the night before. There was no way she was going to tell Daniel she couldn't go to lunch with him. Besides, she needed a break. She'd been going nonstop for almost five hours.

Forwarding her phone, she picked up her purse and stood. "I'll be back in an hour, Mr. Jacobson."

"Ms. Foster, I need those numbers compiled today." The tone in her boss's voice sent a chill through her body. She felt like a misbehaving child being scolded for needing to eat.

Daniel placed a hand at the small of her back, silently showing his support as she answered. "I should have them on your desk before the end of the day."

Then, before she could lose her nerve, she walked away.

It wasn't until the elevator doors closed behind them that all the air rushed out of her lungs and the panic began to set in. What had she done? He was going to make her pay for that. She'd come back to even more work and she was barely treading water as it was.

Daniel's arms wrapped around her, pulling her against his chest. "Breathe, sweetheart. You did good." He kissed the top of her head. "It will be okay. I promise."

They reached the bottom floor and the elevator doors opened. He ushered them outside, guiding them to his SUV.

She didn't ask where they were going. All she cared about was she was away from her boss. The demands of her job were weighing on her and she had to be honest with herself. She wasn't sure how much longer she could keep it up.

They pulled up in front of a restaurant she wasn't familiar with. He parked the vehicle and helped her out of the passenger seat.

The restaurant wasn't fancy. There was even a sign stating they should seat themselves.

She waited in a booth while he went up to the front to place their order. He came back with a tray full of food and two plates. "Eat."

Ali did as she was told. She reached for the macaroni and cheese, and then some of the shredded meat.

Daniel loaded his own plate with several items and began eating. He waited until she'd taken several bites before asking, "How was your morning?"

"Stressful as usual, but not any more than usual."

He nodded. "Do you know a woman named Brenda Renyolds?"

Ali thought about it, but the name didn't ring a bell. "I don't think so. Should I?"

"I believe she'd the reason your boss is trying to get rid of you."

She stopped eating. "What do you mean, trying to get rid of me?"

Instead of speaking, he showed her the files, pointing out the relevant details. She read through the performance reviews and felt both sick to her stomach and vindicated at the same time. It wasn't her. It wasn't anything she'd done or didn't do.

Then he turned the page. "She was their replacement."

Ali met his gaze across the table. "All three times?"

He nodded.

She sat, her gaze unfocused as she processed the new information. It's not as if she'd had any warm, fuzzy feelings for her boss before, but now she felt disgusted by him. How could he have done this, not once, but three times? And what about his wife?

Daniel pushed her plate toward her. "Eat your food."

Picking up her fork, she took another bite, not really tasting what she was eating.

"I want you to quit."

She stopped mid chew.

"You can come work for me, either permanently or until you find something else."

As much as she hated it, her mom and Bradley came to mind, and it must have been written all over her face. "I—"

"I don't care what other people think and you shouldn't, either. You and I know the truth and that's all that matters." He took her hand in his. "I won't stand by and watch you being mistreated. Your well-being is my responsibility until you decide you no longer want it to be. And even then, I'll still be there in any capacity you need me."

Tears sprang to her eyes. He meant every word. She knew he did. She could feel it deep in her soul. "What if I always want it to be your responsibility?" It wasn't quite the same as saying I love you, but maybe it was more.

He studied her face for a long moment. "Are you sure?"

"I'm sure." Ali hadn't been surer of anything in her life.

Daniel held her hand on the drive back to the hospital administration building. He walked her to her desk and gave her a quick kiss. "Put in your notice, but don't be surprised if he dismisses you right away."

"Yes, Sir." They were alone. Her boss's office door was open, but he was nowhere in sight.

"Call me when you leave. No matter what time. I'll meet you at home."

Ali nodded.

He gave her one last kiss, then turned to go, leaving her alone.

She took the next thirty minutes to gather her personal belongings and get her desk in order. Daniel was right. As soon as she put in her notice, Grant Jacobson would let her go. Based on what Daniel had found, it was what he'd wanted all along.

When her boss strolled in at one thirty, he glared at her. "Did you enjoy your lunch, Ms. Foster?"

Trying not to react to the ire in his voice, she plastered a smile on her face. "I did." Then, she handed him her resignation letter. It was short and to the point. There was no sense in drawing it out. She couldn't change the outcome and Daniel was right, she didn't deserve the way she was being treated.

"What's this?" he demanded as he read over the letter. When he looked up, there was a look of satisfaction on his face. "I knew you couldn't cut it."

Ali didn't bother to argue the point.

"I won't have you making a mess of things for your replacement. Gather your things and exit the building." He picked up the phone on her desk and hit the button for security. "Yes, I need someone to escort Ms. Foster from the premises."

Her heart raced as he disconnected. He stood, arms crossed, watching her as she placed all her personal items in one of the boxes the printer paper came in.

She was ready to go before security got there, but he refused to allow her to leave, insisting he wanted someone to walk her down to make sure she left the building.

Ten minutes later, security arrived. It was Charles, an older gentleman who'd always been nice to her. She walked toward him, meeting him halfway. "Could you walk me out?"

"Of course." He shot a quizzical look in her boss's direction but followed her when she continued toward the elevator. Pressing the button for the first floor, he waited for the doors to close. "Is everything okay, Ali?"

"Yes. Everything's fine." And despite her worry this would only confirm Bradley's opinion of her, she was okay. More than okay.

CHAPTER 28

Daniel swung by the office to pick up some paperwork, then made his way home. He was halfway there when Ali called. "You were right. He had security escort me to my car."

"Are you all right to drive?" he asked. She didn't sound distraught, but he wanted to make sure.

Ali sighed. "Yeah. My emotions are all mixed up at the moment, but I'm good."

He nodded even though she couldn't see him. "I'll meet you at home."

"Okay." She paused. "Daniel?"

"Yes?"

She hesitated. "Thank you."

He had a feeling that wasn't what she'd been about to say, but he let it go. "Drive safe."

They disconnected as he took the exit ramp off the highway. Seven minutes later, he was pulling into his garage.

The house was silent when he made his way inside. Bradley's car was parked in the garage, so he knew at least he was there somewhere.

After a quick search of the downstairs, Daniel went to the French doors at the back of the house and glanced outside. His son was sitting at one of the patio tables, his laptop open in front of him, but he kept looking up.

Daniel followed his line of sight and wasn't surprised to see Zelda lounging poolside. What he hadn't expected to see was her wearing one of the skimpiest bikinis he'd ever seen. The woman had a body, he'd give her that, but he felt no attraction. And by the look on his son's face, Bradley didn't either.

Opening the door, he stepped outside. Bradley's head turned, a look of surprise on his face.

"Decided to work by the pool today?" Daniel asked.

At the sound of his voice, Zelda turned her head. She smiled and sat up, her breasts nearly falling out of her top with the movement. "Get done with work early today?"

"I did." That was a lie. He'd brought his work home with him, but she didn't need to know that.

Bradley answered Daniel's original question. "Zelda wanted some sun, so I decided to join her while I worked."

"He's such a spoilsport. I tried to get him to put down that thing and enjoy life a little, but he insisted he had to work." She pouted and while he knew she meant it to look cute, it didn't work.

Speaking of work... "Ali said you move around a lot. Were you planning to stay in the St. Louis area for a while?" Daniel asked.

She didn't seem bothered by the subject change. "I haven't decided yet. I never know how long Ali will need me."

Daniel schooled his features. Zelda wasn't the first gold digger he'd encountered. Now that she knew he had money, she was going to milk it for everything she could, even if it meant using her daughter to do it. "I wasn't aware you and Ali were all that close."

Zelda waved her hand in dismissal. "She's over dramatic sometimes. We talk all the time. We're like sisters."

It was hard not to react to that one. Sisters his ass. "Even still, I'm sure you'll be needing your own place and a job soon enough if you're planning to stay in St. Louis. Bradley here can help you with the job search and maybe you can take over Ali's lease. It's a nice apartment, despite the noisy neighbors."

He saw her mind working, but before she could formulate a comeback, he heard Ali's car come up the drive. "Excuse me."

Bradley opened his mouth to say something, but promptly shut it. His son wasn't stupid. Anything he wanted to say, he wasn't going to say in front of Zelda.

Ali was climbing out of her car when Daniel walked out. He came to her side and pulled her into his arms. He knew how hard it had been for her to quit. "I'm proud of you."

She chuckled. "Is it wrong I feel relief and anxiety at the same time?"

"Not at all."

He had many of the same mixed emotions. Not about her or her quitting her job, but about their future. She'd said earlier she wanted her well-being to always be his responsibility. Was he reading too much into that? Looking into her eyes now, he didn't think so. He knew the connection they had despite their age difference.

Cupping her face in both hands, he pressed his lips to hers. "I—"

The door that led to the house opened. Not releasing her, he turned his head to see who it was. Bradley. "Get out."

His son blinked but backed away and closed the door behind him.

Daniel returned his attention to Ali. "Now, where was I?"

She leaned into his hand. "You were kissing me."

The feel of her mouth moving against his brought home what he'd been about to say before their interruption. Not moving his lips far from hers, he met her gaze. "I love you."

Her fingers stilled on his back. "I love you, too."

A slow smile pulled at his lips a moment before he kissed her again.

They broke apart a few moments later, and he carried her things inside. Bradley was standing by the kitchen island, waiting for him. "Dad, can I talk to you?"

"I'll take this to our room," Ali said, lifting the box of her things out of his arms.

Once she disappeared down the hall, Daniel turned on his heel and headed toward his study. Bradley followed, closing the door behind him. "Did Ali lose her job?"

Ever the observant one, his son. "She turned in her resignation."

"Did you find something out about her boss in the file?"

Daniel walked to the other side of his desk and sat down. "He's been having an affair for at least the last seven years. Every time he gets a new job, he hires her to fill a recently vacated position."

Bradley processed that information. "How did you figure that out?"

Removing the papers from his briefcase, Daniel laid everything out for his son.

"So that's why he was treating Ali like shit? To get her to quit so he could give his mistress a job?" Bradley asked.

"Yes."

Bradley tucked the papers back into the folder. "What are you going to do?"

His son knew him well. There was no way he was going to let this go. It was bad enough what Jacobson had done to him years ago, but after treating Ali the way he had and leading another woman to feel as if suicide was her only option, he was feeling the need to make the man pay. "I have plans." Then he steepled his fingers together as he sat back in his chair. "Now, tell me what's been going on with Zelda today?"

Bradley shared how his morning had gone keeping track of Ali's mother, including how she'd made herself very much at home.

After they were finished, Daniel went to find Ali. The work he needed to do could wait and he wanted to make sure she really was okay.

It wasn't hard to locate her. The raised voices coming from her old room carried throughout the house.

Or, should he say one raised voice. The only one yelling was Ali.

The door to the room was open when he approached, which helped the sound to carry. Bradley was a step behind him, also taking in the women's conversation.

"I told you, I don't know, Mom. It just happened. Daniel and I will figure it out," Ali said.

Zelda laughed. "There's nothing to figure out, honey. He's loaded. You just need to dress yourself up a little nicer and before you know it, you'll have a nice ring on your finger. You'll be set for life."

"Mom, it's not like that."

"Of course it's like that. Men like him expect to be used. They get it. It's part of the deal." Zelda paused. "I mean, you must be a decent lay. I've seen the way he looks at you."

Ali gasped. "I can't believe you said that."

"Why not? It's true. You have that man wrapped around your finger. Now, all you need to do is make it all legal so if he loses interest somewhere down the line, you'll get a nice paycheck out of it."

He heard a loud smacking sound followed by a shriek from Zelda. He rushed into the room. Zelda sat on the end of the bed, a hand cupping the left side of her cheek. They both looked up at Daniel's and Bradley's entrance.

Daniel didn't wait for an explanation. He'd heard all he needed to hear. "I think it's time for you to pack your bags and leave," he said to Zelda. He'd tried to give her the benefit of the doubt because she was Ali's mother, but this was too much. Ali didn't need this.

"I'm not sure what you heard, but—"

"I know what I heard." Daniel moved to Ali's side, placing a hand on the small of her back. "I also know you had no qualms asking me about my finances last night after knowing me for less than three hours."

"What?" Ali stiffened under his hand. He hadn't shared the conversation he'd had with her mom the night before when he'd gone into the kitchen.

"I wanted to make sure you're good enough for my baby girl."

"Even if I was dirt poor, I'd be willing to do whatever it took to make your daughter happy. My bank account has nothing to do with that."

"I'll drive her into the city," Bradley said.

Moisture filled Zelda's eyes, but Daniel wasn't sure he could trust it was real. She was used to using manipulation to get what she wanted. "I don't have anywhere to go."

Daniel turned to Ali. "Get your mother's things together for her." Then he addressed Zelda. "Ali's apartment is paid for till the end of the month. You can stay there until then. After that, you'll have to make other arrangements."

Realizing she wasn't getting anywhere with him, she turned her attention to Ali. "You'd throw your mother out on the street."

Ali stopped what she was doing and faced her mom. "I love you, Mom. I always have, but you can't stay here."

He knew by the look on Zelda's face that Ali had never pushed back against her mother's wishes before.

Ten minutes later, Zelda slid into the passenger's seat of his son's car. Bradley looked at his dad. "Are you sure it's a good idea to let her stay at Ali's apartment?"

"No," he answered honestly.

Bradley nodded.

Ali held out a hand and dropped a key into his son's palm. "She'll need that to get in."

Closing his fingers around the key, Bradley placed it in his pocket. Then he got in his car, started the engine, and backed out of the garage.

* * *

ALI BURIED her face in Daniel's chest the moment Bradley's vehicle was out of sight. She couldn't believe her mom had said those things. Okay, she could, but that didn't make it any better.

Daniel's arms enveloped her, holding her tight against him. His lips brushed against her hair. "It's been an eventful day."

That got a chuckle out of her. "Yes, it has." Ali let the warmth of his arms seep through her. She hadn't been able to lean on anyone like this since her grandmother died.

"Why don't we see if they left us any cinnamon rolls? I think we could both use a little sugary comfort food."

She nodded and went to separate herself from him, but he tucked her into his side, keeping her close.

There were three cinnamon rolls left. They each ate one and left the third for Bradley. The sugary goodness tasted great, but it didn't do much to change the way she was feeling inside.

Daniel cleaned up their dishes, then led her to the couch. He sat down, stretching his legs out, before guiding her onto his lap. She leaned against his chest, her head resting on his shoulder.

They sat for a while, neither saying anything. She knew he was waiting for her to speak, but she didn't know what to say. Her mom was...well, her mom. And her boss? She hoped she never had to cross paths with the man again.

"I'm trying to be patient and let you gather your thoughts," Daniel said. "But I need you to talk to me. Stop trying to hold it all in."

Ali tried to put into words what she was feeling. "I feel like I'm a bad daughter, even though logically, I know I'm not." She paused and he let her go at her own pace. "Every time she shows up, I think, I hope, things will be different, but they never are. Except, this time."

He laced their fingers together in a silent show of support.

She looked out the large window, watching a set of birds as they danced around each other on the grass. Two cardinals. Male and female. Each knowing their role. Each knowing their place.

Ali knew her place. It was with Daniel. Not because he was wealthy, but because he took care of her. He loved her. "I never knew why my mom hopped from boyfriend to boyfriend until today. She told me she left my dad because he refused to give her the type of life she wanted. That she felt she deserved."

He gave her hand a squeeze but didn't say anything.

"For all these years, I thought my dad abandoned me. That he didn't want us, but that wasn't the case at all. She'd used him, thought by getting pregnant, he'd marry her."

Daniel pressed his lips to her temple. "Do you know who your dad is?"

She shook her head. "No. She never told me."

"They have those DNA tests now. If you wanted to try and find him, we could explore our options," Daniel said.

"Can I think about it?"

"Of course."

They sat in silence for another few minutes before she spoke again. "What am I going to do for a job?"

"You don't have to work at all if you don't want to."

She bit her bottom lip, worrying it between her teeth. Her mother's words ringing in her ears. As much as Ali knew she wasn't with Daniel for his money, people would perceive it that way, especially if she didn't have a job of her own.

When she didn't say anything, he turned her to face him. "Did you mean what you said earlier about wanting me to always be responsible for your well-being?"

"Yes."

He kissed the tip of her nose. "Then let me take care of you. I have the means and I don't care what anyone else thinks. You can take care of the house, and if you want to help me with my flips, you can do that as well." He tucked a strand of hair behind her ear. "I want you to be happy."

She cupped the back of his head and brought his mouth to hers. "I love you," she whispered.

"I love you, sweetheart." He kissed her again, this time slow and deep. It was only the sound of the garage door opening that had them pulling apart. He gave her one last kiss, then settled her against him once more.

A few moments later, Bradley strolled it. He took in their position on the couch and lowered himself into a chair on the other side of the room. The weariness in his features said it all.

"You okay?" Ali asked.

Bradley met her gaze. "Yeah." He paused, then met her gaze. "I owe you an apology."

She stilled.

"I guess I owe you both an apology." Bradley ran his hands over her jeans. "I've met a lot of people at the law firm. A lot of not-so-great people. Some who are only out for themselves and don't care who they hurt in order to get what they want." He met her gaze from across the room. "I thought you were that type of person, Ali. I thought..." He blew out a breath and ran a hand over his face.

"Did something happen with my mom?"

Bradley laughed, but there wasn't anything joyful about it. "Today has been...enlightening, to say the least. And the last couple of hours? Well, let's just say I'll never forget them."

"I'm sorry."

"You have no need to apologizes, Ali. You've been nothing but nice to me since I got here, despite the way I treated you."

"I get it," Ali said. "You want to protect your dad."

"That's no excuse. I'm getting jaded in my old age."

Daniel snorted.

"Anyway." Bradley stood. "I'm gonna go grab a shower before dinner."

"Wait," Ali said, making him pause. "What happened with my mom?"

"I took her to get some groceries, then dropped her at your apartment." He shivered and she didn't think it was because he was cold.

"She made a pass at you, didn't she?"

He held her gaze for a long moment but didn't answer. "I'll be back in twenty minutes, then I'll get dinner started. It's the least I can do on my last night."

"You're leaving?" Daniel asked.

Bradley walked backward toward the stairs. "Don't want to outstay my welcome. You may not invite me back." He winked at them, turned, and headed toward the stairs.

CHAPTER 29

The next day, Daniel took Ali to get the rest of her things from her apartment. Her mother was there and tried to get Ali to reconsider. Not the moving in with him part. The kicking her out part.

Ali held firm, though, and he couldn't have been prouder of her. Zelda Foster was a master manipulator. She tried to play on Ali's emotions, even pulling out the 'I gave birth to you' card.

He was tempted to say forget it and just buy Ali replacements for all her things, but he knew there were some items he couldn't go to a story and buy. Her art for one. Ali had talent. Her eye for color was spot-on and he wanted to nurture that side of her. He was already thinking what he'd need to do to convert one of the upstairs rooms into an art studio for her.

It took over an hour to pack up the rest of her stuff and load it into his SUV. The furniture was going to stay—at least for now. If Zelda decided she wanted to take over Ali's lease, she wouldn't have to worry about furnishing the place. If not, they'd donate anything Ali didn't want to keep to charity.

As they were pulling away, he noticed the tears in Ali's eyes. He drove to a nearby parking lot, found a spot, and pulled her into his arms. "It's okay."

"Why does she have to be that way?"

He rested his cheek against her head as she nestled her face into the crook of his neck. "I don't know."

"I've tried to be a good daughter. Even though she wasn't there for me as a kid, I tried to be there for her."

"Sometimes there's no pleasing people, no matter what we do. It's the way she is. Nothing you do or say is going to change that. It's up to her to decide if she wants to change the way she lives her life."

Ali snorted.

They sat there, Daniel in no hurry to get home. He'd called Kevin at the office and let him know he wouldn't be in today. Luke was finishing up the renovations on one of his current flips, and he had a stack of new listings to go over at home. If he missed out on a deal because Ali needed him, he was okay with that.

Over the next two weeks, he and Ali found their footing. She spent some time every day while he was at work painting in her new studio. He enjoyed coming home from work to see her latest creation.

But he could tell she was getting restless. Kim was at work all day and so was he. She wanted to do something besides take care of the house, which she was already doing an excellent job of. By the end of the first week, she'd cleaned out the cabinets in his kitchen and reorganized them. She'd also made a good dent on deep cleaning the first floor. The only thing she had left to tackle was their bedroom suite.

As they were lying in bed that evening, her limp and warm from their play, he approached the subject. "Would you like to come into work with me tomorrow? I need to take a tour of my active projects. I wanted to get your opinion on a few things."

Ali had been playing with the hair on his chest, but she stopped her movement and looked up at him. "You want my opinion on your flips?"

"I do." He ran his hand down her side, enjoying the feel of her soft curves beneath his palm. "I have five projects going right now and they need to be visited throughout the construction process. I can't always get out to them as often as I'd like and I thought if you were still wanting a job, you might be interested in assisting me."

She didn't respond right away. "Are you making up a job for me?"

His chest vibrated under her hand. "Yes." She opened her mouth to say something, but he continued before she could. "But it would also help me out. I'd like to take on more projects, but I don't have the time to stay on top of them. One of the hardest parts of a successful flip is keeping things moving and on budget. Luke is good at watching the budget, but he can't be everywhere at once. Despite how much he tries."

"So what would you want me to do, exactly?"

There was skepticism in her voice, but he could work with that. "You'd drive around to all the properties a couple times a week to make sure things are getting done. If it's not, then you would address it."

"Address it how?"

He smiled. "You'd come to me or Luke and let us know so we can get it fixed."

"That doesn't sound too difficult," she said.

"You might change your mind about that."

She'd started playing with his chest hair again. "Why's that?"

"Because occasionally you'll come across neighbors like Grant Jacobson."

Her hand stilled again. He'd told her what he'd found. They'd spent an entire evening going over the file together. "Have you decided what you're going to do?"

He knew she was no longer talking about his flips. "The plan's already in motion."

Once he'd gotten Ali moved in, Daniel had reached out to Peter and they'd discussed how Daniel wanted to proceed. He wasn't allowing Grant Jacobson to get off with a slap on the wrist. He wanted to see that bastard's entire life crumble around him.

One of the best things about the city was there was almost always a building nearby with a direct line of sight into another. It was only a matter of finding the right angle. And having the right equipment.

"You're not doing anything illegal, right?" she asked.

"No."

She nodded and cuddled closer.

He kissed the top of her head. "Good night, sweetheart."

Ali hummed. "Good night."

Two days later, Daniel came home from work to find Ali in the kitchen. He set his briefcase on the counter, grabbed her by the waist, and turned her to face him.

She circled her arms around his neck and smiled up at him. "Dinner's almost ready."

"Hmm." He covered her lips with his, letting his tongue explore her mouth. She tasted like strawberries. He snaked his hand under her skirt and palmed her ass.

Ali moaned, the sound going straight to his cock.

Daniel broke the kiss long enough to switch off the burner before turning her to face the island. He placed his hand on her back and pushed her down so she was bent over the counter, her ass level with his waist.

Lifting her skirt, he ran his hands up her thighs to her panties. The smooth pink satin framed her cheeks.

He dipped his fingers between her thighs, running them over her already damp panties. "Have you been a good girl today?"

"Yes, Sir."

"Hmm." He removed his fingers and gave her ass a gentle swat.

Her forehead dropped to the cool granite as he massaged the flesh he'd abused. She spread her legs, giving him better access to her body, and he took full advantage.

"Did you miss me today?" He slid his fingers beneath her panties, then retreated, teasing her.

"Yes, Sir. Very much." She'd stayed home today, tending to the house, while he'd been at work. Cassandra and her fiancé, Jesse, were coming to visit tomorrow and Ali wanted to make a good impression. Especially after what had happened with Bradley.

Hooking his thumbs into the sides of her panties, he lowered them over her hips and let them drop to her ankles. He kneeled, lifting her feet one by one to untangle the fabric, and tossed it aside. "You won't be needing these anymore tonight."

He kissed his way up her legs until he reached the apex. Her sex was glistening, and he took a long lick.

Ali moaned as he explored her with his tongue. The sounds she made went straight to his cock. He'd missed her today. Yesterday, she'd come into the office with him. They'd researched listings and he'd introduced her to his team. Not having her there today affected him more than he thought possible.

Standing to his full height, he popped the button on his slacks and lowered his zipper. His erection strained to get free, wanting inside her.

He pushed his pants and underwear down, letting them pool around his ankles. Holding on to the base of his cock with one hand, he guided it to her entrance.

The warm heat of her sucked him in and he groaned. He pushed inside, feeling her muscles contract. Soft and wet and all his.

He began to move, watching as their bodies came together. All the times he imagined being with her, he'd never thought it would be like this.

Pressing against her back with one hand, he gripped her hip with the other as he felt his orgasm drawing near. He didn't want this to end so soon, but he also had plans for them tonight.

Sliding his hand forward, he found her clit. "Let go."

A soft whine left her lips as he began to circle her clit with firm pressure. Her fingers flexed, unable to find purchase against the slick granite.

His balls tightened as he continued to thrust. Just when he thought he wouldn't be able to hold on, her pussy clamped down like a vise grip on his cock. That and her high-pitched cry released the last hold he had on his control, and he came with a loud grunt.

* * *

AFTER REGAINING the use of her legs, Ali went to the bathroom to clean up while Daniel put the finishing touches on their dinner. He hadn't returned her panties, which meant cool air brushed against her sex with every step she took.

They chatted about their day as they sat at the table, then curled up on the couch to watch a movie. Daniel wasn't as big of a TV buff as she was, but he enjoyed a good movie.

Halfway through the movie, his hands began roaming under her skirt. At first, they kept to the inside of her thighs, coaxing her to open her legs.

As the movie progressed, he went higher, lifting her leg over his to spread her wide. His fingers skimmed her pussy, barely touching her and making her want more.

By the climax of the movie, she was a bundle of nerves. He'd been careful not to do more than brush her clit for the last half hour.

Her chest rose and fell as the ache between her thighs grew and her fingers dug into his legs. The music on the screen rose and he finally touched her clit. "No coming yet," he whispered in her ear.

She bit her lower lip, closing her eyes, trying to hold back her orgasm. He loved to tease her, to draw out her climax, and as much as it drove her crazy, she loved it, too.

Something happened on the screen and the music picked up its tempo. Daniel increased his as well. His fingers moved in time with the music, using it to increase the sensations pulsing through her body. She was hanging by a thread and then...

The music reached its climax, and she heard him whisper, "Now."

Relief and pleasure hit her as she let herself go. She came so hard she screamed out. Not a little whine, but an all-out scream. He'd been teasing her for over an hour and everything she'd held onto, everything she felt over that time, left her in a rush.

It took her several minutes to hear anything but the blood pounding in her ears. He kissed the skin above her collarbone. "Feel better?"

"Mmm."

His chest vibrated beneath her.

She leaned her head back and looked up at him. "I love you, Sir."

He cupped the side of her face and lowered his mouth to hers. The slow kiss had her wanting to melt into him.

Picking up the remote, he turned off the television. The movie was over. She'd completely missed how it ended. Not that she'd been paying attention much after he'd started playing with her anyway.

He helped her to stand, then got to his feet and led her around the house as he turned off the lights and set the security alarm. They made their way into the bedroom, and he slowly stripped off her clothes, placing little kisses on the skin he exposed. By the time she was naked, her body was humming again.

She stood there as he removed his own clothing, a cool breeze blowing in from the window, chilling her. It was the end of April in St. Louis and while the days were warm, the nights could still hold a chill. Tonight was one of them.

Daniel lifted the blanket on the bed for her. "Get under the covers."

She settled herself on the bed, pulling the covers beneath her chin. Since they'd been together, she'd realized how different their body temperatures ran. He was always hot, and she was always cold. When he was in bed with her, it didn't matter. He'd hold her close, or she'd cuddle by his side, and everything was perfect. On her own, though, she tended to huddle under the covers, seeking warmth.

Throwing both their clothes into the hamper, Daniel joined her in bed. "Come here."

Ali closed the distance between them, letting his heat seep into her.

He rubbed his hand along her arm several times. "Better?"

"Much."

Daniel chuckled. "It's not that cold in here."

"Says the man who had no problem diving into forty-degree water." She'd woken early one morning last week and found him swimming in the pool. The thermometer on the deck read sixty degrees, so she knew the water had to be cooler than that. She'd bent down to test the water with her fingers, and it had felt like ice cubes.

He gave her a squeeze, his chest vibrating again with amusement. "You get used to it."

Ali remained quiet. He might get used to it, but she didn't think she ever could. She even thought the water at her old gym was cold and they kept it heated to seventy.

Kissing the top of her head, he shifted beneath her. "Get some rest. We have a big day tomorrow."

They'd talked about Cassie and her fiancé coming to visit. Ali was nervous, but she was trying to keep an open mind. Daniel said Cassie was happy for him and couldn't wait to meet Ali. She was hoping the visit would go well.

But at least she wasn't the only one in the hot seat. This would be the first time Daniel was meeting Jesse, Cassie's fiancé.

Beneath the covers, Ali crossed her toes.

CHAPTER 30

Daniel was up at five the next morning. He tucked Ali in, making sure she wouldn't get cold, and headed upstairs to the gym. Going to the treadmill, he set the machine for a brisk walk.

After warming up, he ran five miles, his feet pounding hard on the rubber. Releasing some of his pent-up energy felt good. Granted, he could have gotten that release another way, but he wanted Ali to sleep as long as possible. She'd been on edge the last couple of days. Making a good impression on Cassie was important to her.

He wiped the sweat from his face as he slowed to a walk, then downed the remaining contents of his water bottle. Ali was still asleep when he returned to the bedroom. He stood at the foot of the bed, watching her for a few moments. There was something about seeing her in his bed, her chest rising and falling under the covers, that brought a smile to his face.

He tried not to think about the time he'd wasted. Time they could have spent together. He'd thought for sure he couldn't give her what she needed, not long term, but he was beginning to reconsider that notion. She was happy, which was all he wanted for her. Forcing his feet to move, he headed into the bathroom.

As he rinsed the soap from his body, he heard the soft click of the bathroom door being closed. His cock twitched with the knowledge Ali was in the room.

Wanting to see what she would do, he kept his back turned. It wasn't until he felt lips press against his spine that he looked over his shoulder to meet her gaze. Her blue eyes sparkled back at him as she placed another soft kiss to his skin. "Good morning."

He dipped his head under the spray, rinsing the last of the soap away before he turned to face her. Not speaking, he cupped her face and brought her mouth to meet his.

Her fingers slid up his chest and circled his neck, tangling in his hair. She arched her body against his, straining to get closer as he deepened the kiss.

Releasing her lips, he trailed kissed down her neck. Her eyes flittered open. "May I touch you, Sir?"

"Yes." He scraped his teeth along her collarbone, smiling when her breath hitched in her throat.

Ali reached for the soap with one hand and twisted it between her palms to create a good lather. She placed the soap back on the ledge before taking hold of his erection with one hand and cupping his balls with the other. He closed his eyes, letting himself enjoy what she was doing to him.

She ran her hand along his cock from base to tip in a steady motion. Her other hand massaged his balls with such care, rolling them around in her palm. He groaned and captured her lips with his again.

As she continued to touch him, he kissed her harder, tilting her head back as far as it would go, demanding she kiss him back with as much passion as he felt. Never had a hand job felt so good and he knew it was because it was her.

He ripped his mouth away from her, quickly rinsed off the important parts of himself, and turned off the water. As wonderful as her hand felt, he wanted to come inside her.

Turning her toward the bench along the back wall of the shower, he bent her over so her hands could rest on the seat. He ran a hand over her ass before going lower and pushing his fingers inside to see if she was ready for him.

She pushed back against his hand, and he couldn't wait any longer. He lined himself up and plunged his cock into her welcoming pussy.

Neither of them lasted long. He was on the edge before he'd thrust inside her and she wasn't far behind. A little attention to her clit was all it took to send her soaring.

Once they were both breathing normally again, he dried them both off so they could get ready for the day. Ali fretted over what to wear, so he picked something for her, not wanting her to stress about something that didn't matter.

He made his way into the kitchen to start breakfast while she finished her hair and makeup. When she finally made her appearance, she still looked uncertain.

"What's wrong?" he asked.

She shrugged. "I want her to like me."

He gave her a brief kiss. "She'll love you."

Ali looked less certain, but she let it go. "What's left to do?"

"You can set the table."

Without another word, she went to get the plates.

They were halfway through breakfast when the sound of a car coming up the driveway drew their attention. Ali stilled, her fork halfway to her mouth. "They're here."

Daniel nodded, then went back to his breakfast. "Finish eating. It will take them a few minutes to park and get their things."

Cassie and Jesse were only staying one night. The company was heading into their busy season, and he had to be back in the office on Monday morning.

A car door opened and shut. Daniel glanced at Ali. She was eating, but her gaze was on the front door.

He placed a hand over hers. "Relax."

She nodded.

The sound of another door opening and closing, then he heard his daughter's voice. He pushed away from the table and stood. "I'm going to let them in."

"I'll clean up," Ali said.

Daniel couldn't deny he was a little nervous himself. What Jessica had heard kept playing in his thoughts. Being in the lifestyle, he tried not to read too much into it. Jessica could have been mistaken. Maybe something fell or there was a movie on television.

There was also the possibility his daughter and her man enjoyed a little kinky fun. While it was hard to think about his daughter's sex life, he would be a hypocrite to have a problem with it.

He opened the door as they were walking up the front steps.

"Daddy!" his daughter yelled. She dropped her purse and ran into his arms.

Daniel hugged her close. He hadn't seen her in person since Christmas.

She took a step back, keeping one hand on him, and motioned her fiancé forward. "Dad, I'd like you to meet Jesse."

Jesse dropped their bags and held out a hand. "It's good to meet you, Sir. Cass has told me so much about you."

His firm handshake and the way he met and held Daniel's gaze boded well for Jesse. "It's nice to finally meet you." Daniel looked at his daughter. "I figured you both would be more comfortable in one of the upstairs bedrooms."

Cassie went up on her tiptoes and pressed a kiss to his cheek. "Thanks, Dad."

Daniel chuckled and led them inside. "Go put your things down, and I'll introduce you to Ali." They began to move toward the stairs when he stopped them. "Have you had breakfast?"

Jesse was the one to speak up. "We ate before we left."

"That was over two hours ago." He met his daughter's gaze again. "Pancakes?"

Her face split into a smile. "I'll never turn down your pancakes."

When Daniel walked into the kitchen, Ali had cleaned up their dishes and was already getting the griddle ready for pancakes. He walked up behind her, wrapped his arms around her waist, and kissed the side of her neck. "I guess you heard."

"I don't blame her. Your pancakes are pretty awesome."

By the time Jesse and Cassie made their appearance, Daniel was pouring batter onto the griddle. He finished what he was doing, wiped his hands on a dish towel, and turned to make the introductions. "Ali, this is my oldest, Cassie, and her fiancé, Jesse."

"Hi—"

Ali didn't get out more than that before Cassie was embracing her.

"Oh."

"Sorry," Cassie said, releasing her. "I'm just so happy to finally meet you. Dad's been telling me all about you and I can't wait to get to know each other."

Ali smiled. "He's told me a lot about you, too. I'm glad you were able to come visit us this weekend."

Daniel flipped the pancakes as Ali and Cassie talked. His daughter made herself comfortable, sitting cross-legged on one of his kitchen chairs as she asked question after question. Jesse hung back, content to let the women talk.

Staking the pancakes on a single plate, Daniel carried them to the table. Then, he went back for the syrup and butter.

Cassie put three pancakes on her plate, slathered them with butter, and drowned them in enough syrup to cover twenty pancakes. She cut herself a bite, stabbed it with her fork, and brought it to her mouth. Her eyes closed and she released a contented sigh. "I'd forgotten how good these are."

Daniel laughed.

"You're so lucky," Cassie said to Ali. "You get to eat Dad's pancakes every day if you want."

They all chuckled.

"Thank you for the breakfast, Mr. Ross," Jesse said.

"You're welcome."

They spent the rest of the morning sitting around the table talking. Daniel watched the interactions between his daughter and Jesse to see if he noticed any red flags. Granted, it had only been a few hours, but so far, he'd seen nothing. Cassie seemed perfectly at ease. She even made a few jokes at her fiancé's expense, and Jesse took it in good fun.

"What do you say to some shopping?" Cassie asked Ali after they'd finished lunch.

"Sure. Did you have somewhere in mind?"

His daughter got a mischievous look in her eyes. "I need to do some shopping for the honeymoon, and I could use a female perspective."

It didn't take a genius to know what type of shopping she was talking about. "Um, wouldn't you feel more comfortable doing that with your friends?"

Cassie sighed. "No. They tend to have a one-track mind."

Daniel stood. He might be open-minded when it came to sex, but even he had his limits. "Jesse, maybe you could help me with some things out back while our girls are gone."

"Sounds good."

As the women were getting ready to leave, Daniel pulled Ali aside. "Have fun and call me if you need anything."

"Try not to give Jesse too much grief. He seems like a good guy."

Daniel grinned but didn't answer. He gave her a brief kiss, then backed away.

"Ready?" Cassie asked.

Ali gave him one last look, then turned to his daughter. "Yeah. Let's go."

* * *

ALI TURNED TOWARD THE HIGHWAY. "What exactly are you looking for?" When Cassie said she wanted to shop for the honeymoon, she wasn't sure if she meant lingerie or toys. Or both. "There are a few different places we could go."

"I want something special to wear on our wedding night. It would be nice if it can fit under the dress, but it doesn't have to." Cassie twisted in her seat, so she was angled toward Ali. "My best friend, Brie, thinks less is more. She showed me a picture of a model in nothing but strings. I just don't think that's what I want to wear on my first night as Jesse's wife, you know?"

"Did you tell her that?" Ali felt like she needed to tread carefully. She'd only known Cassie for a few hours.

Cassie leaned back against the headrest. "Brie's a lot more open about that kind of stuff than I am. She has no problem putting herself on display." She paused. "It's not like I don't want Jesse to see me naked or anything. Of course, he does, but it doesn't feel right to wear something like that on our wedding night. I want something...classy."

That made sense. "I'll take you to one of my favorite lingerie stores. They have a variety of options."

Smiling, Cassie refocused on the road as they headed into town. She was quiet for a while and Ali didn't try and force conversation.

When they arrived at the store, Cassie went straight to a rack of baby doll nighties. She removed one and held it against her front. "What do you think? Too much? Not enough?"

The lingerie had solid panels over the breasts and a solid pair of panties but was shear pretty much everywhere else. It was pink, and while pretty, maybe not the right color for a wedding night. "Do they have it in white?"

They searched the rack and the ones surrounding it, but there was no white. Cassie was bummed.

Ali placed a hand on her arm. "It's okay. We'll find something else you like even better."

A few minutes later, Ali saw a similar baby doll. The best part was, it came in white. She held it up to Cassie. "What about this one?"

"Oh, that's pretty." Cassie looked over at Ali with a sheepish look on her face. "I think Jesse would like me in this one."

Ali was thinking if Jesse was anything like Daniel and the other men she knew at the club, he'd like it a lot. Unlike the first baby doll Cassie found, this one had lace cups and a hook in the front. "I'm sure he would like you in anything." She paused and then added, "Or nothing at all."

"True." Cassie giggled. "Nothing I wear to bed stays on very long."

It was then Ali noticed Cassie's bracelet. It was a silver band with a heart, but inside the heart was a keyhole. "That's a unique bracelet."

Cassie blushed. "Thanks. Jesse gave it to me."

"May I?" Ali asked, motioning toward the bracelet.

Lifting her arm, Cassie showed Ali the bracelet.

Trying not to be too obvious, she inspected the metal ring around Cassie's wrist. There was no clasp, which meant it unhooked at the heart. She was willing to bet Jesse had the key.

Keeping in mind who she was talking to, Ali smiled and removed her hand. "Did you want to look for anything else while we're here?"

They ended up spending another hour in the store. Cassie found three more outfits for her honeymoon, although these weren't quite as sweet and innocent-looking as the first.

After loading their things in the back of the car, Ali headed toward the house.

"I hope Dad and Jesse haven't killed each other while we were gone."

Ali chuckled. "Are you worried?"

"Dad can be..."

When she didn't go on, Ali chimed in, "Protective?"

"Yeah." Cassie sighed. "And I love him for it, but Jesse's good to me. He takes care of me."

"Your dad wants the best for you. If that's Jesse, then there's nothing to worry about."

"Speaking of Dad." Cassie shifted in her seat again to look at Ali. "James said you and Dad met at a club."

Ali nodded, not sure if she was going to like the direction the conversation was going. She and Daniel had discussed what they'd tell his children if they asked for more details on how they'd met. They'd both agreed to be as honest as possible without violating the privacy of the club or its members. "That's right."

"Did he approach you, or did you approach him?"

This, she could answer. "I work one night a week at the club and we met while I was working the coat check."

"Oooo. That sounds fancy. What kind of club is it?" She paused. "I mean, James made it sound like a dance club, but that doesn't sound like a place Dad would go. And most dance clubs don't have a coat check."

Ali was counting down the minutes until they reached the house. "It's a private club."

Cassie scrunched her nose up. "Like a stuffy cigar club or something?"

Instead of answering, Ali laughed.

Luckily, Cassie changed the subject. "He seems happy. It's been a long time since I've seen him smile so much."

Ali glanced over at her, not sure what to say.

"It was hard on him when he and Mom split up. He'd try to put on a good face when we came to visit, but I knew he was lonely." She sighed. "I know Bradley was worried about you being too young for him, but I just want him to be happy."

They pulled up to the gate and Ali put in her code. "He makes me happy, too."

Ali parked her car in the garage beside Daniel's, and they both made their way inside.

"I'm gonna put these in our room," Cassie said.

Once she bounded up the steps, Ali went in search of Daniel and Jesse. Since he'd said they were going to work on something out back, she checked there first.

She opened the French doors and found the two men sitting at one of the patio tables. They each had a beer in their hands.

Daniel saw her first. "You're back." She walked over to him, and he pulled her down to his lap. "Did you have a good time?"

Ali nodded and turned her attention to Jesse. "Cassie's upstairs putting her bags away."

He scooted the chair back. "I'll see if she needs any help."

Daniel's gaze followed Jesse as he went into the house.

"Well, what's the verdict?" Ali asked once they were alone.

Daniel snorted. "He'll do."

"Cassie's head over heels for him."

"I know." He took a drink of his beer. "He appears to be for her as well."

Ali debated whether to mention the bracelet, but she figured if he hadn't noticed it yet, he would eventually. It was better to get out in front of it. "I think they're in the lifestyle, too. Or at least dabble." She paused. "She's wearing a bracelet that has a key lock."

Daniel nodded.

When he didn't say anything more, she asked, "Are you okay with that?"

He met her gaze. "Be kind of shitty of me if I wasn't."

Placing a hand on the side of his face, she pressed her lips to his. "Did you want another beer? Or I could get you something from the liquor cabinet."

Daniel shook his head. "I'm good."

Getting to her feet, Ali went inside. She passed Cassie and Jesse on their way back out. "Did either of you need anything to eat or drink?"

"No, we're good," Jesse said, answering for both of them.

Ali poured herself a glass of lemonade and rejoined them on the back patio. They ended up spending the rest of the day lounging around the pool, talking about work and the upcoming wedding. Jesse and Cassie were hoping to get married this fall. They'd been dating for over a year and didn't want to wait any longer.

"I want to bind her to me in every way possible," Jesse said. He picked up Cassie's hand and brought it to his lips, kissing her engagement ring.

As she and Daniel lay in bed that night, Ali thought about her life and how much it had changed over the last month. She'd gone from pining after a man she thought didn't see her as more than a friend, to living with him and sharing his bed.

"You're thinking awfully hard about something." His chest rumbled beneath her ear.

"Thinking about how different my life is now compared to a month ago."

He hummed. "That it is."

His fingers traced circles on her hip, making her keenly aware of how naked she was. Cassie and Jesse had gone upstairs hours ago and after cleaning up from dinner, she and Daniel had retired to their bedroom as well.

"I spent many nights dreaming of you in my bed. Thinking I couldn't have you." He moved her to lie on top of him. "I wasted so much time."

She rested her forehead on his. "I'm here now."

"And you're going to stay."

"Yes."

Cupping the back of her head, he brought her mouth to his as he lifted his hips to press his erection against her sex. As they came together, she knew she was where she was meant to be.

CHAPTER 31

Daniel was in his office working at his computer three days later. Cassie and Jesse had headed home Sunday afternoon, promising to come back for a longer visit later in the summer when things weren't so hectic.

Ali was visiting two of his projects today but had promised to swing by the office with lunch before heading home. Having her work for him came with some definite advantages. She had an eye for detail he appreciated. She was also good at mediation, which he hadn't expected.

Monday she'd been at the Clawson house. It was a new project and Luke had found some issues that needed to be addressed before anything could get started. Daniel had asked his designer to meet Ali and Luke there, figuring it would be a run of the mill type of situation.

It wasn't.

As it turned out, there was asbestos in the floor tile. His designer wanted to tear it up. Luke insisted it was better to leave it and put the new flooring on top.

Ali said it had gotten heated before she stepped in and made them provide her with the numbers for each option. Then, she'd informed them she'd look at the long-term projections and let them know which direction they'd be going in for the project. Luke had been so impressed, he'd called Daniel and thanked him for sending Ali.

In the end, they decided to tear up the old flooring. Not because of the cost, but because Daniel didn't want it to become a problem later down the road. He hadn't decided if he was going to rent the house or flip it yet, but if he'd kept the flooring, his decision would have been set in stone.

A knock sounded at the door, and he yelled for whoever it was to come in without looking up from his screen. A whiff of cherries and lavender pulled his attention to the new arrival. "How'd the walk through go today?"

Ali strolled into his office carrying two bags. She walked around the desk, coming to a stop in front of him. He took the bags from her and set them on his desk. "They were framing the new bathroom and updating the plumbing in the kitchen."

He rested his hands on her hips and spread his legs to pull her closer. She was wearing a dark blue pants suit a few shades darker than her eyes. It pulled tight at her waist, showing off her figure. It also did great things for her ass—a view he very much enjoyed earlier that morning at the house.

"Are you hungry?" she asked.

"Starving." Her working for him also came with a few disadvantages...like how big of a distraction she was. If she was in the building, he wanted his hands on her.

Ali chuckled. "I meant for food."

"That, too."

She bent to kiss him. "I brought chocolate cake for dessert."

He kissed her again, relishing the taste of her. How had he gone so long without acting on his feelings? He was kicking himself for missing out on this every day for the last two years.

Unbuttoning her jacket, he ran his hands up her sides to rub his thumbs over her nipples. She closed her eyes and swayed into him as her nipples pebbled at his touch.

Daniel groaned when another knock sounded at his door. He dropped his hands back to her waist, not willing to stop touching her altogether. "Come in."

Kevin ambled in with another envelope. "This just came for you by currier. I had to beg him to let me sign for it."

Taking the envelope, he felt his pulse accelerate. It had to be from Peter. It was the same type of envelope as before. "Thank you, Kevin."

His assistant was about to leave when Ali stopped him. "I brought lunch. There's plenty to share."

"Thanks, but I'm heading out." He smiled. "I have a date."

"Oh," Ali said. "Have fun."

He smirked. "I plan to."

Alone again, Ali's gaze went to the folder. "Is that what I think it is?"

"Yes." He broke the seal on the envelope and pulled out its contents.

The first page was a note. "Everything is in place. All I need is your go ahead."

Daniel pulled Ali into his lap and flipped to the first photograph.

They say a picture tells a thousand words and as they made their way through the stack, that had never been more true. There were pictures of Grant Jacobson and Brenda Renyolds having lunch together, going into her building, and even sharing a kiss.

But those were only the beginning. The best and most damaging photographs were the shots taken through Jacobson's office window. Not only was he employing his mistress, he was also fucking her during working hours.

All the evidence was there. He'd broken company policy by employing someone he was in a relationship with, and he was cheating on his wife.

Daniel picked up his cell and pulled up Peter's contact information.

Daniel – Do it.

There was no response other than the little checkmark beside his message to let him know it had been read.

"What happens now?" Ali asked.

"Copies of these pictures will be in the hands of the hospital board by the end of the day. One's also being sent to his wife." Daniel tucked the pictures back into the envelope. "The woman needs to know the scum she married."

Ali was quiet.

"What is it?"

She met his gaze. "I should feel bad about ruining his life, but I don't. Does that make me a bad person?"

Daniel tucked a strand of hair behind her ear. "If that makes you a bad person, then I must be the devil. I want to see the bastard burn, but tearing down his career and his marriage will have to do."

"His wife's going to be devastated."

He did feel a little bad about that, but it wasn't him who'd cheated on her. "She needs to know."

Ali nodded.

Daniel patted her thigh. "Come on, let's eat."

Ali headed home after lunch and he tried to focus on the contract he was reviewing while he waited to hear back from Peter. It was a long afternoon.

At three o'clock, he couldn't take it anymore and decided to call it a day. Packing up his things, including the stack of pictures Peter had sent over earlier, he said goodbye to Kevin and headed to his SUV.

He was almost home when his phone dinged with a message. He pulled into his driveway, stopping at the gate, and checked his phone.

Done.

It was from Peter.

He released a loud breath and punched in his code. Jacobson's fate was now in the hands of the board and his wife.

Figuring they both needed to decompress, after dinner Daniel led Ali out to the hot tub. They'd only used it a couple of times so far, but he was hoping to change that.

She leaned back against him, her head resting on his shoulder. "It's so beautiful out here."

They'd watched the sun set and the moon rise in the sky. He'd bought this house after his divorce and while he'd come out to enjoy the stars once in a while, he'd never shared it with anyone before. "Quite different from the view in the city."

Ali hummed. "Very."

They lay back, watching the stars until he felt his skin begin to get that prune like consistency. "Ready for bed?"

She turned her head to meet his gaze. "Yes, Sir."

His cock, which had already been at half-mast having her naked against him, grew harder at her use of his title. He was tempted to take her there, but given they'd already been in the hot tub for way too long, he helped her out and dried them both off.

Leaving the towels on a nearby chair to worry about in the morning, he picked her up fireman style and carried her into their bedroom.

* * *

ONE OF THE biggest advantages to working for Daniel was not having to rush to the club after work. Okay, there were a lot of great reasons, but that was up there.

Ali met him at his office a little after four and they stopped to have dinner before heading to the club. He gave her a kiss before she headed off to the locker room to change into her outfit for the evening.

Daniel still let her pick her clothes on the nights she was working, and she was grateful for that. It was bad enough being exposed when he was at her side. She wasn't sure she could do it while she was in the lobby by herself.

Cooper met her upstairs and they went to work getting the playrooms set up. She laid out most of the requested toys, but Cooper adjusted the equipment. While she could probably move the tables and benches if she had to, it was much easier for him to do it.

They worked together, getting everything ready, then she headed downstairs to make sure the locker rooms were stocked. As she was coming out of the ladies' locker room, she heard someone talking.

She rounded the corner and ran into Katrina. Literally ran into her. If Ali had been wearing her heels, she could have fallen on her backside.

"Are you all right, Ali?" Katrina asked, reaching out a hand to steady her.

"Yeah, I'm fine." Her heart was beating faster than normal, but other than that, she was good. "I'm sorry. I didn't see you."

"It was my fault. I was distracted."

Ali took in the look on Mistress Katrina's face. She'd known the woman for over two years and Ali had never seen her so agitated. "Is everything okay?"

"Yeah." Katrina sighed. "Or it will be." She waved a dismissive hand in front of her face. "Nothing I can't handle." Then she changed the subject. "What all do you have left to do for setup?"

"Everything's ready except the front."

Katrina nodded, but Ali couldn't help but feel something was wrong.

"Are you sure you're okay, Mistress Katrina?"

Pulling back her shoulders, Katrina stood to her full height. "I'm sure." She glanced at the clock, then back at Ali. "Excuse me. I need to run upstairs."

Ali watched as Katrina walked up the stairs. She was still baffled by the exchange. Katrina was never distracted.

"Something wrong?" Daniel's voice pulled her attention away from Katrina.

"Yeah." She paused. "I mean, no. Nothing's wrong, Sir. I just ran into Mistress Katrina, and she seemed a little distracted."

"Distracted how?"

Ali shook her head. "I don't know. I think she was talking on the phone, but I didn't hear what was said."

"Well, I wouldn't worry too much about it. I'm sure Katrina has it under control."

"Yes, Sir."

"Isn't it about time for you to get out front?" he asked.

Looking at the clock, Ali realized how late it was. She was supposed to be out front by six thirty, and it was twenty-seven after. "Yes, Sir."

It took her less than five minutes to get the front organized and ready, which was good because members began showing up soon after. A little after seven, Daniel walked out of the club and opened the foyer door that led to the outside.

A woman around her age with beautiful auburn hair stepped over the threshold. She was wearing a long raincoat and tall black boots. He led the new arrival over to where Ali was standing. "Sarah, I'd like you to meet my submissive, Ali. She's one of the girls who works the coat check here at the club."

"It's nice to meet you, Ali." Sarah's shy smile spoke volumes. She was nervous.

"Welcome to Serpent's Kiss." When she didn't make any movement to remove her coat, Ali asked, "Would you like me to take your coat? Katrina tends to keep the club on the warm side since most of the submissives aren't wearing much."

Sarah laughed and removed her coat. Underneath, she was wearing what could only be described as a little black dress. It was tame compared to what some of the submissives walked around the club in, but it would raise some eyebrows if she wore it in public.

The club door opened again and Mistress Katrina made her way over. She extended her hand. "You must be Sarah."

"Yes."

"I'm Mistress Katrina, the owner of this fine establishment."

"Oh." Sarah's eyes widened in surprise. "Thank you for letting me come tonight."

"We welcome anyone who wants to indulge in the lifestyle safely and privately."

Sarah nodded. "Daniel went over the rules with me. Privacy is a big concern for me."

"You won't have to worry about that here. Relax and have fun. If you want to play, let Daniel know and he can find you a suitable Dom to play with."

"Thank you, Mistress."

"Call me Mistress Katrina."

"Yes, Mistress Katrina."

The first part of the night flew by. Then, as per usual, she was on her own for a while. It gave her time to read her book.

A few minutes after midnight, Daniel came to get her. "How was your evening?" he asked as he helped her with her jacket.

"I made it through five chapters of my book."

He laughed. "That boring, huh?"

"Five people came in and two people left between eight o'clock and eleven."

Daniel tucked her into his side as they walked out into the night. "My night wasn't much better. I was missing my submissive."

They reached the car and he opened the door for her. Instead of getting inside, she turned and slid her hands under his jacket. "I don't have to work tomorrow night."

"And I assure you I plan to take full advantage of that." He brushed his lips against hers and his hands went to her ass. "But the night isn't over yet."

A shiver of pleasure washed over her as she thought of the possibilities.

EPILOGUE

Two weeks later

Daniel opened his email to find something from Peter. He hadn't heard from the private investigator since his last text two weeks before. Not that he'd been expecting to. Things had been put in motion and it would take time for them to unfold.

The email contained two attachments. One was a link to a press release announcing the departure of Grant Jacobson from the hospital. The announcement was brief. There was no mention of the reason for his leaving, but he hadn't expected it.

The other to a court document that had been filed in civil court. Tabitha Jacobson had filed for divorce from Grant Jacobson. He scanned over the document and found this one was a little more interesting. The reason listed for requesting the divorce was infidelity. And she was seeking fifty percent of his assets, as well as their home and a nice sum in child support for their two children.

Daniel leaned back in his chair, steepling his hands in front of him. He hadn't known there were children involved, but it wouldn't have changed anything. It only added to Jacobson's sins.

The lawyer handling the divorce was listed on the paperwork. He picked up the phone and dialed.

"Masterson, Langley, and Bradshaw," the woman on the other end of the line answered.

"I'd like to speak to Jeffery Bradshaw."

"Is this about a case?" she asked.

"Yes."

The woman paused. "He's with a client at the moment. I can take your name and number and have him give you a call."

While it wasn't what he wanted to hear, he gave the woman his name and number, then moved on to his own work.

Jeffery Bradshaw didn't return his call until the end of the day. "Mr. Ross, I understand you're calling about a case?"

"That's correct. I understand you're representing Tabitha Jacobson in her divorce."

"I'm sorry, Mr. Ross. I can't discuss my clients or the cases I'm currently working on. I'm sorry—"

"I want to cover the cost."

There was a long silence on the other end. "I'm sorry?" This time, it was a question.

"Whatever Mrs. Jacobson owes you, now or in the future, I want you to send the bill to me."

"Are you a relative or something?" he asked.

"No."

"Then why?"

Daniel didn't want to get into what he'd found out or why he'd gone digging in the first place. "Let's just say I'm not a huge fan of Mr. Jacobson."

When Daniel didn't go on, Bradshaw took a different approach. "This could be a messy divorce. Lots of litigation. The cost could be quite high."

"I'm aware of that." Daniel paused to let that sink in. "Just send the bills to me and I'll make sure they're paid."

Again, there was a long silence. "What should I tell Mrs. Jacobson?"

He thought about it for a moment and remembered the conversation he'd had with Ali where he'd told her if she was a bad person, he must be the devil. A smile tugged at his lips. "Tell her she has a guardian angel." He wanted to say something along the lines of '*take him for everything he's worth*', but he reined himself in.

Daniel hung up the phone a few minutes later after giving Jeffery Bradshaw an address where to send Tabitha Jacobson's bills. He chuckled to himself, feeling a lot lighter knowing Jacobson wouldn't be able to try and back his wife into a corner and settle for less than she deserved.

Shrugging into his jacket, he shut his computer down and picked up his briefcase. Ali was home waiting on him, and he couldn't wait to see her.

There'd been no sign of her mother. No text. No phone calls. The woman was in the wind. And despite everyone and their brother being on social media these days, she had nothing. Bradley was right. She was a ghost when it came to her online presence.

Over the last month, Ali had begun leaving her mark on his home. It was little things. She'd added some candles to his living room and bought a dishtowel with some flowers on it to hang from his oven door. They brought a feminine touch to his house and it never failed to make him smile.

It had been years since he'd shared his space with someone else, but the little bumps they'd had were nothing compared to what he'd gained. She made his house feel like something more than a place he slept and worked and ate his meals.

Footsteps sounded on the steps and a moment later he saw her. She had her hair pulled back in a ponytail and some paint on her cheek.

Her smile lit up the room as she walked toward him. "Hey."

He wrapped her in his arms and brushed a kiss against her lips. "Hey."

"Dinner's in the oven. It should be ready in about twenty minutes. I just need to make the salad—"

Daniel cut her off with another kiss, letting his hands roam down her back to cup her ass. She melted into him, digging her fingernails into his back. "I can work with twenty minutes."

Then he picked her up and carried to his bedroom. There was a lot he could do in twenty minutes, and he planned on utilizing every second. Now, and for the rest of their lives.

✳✳✳

Want more of Daniel and Ali? CLICK HERE to read a bonus scene.

Ready for Cassie and Jesse's story? CLICK HERE to purchase Falling for the Boss's Son.

CAN'T WAIT FOR SHERRI HAYES' NEXT BOOK?

Let her know by leaving a review and telling her what you liked about
CLAIMING HIS KISS (SERPENT'S KISS #4)

ALSO BY SHERRI HAYES

<u>Finding Anna</u>

Slave (Finding Anna, Book 1)

Need (Finding Anna, Book 2)

Truth (Finding Anna, Book 3)

Trust (Finding Anna, Book 4)

Finding Anna Boxed Set (Books 1-4)

Indulge: A Finding Anna Novelette

Change (Finding Anna, Book 5)

<u>The Daniels Brothers</u>

Behind Closed Doors

Red Zone

Crossing the Line

What Might Have Been

Daniels Brothers Box Set (Books 1-4)

<u>Serpent's Kiss</u>

Welcome to Serpent's Kiss

Burning for Her Kiss

Longing for His Kiss

His Forbidden Kiss

Claiming His Kiss

<u>Liberty Crossroads</u>

Seducing Janey

<u>Strictly Professional</u>

Strictly Professional

A Christmas Proposal

<u>Head Over Heels</u>

Falling for the Boss's Son

<u>Novellas</u>

Tangled In His Embrace

<u>Box Sets</u>

Finding Anna Boxed Set (Books 1-4)

Daniels Brothers Box Set (Books 1-4)

Boys In Blue: Everyday Heroes

ACKNOWLEDGMENTS

Thank you to Mack and Rae who make sure all the BDSM elements are accurate. They are the first ones to see the story, including all my typos.

Beta readers are key to catching inconsistencies and plot holes in a novel. Authors are focused on moving the story forward and sometimes we forget what we wrote ten chapters ago. A big thank you to Marci who went through Claiming His Kiss with a fine tooth comb.

Editors and proofreaders are the unsung heroes of the book world. Without them, our books wouldn't be nearly as good. They painstakingly go through each and every word to help us clean up and polish our work. Thank you to Emily Lawrence and DeAnne Taylor for all the work they did to help get this story ready to be published.

Covers are often the first thing a reader notices about a book, so a great cover design is important. A huge thank you to Amy with Qdesigns for the beautiful cover.

ABOUT THE AUTHOR

Sherri picked up her first romance novel when she was twelve and immediately she was hooked. She would stay up reading long after everyone else in her house had gone to bed, needing to see the hero and heroine get their happily ever after. But Sherri never imagined becoming an author.

At the age of thirty, all that changed. After getting frustrated with the direction a television show was taking two of its characters, Sherri decided to try her hand at writing an alternative ending to give the characters the happy ending they deserved.

Since then, writing has become a creative outlet that allows her to explore a wide range of emotions, while having fun taking her characters through all the twists and turns she can create.